His Destiny:

An American Flier

Alden Smith Bradstock III

Black Rose Writing

www.blackrosewriting.com

The final approval for this literary material is granted by the author.

First printing

This is a work of creative non-fiction. Some of the characters are real and much of the action is true. Any resemblance of the fictitious characters to real persons, living or dead, is purely coincidental.

ISBN: 978-1-61296-235-1

PUBLISHED BY BLACK ROSE WRITING

www.blackrosewriting.com

Printed in the United States of America

His Destiny: An American Flier is printed in Adobe Caslon Pro

AUTHOR'S NOTES

The *His Destiny* chronicles are intended to bring political, social, and military conflict to the household through compelling and exciting storytelling. This project presents to the reader some of the armed professionals that served and defended our Freedom and way of life in the first quarter of the twentieth century. The details of their lives and struggles show how devotion and dedication to Freedom were then, as they are now, the ties that bind our liberty, safety, and security.

The chronicles also show us how the control of American power projection was formed over the years. For it is a simple fact that we must learn the lessons of past experiences in military conflicts to prepare for the next conflict. As sad and hard as it is to believe, history tells us that the next conflict is just around the corner.

I am proud to have served in the armed forces of the United States of America. I began my career in the profession of arms just after America struggled with the questions of military means during the Vietnam War. I witnessed the mistreatment of American service personnel by people who incorrectly believed that the service personnel themselves were the cause of the inappropriate application of the military art. I participated in the transition of our armed forces to an All-Volunteer force and the early integration of women in the forces. I went on to command men and women in Europe during the Cold War. During my military education and development, I learned two overwhelming realities of the application. Military service requires unyielding determination and devotion to the cause of Freedom and power projection by military means is a necessary reality of that Freedom.

Each novel of the *His Destiny* chronicles is dedicated to certain individuals. But, the chronicles, as a whole are dedicated to the American professional service personnel who offer and devote their entire existence and, at times, their lives to the cause of Freedom.

I hope you enjoy the story lines of this novel. Take the time to absorb the various postulates presented in the novel and feel the trials, tribulations, and devotion of those that served. Let us not forget what has been done in the past so that we may properly prepare for what has to be done in the very near future. Liberty and Freedom are easily lost. The work to restore them is hard, costly, and very dangerous.

As one figure in the novel says, "Ego is the torch that lights the fire of hatred and discrimination in mankind throughout the world." We have to work together to find a way to avoid military conflict but be prepared to quickly and appropriately respond in controlled ways to keep the fire from burning us again.

ACKNOWLEDGEMENTS

This work would not have been possible without the support and assistance of many people and organizations. Research is the key to worthwhile creative non-fiction. Organization, theme, and pace are the keys to effective storytelling. Dedication; hard work; and the support of professionals, friends, and family members are the glue that binds the keys. They certainly glued me to the task of making this project a reality.

I began my research for this project when I took my first history lesson in high school in 1971. The research continued when I entered the United States Military Academy at West Point. The cadets and instructors at the academy taught me how to study and learn complicated concepts. The course of instruction brought the History of the Military Art and the study of the profession of arms to me. The military leaders I served with, the soldiers that I commanded as a young U.S. Army officer, and the family members of those soldiers showed me how dedicated service and sacrifice are the realities of professionals at arms. To those soldiers and their family members; what they did, what they still do, and what they taught me, I give my heartfelt thanks.

The professionals that helped me bring this story to you included the many friends that read and critiqued the manuscript; my editors, Sarah Cypher and Stephen Hensen; my literary attorney, Scott Johnson; and my publicist, Reagan Rothe. Thank you for your unyielding help.

Diligent and hard work requires the acceptance and assistance of family members and friends. My wife, Samia gave me great encouragement and support, as she always does. The final product would not have come to this without her ever-present guidance and assistance.

George Washington said, "All I am I owe to my mother. I attribute all my success in life to the moral, intellectual and physical education I received from her." How true is that for all who strive to achieve great things? The support my mother gave me over the years helped mold and bond me to the work that had to be done.

My friends, associates, and West Point classmates gave me great help and encouragement. Without that solid base, I might not have moved forward with the idea of putting my thoughts to paper.

Research today is much different than it was when I was growing up. The Internet brought to me the immediate access to some very heartwarming and heart-retching historical facts. My thanks to Wikipedia and other websites that were structured to help bring their messages to the masses.

Then, to Aunt Win. Your grace and beauty over the 100 years of your life are hard to match and greatly missed. I am very happy to be able to extend your life's story in prose so that others can continue to learn what you, in your ever teaching ways, explained to me.

To my readers, I give you my deepest thanks. This book was written for you and your understanding of its messages. The messages cannot help you learn and go forth until you pick up the book and turn to its first page.

Thank you for taking the first step.

Some of the proceeds from the sale of this novel will be donated to

The Wounded Warrior Project.

For more information on the Wounded Warrior Project, please visit

www.woundedwarriorproject.org

WOUNDED WARRIOR PROJECT

To Samia

His Destiny:

An American Flier

CHAPTER 1: WE'RE JUMPED!

Verdun, France - June 8, 1917

"We're *jumped!*" The 18-year-old pilot couldn't believe it. They had scanned the sky continuously. But the tracers raining down on them were telling. Jimmy Smitts didn't know why, but his reaction was dramatic and immediate. Perhaps he reacted so quickly due to inexperience and fear. Then he realized it was a natural reaction because it had happened so quickly. Pulling back on the stick of his machine hard and to the right saved his life.

His French-built Nieuport 11 biplane responded sluggishly at first. The aeromachine was light and highly maneuverable with one exception. It was underpowered. The wind had to catch the ailerons before the maneuver would start. It seemed like minutes to Jimmy but took only seconds. His aeroplane jumped briskly up and to the right. Of thousands of avenues available to him in the combat of three dimensions, his was the only safe haven in the hail of bullets and tracer rounds that filled the sky. There had to be many of them attacking their flight of four French biplanes, he thought. There were just too many tracers flying around the sky.

He looked up and over his right shoulder as his aeromachine snapped vertically. He strained against gravity and centrifugal force to see what was happening. As he looked up, he realized how they had missed the bastards. The sun blurred Jimmy's vision for a split second. Suddenly a large dark-black Maltese Cross in the flash of the flaming red background of his enemy's aeroplane filled his vision. The Cross was so close, it shocked him. It was large and fast—and so *close*.

The swept-back wingtips of the German-made Albatros were unmistakable. He just couldn't identify what model of Albatros they were up against. He had only heard stories of "Dee Twos" and the newest "Dee Threes" from the other fliers. He praised the Lord that they weren't the newer Fokker models he had heard about. Jimmy knew how important it was to know the make and model of the enemy aeroplanes he was fighting. But he didn't have time for that. For now, all he could do to stay alive was *fly*.

His quick vertical maneuver must have shocked the Hun that was so determined to kill him. The German pilot was spinning his aeroplane to his left to avoid a midair collision with Jimmy's machine.

As Jimmy rose and banked, he saw Clive out of the corner of his eye. Clive was cutting hard to his right. His move made it hard for the enemy to follow him. But they were on him. Jimmy couldn't tell how many were attacking Clive. He just knew his vision was filled with red aeroplanes and they were buzzing after Clive like bees from a hive.

What little Jimmy knew of Clive Samuels flashed through his mind. He was a wiry man with wiry red hair, and he was much older than Jimmy. He was nice but aloof and somewhat irresponsible for his age. He had not yet befriended Jimmy. Then again, Clive hadn't really befriended anyone in the squadron.

Looking forward while suspended in air, a vision of his mother came to Jimmy for the first time since he arrived in France. Thelma Morehead Smitts was standing before the front porch of their farmhouse. A 13 year old and very excited Jimmy was running to his mother having just finished his first ride in Father's new aeromachine. Jimmy was headed to the comfort and warmth of his mother's arms. How he wished he could feel that comfort and warmth now. How he wished he could be home in *Wisconsin* now, now that the bullets were flying.

* * * * *

Madison, Wisconsin, U.S.A. – May 15, 1916

She danced. Oh, how she danced. She looked up into Eugene's strong eyes as he turned her during the Viennese waltz. She had never been happier. Eugene's businesses were doing well, the children were wonderful, and this fundraiser had been organized to help put Eugene in the United States Senate. It was everything she had hoped it would be. Soon, they would be headed to Washington.

Eugene Francis Stevenson was a graceful dancer. His tall, athletic build and experience on the soccer field at DePaul University made it easy for him to learn how to ballroom dance. He knew he had in his hands the most beautiful woman at the fundraiser. "Hell," he said to himself, "Loraine is the most beautiful woman in the world. She's given me three wonderful children and, boy, can she dominate men in a room."

They walked back to the head table arm-in-arm when their third dance ended. Loraine reminisced about the amazing speech Eugene had presented not thirty minutes before the dancing started. He proposed to keep America out of the evolving doom on the other side of the Atlantic Ocean. But he called for "Food for the Troops!" The attendees were overwhelmed with excitement. Mr. Stevenson was asking his constituents in Wisconsin to increase wheat and barley production to sell to the federal government. What a grand idea, many thought. Loraine was overwhelmed with excitement over the idea and how well it was received by the attendees.

Some in the room were skeptical. They knew Mr. Stevenson transferred from his family's Democratic heritage to become a Republican candidate for the U.S. Senate. He and his family of five were also very recent residents of Wisconsin. The skeptics saw the move of the family from Hyde Park outside of Chicago to Madison, Wisconsin, as an attempt to find an easy road to a seat in the Senate.

Eugene had orchestrated a perfect campaign in preparation for his Senate run. He knew that William Wolfe and the other candidates were going to have a difficult time getting elected due to their liberal views. But Eugene knew he had to watch his adversaries. There were many in addition to the sitting Senator Wolfe. His adversaries had much to chime about. Stevenson had converted from a liberal to conservative party and moved his family to Madison just in time to meet the residency deadline for the nomination of his new party. He also purchased the American Hotel in Madison to solidify his qualifications as a Wisconsin resident and influential businessman.

The election year of 1916 was going to be a new age for the

Eugene Francis Stevenson family, he thought. But he had to be careful. The hotels he owned were doing well, and it looked like Wisconsin was embracing its new candidate. But he didn't know who his political friends really were.

* * * * *

The action around him brought Jimmy back to reality. He could not go home. He had to concentrate. He tried to remember Clive and the others as objects rather than people as his machine started to strain against the vertical flight. He knew from his flying aerobatics in Wisconsin that he had only seconds to perform another maneuver. Otherwise the small biplane's wings would lose their flying ability and make him fall and spin uncontrollably like a flat stone.

He had done something only twice before in testing his machine. It worked but was on the brink of disaster both times. "Okay, push hard right rudder," he said to himself. "Just as the aeroplane slips right, the stick has to go unnaturally to the front *left*," he remembered. Timing was everything. He didn't understand the principles of the move, but he knew from the first time he accidentally made this 'mistake' that it worked.

The aileron of the upper right wing lost its maneuvering capability. Jimmy later learned it was called a stall. As his machine started its spin, he knew he would soon have to push the stick hard against multiple forces to the front *right*. The momentum of the vertical turn, combined with the reverse airflow over the down right-wing aileron would snap his machine around in a whirlwind. For this to work he had to recover the stick and he had to do it at the right moment. With his eyes closed to avoid getting dizzy or passing out, he thought, "Do it now!" *Push the stick hard against the rotation, hard. Now, pause, pause, pause, and, center the stick.*

When his vision cleared, he was in a controlled dive. His aeroplane had rapidly cart-wheeled 180 degrees. It had gone from vertically up to vertically down in an instant. The move couldn't have come off more perfectly. And it was quick. It was so quick he had to force the world to stop spinning around as he dove toward the enemy.

The Hun was 1,000 feet below, and Jimmy was screaming toward him. The only problem was his enemy was behind Sergeant Walters, their flight leader.

Jimmy could see enemy bullets and tracers tearing Walters's fuselage to shreds. The burning glow of the green phosphorous in the German tracers showed Jimmy the path of destruction of the German's bullets. The stream of green impacting Walters's machine seemed to be continuous although only every fifth bullet that left the German Spandau machine guns was a tracer round. Jimmy, like his Allied partners, had white magnesium tracers in his machine gun. The Germans behind Walters were using their green tracers with precision.

The Indian head insignia of the Lafayette Escadrille squadron on the left side of the Sergeant's canvas fuselage was gone, shot away by the bullets. The canvas covering the fuselage was burning at its edges from the tracers that had passed through Walters's machine.

Walters was an experienced flier and one of the best of the Lafayette Escadrille. But the Huns had the advantage on him. In his right and left jinking, Walters avoided most of the lead that was in the air around him. But Jimmy could tell it was only a matter of seconds. Just then Walters's biplane turned to the right and flew right through a hail of bullets. The green tracers showed the intersecting paths of Walters's machine and the arcing lead of death. From 400 feet away and closing, Jimmy could see smoke, sparks, and engine fragments bursting from Walters's aeroplane. Bullets had pierced the cockpit but not entirely destroyed the machine. As he neared, Jimmy could see his flight leader slumped at the controls. The pilotless biplane continued on in level flight.

The victor knew his target was done for. The German pilot and his wingman started a lazy right turn to look for other opportunities. As they started their turn, Jimmy's bullets and white tracers slammed into the engine of the victor and cut through the top wing of the lead Albatros. Smoke and oil covered the German pilot. Jimmy had done it! He had gotten back at the enemy who ended the life of one of the greatest pilots Jimmy had ever known.

Retribution felt good. But Jimmy knew that he would never again enjoy the fatherly comfort of Sergeant Wesley Walters's encouragement, that pat on the back that Walters always gave him. The sergeant's large frame, thinning hair, and soft smile had always been welcome sights. Jimmy had just scored his first victory. But he also felt his first painful loss in the war.

Things were definitely not over. Jimmy had plenty of work to do as he passed only twenty feet over the second German flier. The two aeroplanes passed each other in cris-crossing flight paths. Jimmy took his Nieuport to the left. The red German Albatros continued on to Jimmy's right.

As he turned his aeroplane up and to the left, Jimmy remembered Sergeant Walters's words, "Keep your head on a swivel, young man. Head on a swivel—always. That's the only way you'll make it through this blood-thirsty war. You can beat the one's you see. It's the hidden enemy that will get you," Jimmy remembered. "Don't focus on one Hun. Keep looking, boy," Sergeant Walters had said. "Keep looking."

But Jimmy couldn't help staring at the bright red Albatros coming into his view as he made his left turn. The German machine was spitting venom of hot lead and green tracers at Sergeant Walters's wingman, who had flown off to the left of the aerial battle. What is his name? Jimmy wondered. Is it Jones or Johns? That's right. It's Johns, he said to himself. Corporal Johns.

Jimmy was faced with a number of problems. The Hun was pounding Johns' ship and there were actually two of the red devils chasing him. The other problems were Jimmy was losing airspeed and the distance between him and his targets was too great. Jimmy had no chance of closing the gap. The Albatros fighters were too far away and much faster than his Nieuport.

All of a sudden, everything changed. Johns pulled hard right in a desperate effort to avoid the buzz saw that was the enemy machine gun fire. The bullets were cutting through the upper wing and struts that held Johns' aeroplane together. Both Albatroses almost overshot Johns as he turned hard. The Germans reversed and started coming back onto the lighter but slower Nieuport 11 that Johns was so expertly piloting.

Jimmy felt a tickling sensation of weightless in his stomach as he performed a perfect barrel to change his flying path from left to right. He wanted to come in from above and to the inside of the enemy. Lord, Jimmy thought, this machine is slow, but it sure can *move*. It is nothing like the sloppy Curtiss Jenny he had flown in Wisconsin as a youth. His barrel put Jimmy in perfect position pointing ahead of his adversaries. And he was closing on them due to the inside turn created by Johns' desperate attempt to survive.

Jimmy opened with a continuous burst of fire right after Johns' machine passed in front of him. Each Albatros flew right through Jimmy's white tracers, one right after the other. As the bullets passed through the first enemy plane, the second German pilot looked up at Jimmy in amazement. His eyes were fixed on Jimmy just as the bullets and tracers danced right down the German's fuselage and through his body. In seconds, the tan Nieuport flown by Johns and both red Albatroses flown by the Germans had entered and passed through Jimmy's view in rapid succession. The action was over quickly.

A satisfying feeling came over Jimmy once again as he slowly turned left out of the engagement. His bullets had hit home and he had saved a member of his flying group. But there was no time to dwell on what he had done. Enemy tracers started whizzing by Jimmy's machine. He heard the impact of the bullets as they passed through his right upper and lower wings. Some bullets splintered the wooden V-strut between the wings. Other bullets passed through canvas, metal, and wood. The bullets must have just missed his head.

In rapid sequence, Jimmy pulled the stick to the left, centered it, and then pulled back hard. He had done this maneuver thousands of times in the five years since he first sat in an aeroplane. Making quick turns like this was second nature to him.

The quick turn strained the wings, struts, and guy wires holding the wings together. Some guy wires stretched to their limits and sang out in high-pitched unison as the wind rushed past them. The opposite wires went limp as they unloaded from the bending and twisting of the wings. The loose wires vibrated in a guttural noise.

Jimmy heard more than saw that he was straining his machine to its limits. He hoped it would stay together. He knew that some Nieuports folded like fans when their main spar failed due to the excessive force of a turn or dive. But he couldn't stop turning hard. A determined Hun was coming at him from above.

Jimmy looked right and up to find his assailant. The action had been so swift his adversary was already gone. He had passed harmlessly by Jimmy's aeromachine.

For the moment, he was safe. Jimmy unloaded the strain on his machine and started to climb. He had learned at the age of fourteen that altitude was everything. It allowed you to maneuver, pull more aerobatic stunts, and use the weight of the machine to gain important speed in a dive. "Go up, son, go up" his father had told him. He saw his mother smiling at him again in soothing support of his life. But the reality of the situation and the wisdom of Walters's words came back to him. Knowing how his mother wanted him to live, he put his head on a swivel and searched every piece of aerial territory around him for his enemies.

He then saw the total chaos that was below him. Enemy Albatros fighters were in a Dance of Death with the two remnants of his flight of four Nieuports. Red machines were everywhere below him, zigzagging and turning to try to gain advantage over the two wounded birds. He finally realized that each red machine had a different color scheme to it. Some had white tails. Others had tan fuselages. None were completely red, but their brilliant colors seemed to blend and then fan out at times. He saw two red devils much lower than the others. One was trailing black smoke and streaming toward the fate of the first machine Jimmy had shot down. The first machine had obviously exploded when it hit No-Man's Land of the Verdun battlefield 6,000 feet below him.

The sight below Jimmy mesmerized him. How many red machines were working to gain the advantage on the two smaller tan biplanes? Eight. Yes. Eight German fighters were in the Dance. That meant that eleven, including the three he had shot down, had pounced on them. It didn't make sense. The Germans, like his group at the

Lafayette Escadrille, flew in even numbers. He scanned the sky. There *were* twelve. A lone pilot was flying above the others and about 2,000 feet above him. The German was waiting to pounce on any other Allied aeromachines that tried to join the Dance.

So that's how an enemy pilot was able to attack me from above. The Hun that was above Jimmy had a wingman. *The wingman must have thought he could get a jump on me and take me in one swift diving pass.* Jimmy realized how lucky he was that the closing speeds and firing angles for the Hun were too great for him to kill Jimmy. The Hun had come close but failed to hit his mark.

Jimmy now knew that his group was jumped by ten enemy aeroplanes coming out of the early afternoon sun. Two more planes flew higher than the other ten to provide security and act as a reserve. How cunning and yet masterful, thought the young pilot. Jimmy could tell he and the other fliers were up against a large number of capable opponents. This flying war was going to be a real struggle. And it had just begun for the young flier.

Jimmy wondered what to do. The urge to flee from the melee came to him. The sight before him made him shiver. If he joined the Dance below, the higher threat would definitely attack him. But the Hun was not turning to engage Jimmy. The German watchdog might have lost track of Jimmy's position. Perhaps he thought his wingman had scored. He must be concentrating on the combat 2,000 feet below him. To continue into the circling mass, Jimmy had to find a way to help his fellow fliers without being attacked from above.

Then it happened. The German flier above Jimmy turned *away* from him. That meant the threat really didn't know where Jimmy was. Perhaps he thought Jimmy had been shot down or was high-tailing it to safety like the Whitetail deer Jimmy had hunted back home.

That did it. The high pilot's turn brought Jimmy into immediate action. Shedding his urge to flee, Jimmy's youthful naiveté and feelings of invincibility put reason aside. His adrenaline put everything in slow motion. He pulled back on the stick. As the aeroplane rose, Jimmy kicked left rudder and took the stick to the left then forward. Just another perfect diving barrel, Jimmy thought.

Barrels were second nature to Jimmy, and he loved doing them.

Coming out of the roll, Jimmy was pointed directly downward at the circling mass of confusion. Ten aeroplanes were turning and spinning. The sea of cris-crossing red and tan almost filled the sky in front of him. *My word, it is beautiful,* Jimmy thought. But it was also deadly. As he streaked toward the mass, Jimmy knew he had only one shot, one chance to save his friends. But he could save only one. The mass was too great, and it was separating at times, many against each of the two tan Nieuports.

Jimmy was low on petrol. He also knew his last long burst of fire put him desperately low on the .303 ammunition in the drum of his Lewis machine gun. He shuddered to think that he would be close to death from the red devil that was flying above him if he dove into the Dance. But he pushed on.

So, which 'friend' should he save, wondered Jimmy. *Left toward Johns or right toward Clive?* He sensed he should turn toward Johns because he knew him to be a better flier than Clive. *I have to save the most capable of the two.* Many of the decisions he had to make throughout the engagement had been made for him. Things happened so quickly, they had just happened. The decision he was faced with now was no exception. Johns' aeromachine was hit as Jimmy looked on. Even at 1,000 feet away and closing, Jimmy could see bullets and tracers impact Johns' fuselage. It looked to Jimmy like the entire cockpit was engulfed in tracers.

In shock, Jimmy applied slight right rudder. He brought the screaming engine and propeller of his machine on to the four Albatroses that were chasing Clive. As Jimmy dove, he looked up and to the right where he expected the high menace to be. Jimmy saw him. The high German was starting his descent toward Jimmy. Jimmy diverted his attention back to the melee. He sensed that his only hope was to undershoot the mass of red before him. This, he hoped, would get him out of the fight alive. He would use his airspeed to rise through the mass and try to avoid a collision. He hoped the maneuver would scatter the Germans behind Clive.

Jimmy knew his flight path would not allow him to shoot down any of the Germans. Perhaps, if he fired on his way through the mass, the Germans would think he was on them. Passing above the Huns and escaping to the west in a high speed turn was his only chance of survival. The dive would allow him to gain some altitude and avoid the predator coming in from above.

Jimmy also hoped the high enemy flier chasing him would expect Jimmy to stay with the other German fliers in his attack. The descending predator would try to line Jimmy up for a kill. *He is going to try to shoot me down,* Jimmy thought. *He will turn to where I'll go if I try to shoot down the other Germans. My turn to the southwest will put the predator out of position.* Jimmy could tell the German's speed and firing angles would be completely off in the split seconds of the closing engagement. *At least, that's what I* hope *will happen,* he thought.

It worked. Jimmy hit the low point in his dive 200 feet short of the mass of red. As he pulled up, he started firing at nothing. He passed just over and in front of the first of four Albatros killers. He aimlessly fired his Lewis gun as he passed. The shock of seeing another Nieuport buzzing them sent all four German pilots breaking off at different angles. The dive gave Jimmy plenty of airspeed to climb and turn slowly to the left. He would head toward the west then south toward home. The lazy left turn did not sacrifice the speed of his machine.

Jimmy's low-to-high left turning pass made the high predator miss Jimmy's aeroplane with his burst of machine-gun fire by at least 100 yards. Jimmy's left banking turn and the Hun's diving approach from Jimmy's left to his right made for an easy escape.

He put his head on a swivel again. He scanned the sky and saw nothing but open sky between him and his aerodrome. He looked back to his left to see the Albatros aeroplanes forming up and heading toward the east-northeast. The fight was over.

As he looked back a second time, Jimmy saw the last Albatros flier climbing out of his dive to form up with his German comrades. Jimmy started to look to his front when he noticed the last German rock his bright red wings twice. It was as if the flier was giving Jimmy an aerial salute. Not knowing if the gesture was meant for him, Jimmy rocked his wings twice as well.

Finally in level flight toward safety, Jimmy realized he was soaked in sweat. It felt as if he was sitting in a pool of water. He just hoped he hadn't relieved himself and wet his pants during the engagement. *That* would be hard for him to explain to the others.

For the first time in twelve minutes, Jimmy took a deep breath. Various sensations started coming into his consciousness. His left arm hurt like hell. He had pulled his crossed shoulder straps as tight as he could make them when he first sat in his machine. But he realized the force of one of the turns he made must have slammed him against the padded edge of his cockpit. The impact was so hard that Jimmy's shoulder felt as if it was broken.

When did *that* happen, he wondered? It must have happened during the very first vertical maneuver he made in the fight. That was the only time he remembered his aeroplane snapping around so quickly. His shoulder had bounced off the cockpit the first two times he pulled that accidental stunt. But it never hurt so much before. He must have really spun his machine around this time.

Jimmy's six-foot frame and athletic build fit well in the cockpit. He was in great shape from having helped his father around the farm in Wisconsin. Perhaps, had his shoulders been broader, he might not have bounced so hard around the cockpit during his spinning maneuver. He removed his flying goggles and leather cap to let the wind rush through his wavy light-brown hair. *Oh, how good it feels to finally relax and cool down,* Jimmy thought, reflecting on his survival.

Why he hadn't felt the pain anytime during the aerial combat, he didn't know. He had even used his left arm to charge and fire the Lewis machine gun on his top wing. All he knew was his shoulder sure did hurt now. He continued to survey himself and the condition of his aeroplane. His feet hurt and both knees and his right hand were cramped. His fingers felt frozen to the stick. He pried them away, one at a time, with his left hand.

His aeroplane was in pretty bad shape. One of the guy wires had pulled away from his main left V strut. Both of the right wings were shot to hell. Canvas flapped in the wind as he continued to fly to the south. The canvas was burned around its edges, just as he'd seen on Walters's fuselage. But nothing was burning. The wind must have doused the flames ignited by the enemy's tracers.

He finally started to relax his body in the basket seat of his cockpit. Thank goodness the rattan webbing was comfortable as it formed somewhat to his body. But his body ached all over. The sweat he was sitting in didn't make the return flight feel any better. As a matter of fact, the water was pooling around his torso and buttocks, and it was getting cold. It was nice to finally relax and let go. The wind swept past him as he breathed deeply. His mind went blank for a few seconds. He was mesmerized by the spinning propeller, the rhythm of the engine, and the beauty of the deep blue sky on the horizon floating before him.

Jimmy was immediately startled by rapid movement to his right rear. Rather than saluting him by rocking his bright red wings, had his adversary actually been signaling his comrades to attack? His muscles tensed and he jerked his head around to his right to see what was amiss. He saw the blur of a tan figure sliding into formation beside him. It was another Nieuport 11. In sheer elation, Jimmy saw Clive's smiling face looking right back at him. *Holy Moses,* thought Jimmy. *How in the world did Clive get out of* that *gaggle? He got out of that gaggle only because of me,* that's *how.*

With its tail rudder and ailerons in tatters and its fuselage and wings pierced like Swiss cheese, Clive's machine looked as if it was finished. Jimmy was amazed the thing could actually stay in the air.

Clive waved at Jimmy. He pointed his whole hand straight to his front. Jimmy acknowledged the direction of flight. Clive was not the best flier of the two of them. But he knew the best and fastest way back home to their aerodrome at Luxeuil-les-Bains, or the "Lux" as the American fliers called it. After all, Clive had two months and seventeen missions more than Jimmy. *He's not as good as me as a flier, but it is only right that Clive should lead the way home.*

There were four avenues to the Lux from the areas around the Verdun battlefield. The fliers usually followed the rivers. The Marne, the Aisne, the Muese, and the Moselle rivers generally ran north to south in this corner of France. Flying south between the Aisne and Muese rivers, the fliers would turn left toward the Moselle at a point where the Aisne ended at its headwaters. They would keep the Moselle to their left as they passed over the French town of Epinal. The town was a center for local merchants and quaintly situated on the Moselle River that flowed north until it met the Rhine River at the *Deutches Ecke,* or German Corner, deep inside of Germany.

With the trenches of the terrible carnage of No-Man's Land far behind them, the pair of survivors used the direction of the sun, the Vosges Mountains, and the forest of southern Alsace to guide them home as they left the Moselle. The mountains and forest were in the distance to their left. Soon Jimmy would be able to see the church steeple in the village of Saint-Sauveur to the south of Lux.

There it was. And he would soon see the small ponds north of the aerodrome. These ponds, like the town, had their own name among the American fliers. Because they lined the fliers up on their final approach to the landing field, the fliers called them "the Mark."

Descending to 500 feet, Jimmy and Clive turned in unison as they circled the Mark on their left. They could see the wind flag of the aerodrome in a slight westerly breeze. Jimmy signaled to Clive that he should land first. Jimmy doubted that Clive's damaged aeroplane could remain in the air much longer. Clive nodded in agreement and pointed to himself as a final signal of confirmation. Jimmy followed Clive down as he lined up to land.

The aerodrome was in a precarious location. The Allies must have located the landing area to minimize German observation of its location. The fliers joked that it was in the low country because no self-respecting Frenchman would want to own such land. But its location, regardless of the reason for it, made line-up and landing a little touchy.

Trees on the south side of the Mark obscured the landing field. The center of the field was slightly lower than the touchdown area and the opposite end of the landing field. Fliers had to accurately control ailerons, rudder, and throttle to make sure their aeroplanes touched down on the slight down-slope of the field. The down-slope in landing was perfect for taking off. The upward angle of the field put the wings of the Nieuports into the wind so that they seemed to jump off the field. Cross winds made landing difficult, but they helped in takeoff.

Clive made his approach. Jimmy flew in parallel until Clive was 100 feet above the field. Jimmy climbed and turned left to start his circle around the Mark and into landing. Jimmy could tell, looking down at the aerodrome, that the other three groups of pilots had already returned to the field. He didn't know, however, whether the other groups had lost any fliers like his group had.

He passed over the farmhouse that was aerodrome headquarters. The tee shape of the farmhouse below him made Jimmy think of its form and function. It was a two-story structure that had been built many years before the owner gave it to the French government for the war effort. He could tell when he first entered the building that the owner really wasn't giving up much. The floors were not level and creaked everywhere. The roof leaked in three different places. The windows didn't fit in their sashes, and many wouldn't even open. The front of the farmhouse had been opened up to provide suitable space for briefings and debriefings. The kitchen and living areas of the house served as the operations and planning rooms. The recreation area, built upstairs by removing more walls, included a bar, lounge area, and tables to play cards.

As he passed over the farmhouse, he thanked the good Lord that they slept in a separate barracks—a one-story structure built in haste by the French next to the farmhouse. It was flimsy but helped meet the ever-increasing demands of the war. And it gave the men room to spread out in solitude away from the noise of the recreation area in the farmhouse.

Neither the farmhouse nor the barracks had a dining room. The sight of the Hotel of the Golden Apple, the old French inn of Luxeuil Les Baines where the fliers ate their meals, made Jimmy realize how hungry he was. Located across the carriageway in front of the farmhouse, the inn provided sleeping quarters for the founders of the squadron and fliers with seniority. But its main purpose was to feed the men of the squadron. He felt a soothing comfort in thinking about the warm atmosphere of the inn's restaurant as he yearned for food.

Jimmy couldn't get used to seeing the bright Tri-Colors of the French national flag flying in front of the farmhouse. He knew the flying groups were made up mostly of American volunteers. The squadron commanding officer, staff, and mechanics were all Frenchmen. But the bulk of the fliers were Americans. Jimmy accepted the fact that the Lafayette Escadrille was a French unit, but he hoped one day to see an American flag flying in place of the Tri-Colors.

Flying in good order, Jimmy completed the turns into his landing approach. The wind was no factor as he bounced twice on the slight down-slope. The approach was always tricky, but the landing was even trickier. The Nieuport was so light it tended to bounce on landing. Too much bounce with the odd slopes of the field and you could easily flip the machine. If you landed 300 yards beyond the down-slope, you could tear the landing gear from the aeroplane. Three pilots had done just that, Jimmy had been told. One had died as a result of his mistake.

Jimmy bounced a number of times over the clumps of dirt and grass as he crossed the field. He was "riding the bronco" toward the aeroplane line-up. Rising up on the far side of the landing field, Jimmy approached the spot where he would turn toward the line-up. He continued to give and take power by the throttle until his machine came to rest. He cut his engine. His French mechanic rushed to his side. Henri brought a wooden step with him and climbed it to help Jimmy with his shoulder straps. Jimmy sat staring at the engine cowling as the two-bladed propeller slowed to a stop.

The tension immediately flushed from his body as the propeller stopped rotating and the machine stopped vibrating. He sat still in the rattan seat for a moment. His only sensation came from the sweat in his trousers and the back of his shirt. He was lost in absolute relief from the stress he had just endured. He closed his eyes, trying to erase the memory of German bullets and tracers finding his friends in the tan machines of the Lafayette Escadrille

Jimmy struggled out of his seat and rolled more than climbed from the cockpit. Once on the ground, he tried to settle himself as he regained his balance and got the cramps out of his legs. It would take time for the tingling sensation in his fingers to subside. The ground personnel were there to help. They always wanted to be the first to hear how the mission had gone. *"Mon Lieutenant, como tale vous?"* asked Henri. *"Como vous, Se Bon?"*

Jimmy straightened and tried to regain the strength he seemed to have lost in his legs. He had heard Henri's words and wanted to respond. But it was hard to get the words out thinking of Walters. He also hesitated because the pilots had been instructed to keep quiet about their missions until after debriefing. But Jimmy couldn't turn his back on his trusted aide. He held up three fingers and said, "Henri, kaput three A-Lay-Man por me." Henri understood the multilingual reply and smiled with excitement. *His* flier had kills, real enemy kills! And he returned to the aerodrome with bullet holes that must be repaired! Henri had served three American fliers before Jimmy joined the unit. None of them had made any kills. One had not returned from his first mission. And *this* flier was still alive and must have been in the thick of it all.

Patting the Nieuport 11 and referring to its French name, Henri said, "Les Bẻbẻ, she is a good machine, non?"

Henri looked proudly at his new lieutenant. And he was alive to fight another day. But he was even more proud of the chance to repair the damaged Bẻbẻ.

CHAPTER 2 – AFTER ACTION

Luxeuil-les-Bains, France - June 8, 1917

Jimmy could hardly walk as he left his Nieuport 11 flying machine, *his* Bébé. He ached all over. He looked over at Clive and noticed his weird demeanor. Clive seemed to be more aloof and direct in his movements. Jimmy was puzzled. *Had someone just saved my life, I would have given him all due recognition and thanks for keeping me alive,* Jimmy thought. But Jimmy had a lot more to think about than dealing with the wiry and now egotistical Clive.

As he approached the farmhouse, Jimmy saw Captain Georges Thenault, the French commander of the Lafayette Escadrille. Thenault was a handsome 29-year-old man. He was only 5 feet 8 inches tall, but he stood erect and gave a commanding appearance. He spoke in soft and clear tones with a heavy French accent. His dark-brown hair and brown eyes were typically French. He stood in contrast to the tall, thin Bill Thaw, one of the squadron's founders. Bill was next to Thenault, leaning against the post of the front porch of the farmhouse with his ever-present cigarette in hand. His bushy mustache, 6 feet 3 inch height, and deliberate speech enhanced the Ivy League mannerisms he had adopted while studying at Yale University.

Both officers greeted Jimmy with respect and strong handshakes. "Well done, son," said Bill. "Well done. Take a break in the upstairs bar. There's a table of meat and bread waiting. You're welcome to a shot of whiskey too. We'll conduct your debriefing in about twenty minutes."

Jimmy didn't understand how Bill could possibly know how well he had performed. *I guess we'll see,* thought Jimmy. Right now, the aches and pains were secondary to Jimmy's thoughts. He absolutely needed water and something to eat. As he entered the farmhouse, Jimmy could sense a slightly depressing mood in the other fliers. It permeated the atmosphere. The squadron personnel were starting to hear that at least two aeroplanes had not yet returned from the mission.

Jimmy almost ran up the steps to the lounge. He could smell the fresh meats and bread waiting for him. The spread was somewhat sparse but sufficient for his immediate needs. He piled ham, salami, and cheese on a slice of buttered French bread and wolfed it down. He was famished. As he prepared his second helping, Jimmy sensed that someone had joined him. It was Willie Dugan, who had graduated with Jimmy from the French flying school.

"Jimmy, how did it go? I understand two of our guys were shot down today. Have you heard anything about it?"

"Yeah," Jimmy said dejected. "I was there. The Huns jumped us. They got Walters. I also saw that guy Johns go down."

"No!" Willie exclaimed. "What happened? How did you do? Are you okay?"

"I'm okay but really shaken at what I saw. Walters got hit," Jimmy replied. "He died instantly. I saw Johns' machine take a lot of hits and go down. My machine took a beating too, mostly in the right wings and strut. The mechanics are going to repair it tomorrow."

Willie's eyes widened. "Wow," he said. "Jimmy, I'm sorry you saw all that. But you made it back okay. You took hits and still survived!"

Jimmy nodded slowly. "I got my revenge, Willie. I got a good number of the Germans.

"You did? Jimmy, that's great," Dugan said. "I'm really sorry about Walters and Johns, but you've got to be proud. You got yourself some kills."

"Willie, I need a break. I'm really bushed. Thanks for your encouragement, but I don't have anything left in me to be proud, glad, or anything else. If you don't mind," Jimmy told him, holding up his sandwich as a sign that he needed to eat.

"I understand. Take some time and relax. You need it. But I'm really impressed, Jimmy. I hope I can get some too."

Dugan turned and walked slowly to the other side of the table. He had to give his classmate a chance to recover. Jimmy was clearly down about losing Walters and Johns.

Jimmy was soon called to the first-floor bedroom of the farmhouse that had been converted into Bill Thaw's office. He couldn't help fixing his gaze on the stained plaster walls in the corner of the room and noticing the thick smell of cigarette smoke as he entered. Captain Thenault and Bill Thaw were both in the room. They wanted to hear the details of the engagement that killed two of their number. Clive Samuels had been first to be debriefed. Jimmy was sure Clive had gone first because he'd been around longer. Bill asked Jimmy to sit on the worn couch while they talked about the action.

"Jimmy," Bill started. "I'm really sorry that we lost Walters and Johns. I give you my thanks for trying to keep them from getting shot down. Clive told us he didn't see much of the action. He was working hard to gain advantage over the German fliers he was chasing. Perhaps you can tell us more."

"Oui, Jams," Captain Thenault chimed in. "We are sad. We hope you recover well from your escapades."

Jimmy was confused by what Bill Thaw had just said. Clive had done everything he could to *run* from the Huns, not *chase* them.

During his debriefing, Jimmy described the action in great detail. Captain Thenault was most interested in the details of the vertical cartwheel that Jimmy had performed at the beginning of the aerial combat. He wanted to know how Jimmy learned of the maneuver and what needed to be done to perfect it. Jimmy had the feeling that the good captain wanted to learn about the maneuver so he could use it to his advantage in his own action. Perhaps he would pass it on to the other fliers. Jimmy told himself he really shouldn't judge others, particularly since he was unfamiliar with just about everyone in the squadron. *But that is my maneuver. I perfected it. Why give it away to others who probably couldn't do it anyway?*

"So, Les Boche jumped from above," said Captain Thenault. "They did what they usually do. They came again out of the sun. Sergeant Walters did not have a chance. Do you know, Jams, did Johns have a chance?"

"Not really," Jimmy answered. "They were all over us before we knew it. I was only able to keep them off of my tail by the maneuver I pulled. Even Clive had two Germans attacking him. It started and was over so fast."

Jimmy sighed and looked down at his hands in his lap. He paused, waiting for his emotions to subside. He was trying to get over the sight of Sergeant Walters arching up and slumping over in his cockpit after getting hit. Thenault and Thaw waited patiently, knowing Jimmy needed time.

"But I was lucky enough to get the three that I got."

Jimmy looked up slowly and could tell that something was troubling the two leaders.

Thaw spoke first. "Jimmy, *how* many enemy aeroplanes did you say you shot down?"

"Three." He raised a finger each time he counted a kill. "I got the one that got Walters and then the first of the two that were after Johns. The second German flew right through my bullets. He was right behind the first German and had no chance of evading the lead. I almost got one of the four machines that were shooting at Clive, but the angles were all off and I had to break off my attack. Why do you ask?"

Bill was the first to react, probably because he understood Jimmy's words long before Captain Thenault translated the words for himself. "Jimmy, Clive didn't explain the action quite like the way you just described it."

The entire debriefing took only thirty minutes. To Jimmy, it came and went like a tornado. But he was stunned. Clive had confirmed only one of Jimmy's three kills. But that wasn't the worst of it. Jimmy basically dove into the melee to save Clive's life. Clive not only didn't confirm two of Jimmy's kills, he was trying to take one from Jimmy for himself. Clive actually claimed to have downed one of the German fliers.

That was the last thing Jimmy expected to hear. One of his own flying partners, someone he was supposed to rely on and who was supposed to rely on him, was stealing a kill. Was it possible that during the heat of battle Clive had turned and taken a shot at the German Jimmy had killed and only *thought* it was his victory? No,

Jimmy *knew* it, there was no way. He didn't know whether he should object, let it go, or just go over and kill the wiry little red-headed bastard.

As he stood up at the end of the debriefing, Captain Thenault told Jimmy, "Jams, you know all kills must be verified by another. Mr. Samuels confirmed your first kill. He saw it crash in No-Man's Land. But he said he did not see the other Boche that you say you shot at go to ground."

Jimmy just stared at Captain Thenault. *Right,* he thought. *Clive had taken one of my kills for himself and said he couldn't confirm whether I had hit the other German for my second kill.*

Bill could see Jimmy tense up. To Bill, Jimmy was upset at not getting credit for three kills. He cut in, "Jimmy, Clive said that he was so engaged with the enemy he had downed that he didn't see you shoot down the other Albatros. We'll check with the infantry at the front. They usually confirm our kills. They have nothing better to do but avoid artillery explosions and watch the aerial warfare above them."

Captain Thenault then informed Jimmy that every man in the squadron, once he got his first kill, received two days off from flying missions against the enemy. Jimmy didn't understand it but knew he had to comply. There really wasn't any debate to be had. He knew he was ready to go against anything the enemy could throw at him. He now knew he was the best and could take on any German that flew. But he also knew he had to follow orders. Besides, his aeromachine had to be repaired before he could go up again.

The meal and Burgundy wine at the hotel helped Jimmy start his recovery from the cramps and aches that ran throughout his body. He was alert. He could see more clearly than usual. His vision to the right and left was clearer than it had ever been. But he also seemed to be in a fog. His mind was reacting slower than usual. Jimmy had never experienced this kind of euphoric feeling. He felt as though he was actually walking above rather than on the ground. He wasn't drunk. He had downed only one glass of wine to warm his insides. That was enough to wash the dirt away from his mouth but not get drunk.

As he walked back to the farmhouse, Jimmy figured he needed to find out later why the feelings he had were so weird and unnatural. For now, he had to figure out how he was going to control himself being in the same squadron with Clive.

Willie Dugan came up to Jimmy as he walked into the upstairs lounge. "Jimmy, Clive said he got one kill and you got *only* one. What's the skinny? I thought you said you had three kills."

"Clive stole one of my kills and didn't confirm the other one."

"Clive did *what?*" Willie asked with an astonished look. "Hang in there, Jimmy. Perhaps the infantry will confirm that you got all three kills."

"I'll tell you what, Willie. I don't need to worry about counting kills. Let someone else handle that. What does it matter anyway when your flying partner steals them? I don't need to worry about arguing with others about who killed what Germans. I'm just going to go out, fly, and kill Huns. Counting kills really isn't what this war is all about. Our involvement is all about ending this mess. We have to stop the killing overall. We have to stop the misery. We have to stop the domination of one country over another in Europe. Let's just go up and stop the enemy. But Clive better stay out of my way." After a pause Jimmy said, "Ah, forget it."

"You're right, Jimmy. Forget about Clive. Come on. Let's play some chess. You owe me. I'm down four bits to you already," Willie said.

Jimmy knew Willie wanted to help cheer him up. But he was no match for Jimmy at the chessboard. After Jimmy took Willie four out of four matches, they were surrounded by other fliers.

"Jimmy, I just can't beat you at chess. How did you get so good?"

Others cut in. Names and faces that he had not yet become accustomed to started asking Jimmy questions and patting him on his back. They wanted to know how the mission had gone and what had happened to Sergeant Walters and Corporal Johns.

As he answered their questions and got into discussions with them, Jimmy started feeling a level of camaraderie and mutual respect with his newfound friends. As a newcomer to the squadron, Jimmy hadn't had time to sit and socialize. The other fliers were also a good bit older. He had felt somewhat uneasy and alienated when he first arrived at the aerodrome.

His rank also alienated him. Most of the fliers didn't pay any attention to rank. They were the chosen few in their minds. But Jimmy was given a lieutenant's rank out of the French flying school. Many of the American volunteers were sergeants or corporals. Even though they didn't wear their rank, they were upset when they heard that Jimmy, the new addition to their group, had officer rank. They would later learn that his selection as a lieutenant in the flying school was as justified as any selection. He was young, but he was an extremely capable flier and an excellent gunner.

Jimmy was warm and comfortable in the atmosphere and setting of the lounge. Regardless of what Clive was doing to torpedo his success, Jimmy finally felt calm and refreshed. The fire in the fireplace crackled in the background. It was good to be alive, Jimmy thought.

The other fliers left Jimmy and Willie to themselves for a little while. They could tell he needed some time to relax. Many had gone through what Jimmy had seen that day. They knew he needed to reflect on what had happened.

Jimmy surveyed the lounge more than he ever had before. The fireplace and wood paneling around the room made the atmosphere seem like home. He moved to one of the padded leather chairs, sat down, and reflected. He noticed Clive at the other end of the room talking to two fliers with various hand motions as though he was describing the action they had been in that day. The darkness at that end of the room kept Jimmy from seeing who Clive was talking to. He also couldn't make out what he was saying. He had to be telling everyone how *he* downed a German that day, the German *Jimmy* had actually killed.

The fliers all seemed to have an air of confidence about them, Jimmy thought as he reflected on the last two months of the adventure he was on. They were friendly but not close to one another. Some of the men were egotistical. Others acted crazy, as though the next few minutes would be their last. They wanted only wine, women, and kills. Sure, Jimmy thought, they all had a right to be egotistical to some degree. After all, they were some of the very few fliers in the entire world. They were actually the fewest of the few, commanding loaded machine guns in flight.

Whenever they were gathered in the lounge, the fliers discussed aerial combat and tactics. They sometimes argued. Some played poker. Others sat together drinking. Most of the men smoked heavily, as though the cigarettes would steady their nerves. Everything seemed to be done with a sense of finality to it, more so now that two more of their number had met their ends.

What has the world come to? Jimmy wondered. The worldwide human consciousness now seemed to be all about men killing other men. And it was happening on a grand scale on the ground below the fliers. Jimmy couldn't help but think of the light and dark brown colors of the Verdun battlefield. The battlefield stood out from above like a wide, dark-brown river in a sea of green foliage that covered the French territories of Alsace and Loraine. The Argonne Forest of the French-German border was lush, alive with green. Jimmy visualized the bomb craters of No-Man's Land, where constant artillery barrages had pockmarked the earth, and the dark brown lines that were the killing trenches of the front. He could see where the vivid life of the forests ended at the pure death and destruction of the brown dirt river.

Jimmy wondered about his fellow fliers who battled the Huns above these killing fields. Captain Georges Thenault was a capable commander. He was confident and experienced in leading and in the administration of the flying squadron. He was also a good flier, Jimmy had heard. Some thought their commander tried to avoid aerial combat. They believed he flew only to keep his flying status. As Andrew Courtney Campbell, Cort as he was called, once said, "You'll see how he goes up with many around him for protection. Don't count on him to come to your aid."

Apparently Campbell was well liked by the members of the squadron. They spoke highly of his devotion and determination. His stocky figure and bushy mustache made his comic antics around the aerodrome even funnier. Many in the squadron, however, objected to his antics in the air. Campbell had a tendency to fool around while flying. He sometimes joked too much, almost crashing into the other fliers while in flight.

Jimmy had been told that Raoul Lufbery was a determined hunter, and it showed in his eyes. With Bill Thaw, Lufbery was one of the original fliers of the Lafayette Escadrille. He was eager to jump into an aeromachine, any machine, and go after enemy fliers. He just wanted to kill Germans. To some of the fliers, aerial combat was like dueling between respected adversaries. To Lufbery, the Dance was only an opportunity to kill. He hated Huns and talked about going after them as though nothing in life was as important. He was on a mission to kill them, Jimmy had been told, in retribution for the death of a friend. Jimmy had tremendous respect for Raoul and found him to be very friendly. He felt that Lufbery respected him for his flying expertise. Perhaps that's why they got along so well.

William "Bill" Thaw was a name Jimmy heard when he first got to the aerodrome. Thaw and Lufbery were icons to the fliers. They had started the squadron by convincing the French government it should organize the American volunteers as a fighting force. There was an aura about both men, and Jimmy watched them from a distance. Thaw and Lufbery were of a special mettle like few other men in the hallowed halls of the Escadrille. Jimmy often heard the names of the other founders mentioned. However, many of them like Victor Chapman, Norman Prince. Kiffin Rockwell, and James McConnell had all been killed before Jimmy arrived at the squadron.

In the early days of the Lafayette Escadrille and long before Jimmy arrived at the Lux, the American fliers had developed a reputation as an unruly rabble. The Americans got drunk and often got into trouble. Some, like Lufbery, even got arrested. Captain Thenault did a lot of explaining to local authorities and did what he could to minimize problems between the fliers and the locals. Jimmy could also feel tension between some of the fliers. He wasn't sure whether there were problems between them or the stress of combat had made them fearful or somewhat doubtful of each other. He vowed to stay out of trouble with anyone. He just wanted to fly and make some kind of contribution to the war. *My vow may change if Clive takes another one of my kills,* Jimmy thought.

As he heard his comrades speak solemnly of Walters and Johns, Jimmy remembered some of the other fliers who had lost their lives in the Dance. Victor Chapman was the first of the Lafayette Escadrille to fall. Chapman had gained tremendous respect having been seriously wounded in the head during one aerial engagement. He returned to the squadron during his recovery to continue to take the war to the Germans. He then became the seventh victory of the German ace Loytnant Kurt Wintgens in a hard-fought engagement. Jimmy had been told that Wintgens was one of five Germans who attacked Chapman in a coordinated effort.

The Germans today worked like a team, Jimmy remembered. *They were like a pack of wolves after wounded prey. And, they were good.* He shuddered again thinking of how determined *and successful* the Germans had been.

Norman Prince and Kiffin Rockwell were next in the line of fallen heroes of the group. They died in successive months, September and October of 1916. Prince went down after downing five Germans. After Rockwell came names like Pavelka, Frederick Prince, and McConnell, all of who died in the span of only three months. Genet and Hoskier fell in April, only two months after Jimmy's arrival at the squadron. Bloody April, as it was called, showed that the Huns had perfected their attacks on the Allied fliers, particularly the British to their north. And they had taken their toll on the Lafayette Escadrille.

German ace Oswald Boelke had started it all when he organized the German "hunting squadrons," or *Jagdstaffeln.* He developed the dicta upon which the German fliers would dominate the skies over France in April of 1917. Boelke's aerial-combat techniques included such tactics as gaining an advantage over your enemy, firing at close range to ensure proper alignment, and diving toward your opponent. Boelke also wanted his fliers to use the advantage of the sun and always have an avenue of retreat. To Boelke, killing the enemy was important, but staying alive to kill the enemy at a more advantageous time was just as important.

Jimmy glanced over at the other men huddled round the small square table by the fireplace. He heard one of them say "Bobby," speaking of Robert Johns. Johns had piloted his Nieuport expertly in that day's battle, but now he was dead. He had been alive yesterday but was dead today. So was Walters, and Walters had been one of the most capable fliers in the Escadrille. Bad luck and the Huns had worked together to kill them both.

But it was over and done with. All the men knew the dangers of getting too close to any other flier. Death might be a matter of time or just a matter of luck gone bad. The closer you got to your friends in this bloody business, the more it hurt to see them go. It was an unspoken fact.

Jimmy had earlier seen the names of Walters and Johns being erased from the chalkboard in the planning room. "Kills – 1, Probables – 0, Possibles – 1" had been written next to Jimmy's name on the Flight Lineup. He didn't know the meaning behind the *Probables* and *Possibles,* but at that moment he really didn't care. He had one kill and was waiting for some lonely infantryman to confirm another. The infantrymen could confirm two more kills for Jimmy if it weren't for Clive, Jimmy kept thinking.

As he came out of his thoughts, Jimmy noticed Tom Hewitt and Raymond Bridgman coming over to him and Willie. Hewitt had attended the French flying school with them and had shown that he was very good in the air. Bridgman had just joined the squadron and was a likeable guy. Others continued to relax around the dark room, play cards, or just sip at their wine or cognac. Willie, Ray, and Tom really wanted to hear more about the action Jimmy had been in that day. But they talked at first only about his success and congratulated him. They were trying to help him get over seeing their comrades die in combat. Hewitt was first to break from the line of encouragement. He asked Jimmy to tell them about what happened to Walters and Johns. Ray then asked for more details about what the Germans had done to gain the advantage over them.

Toward the end of his interrogation by the fliers, Jimmy crashed. The change in his feelings and awareness was as if a blanket had been thrown over him. His body suddenly wilted and his vision blurred somewhat. Many backslaps and congratulations later, Jimmy talked his way out of the conversation and left the lounge. He needed rest. He walked out the front door and turned toward the barracks. He finally found peace and quiet in the wood-framed bed he called home. He could feel the supporting ropes through the thin mattress. But he was used to the ropes. They didn't really matter. Nothing really mattered. Nothing was going to keep him awake after what he had been through that day.

It seemed like days, but it was only two hours. Jimmy woke feeling completely refreshed. He opened his eyes to darkness and knew that the sun was far from rising. He didn't know what time it was, but knew he wasn't going to get back to sleep anytime soon. For some reason, he was wide awake and thinking about the mission he had flown just four hours before. Every second of the mission came to him in slow motion. He struggled to try to get the thoughts and actions out of his mind so he could get more sleep. But the thoughts were as real as if he were flying the mission again.

How did the Huns get the jump on them, he wondered? How could all four of them not see such a large formation of enemy aeroplanes as they approached the aerial battlefield above No-Man's Land? The whole episode was surreal. The memory of the flash of the sun in Jimmy's eyes that day reminded him of his youth in Wisconsin. Jimmy was an excellent hunter. His favorite hunts were in the dove fields of central Wisconsin during the fall harvest.

Mourning doves are elusive birds, Jimmy remembered. They are fast and agile. A dove hunt is exhilarating because the birds come out of nowhere. They come from every conceivable location and fly to any other conceivable location. They also fly in various directions—up, down, right, and left as they go from one location to another. When it came to hunting doves, a hunter had to be prepared for the unknown at all times. Now, Jimmy knew he had to be prepared at all times when hunting the Hun.

At age 12, Jimmy had developed an uncanny ability to see the birds out of the corners of his eyes. His grandfather, Opa James, had taught him how to calmly watch and wait for the birds to appear. Jimmy had excellent vision and could pick out the rapid movement of a dove in flight before anyone else that was working the dove fields. With Opa's guidance, he had become an accurate and effective shot. He could bring the fast-moving targets down with simple and controlled movements. Deliberate and fluid motions of the body and the gun were the keys to a successful hunt. Jimmy learned to move the gun as if it were a part of his body.

He learned that day that aerial combat was like a wild dove hunt. The enemy birds came out of nowhere and darted in and out in all conceivable directions. Jimmy remembered vividly how he *felt* more than *saw* the Huns around him. The red devils had acted exactly like a flight of doves that Jimmy had witnessed on a hunt five years before. From the corner of his eyes, he had seen a large black object approaching his position in the field from the direction of the sun. Looking slightly away from the light to avoid blackout, Jimmy watched the single dark object explode into five distinct objects. The mourning doves, arranged directly in Jimmy's line of sight to the sun, were approaching the field one behind the other. Only when they cut to different directions did Jimmy know the object to be a flight of doves.

That's how the Germans had avoided detection as they approached Jimmy's flight of four that day. They had arranged themselves in single file and aligned themselves with the sun. The tactic was brilliant. It was also a very complex aerial achievement, especially for twelve aeroplanes in a line. *And* they were doing it in three dimensions not just two. The American fliers were in front of the Germans, and the sun was behind them. Jimmy was amazed. The effective alignment of a single flight of *twelve* aeroplanes to the sun with Jimmy's flight of four was an excellent execution of aerial maneuvering in three-dimensional flight.

Jimmy's alertness and constant thinking did not end with his analysis of how the Huns were able to jump his flight with so many aeroplanes. He didn't know how to tell anyone what he was thinking. He also couldn't stop thinking about the rest of the action that day.

He now understood that the constant alertness after combat must be why fliers are ordered to take two days' rest after their first kill. He just couldn't stop his mind from racing. The pitch black and eerie silence of the room made it even more difficult for him to think. It was as though he was in a whiskey barrel, cooped up without any sensations. He couldn't even feel the ropes of his bed that he knew were beneath the mattress.

Concentrate, Jimmy thought. *This rapid change from one thought to another is self-defeating. Think.*

He relaxed and tried to relieve the tension in his body. That helped him open his mind and come to understand how he was able to fire his machine gun at the right moments during combat. He understood why he could align his machine with the proper lead on the enemy aeroplanes. The way the hunter fires his gun at birds over the dove fields is exactly how a flier has to align his aeroplane with an adversary in combat. The tracers leaving the weapon help him align his machine. But the flier must set up the alignment long before the enemy is engaged. The only difference between a dove hunt and the Dance of Death is that the hunter is standing still. The hunter moves in three dimensions in the Dance. Jimmy realized he had an uncanny ability to properly set the firing alignment of his machine gun in aerial combat. He had never fired from a moving platform at a moving object in three-dimensional flight before. But he had done it very well in the short twelve minutes of the engagement that day.

Jimmy was getting tired. He stretched and noticed that his aches were subsiding. His body was recovering. Soon he would be refreshed. His mind wandered in swirling passes of red and tan. He was in a tan machine. It was the trainer he flew at the French School of Aerial Preparation. The forty-five days that he was in orientation, learning, and practice had passed in a flash. There were times of boredom. There were times of shear elation and disappointments. The waiting and wondering during preparation caused Jimmy to dwell on what he had done. His thoughts at flying school came back to him.

Why had he volunteered? Why did he take on the challenge of the Escadrille Americaine representatives when they visited Wausau during their Midwest tour? Why did he get a false birth certificate and lie about his age? The representatives had been told of Jimmy's flying abilities. Many private fliers told the representatives that they knew of a legend of early flight in Wisconsin. Jimmy Smitts was a man they needed to interview. Did the representatives of the Escadrille convince him that this was his passion, this was his destiny? Did he just want to fly at someone else's expense? Did he seek adventure and a challenge at such a young age?

It was all of that. Jimmy wanted it all. He volunteered for the adventure, the challenge, and the thrill of the unknown. But he was mostly there *because* of his passion to fly. He knew he was good. He just didn't know how good he was until he was in the French flying school. That's when he fired his first Lewis machine gun. The elation, the thrill, the mesmerizing sight of the arcing tracers leaving the vibrating Lewis, gave Jimmy a level of excitement he rarely felt on the ground. Now he knew from the combat that day that he was not just good. He was the *best*.

Jimmy's mind raced from thoughts of Sergeant Walters and Corporal Johns to *Jagdstaffeln* and mourning doves. He remembered his first flying mission in the war. Then his second. After the excitement and rush of anticipation in his second takeoff to combat, he was almost out of fuel. They hadn't seen an enemy flying machine in an hour of patrolling the skies over Verdun. What was going on? Were the Huns in hibernation? Hell, this is his second patrol and nothing, nothing now, and nothing during the patrol the week before, for God's sake. Something had to give. His flying leader was now signaling for them to turn southwest. We're going home without a fight, he complained to himself. He felt very dejected as he landed. *When will we get into some real action?* Jimmy wondered. *When will this boredom end?*

Combat, when it came at last during his third mission with the Lafayette Escadrille, was the most exciting event of his life. The weaving, maneuvering, and danger of it were all he had hoped and dreamed it would be. It was exhilarating, and he had to have more of it. Jimmy realized it was his destiny.

As sleep approached, Jimmy's vision fogged. He was walking with his Opa in a dove field, then flying 6,000 feet above Verdun, then walking again in some strange place. Then, back at aerodrome headquarters, he watched as Clive stepped up and took his kill. Then Clive reached in and stole his bread at dinner. Clive grabbed his bishop on the chessboard. Then all of the fliers in the squadron were reaching in, taking *his* kills, *his* bread, and *his* chess pieces. The fliers, surrounded by red and tan streaks, came into and out of his vision like angry Huns.

Sleep finally came to him. He was floating in air high above the earth again.

CHAPTER 3: THE DREAM

Luxeuil-les-Bains, France - June 9, 1917

So, if I am of German descent, Jimmy thought, *why am I now in the Great War fighting against the Germans? It was simple. I volunteered to fly. Flying is my passion. I was hooked the first time Father took me to an aerial demonstration of biplanes in the fields around Wausau in the spring of 1908. But my heritage gave me the drive to fight.*

He then saw another vision of his mother, Thelma. She was telling him that his grandfather had changed his name from Otto Schmidt to James Smitts upon arrival at Ellis Island from Germany via Holland in 1873.

"Opa James spoke very little English at the time. He came to 'Amerika' to get away from his Hessian Mercenary heritage. Your great-grandfather fought in the Franco-Prussian wars. He felt that it was Opa's Hessian duty to join the mercenaries of Land Hessen when he was young. Land Hessen is the militant land of central Germany."

Thelma told Jimmy it was every Hessian youngster's "Ba-fail," or order, to join the mercenaries. Hessian men were bigger than other German nationals. They were best suited for the hard and challenging work of defending other peoples for a price.

"Jimmy, your grandmother, Oma Brigitte Burth, grew up in a small town near Coblenz in the German country of Rhineland-Phalz. Land Hessen and Rhineland-Phalz are next to each other in Germany. The people of Rhineland-Phalz do not like the Hessians. They are afraid of them. Hessians are large men. They are also bullies. Hessian men think they can dominate other peoples. They also look to be paid for their miserable and demented trade."

"After all," Thelma said, "selling yourself as a mercenary *is* a trade."

Opa James was never enamored with the idea of fighting for just any cause on anyone's call to arms solely for money. He saw many of his neighbors with terrible war wounds. The fact that men were maimed in combat made Opa realize how futile the duty really was. After all, the wounded men could no longer fend for their families. Many Hessian families suffered because of what the duty had done to the breadwinners of the households in the neighborhood.

Opa had been told that the French were the aggressors in the 1860s. Years of hatred between the two countries brought them extremely close to Armageddon. Many of the European countries were militarized. The Germans were the bane of the continent. They had easily been defeated in the past. But 'Land Prussia,' as the Germans called it, established an effective and efficient military staff structure. Prussians became the source of Germany's militarization and effective mobilization for war.

The Prussian military doctrine had dominated the European continent for seventy-five years after the Franco-Prussian war. It also led to untold devastation and nearly world domination for these early years of the twentieth century.

The French aggression toward Germany in the late 1860s led to false confidence in their ability to defeat Les Boche. The Franco-Prussian War showed the world how much Germany had changed in only ten years. Germany so dominated the war that the world took note. After the war, Germany maintained its pressure on Europe as the continent's main aggressor. The Huns had taken the territory of Alsace and Loraine from the French. The people of both territories were a mixture of French and German settlers. But France and Germany constantly took the land from one another over the years.

Opa James had no stomach for the militaristic society that unfolded in Germany after the war. He wished only to live a life of freedom and compassion. He found his way to a Dutch ship bound for some town in America. It was a town named after the city of York in England.

On the ship to America, Opa had changed his name from Otto Schmidt to James Smitts in order to avoid the complications of immigration. He had heard that Americans had a lot of animosity toward Germans, especially Hessians. Hessians had fought for the

British against the Americans in the American War for Independence. Otto—no, James—was worried about what would happen to a young German with mercenary heritage. After all, everyone was leery of Hessians. He was now James Smitts and coming to America to promote the future of the country, his new country—*Amerika.*

Healthy and determined to live a new life of dedication to family and friends, Opa James followed the German farmers from New York City to Wausau, Wisconsin. A year later, he met and married Brigitte. Oma's family had lived in the Wausau area for a generation.

Looking for adventure and the hope of a secure future, Jocham Burth had moved his young wife and daughter, Brigitte, to the new country in the 1850s. Jocham was an international man. He, of few from central Germany, longed to learn about new cultures. He was not enamored with the idea that Germany was shaping itself into a dominating military force in Europe. He preferred to move his family to safety rather than sit and watch Germany overwhelm and dominate its neighbors.

As an artisan, Jocham could take his trade to America, avoid the cultural friction between European peoples, and prosper. The Burth family lived a very happy and private life. Brigitte met Opa James shortly after he arrived in Wausau and quickly fell in love. She respected and admired his dedication and hard work. He was certainly no Hessian, Brigitte would always say. He was a devoted family man who showed compassion to everyone he knew. He was honest and supportive.

In moving to Wisconsin, Opa could at least communicate with the German immigrants while he worked in the fields and studied his English. He had no idea when he made his decision to move to American that he would find true love and plenty of work. But he was totally different than the Hessians that Brigitte had heard of from her parents and grandparents. At first she was scared of what this man could be. After all, her family told her when she was growing up how unpredictable and scary the Hessians were.

Opa James met and was hired by Mr. Daniel Doede, of distant German descent. Mr. Doede noticed how dedicated and hard working

James was. Whatever Mr. Doede needed done, he could rely on James to do it and do it right. After one year of servitude in the fields, Mr. Doede asked James to help in the General Store on Main Street in Wausau. James was amazed at the many products in the store. The store rarely ran out of the various grains, food products, and farm equipment that it kept in stock. The store also sold firearms of all makes and models.

The bond that formed between James and Mr. Doede laid the foundation for a life in financial security for James and his growing family. It also gave James the opportunity to live his dream of devotion and dedication to family and friends. The firearms in the store gave him the opportunity to show his excellent marksmanship to customers. Mr. Doede was extremely pleased with his hard-working assistant. Business was picking up due to James's abilities. And the most expensive items in the store, the firearms, were flying off the shelves.

Business was good and life was better for the Smitts family. James and Brigitte had three children. The oldest was James Earl Smitts. James was a wonderful child. He worked very hard at school. He did his chores and helped the neighbors. As a young man, James helped Mr. Doede and his father in the general store.

It was at the store that James first met Thelma. The Moreheads frequented Mr. Doede's store. But it was not until she was thirteen years old when they finally allowed Thelma to join them on their shopping trips. The attraction between James and Thelma was immediate and lasting. The deep love that developed between them would endure through many hardships. It also resulted in four wonderful children. Jimmy was the first and learned early how to manage the other children – and his chores around the Smitts farm.

Jimmy was hooked the first time his father took him to an aerial demonstration of biplanes in the fields around Wausau in the spring of 1908. Jimmy was nine years old, and Father was going to buy himself a flying machine.

Mr. Smitts intended to fly for the farmers in the countryside around Wausau. He also hoped to hire out as a flying messenger of some kind. Perhaps he could deliver news or baskets of products. Father told Jimmy how he hoped Mr. Doede would need *their* help moving products from the general store to his customers. It was funny to Jimmy how Mother thought Father was crazy. "Who would actually pay good money to have a flier fertilize fields and deliver news?" she would say. Mother realized that father was determined to start this new hare-brained adventure. It would be easier for her to accept if someone else in the town was doing it. Mother, like many in Wausau, had no idea what an aeroplane was and what it could do. This is insane, she used to say.

The Curtiss Jenny Mr. Smitts purchased was an amazing machine to the young Jimmy Smitts. Its large wings and massive engine were things that few people understood or even welcomed. The modern age was here, and Mr. Smitts was going to be a part of it. Jimmy was elated. He would not find out for another four years that the Jenny was an extremely bulky, slow, and fragile work of early modernization. At the transfer of ownership, both Mr. Smitts and his young son were excited as they became the talk of the town. Mr. Smitts' new business was going to double the production of the fields of Wisconsin. At least that was the skinny around town.

Jimmy couldn't wait to learn how to fly. He watched his father work hard every day to try to make a living. The Jenny was expensive to maintain. Its canvas covering had to be constantly repaired and cleaned. A goose flew into the wing during flight in the winter of 1916. The spar and canvas covering on the wing had to be rebuilt. That accident almost ended Mr. Smitts's enterprise. The fact that it almost killed Mr. Smitts didn't escape Thelma. To Jimmy, the worst was that the accident would delay his flying for about two months.

Wintertime brought complications with proper winterization and maintenance of the aeromachine's engine. Mr. Smitts struggled constantly to make ends meet. But he always showed great strength of character and honesty in working with his clients. Jimmy just wanted to fly. Sitting in his father's lap in the cockpit of the Jenny in flight when he turned thirteen years old was a thrill for Jimmy. But it wasn't until he took off alone on his fifteenth birthday that Jimmy was totally hooked on flying.

One year later, swallowing hard against the fear from his stomach to his throat, Jimmy performed his first barrel roll in the Jenny. Boy, was that close, thought Jimmy. The darned thing almost came apart. It also ate up almost one thousand feet of altitude.

Thank the good Lord Father didn't know I had performed the maneuver. Father would have killed me because it would have ended their chances of putting meat on the table if I had crashed. If Father hadn't killed me, Mother certainly would because it would have scared her to it.

As Jimmy finally fell into deeper sleep, his thoughts passed from one scene to another.

Suddenly doves were everywhere. Opa James was behind Jimmy as Jimmy trained the 16-gauge, single-shot Winchester shotgun on one of the gray fluttering masses above him. Giving proper lead on one bird in the mass, Jimmy waited until the bird was below and slightly behind the gun's front sight. After all, at this distance, the lead shot would drop before impacting the bird as it sped across the sky.

At 11 years old, Jimmy had had a full year of practice leading doves in flight. His practice over the summertime in 1909 gave him the calm and cool demeanor to bring the shotgun up to his shoulder without jerking the weapon. The dove folded up and dropped like a stone. The trick to being a great marksman was to avoid jerking the trigger. One had to ease the trigger back and be surprised by the report of the gun, his Opa had said.

"Vunderbar, Yimmy," Opa said in his fragmented English. "Das war goot und smoot. Great scheest."

* * * * *

Now Jimmy was in a cloud, confused and lost. He realized he was in his second barrel roll. He was preparing to pounce on a mass of red in the Dance of Death. Did the doves change colors? Jimmy wondered. No, Clive was changing the colors. He was taking one of Jimmy's red doves.

Sergeant Stevens couldn't seem to wake the youngest flier in the Lafayette Escadrille. *What's going on?* thought Stevens. *Smitts is covered in sweat. Is he coming down with fever or malaria?* Stevens hoped the newest flier with the latest kill wasn't getting sick. The group needed his flying and killing skills.

Jimmy flinched as bullets flew by. He heard a distant voice calling to him, "Lieutenant!" He realized that he was bathed in sweat. "Aren't you coming to breakfast, Lieutenant?"

Breakfast? In the heat of aerial combat, someone is yelling about *breakfast?*

The fog of the cloudbank was clearing, Jimmy noticed, and he knew that he wasn't in the cockpit executing a barrel roll, or diving on red aeroplanes. It was breakfast time in June 1917, and someone was attempting to wake him. He was no longer in the air above Verdun or in the dove field with Opa.

"Are you okay?" asked Sergeant Stevens.

"Yes, Sergeant Stevens," said Jimmy as he rose to his feet. "I need to clean up and will be over to breakfast in the hotel presently." Jimmy knew he had to collect himself, clean up, and walk across the carriageway to the inn.

The stiffness was still there, but the ache in his shoulder had subsided somewhat. While looking into a mirror in the gang bathing area while shaving, Jimmy saw the large black and blue bruise on his shoulder. He must have banged hard against the cockpit frame. He was lucky the blow hadn't kept him from working the Lewis machine gun.

At breakfast Jimmy thought about the debriefing of the day before and became still more determined to practice his trade. In spite of what Clive had done to him, he was a hunter-killer. His uncanny ability to see movement in all directions and intersect the path of arcing machine-gun tracers with the predicted path of the enemy in flight made Jimmy realize that he was the best there is at aerial combat.

His thoughts were interrupted by the voice of Bill Thaw. "Son, you need to relax today and tomorrow," Thaw said. "The mechanics need time to repair your machine. It is pretty well shot up. Spend some time reading and playing chess or cards. We're planning the missions for next week, and we'll put you in a flying group on Monday."

"Bill," said Jimmy, "I think I'll work on the alignment of my Lewis today if that's okay. I'd like to go to the firing range and tune up."

"Okay, discuss it with the mechanics. Your practice won't be very helpful if you don't have a machine to fly next week."

Jimmy gave it some thought. He realized the mechanics could repair his wings as he fired the Lewis at the range. They only needed to take the equipment to the firing field in order to make the machine right again.

* * * * *

North of Nancy, France – August 8, 1917

The veteran infantryman was stirred by the shouts from his First Sergeant. "Sergeant Witherspoon, take your squad over to the right. Probe toward the right front and see if you can make your way up the slope to the right and outflank that enemy position," yelled First Sergeant Miller over the noise of the action around them.

Sergeant Witherspoon gave hand signals to his squad members. They crawled on their bellies through the woods to their right. The bullets whizzed over their heads and struck the tree branches and leaves around them. The Germans were putting down a heavy base of fire from their bolt-action Mauser rifles. Thank goodness, Witherspoon thought, the Germans didn't have any machine guns with them right now.

The squad had to leave Corporal Roberts behind with the rest of the platoon. He had been shot in the shoulder and couldn't continue on. He was still able to fire his weapon. So he stayed with the rest of the platoon and could at least support the squad. Corporal Roberts was a real loss to the squad. He was an excellent shot, and his willingness to stay in the fight gave everyone the confidence to push on.

Sergeant Witherspoon continued to move his squad as far to the right as he could without losing contact with the rest of the platoon. The First Sergeant had taken over the platoon because both Lieutenant Johnston and Staff Sergeant Mitchell had been wounded. It didn't look as if Staff Sergeant Mitchell was going to make it. He had been shot through the neck and was bleeding a lot.

Witherspoon brought his seven men closer to him when they got to their jump-off point. The men called him Old Sarge because he was the oldest in the platoon. He was just a buck sergeant because promotions were slow in peacetime. Old Sarge signaled for his men to fix bayonets on their weapons. Then he placed them on line abreast about eight feet apart. This array would keep the soldiers far enough apart and prevent more than one soldier from getting wounded by one grenade or burst of enemy fire. Also, an on-line rush to the enemy position would put as many soldiers as possible in the assault and deliver them as quickly as possible onto the enemy.

The company had practiced this kind of envelopment more times than Sergeant Witherspoon could remember. This maneuver was working like clockwork. All Witherspoon needed to do was wait until the First Sergeant ordered continuous fire on the enemy position. Once Witherspoon and his men heard the high rate of fire from the platoon, they would rush the enemy position. The most effective rush would be without firing a shot until the squad was on top of the enemy position. Timing was everything. The platoon would lay down a heavy base of fire. A few seconds later, Witherspoon's squad would rush the enemy with fixed bayonets. Jumping into the enemy trenches, the squad would open fire and kill the enemy with rifle fire and the bayonet. The rest of the platoon would shift its fires to avoid hitting anyone in Witherspoon's squad. At least that's what was supposed to happen.

The American soldiers in the platoon started their effective and sustained fire on the enemy position. Witherspoon paused then, nodded to his squad. The eight soldiers rose and charged the enemy position. They had thirty yards to cross and hoped they could do it as quietly as possible. As they approached the enemy, one German turned to engage the squad. Sergeant Witherspoon ordered his men to open fire only by shooting the German through his chest. He didn't need to speak. His rifle spoke for him. The squad was on the German position in a flash. They jumped into the enemy trench and shot, speared, and beat all of the Germans to death. The action was over. It happened fast. The position was in the hands of the Second Platoon, F Company, 26th Regiment of the 1st Expeditionary Division in the assault.

The fresh soldiers of the American Expeditionary Force had just gained their first ground in the Great War. As fillers for the French Army, the men in the Regiment were gaining the valuable experience of combat.

The American 26th Infantry Regiment had been assigned to the Eastern French Corps under General Castelnau. The regiment was positioned northwest of the French town of Nancy north of the Moselle River. The regiment was one of only a few American units thrown into the mix to bolster the morale of the French forces. The Germans had successfully defended their trenches and renewed their advances through the Somme and Aisne battlefields. The toll on the French forces demanded quick and decisive action. Young and inexperienced American Doughboys filled the voids in the French lines just in time.

First Sergeant Miller brought the rest of the platoon to the enemy position now that the action was over. He looked at the 31-year-old sergeant and said, "Sergeant Witherspoon, you are now Staff Sergeant Witherspoon and the new platoon sergeant for Second Platoon. Lieutenant Johnston and Staff Sergeant Mitchell are both down. You are in charge."

As quickly as it had started, it ended. As quickly as it ended, First Sergeant Miller gave his orders to Witherspoon and was gone. Staff Sergeant Witherspoon was now in charge and had no idea what he was to do next. The First Sergeant had spoken loudly enough for everyone in the platoon to hear his words. There was no question about what had just taken place. The only question was what he was going to do now. Was he to continue to move forward, hold the position, or move back to their previous fighting positions?

Witherspoon went for moving forward. He knew the men were all new recruits. But they were well trained and led by experienced noncommissioned officers like him. If things didn't go well, they could always come back to the German position they had just taken. He also realized that for the first time his men had seen some of their squad and platoon members wounded and killed in action. Witherspoon wanted to keep his soldiers moving and thinking about anything other than the wounded and dead.

"Sergeant James, we're moving out, First Squad lead. Corporal Rogers, you're now the Second Squad leader. Move your men out behind First Squad. Third Squad, reserve behind Second Squad. Second Platoon will advance northeast toward Hill 143."

The orders couldn't have been clearer. Each squad formed into an attack formation in perfect order. The men throughout the platoon knew immediately that First Sergeant Miller could not have made a better selection for their new platoon sergeant. And the men realized they were moving out without an officer.

It took only twenty minutes for the platoon to reach Hill 143. The men had heard gunfire to their right front. But the enemy had not seen Second Platoon moving through the woods up to the hill. Sergeant Witherspoon called for the three squad leaders to join him in the center of the hill.

As he waited for the squad leaders, Sergeant Ralph Witherspoon took a breather. He sat and looked down at his weathered hands. He thought about the southern Pennsylvania coal-mining town he'd left to join the Army. He had to get away from the dangers of mining. His 5-foot 10-inch frame and rugged background served him well through his peacetime training in the Army over the last eight years. *How ironic*, he thought. *I got away from the dangers of mining to be here – facing the dangers of war.*

Witherspoon's train of thought was broken by the squad leaders as they started showing up.

He motioned to his junior leaders to sit with him. "Let's dig in," he told them. "I want Third Squad behind the hill in reserve and to watch our backs. First Squad on the right. Second Squad on the left. Third Squad to send runners to our flanks to hook up with adjacent units. Machine guns to cover any formidable approaches to the position. Everyone prepare for an enemy counterattack. It's getting dark and I want us ready to repulse anything that comes up the hill to our front. No fires. We eat cold tonight. Any questions?"

All three squad leaders simply said no and moved out. The advanced position of the AEF in its first attack of the Great War was just being organized by a newly appointed platoon sergeant and a lot of young Americans with no combat experience.

The night was uneventful. Even though they were scared, the men were ready. They listened to the artillery fire in the distance. Now and again a machine gun would fire under the bright hue of artillery illumination rounds fired by who knew which side? Everything seemed so eerie and threatening. Sergeant Witherspoon sent out two observation listening posts to their front. Each post included two soldiers that would give early warning to the platoon if the enemy advanced on its position.

Witherspoon sat back and listened to the sounds of the night under the pulsating glow of periodic illumination rounds. He remembered how the regiment was only one of a few American units that were capable of being hastily shipped to France to plug gaps in the French defenses. The French army was almost in total mutiny after the disaster of the Nivelle offensive of April 1917.

Nothing threatened the platoon that night. But they were the most advanced position of the entire AEF. Sergeant Witherspoon told his squad leaders they would definitely be attacked in the morning. At the very least, he said, the Germans were going to try to get their lost positions back and push the platoon as far as possible.

As morning broke, they could hear the advance of the rest of F Company on their left. The company commander was trying to establish a solid defensive position with Second Platoon as the base of the company position. But the men of Second Platoon could hear that the company was meeting stiff resistance from the Germans. Clearly Second Platoon was a little too far forward of the rest of the Regiment. Sergeant Witherspoon thought it was time to think about moving back to the position they had taken the day before. As the sun rose higher over the horizon, he thought about sending runners back again to try to make contact with adjacent units and get orders for their next move.

It was too late. Rifle fire opened up before them and bullets flew about their position. The Germans were probing to see if they could find the American front lines. Sergeant Witherspoon called for runners to go to the squad leaders to tell them to hold their fire. He didn't want the men to give their position away to the enemy. The position was strong but it couldn't protect them from an enemy envelopment. He also didn't want the Germans to fire their artillery on them.

Sergeant Witherspoon quickly wrote out his order: "Second Platoon to continue to dig deeper and strengthen its position. All squads to hold fire until ordered or at risk of being overrun." Then the runners were off. Would his orders arrive in time?

Everyone in the platoon that heard or read Sergeant Witherspoon's orders was impressed by their simplicity and conciseness. They could see that Witherspoon knew what he was doing and he did it effectively and with precision.

The probing fire of the German infantry stopped. After a while the German artillery started probing the position. Artillery rounds exploded in front of the forward squads. The artillery rounds were being fired indiscriminately. The Germans still did not know where they were. The rounds were landing all around them. At least they were not landing in the middle of the position and the Germans were not concentrating the artillery fire.

Hell, Witherspoon thought, *the Germans probably don't know where we are. Even I don't know where we are. I know we passed through the area north of Toul, and we are north of the Moselle River. But the exact location of our position escapes me. At least I know which way we need to advance or withdraw. I guess time will tell which way we go.*

Then combat activity came to a standstill. The men of Second Platoon sat and waited for word of what to do. They sat in their fighting positions knowing they had performed well in their first engagement. The platoon had lost its leaders and some of its men. They also had constant trouble with the French rifles they had been issued.

Witherspoon checked to see that the 8mm ammunition of the French rifles was evenly distributed around the platoon. The Americans had been issued the short-barrel version of the French Lebel rifle. The AEF had been brought into the line so quickly that it didn't have sufficient weapons. It had to use French and British rifles, machine guns, artillery pieces, and ammunition until America completed its mobilization. Witherspoon did not like the Lebel. It seemed to him that the French gave the weapon to the Americans because the French didn't want to deal with its problems. It carried eight bullets but was loaded by putting them backward in the front of a magazine tube under the barrel. The process took time and required that the soldier put the weapon behind him or to the ground. The bolt action of the French rifle was also stiff, and the rifle jammed constantly. Rounds did not move down the magazine tube very easily. The bullet casings were flimsy and sometimes expanded when the weapon was fired. That caused them to not eject smoothly. But the platoon was in a strong position with new and very capable leadership. Now it was just down to sitting and waiting to see what was going to happen. The waiting was eerie.

The men ate cold food again at lunch to avoid detection. It looked as if they were going to spend another night in the position when the noise before them broke the silence. Everyone in the platoon could tell that a large force was moving through the woods toward their position. Branches were snapping underfoot, metal was clanging, and voices could be heard in the distance. The lookouts came back to the main position. They announced the arrival of a strong German infantry force to the front and front right of the platoon. Everyone in the unit was on edge.

"Sergeant Witherspoon," one of his runners said. "I hope these damn French rifles hold up for a change. It sounds like we're gonna need everything we got."

"Son, just follow your training," Witherspoon replied. "The Germans don't know what they're getting themselves into. We're gonna whip 'em in no time."

Suddenly rifle fire broke out to the right front of First Squad. The fire grew in intensity and started building up all along the Second Platoon front. Witherspoon could tell that First Squad was completely engaged. A runner came back to platoon headquarters from the Squad. He reported to Sergeant Witherspoon that the Germans were on top of them.

The runner said while trying to catch his breath, "Sergeant Witherspoon, Sergeant James doesn't think the squad can hold much longer."

Sergeant Witherspoon sent the runner back, saying, "Tell Sergeant James that I'm bringing Third Squad up to counterattack."

The whistling buzz of bullets was everywhere. Tree limbs and leaves were falling all around the platoon position as Witherspoon moved the Third Squad into position for its counterattack. The debris in the air around First Squad was thickest. The Germans were pouring lead into the First Squad position when he gave the order. Witherspoon could tell that his decision was just in time. But the fighting was brutal. The Germans put up a stiff fight. Some of the Lebel rifles lived up to their reputation as unreliable weapons. Men were constantly clearing jams. Five men of First Squad were down by the time Witherspoon and the Third Squad joined the fight. The Squad attacked with fixed bayonets. Hand-to-hand combat broke out with the remnants of the German force as the other Germans pulled back some. Sergeant James was shot through the mouth. Two members of the Third Squad were wounded too. Witherspoon started to organize one more push. He had the men get down, pause, and make sure their rifles were loaded.

Suddenly they were interrupted by a loud, strange noise that seemed to come from everywhere, reverberating off the trees and hills. It grew louder and sounded like a machine of some kind. The sound of machine-gun fire erupted from above. As bullets impacted around the German soldiers, a tan machine flew rapidly overhead. Soldiers dove to the ground. Some covered their ears. Men looked up and saw another tan machine racing behind the first. More loud bursts of machine-gun fire from the air could be heard. German soldiers scampered, trying to avoid the thundering fire from above. The Americans looked up in astonishment and stared at the two machines as they turned up, to the right, away from the scene.

"Look at that!" cried Private Henderson. "What are they?"

"They're aeromachines, you Southern fruitcake!" came the reply from the distance. "Those are Frenchman taking out the Germans. And they're doing one hell of a job of it, I can tell you."

The machines continued on and disappeared behind the trees and a hill before the platoon. The noise of the engines died down quickly. Then there was silence except for the men starting to talk to one another about what they had just witnessed. The action seemed to increase the enthusiasm of the Americans.

Sergeant Witherspoon saw the moment and yelled, "Open up, men. Give 'em hell!"

As the Germans stood in shock at what had hit them, the First and Third Squads unleashed a sustained and concentrated fire on the enemy. With the help of the fliers, the counterattack finally drove the Germans back. But the attack came at high cost, and the enemy was still maintaining sporadic artillery fire on other sectors of the platoon position.

Sergeant Witherspoon realized those aeromachines were the only things that helped them push the Germans back. It was time to go. The platoon couldn't stay there and withstand one more German push. Now that the Germans knew where the platoon was, they could easily envelope the Americans with a flanking movement or the platoon would be in real trouble if the German artillery accurately opened up on them. Witherspoon knew the aerial support they had just enjoyed would not be back. They *had* to move back.

"Second Platoon immediately withdraws to German trenches taken yesterday," was Sergeant Witherspoon's order to the runners.

The platoon moved quickly but with precision. They kept up active fire toward the enemy as they withdrew. Their coordination and effective fire made their withdraw relatively painless. It was tough going because they carried their wounded comrades with them through the underbrush.

The platoon finally reached and occupied the German position they had taken the day before. It was a good fighting position and could be well defended. The only problem Witherspoon had was he did not know what was going on to his right and left. He had to send runners out again to try to find out what he was to do. He also needed to evacuate his wounded soldiers. Their pain and suffering were hard for the other soldiers in the unit to watch. *If I can't get the wounded out of here,* Witherspoon thought, *the morale of the other men is going to suffer with their suffering.*

Then the enemy fire started building up again. The action started on the left side of the platoon. Only five minutes passed before a runner came from the F company commander. The runner said, "The Company is under heavy attack from the left. Captain Sandhurst orders the company to withdraw to its original defensive positions. It looks like the Germans are starting an advance along the entire front. The French are withdrawing on our right. The Captain does not know if our right flank is secure. We need to withdraw."

Sergeant Witherspoon appreciated the information his commander had given him. While threatening, it was so reassuring to know what was going on, Witherspoon vowed to keep his men informed as much as possible. He was also reassured knowing Captain Sandhurst to be an experienced and capable leader. A 1902 graduate of the United States Military Academy at West Point, Captain Robert Sandhurst spoke with the Southern draw of his Virginia heritage. Rumor had it that his full name was Robert Edward Lee Sandhurst, named after General Robert E. Lee of Civil War fame. Captain Sandhurst walked, talked, and commanded with the confidence of a well-rounded and capable West Pointer. Whether he was named after Robert E. Lee or not, Witherspoon knew Captain Sandhurst had the same ability as General Lee to quickly analyze any situation in great detail. He also knew that nothing was more important in combat than having a commander make the right decisions and keep his men informed.

The Second Platoon could not move out of its position fast enough. The German infantry was maintaining constant pressure. The Germans pushed the French forces back over the entire general area of the Southern Somme and Aisne sectors. German General Lundendorff's defenses had held, and his successful advances of the fall of 1917 had just begun. It meant the start of many months of constant fighting up and down the line. The Americans quickly lost the tentative footing they had gained. They also lost their offensive initiative.

Sergeant Witherspoon, as he considered this first engagement in frontline combat, thought his soldiers had shown great fortitude in standing up to the enemy fire and dealing with the stress of seeing their brothers wounded and killed. He was proud of what they had accomplished.

After the Allied forces stopped the German advances in the Verdun sector and held, F Company was removed from the line and given a month to recuperate. It later became a filler for another French unit just south of Soissons. One more month of static trench warfare gave the young Americans an in-depth knowledge of death and suffering.

The pressure and constant fighting resulted in Sergeant Witherspoon, Old Sarge, being promoted from buck Sergeant to Sergeant First Class in the span of only two months. It took Witherspoon seven years in peacetime to make it through two ranks in the Army, private and corporal to the rank of sergeant. It took only two months for him to be promoted two more ranks. The good news for Sergeant First Class Witherspoon meant bad news for others. Five sergeants opened the way to Witherspoon's promotions because they had either lost their lives or were wounded. Witherspoon knew the wounded sergeants had been maimed, not just wounded. The Army classified them as Combat Ineffective. To Witherspoon, it really should be classified as murder and human suffering.

* * * * *

Witherspoon sat back and realized how exhausted he was, physically, mentally, and emotionally. He had seen untold atrocities, pain, and suffering in every imaginable way. The wounds he saw and dressed during combat included gruesome head wounds, dismemberment, and gashing wounds in the torso from bullets and artillery shrapnel, the deadly, spinning, knife-like steel shards that spewed from exploding artillery projectiles.

In a rare moment, Witherspoon confided in his platoon orderly, Private Henderson. "Combat is like nothing I had ever been told it would be. Peacetime training prepared me for combat leadership and decision-making. Nothing could have prepared me for the carnage of actual combat. In peacetime it was all talk. Soldiers never screamed and always recovered from their wounds. In combat no one ever fully recovers from what they see and experience."

"Sergeant, the hardest thing for me is listening to men and boys lying on the battlefield, screaming and crying out 'Mother!' Now *that* can chill even the most hardened men to their bones," Henderson replied.

"And I fear this is just the beginning, Henderson. I'm not too sure how the French and British have been able to make it through three years of war. Fact is, I don't know how *anyone* is going to be able to continue."

CHAPTER 4: PREPARATION, PREPARATION, PREPARATION

Luxeuil-les-Bains, France - June 9, 1917

Jimmy watched the last flying group take off from the landing field. The groups were a mix of Nieuport 11 machines and the newer and faster Nieuport 17 fighters. The last group up had most of the newer machines. Captain Thenault's hope was the Nieuport 11s would bring the Huns up. The Nieuport 17s could fly faster and longer than the 11s. The 11s, the Bébé's were to be the bait. The 17s would pounce on the Germans when they attacked the 11s.

The 17s also had two Vickers machine guns mounted in tandem above the engine cowling instead of one Lewis above the top wing. To load the Lewis one had to lower the gun on a rail system, remove the drum, install a new drum, charge the machine gun, and raise the gun on the rail to its place above the top wing. Sometimes the gun got out of alignment in the process. The machine guns on the 17s were modernized with synchronization equipment that timed the firing with the rotation of the propeller. They also had cotton belts of ammunition with twice as many rounds to them as the 57 rounds in the drum of the Lewis. So the Vickers had more ammunition and was easier to load due to the position of the guns right in front of the flier.

New fighters with more power and firepower, he thought with much enthusiasm. *That will help me kill more Huns.*

Jimmy wished he was on the day's mission. Because he flew a Bébé, he would have been one of the sacrificial lambs. But he would gladly have taken the stick of any machine in this action. As it was, he could only stand with Captain Thenault and watch the fliers take off.

"It sure is a sight, isn't it, Captain Thenault?"

"Yes, Jams," said the Captain, looking up at the formations as they left. "I wonder at the sight each time I see it. I also stand in great satisfaction. Men take great risks for France. They may be characters.

But they do this for *France*. I humble at their determination to kill Les Boche. I also appreciate you, Jams. I am told you, in the air, are a good flier."

"Thank you, Captain. I do my best and only hope that I can do everything I can to help end this war."

"I too. My country is in grave danger. We need strong will. We suffered many travesties during the 1870 war with Germany. We need fliers such as yourself to kill Les Boche and stop the aggression against my people."

"Do you think our materiel will improve? Do you know if more Nieuport 17s are on their way?"

"Ah, yes, Jams. We are next in line for more 17s. I also pray Nieuport 28 will soon come. It has much power, more even than the 17. France also has a new machine. It is better even than the 28. I am told we may get some of them soon too."

"That would be great. We can always use more power. The 11 has a hard time staying up in a turn."

"The 17 has the same problem," Captain Thenault replied. "I don't know whether the 28 is better in a turn or not. We have to see. As for the fliers, I hope they come back to fight again. The British have a difficult time of it to the north. Les Boche have new flying machines that are overpowering the British Sopwith Pub, I hear."

"I believe a good flier can get out of any jam, Captain."

Captain Thenault slowly turned his head and looked up at Jimmy. "This is foolish thinking. You must be confident but modest in the air. Les Boche can come out of nowhere and get any flier. Survival in this war has much to do with luck. I fear some aggressive fliers such as Lufbery will find out the hard way. Other aggressive and reckless fliers have already found their end."

I might be aggressive, Jimmy thought. *But I am anything but reckless. And I am good enough to know how to take the fight to the Huns and stay out of trouble.*

Captain Thenault's talk of more capable flying machines excited Jimmy. He was an expert flier and a crack shot, and he would only get better with a faster aeroplane and tandem Vickers spewing out lead at twice the speed. *I can time my firing as each enemy pilot flies into the intersecting point of my aim,* Jimmy thought. *In that way, I will be able to kill more Huns in each engagement. I will also be able to conserve my ammunition.*

Since he had a kill to his name, perhaps he would graduate to the newer, faster, and more powerful 17. Jimmy thought he was better than most of the fliers and should even be first to skip to a 28. Right now, though, he had more important things to think about than whether he would get a 17 or 28. He flew a Nieuport 11, and it was under repair. He hoped to convince the mechanics to repair his machine at the firing range.

Despite the language difficulties, Jimmy could tell the mechanics were not happy with him. They did not want to move their repair shop down to the firing range. It was hard enough to move the aeromachine to the range for firing practice. Once at the range, the mechanics had to prop the rear landing strut up so the Lewis could be fired. Now they had to travel five or six times between their maintenance shed and the range to get enough gear to the range to fix the wings. Then they had to bring the aeroplane and their repair gear back up to the shed.

Jimmy was convincing in his argument with the mechanics. They knew he was a successful fighter. He had one kill and one "Possible" to his name. And he had done it in his first engagement. The mechanics understood what Jimmy wanted. They wanted to help promote him in his expertise. They relinquished with the satisfaction of knowing they were working with a successful hunter of Les Boche.

After three hours of moving the machine and repair equipment, Jimmy and the mechanics were in position. The equipment was set up next to his aeroplane. The mechanics began their hard work on the wings. Jimmy began his hard work on the Lewis. He worked on clearing misfires and jams. He blocked the firing bolt of the three-oh-three caliber machine gun with a spent shell. He worked on lowering and raising the gun on its rail system. He used his clearing tool to remove jammed cartridges. He mounted and removed the round ammunition drum of bullets and tracers as he rehearsed his loading and reloading exercises.

Lord, they couldn't have made this any more difficult, he thought. *How could anyone reload the weapon in the kind of action I was in yesterday? There was no way, at any time in the twelve minutes of combat that I could have disengaged the gun, hauled it down the rail before me, reloaded the gun and reengaged the gun onto the top of the upper wing. The hauling mechanism makes it easy to bring the weapon down, but I was in so many different flying aspects with the machine. There was just no way I could have done all that in the heat of battle to reload this machine gun. I need a 17.*

Jimmy started to engage the targets on the firing range. The mechanics immediately started their foreign banter with wild hand and arm gestures. They were objecting to the vibration of the aeroplane caused by the rapid machine-gun fire. The vibration must have made it hard for them to work on the wings. Perhaps they were also objecting to the noise. Jimmy relented. He realized, to some degree, that Bill Thaw was right. How was he to kill Huns when his aeroplane was grounded? He had to give the mechanics time to repair his machine.

He decided to work on the action of the Lewis without firing it. He removed and remounted the gun. He disassembled and reassembled the weapon until it was second nature to him. After some time, Jimmy realized he had worked on every conceivable problem with the weapon. All he needed now was a little more time shooting on the range. Perhaps he could go back to the farmhouse and practice something else. What he needed while the mechanics did their dirty work was practice at firing at moving targets.

Jimmy walked the 300 yards from the firing range to the farmhouse. Perhaps the Escadrille had some shotguns, he thought. Maybe he could procure some by some means and work on leading his targets. Jimmy met with Thaw in his office, where he was working on paperwork and planning next week's missions.

"How are the repairs to your wings going?" Bill asked.

"The mechanics are still working on them. I had to leave because my firing was disturbing their repair efforts. Bill, what do you think of setting up a shotgun firing range with moving targets? Don't you think it will help us stay sharp and better engage the enemy machines? If anything, it will help pass the time."

Bill sat back and reminisced. He said, "I practiced with shotguns at an aerial school on Long Island in New York. The school was one of the earliest civilian flying schools in America. The school promoted shooting at moving targets when the European countries started rattling their sabers at one another. As usual, the Europeans argued over nonsense like what culture was most influential and important. Americans were talking about the possibility of war and mobilization. That's when the school thought it best to set up a firing range. It helped but it was more fun than actual preparation for aerial combat."

Opa James had often told Jimmy what Bill had just said. The major powers in Europe hated one another. It had always been about who could dominate whom in the European world. It was said that it had been that way for a thousand years. Jimmy wondered what would stop it. Would it take total devastation?

"The threat of war in Europe made the American civilian fliers think that it was only a matter of time before they could be called up for military duty," Thaw said. Fliers everywhere hoped that the American government would form a group of American fliers to defend the nation. If that were the case, the Long Island Fliers would be ready and able. Bill enjoyed using the shotgun shooting range that was built.

"Little did we know," Bill said, "that the government was *reducing* its fighting capabilities at the time, not preparing for war. Here it is, four long years after we built our shooting range, and America still cannot send a reasonable fighting force to Europe."

"Jimmy," Bill continued, "I think your idea of a moving-target shotgun range can help the newcomers to the squadron. At least it would be entertaining for some of the fliers. But I don't think the older and more experienced fliers will use the range for target practice. They just aren't interested in devoting their time to training."

"We could pass the time between missions on the range without having to drag all the aeroplanes down to the fixed firing range. It might also save lives."

Bill tilted his head as he tapped his desk. "I'll tell you what, I'll take your suggestion to Captain Thenault. If Thenault approves the idea, we'll look for the equipment to organize a range for the flying members."

"Bill, something hit me last night when I was thinking of the attack yesterday. The Huns got the jump on our flight of four. I believe the Germans lined their twelve machines up with the sun."

Jimmy continued to explain the German flying alignment and the three-dimensional calculations they had to do to keep themselves between the Americans and the sun.

"That's very tough to do," Bill said. "I have a hard time believing that the Huns did it deliberately."

"Our location in relation to the enemy lines puts us at a disadvantage in the mid-morning," Jimmy said. "The rising sun gives a marked advantage to the Hun. Something has to be done during those hours of the day to minimize the advantage to the enemy."

"Well, it's true that hunting for German flying machines is most rewarding in the mornings. It seems the Huns come out more often early in the day."

"They have to be doing that because the sun gives them that advantage. We have to divert our approach to the Verdun battlefield in the mid-mornings. The situation is worse if the Hun has perfected its alignment of large formations with the sun. If we head west first and then turn to the east, we'll have the enemy in our sights. We'll have a better chance in the first pass because it'll be too difficult for the Hun to shoot us down. We'll be in a passing engagement. Once we pass one another, we'll have the sun to *our* advantage."

Watching Jimmy walk away toward the firing range, Bill sat back in his chair, satisfied in what he saw in his young charge. *He does have spunk*, Bill thought.

* * * * *

Jimmy reminisced as he sat at lunch. His discussion with Thaw about tactics and strategy in aerial combat brought back to him thoughts of his preparation for becoming a full-fledged member of the American volunteers. The French representatives of the military processing center in Paris treated him like a king when he arrived. After all, he'd volunteered to defend France against German invasion, hadn't he? But Jimmy was there to put his flying abilities up against capable adversaries. And the Germans were exactly that.

America declared war on Germany on April 4, 1917, two months after Jimmy arrived in France. But the American Army was a fledgling force. Its divisions were small and without combat experience. Organized flying squadrons were almost unheard of in the American military. The country had not developed any capable aeromachines for military service. The United States had neither worthy machines nor experienced fliers. America couldn't deliver observers over the battlefield or bombs onto it without the assistance of her European partners.

Perhaps false hopes that America could stay out of another European war kept her from properly preparing, Jimmy thought. American's military-industrial complex was nonexistent. War materiel was ancient and very limited in numbers. Her military forces were small and untrained. Without combat experience on a grand scale, the American forces were totally unprepared for the devastation on the modern European battlefields. So America had to turn to her allies for equipment. She had to turn to the hearts and minds of the civilians to fill the ranks of the fighting units. The effort would take at least a year.

Had Jimmy thought American would enter the war, he would not have volunteered for the French Foreign Legion. But America did not mobilize early enough for the war. Even if the newspapers had written of *possible* mobilization, Jimmy would have waited. He would have much preferred to be an American pilot in an American war effort.

But that was not to be. America did not have suitable flying groups with capable flying machines. Fliers were also second in importance to the infantry in the U.S. Army of 1916 and 1917. Then again, Jimmy remembered, the French representatives got to him first.

The French Caudrons that he trained in at the military aerodrome north of Paris were not much better than the Curtiss Jenny that Jimmy had grown up with. They were as large as the Jenny but a little more powerful and more maneuverable. They were machines of old technology, however, and they had been built with an exposed fuselage structure. The wooden cage of the fuselage formed a "V" shape from the wings to the tail section. At least the Jenny had a modern appearance with a thin fuselage that was covered with canvas.

Had Jimmy not shown his excellent flying abilities in the French Ecole de Preparation, he probably would have been an aerial observer. At best, he would have flown large and clumsy Short Bombers or the newer two-seat Brequet Br.'s that had just been deployed.

But Jimmy had shined in the School of Preparation. The French were impressed with his ability to perform loops and slips. He could even loop in the form of a barrel in the large and slow Caudrons. The French were looking forward to Jimmy's transition to the acrobatic and shooting schools. That's when he met the famed French aviator Lieutenant Charles Nungesser. Jimmy vividly remembered how it happened.

"Gentlemen," the French Commandant of the school began, "I have the honor of introducing one of your instructors. He is none other than Lieutenant Charles Nungesser of the French squadron of American volunteers the Lafayette Escadrille. We are honored to have Lieutenant Nungesser with us as he recuperates from his combat wounds. I turn the floor over to Lieutenant Nungesser."

The men stood and applauded as Charles Nungesser limped to the front of the class.

"Gentlemen, I am pleased to be among you. I hope to show what aerial combat is like. I wish to bring Les Boche and his tactics to you. In this way, you will better be prepared to fly against these animals and save France."

Wow, Jimmy thought at the time. *This French aviator is from the Lafayette Escadrille. I may be able to hear about the unit I'm going to.*

Jimmy breezed through the second phase of his training. It was at the Superior Ecole de Perfectionment where Jimmy showed his real stuff. He was the best in performing the three maneuvers taught at the school, the spin, the barrel, and the reversement. Jimmy knew how to quickly lose altitude by spinning vertically downward. He had done spins many times. He had rolled his Curtiss Jenny in its direction of flight first in 1916 but did not know it was called a barrel. He did not know then that one could also pull on the stick, flip over backward, and turn back right-side up to quickly reverse his direction of flight. He found out he could also perform the maneuver by first flipping upside down. The down reversement lost quite a bit of altitude, but Jimmy was able to do it without losing too much by how tightly he flipped his machine. The students and instructors at the school were impressed.

Charles Nungesser was impressed by Jimmy's flying abilities. Few instructors and even fewer students could make an aeroplane perform like Jimmy could, and no one could shoot like him. Nungesser was happy to hear that Jimmy was going to the squadron of his heart, the Lafayette Escadrille.

Because he was the best flier and had Nungesser's recommendation, Jimmy received the rank of lieutenant. Most graduates were given the rank of corporal or sergeant. Those who just barely graduated became corporals. Many of the corporals and some sergeants were sent off to the bomb and observation squadrons. The best part about being a lieutenant was the extra pay. Jimmy was pleased to get that extra three dollars per month for his rank.

Graduating with William Dugan, Thomas Hewitt, and four French fliers after six months of training in the French training machines, Jimmy finally found home at the Lux. It was nice to have Dugan and Hewitt with him. At least he had other new fliers to relate to when he got to the aerodrome.

Jimmy's preparation did not stop when he left the French schools. He, Willie, and Tom went through rigorous exercises and testing at the hands of the Lafayette Escadrille fliers under Bill Thaw's tutelage. They had to get used to the flying controls of the Nieuport 11 and get accustomed to the arrangement of the gauges in the cockpit of the fighter. The new fliers were used to the clumsy arrangement where the machine gun was mounted on top of the top wing of the 11. It was just like the machine-gun mounts of the Caudrons that they had flown in the French shooting school.

Jimmy and the other newcomers had been fortunate to fly their first two missions as "Milk Runs." Those missions were intended to calm the new fliers' nerves and provide them with some time to get accustomed to flying combat formations and the terrain below them. To Jimmy, the Milk Runs were just a waste of time. He wanted desperately to show his stuff against the Germans. After all, he thought, that's why they need *me*, isn't it?

His first experience against the Germans proved him right. Nothing in his preparations to becoming a flying member of the French fighting squadron was as thrilling and challenging as the combat. He had passed the biggest flying test he had ever been exposed to. *And* he had won. He couldn't wait to get another chance at winning.

Jimmy returned to the firing range to check on the progress of the repair to his wings. He was extremely restless. After reminiscing about his training and reliving the high-octane emotions he went through in only twelve minutes of flying yesterday, he just couldn't sit still.

Jimmy was amazed at how fast the mechanics had replaced the spar in his wing. They were gluing the new canvas onto the finished frame. Even the guy wires were all repaired and back in place. They would soon be ready to paint the finished product. The good news was that Jimmy could fire the Lewis as the glue dried.

The firing soon resumed. Three-oh-three rounds were arcing toward the distant paper target. Jimmy adjusted the vertical elevation and sideways deflection of his machine-gun mount so that the firing spread was perfect for targets at 50 yards. That distance was used by the squadron to "zero" the machine guns. It gave the fliers a perfect intersecting point of their aim and the bullets. One fired slightly below an adversary within 50 yards and aimed above the target if it was more than 50 yards away. At a range of over 200 yards, the bullets would more than just drop. They started to plunge. Plunging fire was used by infantry machine gunners, artillerists, and aerial gunners. There were many advantages to plunging fire. But it had to be used in the air only when necessary, as it was inaccurate and hard to control. *Get anywhere within 50 yards of me,* Jimmy thought, *and any target was going down.*

He and his machine were almost ready. The machine needed only the paint that made it a Lafayette Escadrille flying weapon. The mechanics would soon apply the tan color with a slight reddish hue to the wing canvas. He was flush with excitement, excitement he had not felt since his first barrel roll. *How had that Jenny stayed in one piece anyway?* Jimmy reflected.

As he approached the farmhouse, the first flight of Bébé's was returning from the front. He wondered whether anyone had made kills that day. He rooted for all of the fliers, no matter who they were and how they treated him. What mattered to Jimmy was that Allied fliers lived and Huns died.

Jimmy approached Willie Dugan as he climbed out of his machine. As a newcomer, Willie also flew an 11. He had been one of the bait planes flying to bring the Germans into the air.

"How did it go, Willie? How did you do?"

"I don't think there is much to report on by way of action. The Huns must have been keen to Captain Thenault's tactic. They never really came up to challenge us. At least, from my vantage point, I didn't see anything come up. Maybe Lufbery had more luck in his group. You know him. He'll pounce on anything that flies."

"Let's go sit down and relax," Jimmy suggested. "You look exhausted."

"I am. I think I need a bath and some rest. I'm sure Lufbery is going back up again. He always does. I'm out. I need to take a break."

"Sure, Willie. Take it easy."

As Dugan began to leave, he turned to Jimmy. "By the way, have you seen Hewitt? He reported engine trouble over the Bains. He turned back and should have landed a long time ago."

"I was tied up with the repairs to my machine. I haven't seen him. But it looks like his aeroplane is over there at the end of the line."

Then Raoul Lufbery came up to them in a rush. "Where is Le Hewitt?" he asked. As a French immigrant to America, he spoke with a strong French accent. "You are his buddies and know of him. You were with him at flying school. Where he is?"

"Not sure, Raoul. I know he had engine trouble. His Nieuport is just over there. What's up?" Willie asked.

"Engine trouble? That's three time he has engine trouble while flying in the group of mine. The man is a cad, he is scoundrel, that is *what is up*. I shall have his tail if he does it more. We are here to kill Les Boche. We not here to fly for fun leaving the sky anytime things get hot. Oh shucks, forget it. I go back up by myself. You wish to come with?"

Willie replied. "I'm sorry, Raoul. I'm spent and Jimmy is on his two-day R&R. Thenault won't release him to combat until tomorrow. Take Hewitt with you if you think he hightailed it and see if he has the guts to go up."

"Hewitt? I won't fly with him if for life itself. When someone back out on you when you need him most is just suicide. Forget it. I kill Les Boche bastards myself."

Jimmy and Willie smiled at each other. They watched Raoul Lufbery get ready to go up again. Willie said, "That French-American sure is hard to understand, isn't he?"

Jimmy nodded as he looked on in amazement. "I wish I could go. That French-American may be hard to understand, but he is a true fighter."

Evening activities were quiet and relaxing. Jimmy liked how the French chefs at the hotel prepared their food. Jimmy especially liked the veal. They never served veal in Wisconsin the way the French chef prepared it. Born in Alsace, the chef was half-German and made a special dark-brown gravy for the veal. He always cut it thin like the Germans. He usually baked it and served it with the gravy. Tonight the veal was breaded and fried. *Boy, how they can cook,* Jimmy thought as he dove into his meal. He thought the portions could be more, but he was comfortable and content. He needed some rest. He planned to use his time effectively tomorrow. He was going up on his second day of R&R to put his machine to its test. He would soon see how well the mechanics had repaired his spar and guy wires.

The next morning, Bill Thaw told Jimmy, "Take it easy at first. I want you to make sure your machine is properly repaired before you perform tight maneuvers. After I take off with the other fliers, I want you to head straight to the training sector. And take it easy," Bill shouted as Jimmy left, looking over his shoulder with a smile and a wave toward his Nieuport.

Bill Thaw and the other fliers were going out as two-man hunter-killers. Jimmy took off and turned to the southwest. He watched as the hunter-killers flew toward the combat area to the northeast.

Flying through 4,000 feet, Jimmy gave the Nieuport a few lazy turning maneuvers. He noticed the guy wires between the left wings were a little too loose. He needed to return to the mechanics to have them adjust the wires before he started his real tests on the machine.

As he slowly banked to avoid putting too much pressure on the guy wires, he saw the glimmering of the early-morning sun reflect off of a number of flying machines in the distance. They were coming his way. Jimmy was alarmed because he knew his machine couldn't withstand combat flying. He would surely lose a wing in a fight. He slowly turned away from his enemies and started a slow dive. He wanted to distance himself from the adversaries and blend in with the ground to avoid detection. This was now very complicated. He didn't want to run but wanted to live to fight another day.

He kept turning and diving. Staying low kept him from easily finding his way back to the Lux. But it was safer than flying high and getting attacked. He finally saw the Mark after avoiding detection and landed his Bébé.

With tight readjustments to the guy wires, Jimmy went into the real tests on his machine. He hoped he could find the group of enemy machines he had seen earlier as he climbed rapidly to 5,000 feet. It was warm enough at that altitude for Jimmy to be comfortable. It was high enough to give him some safety factor in his maneuvering. Barrel right, barrel left, sharp turns right and left. Now the tricky maneuver to top it all off, the reversement. Half barrel, pull on the stick hard, flip around, and head in the opposite direction. There. A very tight reversement without any problems with the guy wires and wings. *Good, good,* he thought. He felt very comfortable with the adjustments the mechanics had done. Now he could go on to the real fun.

Jimmy performed a tight barrel and cut it hard to his right. This formed a turning barrel. The torque from the rotating engine caused some flying machines to be slower and sloppier in right barrels. Even though his Nieuport 11 turned best to the left, it seemed to turn well in the other direction too. Jimmy knew that he could snap his machine as fast as the propeller torque would allow. His right and left rolls by the barrels were much tighter and crisper than those of any of the other fliers.

I wonder when I will be assigned to a new mission, Jimmy thought as he started his approach to the landing field. *What will it be and against how many of the Huns?*

He was ready and he was flush with excitement. He couldn't wait.

* * * * *

South of Chalons, France – March 1, 1918

The constant rumble and swaying of the troop train lulled the packed car of soldiers to sleep. The overheated car made Sergeant Witherspoon, wearing his wool overcoat dose off. He dreamed of his infantry training at Fort McPherson in Atlanta, Georgia, in the summer of 1914. It, like the fighting in the trenches of last August and September, was total misery. Sergeant Witherspoon's new soldiers of the 26th Regiment suffered from heat stroke and heat exhaustion for the first time in 1914. He had never been exposed to such heat and humidity in the three years he had been in the Army. The worst part about the exercises was the lack of rifles and ammunition for proper training. He could endure the heat if they could fire real rifles on a firing range rather than run around with broom sticks as weapons.

"Sergeant Witherspoon," one of the new recruits said, "this weather is killing me. I need a break."

"Son, there are no breaks in combat. You need to buck up and find a way to get through it. I'm here to train you and prepare you for the worst."

"The worst? I can't imagine anything worse than this," the recruit said. "Besides, what war would America ever get into? The only war we have to fight is against the Georgia heat, mosquitoes, and chiggers."

"Son, stay low. You need to keep quiet and watch the ambush zone. This isn't Central Park. It's a training exercise and we'll fail the test if you keep up your complaining."

"Low? That's easy for you to say. You're testing us and can stand up in the breeze. I have to lay here in the dirt and take the heat and the bugs."

Sergeant Witherspoon was one of the older sergeants in the company in 1914 and took the recruit's comments in stride. Many recruits, soldiers, and sergeants had come and gone. Few soldiers wanted to stay in the U.S. Army. The recruiting posters made men feel like the Army was a noble organization formed to defend freedom and liberty. The reality of peacetime boredom and the lack of quality training made many soldiers leave the service as soon as they could.

Most recruits joined the Army to get away from something. Others were ordered to the service to fulfill a court order for juvenile or small criminal offenses. The Army was no place to be for an enterprising young man or those on their way to college. Witherspoon joined the Army to get away from the danger of the Pennsylvania coal mines.

To Sergeant Witherspoon, the Army's preparations for war were in the stone age in 1914. He worked hard to keep young soldiers on track with proper training for war. The Army gave him some purpose in life. He had to keep reminding himself that there was a reason for being. The United States Army had a distinguished history, but it had been engaged only in small skirmishes since the Spanish-American War. He couldn't see where the Army was really going. He hoped to be a part of it but told himself that if this kept up he would need to find another line of work.

But he didn't need to find another line of work. It finally came down to this endeavor. They had passed the tests of combat and were rejoining the rest of the 1st Division at R&R in Fontainbleau west of Paris. Witherspoon now felt calm satisfaction knowing he had prepared his men well. What they endured in peacetime training helped them make it through their first test of trench warfare. He knew with spring upon them, the train was taking them to tests of new heights of combat north of the Marne River.

CHAPTER 5: THE BRIEFING

Luxeuil-les-Bains, France - June 12, 1917

The alarm clock sounded. The sun was not yet up, but Jimmy knew this was a new day. His two-day R&R was over and he was ready. His machine was in perfect order. He had practiced his flying techniques in the air and in his mind. His Lewis was perfectly zeroed with the proper elevation and windage. He was full of excitement as he prepared for the new day. His shoulder was a little sore, but all of the cramps he experienced from his last combat two days ago were gone.

As he rose to prepare himself for the day's action, he heard a noise on the metal roof of the barracks they called home. He struggled to his feet and realized it was raining. Jimmy felt the cold air move through the barracks, and his feet were cold against the wood floor. He opened the wood steamer trunk at the foot of his bed to get his uniform ready for the day's events whatever they might be. The barracks was Spartan, and the trunks were their only private accommodations. The metal roof kept them dry, but it made a racket when the rain fell. The large raindrops this morning sounded like rocks striking a metal plate. Jimmy thought the noise could wake the Devil.

The early summer rain in Alsace-Lorraine was usually cold. It didn't rain often in the summer but when it did it rained hard and it was cold. Today's mission would be delayed, Jimmy knew. But he hoped it wouldn't be canceled. He had to get in the air and test the alignment of his Lewis against *real* targets. He didn't want to spend another day sitting and waiting for his chance to dance with the Huns again.

At breakfast with the other fliers, Jimmy noted that many of them were resolved to wait out the weather. The wind wasn't up but the rain made it dangerous to take off from the field. The fliers knew the weather could change at any minute. One could be in the air when the weather turned worse. The weather could also clear quickly, making for an eventful afternoon in the air.

The rain never interrupted the ability of the artillery to duel. The constant rumble of various calibers of guns firing across No-Man's Land kept the war in the forefront of the flier's minds. That was one thing the fliers could count on. Artillery dueling ebbed and flowed each day like a river. The fliers could tell when an assault from one side of No-Man's Land to the other was underway. The artillery barrages started with a low rumble and rose to a crescendo of single and long-lasting thunder. The roar could be deafening at times. The fliers knew many men would die and be maimed for life once the thunder subsided. At that moment, it was time for the whistles to blow and loud commands of "Over the top!" to be heard on the battlefield.

They had seen it from above. The experienced fliers witnessed the carnage of the Battle of Verdun from their machines. The Allied advance across the barren land of western France resulted in hundreds of thousands of dead and dying on the field. The fliers contributed to the melee, strafing the enemy trenches and supporting the large Handley Page bombers of the British Empire. The Handleys were slow but brought destruction upon the enemy lines with their racks of bombs.

The older fliers joked about the Caudrons. Thank goodness the Caudrons were being taken out of service as bombers. The small fuselage kites for machines were slow and ugly, explained the older fliers. How anyone would dare sit in the cockpit or gunner's seats of those machines nobody knew. They weren't much more advanced than the Wright Brothers' motorized kite at Kitty Hawk, they said.

During the rainstorm, the experienced fliers continued to explain to the newer pilots how the combat had developed. It took only one year after the first aeroplanes flew over the battlefields of Flanders and Verdun that "experts" determined that the flying machine could be an effective mechanism to promote the killing. Aerial tactics and maneuvers were nonexistent in 1914. Fliers such as Major Lanoe

Hawker, Captain Arthur Knight, Captain George Bailey, and Major "Mick" Mannock constantly came up with better ways in which man could exterminate other men in the sky.

American military leaders had been slow to take note of the advances in military aviation in Europe. The American fliers had argued before stubborn infantry commanders about the attributes of machines in the air. The war on the far side of the Atlantic Ocean was an amazing test bed. The arguments fell on deaf ears. Only after Hawker and Mannock became famed aces over France did American officers start to recognize that flying machines could play important roles in warfare.

Hawker and Mannock had been awarded the Victoria Cross, the highest military honor of the British Empire. Then the names began to fall, Hawker in November, Knight in December, and Bailey in February. They all found their end at the hands of German aerial experts like von Richthofen, Max Immelman, and Werner Voss. Everyone was learning the art in the increasingly threatening classroom in the skies.

Jimmy had heard some of the names before in earlier discussions. But he was awestruck by the details of the engagements. Max Immelman's development of the double reversement revolutionized modern aerial combat. He perfected his combat techniques in a single-winged machine called an Eindecker, or one deck. But an ominous feeling came over Jimmy. As each name was brought into the discussion, the name disappeared as final defeat and death eventually found the flier. Jimmy was determined not to let that happen to him. He would continue to learn and perfect his craft, the profession of killing in three dimensions.

Bill Thaw and Lufbery were some of the first in the Lafayette Escadrille to make kills. As a young lieutenant, Bill saw firsthand how Immelman performed his aerial feat. The double reversement he pulled on Victor Chapman was a sight to behold. Chapman was in a dance with four Germans and had Immelman in his sights. Bill was in the distance and had just finished off his second kill. As he turned, Bill saw Immelman perform a rapid vertical half loop. Upside down over Chapman in a reversement, Immelman pulled another half loop and reversed upside down a second time. The maneuver put Immelman right behind Chapman before he knew what had happened. Immelman scored another victory as Chapman landed his shot-up Nieuport, seriously wounded by a grazing bullet to the head. The double reversement startled Bill. Low on fuel, he had vacated the action to report to the others. The fliers needed to know how to stop or counteract the maneuver.

The fliers spoke of Sergeant Walters, who had come to the squadron as a corporal and been promoted by the French to sergeant in late 1916 due to his courage in combat. Everyone in the Lafayette Escadrille came to respect him. The fact that he had been the last to see Walters alive made Jimmy reflect again on his own mortality.

Jimmy thought of his own maneuvering as the fliers talked. He knew of the Immelman. The French School of Perfection taught the reversement maneuver as soon as word got out that Immelman had performed it. But few could attempt the vertical climb and turn to the opposite direction in the aged Cauldron training machines. They needed more powerful and acrobatic machines. Jimmy was the exception in his class. He had performed many maneuvers in the Curtiss Jenny at home. How crazy he had been back then, he laughed to himself. *Why did you take such chances turning so hard and doing loops in a Jenny, of all things?* But he *had* done those maneuvers. He had pushed the biplane to its limits many times, and somehow it had stayed together.

"Briefing in five minutes, gentlemen! Briefing in five minutes!" came the call. Apparently the rain was subsiding. A charge of adrenalin raced through Jimmy's body. He was going into the air again.

"All right, gentlemen, please take your seats," Captain Thenault said as the men filed into the briefing room. "You will be flying in a group of eight today. Your assignments are on the mission schedule board in the planning room."

Thenault explained the current and upcoming weather to the fliers. He planned to turn the mission briefing and upcoming tactical situation on the ground over to Lieutenant Antoine Maison-Rouge but wanted the fliers to know the weather patterns they would face in the air.

"The aerodrome has been experiencing an early-summer thunderstorm that is clearing. The area to the north of the aerodrome is now clear, and I expect the weather here to clear in the next thirty minutes. This will give you an opportunity to take off without problems. You will gather your gear and prepare to take off as soon as the weather front passes to the southwest. The squadron has been receiving calls from headquarters to go aloft and support the operations that Lieutenant Maison-Rouge will now explain."

Maison-Rouge explained that the Allied forces planned to mass their forces around the southern portion of the Verdun battlefield. In an effort to hide the massing formations, headquarters had ordered a portion of the Lafayette Escadrille to eliminate enemy observation balloons that were aloft to the east of Nancy on the Belfort-to-Metz roadway.

Jimmy tried to hide his disappointment. He was basically being told he would fly against a bunch of pansies. Balloons? He was prepared for real action but was going to shoot at stationary objects the size of a barn.

"Once you reach Boubonne-les-Bains," Maison-Rouge continued, "climb to 5,000 feet and travel north-northeast along the Bains-du-Nancy road."

Each flier was to attack targets of opportunity. The observation balloons were the object of the mission, the lieutenant explained. But the fliers were to attack any German machine that was a threat to the squadron.

Lieutenant Maison-Rouge turned the presentation over to Bill Thaw. The senior American flier reminded everyone how to attack balloons.

"You engage each type of balloon differently," Thaw said. "The mechanics are adding tracer rounds, which are most effective against gas balloons, to your ammunition drums and belts. Gas balloons look like large cigars. Hot-air observation balloons look like large balls in the air. They're round at the top, with observation baskets roped to them."

Fliers were to concentrate tracer fire in one large area of the side of the gas balloons. The tracers would light the gas in the balloons. But the fliers had to open a large hole so that the gas would burn. The gas will not burn without air mixed with it. Sometimes, for the balloon to burn, the hole had to be as big as a motorcar so that the gas could escape and mix with the air.

Bullets rather than tracers were effective in tearing the silk of the hot-air observation balloons. The tracers could seal the edges of the silk and minimize the tear. The pilots were instructed to create a gaping tear by walking their fire from low to high. The demise of the balloon would come when the tear reached the top. Within seconds the balloon would deflate and fall to the ground.

"After you engage a balloon," Bill continued, "you must exit the attack correctly. You must fly hard to the left or right, depending on your approach when attacking the gas balloons. Should the gas ignite, the fireball will consume you if you fly directly over the balloon. Be cautious," he said. "The gas can ignite much later than you think. Try never to fly too close to a gas balloon, and don't fly above one whether it's alight or not. You can fly directly over a hot-air balloon. But the rapidly escaping air will buffet your machine and can cause you to lose altitude."

Jimmy had no idea that attacking balloons could be so complicated. They had to be the largest targets in the world. How could anyone miss?

Lufbery interrupted and delivered the most stunning point of the briefing. "It always takes much fire to bring balloon to ground. Fliers concentrate vision on balloon in attack and continue fire on it. Les Boche usually wait until we are involved in attack. That's when Les Boche attack us. Aviators shooting at balloons get shot down."

"That's right, Raoul," Bill said. "All pilots are to stay alert at all times. You have to coordinate your fire on the balloon and still keep one eye on the sky."

Okay, Jimmy thought. *Head on a swivel.*

At the end of the briefing, Jimmy approached Captain Thenault as Bill Thaw watched. Jimmy asked him if he had any confirmation of his other kills. The captain said he had passed the request up to headquarters. He said it usually took a week or two for confirmation to come from the front.

"Concentrate today, Jimmy," Bill said, having heard the exchange. "Attacking balloons can be fun. But you have to be aware of everything around you. The Hun will pounce on you when you least expect it, lad. Good luck."

* * * * *

Chicago, Illinois - June 12, 1916

Mr. Eugene Francis Stevenson sat back comfortably in the overstuffed brown leather chair. He always enjoyed a cigar and cognac at the University Club in Chicago. He didn't enjoy the constant interruptions by his colleagues. Mr. Stevenson was in the middle of a hard-fought campaign for his nomination to an open seat of the U.S. Senate from Wisconsin. His membership at the University Club gave him rights to the other University Clubs in the United States, including Wisconsin and the District of Columbia.

Stevenson had used his family wealth and political influence to gain a large foothold in Illinois and Wisconsin. *Hell*, he thought. *I have a large foothold throughout the Midwest.*

His father, Adlai Ewing Stevenson, had been a member of the House of Representatives from the great state of Illinois. Adlai went on to become the Vice-President of the United States under President Grover Cleveland. Eugene's brother, Luis G., was the current Secretary of State of Illinois.

Adlai was admitted to the bar as a young attorney at age 23. He had amassed a small fortune working the sawmill that he had inherited from his father. He had met and associated with other prominent attorneys such as Stephen A. Douglas and Abraham Lincoln. Stevenson did not like Mr. Lincoln's platforms. Adlai decided to help Mr. Douglas in his quest for the presidency. Mr. Douglas's campaign speeches needed to bring the German and Irish communities of Illinois and the Midwest to his camp. It was his only hope of defeating Mr. Lincoln in their race to the White House. In that light, Adlai helped Douglas write long speeches that took the form of character assassinations. The speeches were not well received. Their length and wordiness lost the attention of listeners, who failed to see the importance of their message. To Adlai the nation picked the wrong man in Mr. Lincoln. Stephen Douglas was an internationally recognized figure and a very influential and effective orator. Adlai's support for Mr. Douglas ended up being a great setback when the Civil War consumed the nation. At least his involvement in politics gave Adlai and his young family national attention. His business success gave them the comforts of an upper-middle-class home. So Luis and Eugene both grew up in comfort and prestige.

Eugene used his influence and money to buy boutique hotels throughout Illinois and Wisconsin. His businesses flourished and were basically self-sustaining. So he turned to politics as the cash rolled in, particularly from his hotels in Chicago.

The Democratic seats of both the House of Representatives and Senate for Illinois were all in solid hands. Eugene's only chance of getting into the Senate was to fight for the seat that was available in Wisconsin. But he had to transfer from the Democratic Party of his family's heritage to the Republican Party of the conservative German and Irish constituents of Wisconsin.

His campaign theme of "Food for the Troops!" was working for him. Many of the available constituents in the Midwest in 1916 were dead set against America going to war. "Why go fight a war in Europe?" many would ask. "What do we get out of going to war to help foreigners?" So Eugene's theme was risky but caught on as farmers sold more goods. Even his opponent was working the streets claiming, "My opponent wants us in the war. Keep the war *over there.*"

Eugene Francis Stevenson was as cunning as the next man. He reminded everyone he met in his campaign that he was not promoting war. He was promoting the sale of wheat and barley to the federal government. This message caught on quickly as a banner for the prosperity of the immigrant farmers in the German and Irish households of Wisconsin.

Eugene's father, who had passed away in 1914, would have preferred that Eugene become a senator for his beloved Illinois. But a senator was a senator, his father would have said. Eugene knew he was on the right track. As he had many times in business, Eugene could smell victory.

* * * * *

Fountainbleau, France – March 23, 1918

Finally, thought Witherspoon. *We finally made it to Fountainbleau, France, for R&R. I know this is only a respite from the mess. Captain Sandhurst told me we will soon be in the mix of the defense of the French line. I guess we need to make the most of it. This really isn't R&R. This is no party. We're just getting some time to take a break and get ready for the worst of it.*

The men have been in the thick of the fighting of this war for as long as Americans have been on French soil. They dodged German machine-gun fire, cut German wire, and fought their way through rains of steel. They deserve this. No, they need *this.*

"Sarge, ain't this just grand?" Private Henderson said in elation. "We gonna get some *real* food now!"

"Henderson, you need some Pennsylvania English if you're going to talk to me. I can't make out a thing you're saying with that South Carolina drawl."

"Y'all just stand back thar while Old Sarge and I go at it. Sarge, ya dun met yo match wit dat English you-a wantin'," Henderson said as he exaggerated his accent.

The men around them laughed. They were used to this banter. One was a seasoned veteran. The other was an invaluable assistant and one of the best comedians in the company.

"All right, then. Everyone fall in," Witherspoon ordered. "Chow time."

The men ate like they had never had a full mean in their lives. Witherspoon could tell they were enjoying their rest.

As he sat with his plate of warm turkey, potatoes, and peas, Sergeant Witherspoon took in his surroundings. With the exception of the hoards of men and materiel, the town was quiet. Fountainbleau had two churches. One was a large cathedral with two high steeples. The cobblestone main street was framed by masonry two-story homes. Stores occupied the first floor of the homes. The distant blue sky beyond the tranquil setting made him reflect on his small-town heritage. *This is something I could get used to,* he thought.

But, he thought, *there are no ladies here for the men.* There's nothing here but peace and quiet. The constant artillery barrages in the distance reminded him that it was only a matter of time before they would face the enemy again. Word had it that the Germans were pushing the British back in the Somme and the French back along the Aisne. The Americans would soon be called up to fill the gaps.

CHAPTER 6: THE ATTACK

North of Nancy, France - June 12, 1917

The takeoff was uneventful. Jimmy was in the second wave of four machines. His group was trailing the lead group of four by 1,000 yards. They were approaching 3,000 feet of altitude when Jimmy saw the lead flier in the first group waggle his wings twice. That was the signal that the lead group saw Bourbonne-le-Bains in the distance. They would soon turn north-northeast according to the flight briefing.

Jimmy continued to climb. Once the lead group started its turn directly over "the Bains," the rear group would turn slightly in the opposite direction. The maneuvers would bring both groups On Line Abreast. The wide expanse of side-by-side fighters would allow all of the fliers to look for observation balloons. Once the balloons were located, the group that first saw them would have the first shot. During the attack by the first group, the second group would climb to 8,000 feet, circle the area once, and watch for enemy aeroplanes. The first attacking group was to reserve enough ammunition in their machine guns to watch over the second group when it attacked the balloons.

Jimmy searched the sky. He paid particular attention to his rear. *I have a blind spot below me to my rear,* Jimmy remembered. *I may need to use left and right rudder periodically to clear the area behind and below my machine. I'll do that when I fly alone. At least in this formation, my neighbors can clear my lower rear area. After all, I can see below the fliers on my right and left. We need to support one another,* he thought.

They started their turn. The critical part of the mission was about to begin. Each of the fliers fired a machine-gun burst to make sure his weapon was charged and ready. The wide formation continued to climb to its combat altitude. After ten more minutes of flying, Jimmy's leader raised his hand to signal that balloons were coming into view.

That meant that Jimmy's group would attack the observation balloons first. The group started to line up. Jimmy would be the third in the line to dive on the balloons. There were three of them—great gray hot-air balloons tethered to the ground where communication huts had been constructed.

Jimmy came to understand just how critical the mission really was. The balloons were in an excellent position to observe the Allied trenches and dust clouds in the distance. The dust was a telltale sign of horse and autocar activities as the Allies massed soldiers and materiel behind the lines in preparation for an assault.

We must destroy these balloons, Jimmy thought. *Our men in the trenches are counting on us.*

As Jimmy turned to get into position to attack a balloon, he saw a sight that shocked him. Two human figures *jumped* from the basket suspended below the balloon. Were the Germans committing suicide? Jimmy wondered. Were they so scared of the approaching aeroplanes that they ended their lives the easy way? As Jimmy watched the men fall toward earth, suddenly he saw a white sheet billowing above one figure and then the other. It occurred to him that he'd heard of this new device. It looked like a great silk parasol such as women used to shade themselves from the sun. It allowed a man to drop safely to the ground from such heights. There was a French name for it that Jimmy couldn't remember. He would have to ask about it after the mission.

Lieutenant Bridgman and Sergeant Masson, ahead of Jimmy in the formation, banked their machines and lined up on the center of the now-vacant balloon. Tracers started arcing from the first aeroplane. Bridgman fired a continuous burst at the gray mass of the balloon and pulled up and to the left as he finished his run. Masson, Bridgman's wingman, started his run immediately after the first burst of bullets and tracers entered the balloon.

Jimmy was next. He was surprised to see that neither Bridgman nor Masson, although they must have fired fifty rounds into the balloon, had been able to bring it down. How could it stay aloft? Jimmy kicked slight left rudder, pushed his stick down and to the left, and began his descent toward the target. *Now,* Jimmy thought. He pulled slightly back on the stick, lined up, and pulled down the firing handle of his Lewis. The Nieuport shuddered under the vibration of the discharge of bullets and tracers. Jimmy pulled his aeroplane up and walked his tracers along the line in the balloon formed by the shots of his predecessors.

As Jimmy's rounds rose to the middle top of the balloon, it happened. The Lewis gun jammed. He climbed and banked to his left as his wingman fired. Jimmy watched as Corporal Ford's rounds struck at the top of the balloon. Suddenly the mass of gray billowed and folded in on itself. "Yes!" Jimmy yelled. That meant Ford would get the kill. It also meant that Jimmy had time to separate from the group and clear the jam from his weapon.

Jimmy signaled his flight leader. Bridgman acknowledged and allowed Jimmy to fly higher and to the right of the remaining fliers. Jimmy looked around before hauling his weapon down from the top wing and working the charging handle on the Lewis. He worked it a number of times and finally dislodged the cartridge that was jammed in the breach of the weapon. *Back to work,* Jimmy thought.

His group was climbing to take up its position above the other group. Jimmy formed up with the other three and watched as the next group of four started its handy work. As the transition was unfolding, Jimmy saw Corporal Ford rock his wings. He had seen movement to the east. Jimmy was elated. He would now have another opportunity to engage enemy aviators. As he made his turn, Jimmy noticed that the other two observation balloons had descended. The German crews were feverishly winding the tether lines to return the balloons to the ground.

Where were the enemy fliers? He scanned the horizon until he saw the dark specks against the sky. There were two of them. Jimmy also noticed that the second group of Americans was breaking off its attack on the balloons. They were giving up on the object of the mission and starting to fly up to meet the threat. Jimmy knew an attack on the enemy machines was supposed to be left to the high group. But the low group was taking advantage of its closer position to the enemy.

Lieutenant Bridgman took the initiative as well. He pointed to their right front. It was clear to Jimmy that Bridgman intended to close on the enemy by flying east-southeast. That flight path would intersect the Germans if they tried to return to their aerodrome. *Let the other group scare the Huns,* Jimmy thought. *We'll take them when they're low on petrol and ammunition.*

The two enemy fliers continued toward them but then suddenly turned northeast rather than south toward their aerodrome. The other group was out of range, and Jimmy's group had no chance of closing the distance to the enemy. As Jimmy looked back and down at the balloons, he realized that the enemy fliers had done their job. They had lured both of the American attack groups away from the balloons. That job completed, the two enemy fliers flew safely away from the danger of eight Nieuport fighters.

The older fliers had warned Jimmy that the Hun usually did not fight over the Allied-controlled territory. The Germans were cunning. They stayed in the air behind their own trenches as much as possible. In that way they could wait for the Allied fliers to cross No-Man's Land before getting into a fight. Jimmy now witnessed Boelke's dicta firsthand.

By staying close to their aerodromes, the Germans conserved their petrol. They could fly longer in the attack because they shortened their times to climb and return to the safety of their landing fields. Allied fliers attacking across No-Man's Land used precious fuel to get to the fight. When an Allied flier ran out of fuel, it amounted to a German victory. A kill was a kill even if the Allied flier landed with a dry petrol tank. The only important point was that the flier had to land in German-occupied territory.

As long as they fought on their side of No-Man's Land, the German fliers had a good chance of landing behind their own lines if shot down. Landing in No-Man's Land was suicide, the experienced fliers had told Jimmy. If you ever needed to land between the trenches, you might as well shoot yourself. Your machine wouldn't survive its landing in a battlefield covered with bomb craters. If you were lucky and your machine missed a crater, it would get tangled in the wire that covered the fields. You won't survive, they had said, if your machine doesn't survive. Even if the bomb craters and wire didn't get you, machine-gun fire or snipers would. Fliers could be killed by friendly fire, Jimmy learned, just as easily as they could be killed by a German bullet.

The Germans wanted a fight. They often approached enemy lines to coax Allied fliers into a confrontation. But they could also be cold and calculating. If *Allied* fliers wanted to fight, Boelke theorized, why not let them come to us? Germans had to cross No-Man's Land to protect their observation and bombing machines, but they tried to make the aerial combat take place to the east of the brown river of dirt and murderous crossfire in No-Man's Land. The safe haven for the Germans was to the east of the dirt.

Low on petrol, Jimmy's group turned toward the Lux. There was no need for all eight fliers to return together, so his group would land first. Jimmy didn't have any kills from the mission, but he had learned valuable lessons. For one, balloons were extremely hard to bring down. For another, a flying group should always stay with the plan of the attack. Had the second group followed through with its mission, they'd have destroyed at least one more balloon, and the two enemy fighters might have continued on to the scene. The attempt of the two German fliers to divert the Allied attack on the balloons might have resulted in aerial combat. Jimmy's group might have had a better chance at taking the Huns.

The return flight to the landing field was uneventful. Once he was on the ground, Jimmy watched the second group come in before climbing from his machine. The debriefing, Jimmy thought, could be very ugly. Maybe it should be. Both groups deserved to be chastised. They left the balloons only to chase the shadows of distant German fliers.

* * * * *

Hyde Park, Illinois, U.S.A. – June 12, 1917

Loraine and Eugene thoroughly enjoyed their time back in Hyde Park. They were relaxing between Senate sessions in Washington. The resort town along the banks of Lake Michigan was bustling with the activity of the rich. Paul Cornell sure did have a wonderful idea building his Hyde Park House hotel and starting the town, Loraine thought. Eugene's idea of building their summer home on the lake and his own hotel in Hyde Park was a capital idea even though not well received by Mr. Cornell. They were happy, but Loraine could tell that something was troubling Eugene.

"Darling, what's bothering you?" Loraine asked her husband. "I can tell you're upset about something."

"It's nothing to worry about, Loraine," Eugene replied. "Everything will be fine."

"Oh, you are not getting off *that* easily. I will not permit you to take anything on by yourself."

She sat down in a defiant posture on the edge of their living-room sofa. The room was large and had a ten-foot-high ceiling for better ventilation in summer. Although large, the room had a warm feeling to it and was appointed in the dark mahogany and red silk of Victorian décor of the times. Eugene could sense Loraine's determination to hear about his business problem. Her energy radiated in the warm surroundings of the room. She needed to say no more. Eugene could feel more than hear her demand to know what was going on. More so, he could see it in her eyes. They were wide open and unflinching.

Eugene lowered himself into the overstuffed chair facing her. He sat back with his arms extended on the high armrests of the chair.

"Well, it appears that every one of our hotels has been cited by the Chicago city inspectors. I have numerous city violations in each hotel. It seems the city has something against us. It's as though we're being attacked."

"I'll tell you what *is* against us, Eugene. Mr. Colosimo is against us, that's what. He's been trying to take over businesses all over the district. I'm sure he cannot stand to know that you own your hotels. He wants them for himself *and* his group. At least he calls it his group! His group is nothing less than women for money. And he wants to put his 'action' into your hotels."

Eugene could see Giacomo Colosimo in his mind, standing before him. He was a large and overweight Italian and a major player in the illicit business circles of Chicago. He was called Big Jim for his size but was better known to his friends as "Diamond Jim" Colosimo because of the numerous diamonds he wore. He had, over the years, become a major figurehead of the Chicago crime scene. He owned more than 200 brothels and was heavily engaged in racketeering and bookmaking. Rumor had it that Diamond Jim would get involved in any business venture, illicit or otherwise, if it meant easy money. Rumor also had it that he was successful only because he paid off Chicago policemen, inspectors, and politicians. Colosimo was in everyone's pockets, people would say.

Eugene reflected in silence. As always, Loraine was right. Colosimo had to be paying city inspectors to cite his hotels.

"Loraine, you have done it again. You've figured out what's going on. It has to be true. This Mr. Colosimo has to be paying off inspectors to take us down. Now, I have to figure out what can be done to stop him."

"You have a fight on your hands, my love. Mr. Colosimo epitomizes everything that is evil in this world. His tentacles are everywhere and meant to take advantage of the vices of unknowing and respectable people. He means nothing but trouble for us."

Eugene slowly nodded. He now knew he had two major fights on his hands, one to keep his political position solid and the other to keep his businesses in *his* solid and honest hands.

"My dear, he might think he's attacking us. But, as they say, a great offense is the best defense. We will overcome, my love. We *will* overcome."

* * * * *

Cantigny, France – May 12, 1918

The smell. The blood and vomit mixed with the mud to form a soup of pungent metallic odor that made strong men weak. The French had left *this* defensive position in worse shape than others they had occupied. The rain destroyed the trenches and made the air heavier. It caused the odor to permeate the air in the trenches. The men shivered all night as it poured on them. The sides of the trenches tended to collapse, contributing to the soup.

In some areas the soup was so deep that it spilled over the men's leggings and into their boots. Sergeant First Class Witherspoon was most concerned about trenchfoot. Although it was raining and cold, he made his men remove their boots to dry their feet.

The soup, odor, rain, and cold made life in the trenches miserable. If the mud didn't spill into their boots, it stuck to them like glue, making it tiring to walk. The occasional crack of a passing bullet from a German sniper's rifle made everyone remember the dangers they faced.

Sergeant Witherspoon knew the men couldn't take much more of this. They had fought with the French north of the Moselle River near Toul and along the Aisne River west of Reims. They had been in these horrid trenches near Cantigny northwest of Montdidier, France, for twenty-two days. Word had it that they were about to be faced with another German drive through the Aisne to the Marne River. Their morale was waning. Their health was deteriorating. Their loneliness was chronic. He knew that the clearing clouds would be the first sign of the approaching fresh air. He also knew it would be the sign of a fresh advance and the beginning of a new level of carnage in the fields of Soissons. He only hoped that they would be pulled from the line before the carnage began.

Captain Sandhurst and the company First Sergeant came over to Witherspoon. "Sergeant First Class Witherspoon, Regiment has told us that the Germans are coming over the top tomorrow. We have a considerable amount of artillery massed in our defense. Prepare the men but, most importantly, make sure the machine guns are ready. The Germans are attacking the British at Ypres, and we believe that is only a supporting attack. The main attack is to come right down our throats."

"Sir, my men are spent, but they are ready to give it their all," Witherspoon replied.

As Sergeant Witherspoon worked along the company defensive position and discussed the coming threat, the men seemed to energize into constant activity. Their industriousness caught on like a wave along the line and seemed to help calm their nerves. They worked on the sandbag parapets in front of the trench and the sandbag parados behind it. The parados were brought up higher than the front parapets so that the enemy would not see the helmets of the men against the sky as soldiers peered or fired over the parapets. Observation and firing slots were improved in the parapets. Ammunition was distributed and the company leadership made sure every man ate something. Some had trouble eating before a fight. Their nerves kept them from feeling hungry, so they were told to eat even though they didn't feel like it.

The Germans started with another horrendous barrage of artillery fire at 4:30 a.m., 0430 hours. Witherspoon and his men hunkered down while the barrage started impacting in the distance to their front. He knew the massive Allied artillery fire would stay silent and start only after the Germans were exposed on the battlefield. Witherspoon heard sporadic harassing artillery fire in the distance, which meant that the large-caliber artillery was trying to interrupt the German artillery fire. Counter-Battery Fire, Witherspoon remembered. "Go get 'em," he whispered.

He looked down the line of waiting men. All stayed low but were ready to step up on the firing step that was formed in the side of the front wall of the trench. Three feet above the wooden duckboards that formed the floor of the trench, the step allowed men to fire at the advancing enemy. They could step back down onto the ductboards to find better protection from the artillery in the deeper part of the trench. Their faces were contrasts of grins on their lips and frowns on their brows as the artillery worked its magic over the fields before them. Their hope for ineffective enemy fire was overshadowed by their fear of the unknown. Would they, *could* they make it through another artillery barrage alive and unhurt?

"Men, hold tight," Witherspoon said in a calm and reassuring way. "The German artillery is going to pass over us without any problems. We're deep enough here. Then, just step up when we say so and give them hell as they come across the plain. The mud is going to hold them up so we can knock them down. Make every shot count just like in your training. We are the 1st Division, and they're not going to get past us."

He could see the fear in their eyes even in the darkness, the white circles standing out as they looked at him for further reassurance. The overcast skies made it hard to see beyond the sixth man in the trench, but Witherspoon could see a lot of white circles looking about much farther down the line.

The ground shook. Small balls of dirt cascaded down from the trench walls. Only the sandbags of the trench parapet and parados held their own. "Steady, men," Witherspoon said. "Steady."

The barrage continued to approach and then hit near but above their underground refuge. The noise was deafening. Men tried to stay as low as possible and shuddered as the nearest explosions took the air from their lungs. Witherspoon could see white knuckles of some of the men as they gripped their rifles too tight, possibly in hopes of squeezing out an end to the carnage that was raining down around them.

As the German artillery shells passed, the sides of the trench lit up from the illumination rounds fired by the American and French artillery units in the rear. Bright light and dark shadows bounced back and forth over their helmets and along the trench walls. Witherspoon could tell that everyone in the trench was scared beyond anything he had seen before. *I've got to stand strong,* he kept telling himself, *I've got to stop this shaking and be strong so that they can see that I'm not as scared as they are.*

"Okay, men, mount up on the firing step. Stay low and watch for them. Don't shoot until we give the order. We don't want to give away our position. The Germans can't tell as they advance across the field exactly where we are. Hold your fire. Machine guns manned and ready?" Witherspoon asked as he walked down the line.

"Ready," came the reply from four different positions.

Suddenly the sky lit up from far behind the trenches followed by a distant and constant rumble, ebbing and flowing like the sound of a nearby train. Witherspoon knew from experience that the American and French artillery rounds were on their way to the German infantry in its assault across No-Man's Land.

He peeked over the top of the trench wall and through an observation slot in the sandbags. At 0530, the artillery explosions in the middle of No-Man's Land flashed brightly, almost blinding him. The crack of each explosion followed the bright light by three seconds. That meant the Germans were 1,000 yards away and advancing. Witherspoon stepped down into the trench and walked behind the men standing on their firing steps as the Allied artillery barrage continued to rumble.

"Men, they are 1,000 yards away. Let the artillery do its work. It's tearing them to shreds now. There won't be many of them when it's time for us to go to work. Steady yourselves. We're gonna get through this together. We got through the German artillery barrage. The German infantry won't get anywhere near us. Once we've done our work, we're goin' over the top and push them back to Germany. You'll be shakin' hands with the Kaiser in the morning."

Witherspoon's humor helped somewhat until the Allied illumination rounds exposed a number of gray forms advancing over the battlefield toward their position. Rifle and machine-gun fire broke out on both sides of F Company. He stepped up into an observation platform, his heart pounding. The noise immediately around him rose to a deafening level as soon as he yelled, "Fire!"

* * * * *

The men were elated. They had stopped the Fourth German Drive through the Soissons Salient, jumped over the sandbag parapets and advanced behind the retreating Germans. The American and French artillery had blasted big holes through the retreating infantry. The artillery had done its work, but the remaining shell holes and churned-up mud slowed their advance against the enemy. Determined, they were able to push on and occupy the German trenches. In addition to what the 1st Division had done to advance through Cantigny, four divisions of the AEF with contingents of U.S. Marines helped the French stop the Germans at Château-Thierry and Belleau Wood. To Witherspoon, the current lull was like a welcome vacation. But he knew it was only a matter of time before they would be at it again.

Captain Sandhurst and the First Sergeant approached Witherspoon as he rested against the trench wall. Two days resting in the trenches made Witherspoon's muscles ache as he stood and saluted his commander.

"Sergeant First Class Witherspoon," Sandhurst started, "General Pershing has successfully argued with the French to keep American units under American command. Six more divisions have arrived in France. F Company is being withdrawn from the line as part of an overall reorganization. Because of your combat experience, you will be promoted to First Sergeant and transferred with a third of F Company to one of the new divisions. You are going to be a company First Sergeant in a division called the 82nd Division.

"Sir, I've been with the 1st Division for seven years. How can they move me to an unknown and inexperienced unit with an unknown and inexperienced company commander?"

"Well, Sergeant, you will have a *very* known and experienced company commander. As they say, 'The needs of the Army come first.' I am leaving the 1st Division after five years, going with you, and will be your new company commander."

Sergeant Witherspoon looked at him with admiration and great satisfaction.

"Well, sir, we obviously have a lot to do together to get the new company ready for the worst."

Witherspoon reflected on the tasks that lay ahead for him as a new company First Sergeant. He was comforted knowing the misery was about over, at least for the foreseeable future. They would soon join their new company, their new division and be a part of the largest American fighting force to be organized since the American Civil War. *At least for now, I'll be able to relax before the coming fury,* Witherspoon thought.

But the reality of war struck home one more time an hour after his promotion to First Sergeant. As Witherspoon helped one of his soldiers remove mud from his boots, a German sniper's bullet struck the soldier, wounding him fatally. Sergeant First Class Witherspoon performed the last act of his involvement in the 1st Division. He helped carry his soldier's body to a waiting ambulance.

CHAPTER 7: THE MISTAKE AND ELATION

Luxeuil-les-Bains, France - June 12, 1917

The debriefing didn't take place as Jimmy thought it would. He could see the attitude of the fliers and camaraderie between them was more important than destroying German observation balloons. Captain Thenault and Bill Thaw didn't admonish the flight leaders and fliers for abandoning their mission against the gray masses. *I guess,* Jimmy thought, *that chasing enemy aeroplanes was more important to the squadron than fulfilling a mission against static air-filled silk.*

The two leaders worked the room like professionals and got the fliers to suggest that the mission could have been flown better. The flight leaders agreed that the two enemy aeroplanes did not present an overwhelming threat to the mission. One said it appeared to him that he and his flight could lure the Huns into a trap. He had hoped that their direct approach would cause the Hun pilots to turn to their aerodrome. That would have given Bridgman's group the chance to cut off the retreating fliers. Everyone agreed that it was a valiant but fruitless effort to engage the enemy.

The debrief turned to a discussion of enemy tactics. Fliers discussed how to improve their angles of approach. Jimmy was able to present how his machine gun jammed halfway through his attack and how he cleared the jam in time to rejoin his group. Other pilots expressed their frustration with the jams they had experienced in the past. In many cases, the fliers could not clear the jam.

Causes for jamming were brought to the floor for discussion. It sounded like head spacing and timing between the firing bolt and the breach of the machine gun were the most prevalent culprits. Captain Thenault gave the task to Lieutenant Maison-Rouge to speak with the lead mechanic about checking all of the machine guns. Other fliers said it was very important in the fall weather to keep the weapons well oiled. Air moisture sometimes caused water to form on the weapon. Friction and heat were any machine's worst enemies, particularly a machine gun's. All fliers were encouraged to oil their machine guns liberally before and at times during flight.

Ken Marr stood up to speak. He had arrived at the squadron one day before Jimmy, Dugan, and Hewitt. He had attended a different French flying school than the others, but was a very capable flier.

"Captain, I believe the main reason behind the jams is the bullet casing. The casings are brittle and thin. They tend to expand and sometimes burst in the chamber or as they're being ejected from the gun. Something has to be done to get us better ammunition."

"I'll take that up with superiors. But, sir, I do not believe government can control the quality of munitions. France, as you know, is in a great struggle and resources are few."

"Anything more?" asked Captain Thenault.

"We need to find a way to put more ammunition in the ammunition drums. The Germans can fire up to 250 bullets and tracers at us, and we have less than a third of that number." The speaker was Walter Lovell, who had been with the squadron since February and was a dependable flying partner.

The discussion turned back to the need to destroy the observation balloons. Jimmy wanted to jump up and say the mission that day had failed miserably. He kept quiet for now as all agreed that another mission should be organized for the next day. Lufbery and Bill Thaw suggested that smaller formations should engage balloons. The squadron could send out two-man hunter-killer teams to look for other targets of opportunity over the battlefield. Individual fliers could attack balloons or other observation machines if the Hun decided to send them up.

Before he dismissed the group, Captain Thenault said he had an announcement to make. "Gentlemen, it is my pleasure to announce we receive from a British infantry unit confirmed kill on the 8th, instant. Staff of the Lafayette Escadrille awards a kill to Corporal Clive Samuels. That kill came in the same mission with kill that has already been awarded to Lieutenant Jams Smitts."

The room broke into loud applause and roars of congratulations for Clive and Jimmy. It wasn't often that two kills were made in the same flying mission. Jimmy was humbled, yet extremely proud of his kill, even though he knew the second kill was actually his. His flying comrades were patting him and Clive on their backs and clapping when Captain Thenault asked for calm.

"The British unit also reported Lieutenant Smitts hitting a third enemy machine." As the whoops and screams subsided, Captain Thenault was heard to say, "But, but, the machine was able to continue its flight to safety. There are no reports the machine was shot down. Unfortunately, that machine cannot be a kill."

All in the room overlooked the negative news. As the room of fliers settled down, Captain Thenault delivered another announcement. "I wish to report the German flying unit was identified by the Englishmen. The downed machine had the symbol of the famed German Jastas 5. We believe flight leader Lieutenant Smitts faced was in fact Herr Werner Voss, famed German ace of Jastas 5. That is all, gentlemen."

The room went wild as Captain Thenault left. The fliers all rose up in celebration and swept Jimmy off to the bar to memorialize his kill and the fact that Lieutenant James Smitts bested one of the best that the Germans had to offer, Lieutenant Werner Voss.

Jimmy didn't know what was more important to him, a positive and confirmed kill or surviving aerial combat with Werner Voss. Jimmy was sure the Ace had saluted him. Why else would an Ace waggle his wings as they both left the aerial battlefield above the assembled masses of men and machines?

The drinks never stopped coming. Jimmy was in a constant fog throughout the night. He couldn't stop thinking of Werner Voss, *the* Werner Voss. Had Jimmy not buzzed the red hoard of Huns that day, he was sure Werner Voss would have scored another victory—Clive Samuels. Instead of the squadron losing another flier to Voss, Jimmy had received a salute he would never forget.

The next day, Jimmy awoke with nothing less than the worst feeling he had ever felt. His head was bursting. His stomach was ready to unload its contents. He wondered if he would ever recover from the awful feeling. Suddenly he had to run to the latrine and empty his stomach. This was not the start of a good day. Pale from the affects of the alcohol the night before and his episode with the latrine that morning, Jimmy approached breakfast. He wondered if he would actually live through breakfast. "Lord, please let me get through this," Jimmy thought. "I swear I'll never drink like that again."

Jimmy was not on the flying roster for any missions that day. It was as if the leaders knew they'd find him unprepared to fly. They had seen this before. One never plans a combat flight for an aviator after news like that comes out. Jimmy was disappointed when he didn't see his name on the chalkboard for a mission. This time, however, he was resigned it. He would spend the day recuperating in bed, no target practice on the firing range and no shooting on the new shotgun range. No assembly and disassembly of his Lewis. No, Jimmy would rest this day.

In the late afternoon, the many small hunter-killer teams returned to the field. Two had scored victories. Lieutenant Dolan had downed an Albatross C. III. observation aeroplane. Lieutenant Rumsey downed the squadron's fifth observation balloon. Clearly the Huns were trying to determine what the Allies were up to behind their front lines on the south side of the Verdun battlefield.

Torrential rains over the next two days cancelled all plans for flying. The fliers tried desperately to stay dry and avoid boredom. They could tell by the constant artillery barrage that the boys on the front lines didn't have to worry about being bored. It seemed like the Allied assault was about to begin.

Downtime gave the fliers opportunity to discuss the combat and events throughout the theater. The Germans were advancing on many fronts. The Russians weren't very successful on the Eastern Front. Some campaign called the Dardanelles was a disaster for the Allies. Bucharest was afire. The Italians were making some advances. Germans were even occupying areas of North Africa and Palestine. Jimmy was amazed to hear how one country could so dominate distant areas throughout the world. Jimmy was from a small town. His view from the sky helped him understand how expansive influence could be. But he couldn't grasp how Germany, a country the size of only one state in America, could occupy and control so much land around the world.

But the fliers were confident. They believed in their cause. They also believed they could persevere in this miserable war even against the equipment that dominated on the ground and in the air by the superior war-fighting machines of the industrious Germans.

Things had not gone well to the north. German fliers had destroyed many British machines during Bloody April and in the Battle of the Aisne River. Sad feelings made their way through the older fliers. The squadron had had its own Bloody April. It started toward the end of March when Sergeant James McConnell became the squadron's sixth member to fail to return to the aerodrome. According to his wingman, McConnell flew too low to the ground in pursuit of a kill and was shot down by enemy machine gunners on the ground.

The experienced fliers didn't fear ground fire, but that attitude would change as the war dragged on through 1917. German gunners were sharpening their skills against aerial targets. Two more fliers in the theater would be lost to accurate gunfire from the ground before the year was out. Word would spread rapidly as fliers became aware of the danger from below.

April also brought the deaths of Genet and Hoskier in close succession. Genet was as young as Jimmy and died when his wing separated from the machine as he corkscrewed in at full engine power. Hoskier never returned to the aerodrome. His death was confirmed a week later by the Germans in a report they sent to the aerodrome by way of the French infantry.

The fliers said the tactics and discipline brought to the group by Captain Thenault were proving to be very effective. Squadron mates were surviving complicated engagements with the enemy. And, according to Thenault, advances in flying technology were on their way.

The British had fielded a new aeromachine called the Sopwith Camel, which was maneuverable and fast. It quickly became the talk of the Lafayette Escadrille. Jimmy had grown up knowing how important it was to fly higher, and his fellow fliers knew how important altitude was in combat. The fliers who had the Nieuport 17 liked it. It was light and fast and could turn on a dime, the fliers said. But, like many flying machines of the day, it couldn't turn without losing altitude.

Recent German advances in aviation were starting to take their toll on Allied squadrons. The Fokker Dr. I triplane was a very capable machine, and improvements in their beloved Albatros were showing results. The weapons were now so effective that the British experimented by tinkering with the engines on some of their biplane Sopwith Camels.

The discussion among the fliers was interrupted by loud and increasingly frequent explosions in the distance. Something was up to their northwest. Worries were confirmed in the next flight briefing on August 16th. The British were demanding that the French take pressure off of them as the Third Battle of the Ypres continued to drag on in the muddy fields of Flanders to the north. The battle had been joined for the third time on July 31st and hadn't stopped. The British needed the French to do something in the area around Verdun to help minimize the slaughter in Flanders.

* * * * *

Southwest of Toul, France – August 1, 1918

The new First Sergeant was returning to duty on the front line. He and Captain Sandhurst had worked their new company, Chester Company, 163rd Regiment of the 82nd Division, into fighting shape. After a short orientation and some field training south of Toul, the company was on its way to occupy the trenches before the Saint Mihiel Salient for the first time in its combat experience. They all hoped that the unit they were relieving had done something to improve the trenches, strengthening their wooden sides, installing duckboard platforms above the wet trench floors, or improving the communication trenches that led to the latrines.

Sergeant Witherspoon wasn't very hopeful that they were headed to more comfortable and secure conditions at the front. He knew how hard it was for the units to fortify and improve the breastworks. Units were usually exposed to daily artillery fire, machine-gun fire, and the accurate rifle fire from enemy snipers. He had difficulty improving the position his unit had occupied in the past. He could only imagine how bad the conditions would be when the unit arrived at the front. He hoped they were much better than the last fortifications they had left.

"Oh, my Lord, First Sergeant. Look at this mess," one of the squad leaders told Witherspoon when they arrived. "How could anyone live in conditions like this?"

"We'll just have to start right away to get this miserable place in better shape," he replied. "You're right. This is about as bad as I've ever seen it. We're going to need some support. I'll see if Captain Sandhurst can get some help from Regiment. Let's get the platoon sergeants to the company headquarters in thirty minutes. We'll talk about what needs to be done once they get a handle on how bad this really is."

Obviously the unit that had occupied the trenches had done very little to make them livable. The bottom of the trench was a quagmire of mud, water, and debris. There wasn't much wood left in the sides of the trench to keep the mud from collapsing. The observation and machine-gun positions were almost nonexistent. Sergeant Witherspoon knew he was in for a real test. His men were not going to like what they had to do to make the defensive position tenable.

The first rifle shots and artillery fire started just as the platoon sergeants reached the company command post. Every leader in the company told the same story. This position was the worst they had ever seen. Captain Sandhurst watched as his First Sergeant explained everything that needed to be done to get the company sector into better shape. The commander proudly watched as his platoon sergeants accepted their orders with the look of determination that would make the position the best it could be.

The regimental headquarters did not have anything to offer to the company to help get the position in fighting order. There were no materials available and the engineers were working on other tasks. The Regimental Operations Officer told Captain Sandhurst it was up to him and his company sergeant to get the position in better shape.

The hard work of getting ready to endure another full month of frontline combat was just beginning. Sergeant Witherspoon turned to his commander as the platoon sergeants left the headquarters. "Sir, this is the worst I have ever seen it. Whoever commanded the units that were here should be shot. The only good thing about this is it will give the men something to do. But I've got to insist that Regiment provide us with more hot meals. The men deserve that as a minimum since Regiment put us here."

"I'll see what I can do, First Sergeant. You know how hard it is to get hot food to the front. I'm going to Regiment in about five minutes to give my report. I'll let you know what they can do for us."

"Thank you, sir. I know you'll give them the facts. It will be very hard to defend this position if we don't get some support."

Sergeant Witherspoon told his company orderly to follow him as he turned to inspect the rest of the company sector. The company sergeant wanted to look first at the latrines to make sure he could keep his men as healthy as possible. The latrines were the main source of illness and disease at the front. Witherspoon was determined to make sure his men survived the coming fury. But he had to sit down and take a deep breath to try to calm his nerves. He needed to be strong as he knew the next attack would soon materialize.

CHAPTER 8: CONTACT

Northeast of Nancy, France – August 8, 1917

"Contact!" Jimmy yelled to Henri as he activated the start switch in his cockpit. Henri flipped the double-bladed propeller of Jimmy's Nieuport 11, *his* Bébè. This could be the last time he would pilot an 11, Jimmy hoped. Word was that more 17s were on their way to the squadron. Word also had it that the French had developed a superior aerofighter. Its name wasn't known to the group, but everyone was charged up knowing that something very good was on the horizon. They could always use more maneuverability, power, and firepower.

Jimmy's attention, though, was on the task at hand. He would be in a flight of two with Sergeant Didier Masson. Sergeant Masson was a ten-month veteran of the Lafayette Escadrille. He was a good, well-respected aviator. Everyone was eager to fly with him and equally eager to *party* with him.

The flights of two seemed to bring good results. The large formations that were employed at times seemed to keep the enemy from jumping into engagements with the American fliers. The German aviators preferred to duel rather than join a slugfest. That would change in the next month or so as the Germans turned to massing their fliers in larger and mutually supporting formations. But for the moment, small hunter-killer teams were the order of the day.

Jimmy and Masson took off and headed west to avoid the early-rising sun of August. It was much more difficult to see enemy aeroplanes in the sky between the hours of 9 and 10 due to the angle of the sun or the haze in the distance. The haze, more than anything else, made it difficult for the Americans to pick out distant enemy aeroplanes in the eastern sky.

As the two gladiators turned north, they scanned the horizon for landmarks. They were also wise to the pounding that was going on below them. The Second Battle of Verdun was in full swing. The destruction was evident even from the sky. Jimmy did not often look down at the ground as he flew over the battlefield. He normally paid constant attention to the sky around him. Only then could he pick out his adversaries in time to protect himself. But this day was different. Jimmy could see large puffs of black smoke rising on each side of the dark brown of the battlefield. He could tell that the artillery duels were underway in the distance below him. The green fields of the Somme, Aisne, and Verdun areas were so torn up by war that the battlefield looked from above like a continuous wide river of brown death. The brown river meandered from the northwest to the southeast of the French countryside. Jimmy could see the lush green forests of Alsace and Loraine to his right front. He could also make out the lush green countryside of Germany in the distant haze. The massive green of all of Europe was only torn up in the western half of France. Jimmy felt sadness flush through his body thinking of how miserable it must be to be fighting in the killing fields.

He quickly broke his train of thought about the devastation below. He knew he had to stay alert. Then, immediately after passing into the Verdun Theater of Operations, Sergeant Masson signaled that he saw two large forms in the sky in the distance. The Germans must have sent their Gotha multiengine bombers to Verdun. The Gothas were lining up to bomb the advanced trenches of the French line. Jimmy acknowledged Masson's alert and planned an immediate assault with him in the lead and Masson flying cover on the first pass.

Both fliers put their goggles over their eyes and started their descent to the large targets. The massive forms continued to grow as the pair advanced. The fliers could see the rear gunners of the Gothas preparing for action. They were charging their Spandau machine guns and taking aim at the Americans. Jimmy started his jinking as tracers arced up from the rear Gotha bomber.

Okay, Jimmy he said to himself, *a little lead and go for the center front of the fuselage, just behind the main wing spar.* These behemoths needed a lot of bullets to stop them in flight unless you hit the pilot. Jimmy had by now grown out of the choking feeling he had when shooting at another human. He learned from the combat to think of the Germans as forms rather than men. Now it was time to use his development as an advantage. He pushed on with determination. Jinking hard now, to the left then the right, Jimmy avoided the trail of bullets and tracers that rose up to him. His rapid crossing path made it difficult for the German gunners to find their mark.

Jimmy let go with a curving line of fire into the fuselage of the huge machine. He was sure he found his target as he passed under the bomber. The trick was to pass underneath the first bomber and turn to keep his machine out of the line of fire from the rear gunner of the second Gotha.

Now! he thought. *Turn sharply left below the other machine. Continue the curving path to come around from below the two bombers. Look back and check on Masson.* Yes, he was right where he was supposed to be. Jimmy was reminded how good Masson really was by seeing him in perfect position behind him in his very tight turn.

Let's bring it around and see what we did on the first pass, Jimmy thought. *We'll take them from below and behind and fly in the gunners' blind spot.* If the first machine was stricken, Jimmy would have to be careful. As the aeroplane lost altitude from its dead pilot, the rear gunner could still engage the two predators. The gunner of the stricken bomber had proven to Jimmy that he was a capable shot. Jimmy's machine would have been riddled with bullet holes had it not been for his maneuvering during the attack.

Coming around, Jimmy could tell his first pass had been successful. The rear Gotha was banking and diving. The pilot was nowhere to be seen. He must have slumped into the cockpit and pushed the stick forward. Now pilotless, the bomber continued to slowly bank and start down toward its fatal end. Suddenly Jimmy saw a shocking reality of the war. The German gunner in the back seat of the Gotha stood up, steadied himself in the falling bomber, and saluted the Americans. Jimmy realized the gunner was accepting his fate with dignity and honoring his most capable adversaries on his way to certain death. Jimmy stared at the scene. It shattered his thoughts of Germans as forms. They were in fact *men*. The bomber continued its slow and graceful downward fall from the sky. The rear gunner maintained his military stance at attention and final salute to his enemies.

Jimmy tried hard to control his emotions and turn his attention to the task at hand. He didn't understand what he actually felt. Perhaps it was a mixture of pride in what he had accomplished in downing the bomber, sadness at the loss of human life, and shock at having been so honored by such a heroic and worthy opponent.

Jimmy turned and focused on the second bomber and the Germans. They were again forms rather than humans. The second bomber had banked as soon as the action started. The large form was diving to increase its speed. The pilot was also trying to get support from the trenches by flying low over his friendly lines. Separating from the Americans, the enemy pilot was high-tailing it toward friendlier fields. Jimmy realized he needed to conserve ammunition. He always tried to use as little as needed to make his kills. He wanted to reserve some ammunition for self-defense when he returned to the aerodrome. He and his flying mate circled and watched as the first bomber continued its downward flight. The second Gotha was out of range of the two, so they watched the approaching death of Jimmy's downed target. Jimmy's second "official" kill was about to score.

After Jimmy saw the Gotha bomber rip apart at impact, he signaled to Masson that they should make a lazy wide turn over the battlefield. Jimmy wanted to look for more targets of opportunity. He also wanted to give Masson an opportunity to take advantage of any "low-hanging fruit" like the Gothas. Perhaps they would encounter an observation aeroplane. The Germans were now using aero picture-taking from older Albatros and Fokker Eindecker aeroplanes. The mono-aeroplanes were odd-looking machines. They had one wing toward the bottom of their fuselage and wing guy wires ending at a vertical post in front of and above the pilot. The mono-aeroplane looked as though it could easily fold in half. At least the biplanes had wing spars and extra guy wires that kept the machines together.

The mono-Fokkers were also underpowered, making them fairly slow. They had one Spandau machine gun mounted in front of the vertical spar. The spar obstructed the pilot's aim. Jimmy knew he would have an advantage over the mono-planes with his superior Nieuport fighter.

Circling above the battlefield and No-Man's Land, Jimmy saw nothing but open sky. He signaled to Masson by pumping his open palm downward that they should do a low patrol on their way back to the aerodrome. They made a lazy turn to the south and descended to 3,000 feet when Jimmy noticed a large formation of gray soldiers advancing up a hill. *Germans!* he thought. They looked like ants clambering after abundant food. He turned slightly in his cockpit and motioned to Masson that they should help the Allied soldiers that were about to be surprised by the large mass of gray. Jimmy moved his open left hand slowly back and forth in the direction of the hill. Masson replied by holding up his left thumb and forefinger in a circle signifying his understanding of Jimmy's suggestion that they attack. The pair banked their machines in unison slightly to the northwest and the evolving conflict below them.

Jimmy could see the smoke and explosions of artillery as he continued his downward advance toward the battle that began to rage below him. The noise on the ground must be deafening. He could almost feel the thunderous explosions over the drone of his engine and the wind as it swept past his ears. The Allied soldiers were giving and taking brutal punishment as the gray mass advanced on them. The Dance on the ground seemed to unfold in slow motion. The rain that had kept him from flying for days must have transformed the Verdun battlefield into a massive quagmire, with mud sticking like paste to men, horses, and weapons.

The artillery barrages were exploding above the ground with the new aerial-burst technology. The sharp, burning shards of metal could cut men down like a sickle cuts wheat. If the sickle didn't get you, the pressure wave of the artillery burst could tear your eardrums and organs, causing internal bleeding. His thoughts of the struggle below made Jimmy press on and suppress the feeling of deep sadness at the need to shoot directly at other men. But he had to do something to help save his comrades. With Masson directly behind him, Jimmy opened with a long burst of fire into what he visualized as a gray blanket billowing up and over the hill. Rising, he turned to watch Masson cut men down as he had.

As he climbed, Jimmy remembered that the Germans were applying the aerial-burst technology to antiaircraft fire. No longer did the fliers have to watch out only for machine-gun fire from below. Air bursts were starting to sprinkle the sky with deadly shards of metal. Jimmy knew the killing in this war was going to new heights, including the heights at which he flew.

Low on ammunition and petrol, Jimmy and Masson turned to the south and home. They had done a good day's work. The cramps in Jimmy's legs and back told him how hard he had worked at his craft.

Jimmy foresaw weeks of more hard work in the skies over No-Man's Land. He thought about how his fast and agile new flying machine, the Nieuport 17, would give him more opportunities for kills. He knew as good as he was that he deserved a 28. He would miss his Bébé but just couldn't wait to get out of the 11. It served him well, but he could make his German adversaries fear him more in one of the newer machines. He adjusted his throttle as he approached the landing area, Masson close to his left rear.

The aeroplanes worked in perfect unison as they flared on touchdown. The two tan flying machines landed like geese of war. The setting sun painted them with a redish glow before the dark green trees at the head of the landing field. The well-choreographed landing was a sight to be seen. The crimson sky in the background framed a beautiful, soothing picture. But it was a picture of war, war at its deadliest.

* * * * *

Southwest of Saint Mihiel, France – August 11, 1918

The explosions came in erratic, deafening blasts. Some were muffled by the mud. Others went off with a loud crack sometimes followed immediately by a terrifying *ca-BOOM*. The *ca-booms* were the worst. They were the new timed fuses that caused the projectile to explode above the ground. The rotating hot metal shards called shrapnel cut through flesh like buzz saws as they spun toward the ground and into the trenches.

It was Captain Sandhurst who brought the reality of their situation to Sergeant Witherspoon. "We have our work cut out for us. The French have been trying desperately to find the right force structure to hold and ultimately defeat the Germans. The egos of the French and British commanders caused them to use us as fillers for their forces rather than to allow an American Army to hold its own. The French and British have little respect for our ability to contribute effectively to the war effort. The two allies know the last time the Americans commanded soldiers in real combat happened during the American Civil War, more than fifty years ago. The Allies do not believe that we can fight as an independent command structure. But General Pershing refused to allow his soldiers to come under the orders of foreign forces. Now it's time for the Americans to face the cauldron of fire as an organized and cohesive army."

"Sir, filling in for the French forces last year afforded us excellent training and experience. We are as battle hardened as any in the AEF. That's why they placed us in the most tenuous position of the American sector. I believe the company is well prepared for the new offensive in support of Field Marshal Pétain's plan to push the Germans back to Germany."

Witherspoon had received his promotion to First Sergeant and joined Captain Sandhurst in the 82nd Division before it occupied the trenches in its position in the line of the new American sector. He had grown used to the noises of war as they cracked and rumbled through the air. He had watched new, young soldiers suffer with their inner fears as artillery barrages came and went. The shock wave that hit your chest and stung your ears was a welcome relief to the incessant explosions. Sergeant Witherspoon would joke with the youngsters as they passed by. "When you feel the shock wave, gentlemen, you at least know you have a few more minutes on the sunny side of the mud. When you don't feel the shock, it'll be up to us to take care of you. You won't have to worry about a thing. We'll carry your mangled body back to your Momma."

The jokes seemed to relieve the stress in most soldiers, but only for a second or two. Even Sergeant Witherspoon, with his five months of combat experience, felt the inner monster of fear well up in him every now and again.

The "whiz-bangs" scared the young soldiers the most. Their sound as they whizzed through the air foretold a coming explosion. But whiz-bangs, Sergeant Witherspoon knew, were the least threatening of all artillery fire. Their low trajectories meant the projectiles, or "projos," had little chance of entering the trenches. Their explosions came low to the ground, while the soldiers remained protected below the surface.

It was the loud rumble behind enemy lines that gave Witherspoon the chills. It meant high-angle attacks by large-caliber mortars or howitzers. The 240 millimeter mortars and 120 millimeter high-angle howitzers that the Germans fired could decimate an entire platoon if the projos found their mark and landed in the trenches. That had happened to Sergeant Witherspoon in 1917 during a battle to the west of their current location. That's when the 26th Regiment of the 1st Division filled some of the French front lines of the expansive Verdun battlefield. Witherspoon had survived the explosion only because it had happened just around the corner of the trench he was in. The corner absorbed the shrapnel and shock wave that would have killed him and his entire platoon.

Witherspoon couldn't swallow hard enough to keep his stomach from trembling as loud booms went off in quick succession in the distance. "Okay, gentlemen!" he yelled. "We have about thirty seconds. The big ones are on the way. Stay low, put your heads down slightly, and open your mouths. Absorb the shocks when they come." The Sergeant waited, counting. Then he yelled, "Five seconds!" He heard the platoon sergeants repeat his warning down the line of the trenches: "Five seconds," came the echo. "Five seconds."

Suddenly the muffled explosions cracked and boomed in quick succession. The ground shook. The dirt of the trenches jumped. Shrapnel ripped through the air. Then came the shock waves, one immediately after the other. One explosion came close enough that it squeezed the air from the lungs of the crouching soldiers.

"Stay low, men," Witherspoon shouted, "stay low. Here comes the debris."

Mud, water, and clumps of ground rained down on the soldiers from high above.

"They're hitting us with the 240s, men. Hold tight," Witherspoon yelled. "The rounds are all short again so we should be just fine."

The men heard more rumbles in the distance, and Witherspoon counted again.

"Five seconds!" he yelled again. "Five seconds, five seconds," came the echo.

Wah-woompf, woompf, woompf, the rounds exploded.

Witherspoon knew by the sound of the explosions that the high-angle mortar rounds were not on target. The men would be okay, as long as they stayed and absorbed the punishment, controlled their fear, and resisted the natural desire to run from the threat of death. Because running was not an option, some men went into shock, others into uncontrollable crying. Between explosions and the sound of dirt raining down on them, Witherspoon could hear whimpering and groans of fear from some of the men. A man crying in the trenches tried hard to control what couldn't be controlled.

The fear in his soldier's eyes made Sergeant Witherspoon remember how he was taught that combat could be a nightmare. He even taught his young soldiers how to prepare for the carnage. But everything he learned *and* taught came from history books and military training manuals. He had never actually felt the shockwave and heard the whizzing of death that rained down on them. He now knew from actual combat experience that the death from above killed men in many ways. One did not need to be hit by the flying steel shrapnel. In combat Witherspoon had seen soldiers killed by clumps of dirt and debris that fell from the sky after an artillery explosion. Men had been buried when the trench walls collapsed from explosions. The pressure wave of the explosion alone could kill.

Then there was the shock and devastation of the explosion in the trench he was in near the Somme last year. Half of the French platoon disappeared in the blast. The projectile landed right in the middle of two of the French squads. The sides of the trench were covered in human flesh and blood. There wasn't a body part to be found. Witherspoon was amazed at how much damage the dirt of the trench had absorbed. There was only a small crater in the bottom of the trench. Twenty men simply vanished from the explosion. The only indication that the platoon had been there was scattered parts of rifles, equipment containers, helmets, and boots. It was a sight that gave the Master Sergeant nightmares whether he was asleep or awake. He shuddered for two months after the incident and got over the experience only because the devastation was so complete.

Captain Sandhurst spoke up. "Sergeant, it's time to take a walk. Listen for the tempo of the blasts. We may need to get back here quickly if this turns into a rolling artillery barrage. The German infantry may be following directly behind the wall of artillery shells as it's rolled up to us, just like they had done at Cantigny. The enemy will be right on top of us as soon as the barrage ends if that's the case. We need to be back in this position to command the defense if that happens."

Sergeant Witherspoon knew exactly what Captain Sandhurst meant. The two men had been working together as company leaders only nine months. But Witherspoon could almost predict his commander's orders. The Captain was a confident and inspiring leader. Witherspoon was the perfect selection as First Sergeant. He mirrored his commander's confidence in every way. He knew the company commander would now walk down the trench in one direction. Sergeant Witherspoon was expected to walk in the other direction. They would stop at the ends of the company sector, turn, and walk back to meet each other at the company headquarters. They would pass each other and go to opposite ends of the sector. It was a risky business, but this "walk in the park" would put both the commander and the sergeant in front of every man in the company, reassuring and settling them. Even while putting themselves at great risk, they would walk slowly and walk tall among the men during the barrage. They would reassure the men with their bearing and their demeanor and pause at times to offer words of encouragement to a trembling soul.

Sergeant Witherspoon walked to the north. He patted men on their shoulders as they crouched under the rain of debris. The rumble in the distance started again. The Sergeant knew the rain was coming. "Here it comes again, First Sergeant," one of the older soldiers said. "Right, Jones. The Germans are doing their dastardly deed," the Sergeant responded. "Five seconds, men," he yelled as he crouched between his comrades. "Five seconds, five seconds," went the echo.

Sergeant Witherspoon looked directly at as many men as he could. White, worrying eyes peered back at him from dirt-caked faces half hidden under the flat brims of helmets. Witherspoon patted the men's shoulders and crouched to speak quietly and deliberately to those who shivered most. The men reacted well. *They needed this*, he thought. The barrage was bad.

Witherspoon reached the end of the sector after the last group of shells struck the ground. The next rumble of firing mortars that he expected to hear did not come. He waited and listened. The quiet was more deafening than the explosions. The death and destruction was over for now. The barrage had ended.

It looked as if things were going to return to normal. Death and destruction always came suddenly and furiously, and it was always followed by hours and sometimes days of boredom. "Give me the boredom," soldiers would say. "It beats the whiz-bangs any day of the week and twice on Sundays."

Captain Sandhurst nodded at Witherspoon as they approached one another. "Okay, gentlemen," Witherspoon said. "The company will stand down." The command, like his five-second warnings, was repeated by the other company sergeants. Witherspoon watched, without expression, as the men slowly relaxed. Their shoulders lowered as they stood and stretched to relieve cramping muscles. Crouching under the fear of an artillery barrage was hard work. Shoulders stiffened, hands and feet ached, and leg muscles turned to stone.

Witherspoon and Sandhurst met at the company headquarters area. Witherspoon took to the wired company phone. He cranked the handle on the box and called to his platoon sergeants. "Battle report," Sergeant Witherspoon said into the phone. The words *negative report* could be heard in succession as each of the four platoon sergeants reported.

"Negative report, Captain," Sergeant Witherspoon reported. "One hundred thirty-eight soldiers present and accounted for."

"Thank you, Sergeant," Captain Sandhurst said. "Please see to the ammunition. Post the lookouts. The men can have their breakfast."

Captain Sandhurst turned to Corporal Jones, the communications specialist. "Corporal Jones, you may report to Regiment that Company Chester, 325 Regiment, 163rd Brigade, 82nd Division reports Negative Report. One hundred thirty-eight men accounted for."

It had been a long and difficult trip to this moment in his life. Sergeant Witherspoon never knew he would make it into actual combat. The American military was a fledgling force when the sergeant joined the Army in 1908. He needed the money and the security of a job. His first years in the Army were as boring as they could be. He spent most of his early years writing reports and doing paperwork. Even as a corporal, in the earliest years of his enlistment, he spent most of his time helping the sergeants in his company with their work. Equipment was old, ammunition was very limited, and there were few places where his infantry squad could actually practice its maneuvers. As each of Witherspoon's two-year reenlistments approached, he wondered if he should get out of the Army and stop wasting his time. He really wasn't learning a trade that he could take with him when he left the service. He didn't know why he stayed in the Army.

But it all seemed to pay off when America started talking about joining its Allied partners in the worldwide struggle. Europe was on fire in 1915 and 1916. Reports of the atrocities of war did not fall on deaf ears in the Army ranks. Buck Sergeant Witherspoon started to understand as early as 1916 that he could find himself in actual combat. The prospect of using his knowledge and experience in combat made Witherspoon very excited. The lessons he had been taught in his Infantry Training School and his unit gave him the knowledge of how to fight an enemy. His classroom lessons and the exercises in the field gave him and his soldiers a false sense of security. They experienced easy, peacetime combat. Peacetime combat was all about giving commands to soldiers and planning. It was not about fighting an enemy that fought back. He was good at his work and he couldn't wait to show his stuff. The only problem he faced after eight years of peacetime training in the Army was he was only a buck sergeant. The other sergeants in the company told him all he needed to do was follow orders and do what he was told.

He had no idea how wrong his peacetime training and the stories told by those older sergeants were. He also had no idea how wrong he was to think that combat was a thing of beauty to be applied by professional soldiers like, himself. In the last five months, he came to realize the pain, hardship, and agony that war really caused. War not only destroyed soldiers and military materiel, it destroyed land, property, animals, and civilians. The carnage and hatred that permeated his surroundings in combat were endless. All he knew now was he had to lead his men like they had never been led before. He had to do what he could to keep them alive and bring them home.

Witherspoon heard whimpering from a nearby soldier. It made him shiver for he knew they were engaged in the real thing, where men suffered. Some got wounded. Some died. He tightened his gut to stop his own shaking and control the fear that welled up inside him. *I need to be strong for my men,* he thought. *I need to be strong for myself if I'm going to get through this.*

CHAPTER 9: THE MELEE AND CORKSCREW

Luxeuil-les-Bains, France - August 2, 1917

The artillery thunder in the distant fields continuously rumbled across the aerodrome. It permeated every corner of the buildings and vibrated the glasses in the kitchen and bar that the aviators called home. At times, when the projectiles of the big guns found their marks, the pressure shock of the explosion compressed the lungs of the fliers as they ate their meals and attended their briefings. The carnage in the distance was constantly on the minds of the fliers. They did not know that they were soon to enter a killing field of their own.

The mission briefing was routine. Thenault, Thaw, and Maison-Rouge went through their combat dissertations with the normal precision and professionalism they showed in all of their briefings. The briefings seemed routine to Jimmy, but he knew that nothing should go unnoticed. Weather predictions and tactical scenarios were critical to success.

The squadron would participate in a major effort across the front to down enemy flying machines and equipment. The Hun was using all avenues to his advantage to kill Allied soldiers on the ground and end the pressure on their lines.

Jimmy would be part of one of the flights of four to take off. That made for four flights of four ships for the day. His flight, like the others, was to split into two mutually supporting flights of two fliers. He tried to control his rage as he learned Clive would be one of his number. But he felt satisfied. He was going to fly his new Neuport 17. In his mind, it was about time. He knew he could count on the machine. He also knew he couldn't count on *Samuels*.

The four would patrol and work a quadrant over the Verdun battlefield. Each quadrant overlapped the two adjacent quadrants on its left and right so that the entire squadron was supporting itself. The intent was to spread the coverage of aerial attack over the battlefield while maintaining effective supporting defense. In this way the fliers could expand their observation of enemy-controlled skies. One or two quadrants of fliers could possibly come to the aid of the fliers in an adjacent quadrant if they were attacked by numerous enemy fighters.

Lieutenant Maison-Rouge informed the fliers that they were to strafe enemy trenches when the opportunity presented itself. The fliers knew that the German gunners were training in aerial-engagement techniques and were getting better at bringing down low-flying aeroplanes. But Jimmy was up to the task. He knew that his brothers on the ground wanted to kill the Huns by whatever means and end this melee of death.

It took a full hour for the entire squadron to take off from the field. Each group of four formed up to the west of the aerodrome as it took off and headed toward its assigned quadrant. The first group to go up had the farthest distance to fly to its patrol area. That meant those fliers had the least time to hunt. Jimmy was in the second of the four flights to advance to the battlefield. His group was assigned to a quadrant five miles north of the French town of Nancy.

How many times had he taken this route to the battlefield? He'd been flying for two months now and had two confirmed kills to his name. After his second successful engagement, the possible kills that presented themselves to Jimmy were few. Had the Hun taken a break from the aerial combat? Had he moved his flying assets to another battlefield? Jimmy couldn't understand why there had been so few targets afforded to him in the last few weeks.

His four split up into two as they approached their quadrant. Jimmy was flying with Cort Campbell, a reliable and experienced flier, as his lead. Bill Thaw was flying lead in the other flight of two with Clive. As soon as they were near their sector, Sergeant Campbell signaled to Jimmy that he saw movement in the sky to the east. Jimmy immediately saw at least six dark specks flying toward them at about 2,000 feet above their 8,000-foot altitude. The Huns were almost at the maximum altitude that the Americans wanted to fly in their Nieuport fighters.

Jimmy's new Nieuport 17 was larger and more powerful than the

11 he had flown for a month. He was confident in the capabilities of his new machine. The many hours he spent working the controls, throttle, and machine guns in training reassured him that he was flying the best fighting aeromachine that the Allies had to offer.

Jimmy and Sergeant Campbell started a right-hand climbing turn toward the Huns. They needed to gain altitude to diminish the advantage that the enemy had gained by its high approach. The two couldn't allow themselves to engage six enemy aeromachines that were in a diving run toward them. The enemy would close at high speed in their diving approach and be able to turn more quickly than the Nieuports.

What were they? Jimmy wondered. He wanted to understand the capabilities of his adversaries before he engaged them. They were darker than the red Albatrosses he had engaged in the past, and the fuselages were boxy. Jimmy put his fighting goggles in good order. The approaching fighters could be the more modern Fokker Dees. Jimmy heard that they were painted gray, dark green, brown, and dark magenta. The colors were arranged in a rectangular pattern to camouflage the fighters from observation from above. The dark color of the approaching killers stood out in the light sky and was to Jimmy somewhat ominous.

As the two Americans came around, Jimmy could tell they had almost evened the score. The two were just below the enemy aeroplanes. Then he saw an enemy flight of six flying *behind* the first group of six fliers. *Two against twelve,* Jimmy joked to himself. *Those are pretty good odds in our favor.* He pulled back on his stick and slightly to the right as he rose to face the tracers that would soon be coming at him.

The head-on pass happened in the blink of an eye. The enemy planes passed harmlessly over Jimmy's machine as he climbed and fired. He didn't know whether any of his bullets had found their way home. Gravity and the rapid changes in the angles between the fighters made targeting very difficult. He didn't have a second to think more about it. He executed a rapid left half-roll as he rose above and between the two German formations. The half-roll allowed Jimmy to control his alignment onto the second oncoming wave of German machines. He would have been too lightheaded in his attack had he not rolled inverted. Blood would flow to his head as he pushed the stick forward to bring the oncoming targets into his gun sights. So he rolled to avoid being disoriented.

Turning upside down, Jimmy's body hung suspended in the crossed straps, which were cutting into his shoulders. He had to readjust the grip of his right hand on the stick. He was now farther away from the control device than when he was in upright flight.

Jimmy then pulled slightly back on his stick. He pushed the throttle as far forward as the control box would allow. He needed to feed more petrol into his rotating engine. He needed maximum airspeed to give him more control as he aimed directly at and to the left of his second oncoming target. Jimmy saw the two German fighters to his far left were converging. They were going to concentrate their fire on Sergeant Campbell.

He couldn't afford to complete his roll to upright flight as he aimed at his oncoming target. The jerking of the roll would give him vertigo and throw his aim off. He *had* to aim and shoot upside down. Making final adjustments in rudder and ailerons—in reverse order from upright flight—Jimmy couldn't help wondering what the Germans thought of shooting at an upside-down oncoming aeroplane.

The second wave of six was on them. Jimmy pulled the trigger and his two Vickers machine guns barked in unison at the Hun. Jimmy realized they were fighting the new Fokker Dee Threes, very capable and highly maneuverable fighting machines. He watched as his arching tracers lobbed up and over at the oncoming machines. The angles were off slightly, but Jimmy was sure his rounds were impacting the rear of one of the enemy Fokkers. The pieces of canvas and wood that Jimmy flew through confirmed that he had hit his enemy.

He couldn't pull harder to bring his fighter ahead of the German aeroplane for proper lead on the enemy machine. Had he done that, he surely would have caused a midair collision with his foe. Besides, he and Sergeant Campbell were safe from the enemy fire. The

German aeroplanes were in a slight downward flight path and were firing low. At least that's what Jimmy thought.

The second pass was over just as quickly as the first. Jimmy's aeromachine passed within twenty-five feet of the Hun he was seeking to kill. Even at that high rate of speed, Jimmy clearly saw his adversary looking at him as he passed. Now it was personal and time for Jimmy to use his best aerial maneuvering. Now he had to *fly*.

Jimmy jerked his stick to his upside-down left and centered the stick as his wings quickly cut to the vertical. He had just completed three-fourths of his roll. Jimmy wanted to stay to the outside of the gaggle of enemy planes in the air. He needed to turn to the right or due south. On that outside edge of the aerial battle, Jimmy could minimize the chances of a collision. He could also try to single out an enemy machine without being jumped by an unseen adversary. There were just too many of them in the center of the melee. He could be jumped from any angle in there.

With dwindling airspeed, Jimmy pulled the stick hard into his stomach. The machine responded as the two ailerons of his wings and the two of his tail caught the wind. The strain on his body was hard to endure. The maneuver also slapped Jimmy's body back into the rattan seat. *Squeeze your stomach and grunt*, Jimmy thought. "For God's sake, breathe," he said out loud.

The bird held together only because Jimmy had lost airspeed in the climb. Had he pulled this maneuver so dramatically in a dive, the wings of the Nieuport would have folded like the wings of the dove he used to cut down in Wisconsin by a center shot from his shotgun. Jimmy strained to look above his body. He was actually looking horizontally to find his enemies. As he strained, he saw the dark forms of twelve enemy fighters exploding in every direction. They looked like quail flushed from the protection of a bush during a hunt.

In horror, Jimmy also saw a tan-colored machine spinning and falling toward earth. Perhaps Campbell hadn't climbed as high as Jimmy had by the time the second wave of German fighters attacked them. The left lower wing of the Campbell's aeroplane was gone, possibly torn off in the dive or shot away by the Germans in their first pass. Jimmy stared as Campbell's machine spun in a corkscrew shape downward toward a deadly end.

Jimmy concentrated on the two Huns on the left side of the breaking enemy formations. They were both turning slowly to their left. One was 200 feet below him. The other, to the inside right of the first, was about 400 feet below. He realized as he pulled through his hard right turn that the two enemy pilots were facing the third flight of four from the Lafayette Escadrille. The third group of American fliers abandoned flight to their assigned quadrant and were entering the Dance. Jimmy and his group had more support on the way.

He continued to turn hard. He wanted to get on the inside rear of this next target. Now he had to make slow and deliberate maneuvers. For the first time in many engagements over Verdun, Jimmy now had the sun behind him and to his advantage. Rapid movements would diminish the effectiveness of Jimmy's bright and shining assistant to the east. Sudden jerks of his wings would give away his position. He slowly rolled his machine back counterclockwise. Instead of completing the roll he had begun, Jimmy leveled his wings in reverse of the original roll. He was now flying horizontally and about 200 feet above the Hun. He knew he wanted to take the high flier first. That way he would conserve his flying motions and potential for more airspeed. He could take on the other fighters later as he gained airspeed in his next dive.

Flying at an angle of about forty-five degrees to his target, Jimmy waited patiently as the flying relationships between the two machines were perfect. He also wanted to allow his oncoming friends to engage the enemy. By temporarily staying out of the fight, Jimmy would avoid shooting his supporters as they passed by the Germans. He would also see what direction one of the Huns would take after this upcoming pass occurred. The German was pointing his aeroplane directly at the oncoming flight of four and wasn't flinching.

The American fliers fired first. Concentrated fire filled the air. But the German pilot pressed on. "Lord, you *do* have guts," Jimmy said. The flight of four newcomers to the fray streaked past the German. The beautiful mix of color and motion shinning in the midmorning sun was mesmerizing.

To Jimmy's amazement, the German turned right. Jimmy was now in perfect position on the inside of the German's turn to attack his target. Like a bird of prey, Jimmy eased back on the throttle to avoid overshooting the doomed machine. *Begin a slight downward turn to the right,* he thought. *Apply slight right rudder for the proper lead,* Jimmy corrected. *Now!*

The dual Vickers came to life as Jimmy pulled the trigger. *Wham-wham-wham-wham.* The tracers arched ahead of the Fokker. The pilot who had so bravely faced the line of concentrated fire from the entering Nieuports had no chance. The Fokker caught fire, and the fuselage was quickly engulfed. Jimmy knew that he'd killed the enemy pilot instantly and was thankful that the Hun hadn't felt the torture of the flames.

Kill number three, Jimmy thought.

His immediate concern was to find the second pilot, who had been 200 feet below the first. Jimmy hoped the Hun had scattered when the third flight of four attacked. Continuing his inside slow turn, Jimmy scanned the sky. *Where was the bastard?* A left turn would have put his new target below him and to his right front. He would have seen the Hun by now if the enemy pilot had turned to his right. Jimmy figured out what to do immediately. He reversed without another thought. He threw his stick to the left, put his wings in an eighty-degree left-hand bank, and pulled back hard on the stick after it was centered again. He knew the sky was clear to his right. He needed to locate the lower adversary. He *had* to be to his left.

The sharp reversing move bounced Jimmy around in the cockpit. He was used to the reactions resulting from his rapid maneuvers. He had practiced the moves with his stick so much that he could time the reactions like a metronome. He knew as he came around that he had to look down. The Hun had to be close.

Just then a streak of gray, green, brown, and magenta flashed through Jimmy's vision. The enemy fighter was banking under Jimmy's machine. The German must have thought he could turn left under Jimmy and then perform a right turn to gain Jimmy's rear. The

Hun was in the first half of an *S* shape he was forming in the sky with his machine.

Jimmy pulled his stick back some more, climbing slightly. His next move depended on what the German did next. He would barrel roll into his enemy if he turned right. He would continue his climbing left turn if the German went left. As the Hun flew under Jimmy and straightened his machine to start the second half of *his* turns, he looked right up into Jimmy's eyes. The German presented a smile rather than a look of fright.

The opposing pilot then performed an unexpected maneuver. Instead of turning right or left, he pulled straight up into Jimmy. Jimmy knew the German was trying a reversement. He couldn't have performed a more perfect act. And he did it at the exact moment Jimmy would have done it. "Wow!" Jimmy said aloud. He knew that he was facing a professional killer with plenty of experience.

Okay, Jimmy thought. *Now it's my turn to turn into you.* Snapping half upside down and half horizontally, Jimmy pulled hard again on his stick. The two fighters crisscrossed. The German was in a right vertical climb. Jimmy flew off in a left-slicing dive. He knew he had to continue his hard turn to the left. If he unloaded his aeroplane, the German would complete an Immelman maneuver and have the Nieuport 17 in his sights. Jimmy looked up and to the inside of his turn. He saw the enemy turning against his direction of flight. The two were in opposing and revolving turns. The Hun was trying hard to close on Jimmy's tail and visa versa.

Jimmy continued his tight left turn. The Hun was good, but he couldn't come around. The turning motion and force of his turn kept the enemy machine out of gun alignment with Jimmy's bird. As the first passing turn came to its end, the Hun slipped right rudder and threw a burst of fire in Jimmy's direction. Jimmy didn't know what purpose the burst was to serve. The firing angles were all wrong. The Hun didn't have a chance of hitting Jimmy's aeroplane. Perhaps the German wanted him to startle and make a mistake.

"Careful," Jimmy said to himself.

Jimmy was trying hard to stay inside of the German. He was sure his Nieuport was slower than the Fokker, but it was more maneuverable. As he came out of that first diving turn, Jimmy realized his airspeed was too great. He sensed himself getting out of position. Pulling back on the throttle and raising the nose of his 17, Jimmy hoped to slow enough to stay inside. He barely made it and was able to fire a burst of his own. The pair, turning in and out of ever-tightening circles, was weaving an imaginary basket in the sky.

The German nosed down to gain airspeed as Jimmy brought his ship around. The only safe maneuver the Hun afforded himself was the same vertical reversement he had performed minutes earlier. Jimmy was ready for it this time. He applied slight left rudder, threw the throttle all the way forward, straightened the rudder, and banked enough to go vertically. He was a little early in his anticipation. The German started his vertical run. Jimmy pulled the trigger of his dual Vickers and kicked hard left rudder this time. His bullets sprayed across the sky in a rising and turning arch. Jimmy just missed hitting the German square in the middle of his aeroplane. But his bullets and tracers had hit something as they randomly sliced through the air. Parts of the Fokker were swirling around in the sky.

As Jimmy continued to fall to his left, the German turned to his left in the *same* direction of Jimmy's fall. *Oh, hell,* thought Jimmy. *I've lost all my airspeed, and this guy's coming around.* Jimmy had attempted to end the Dance, and he had almost succeeded. But the effort had put him into a difficult spot. In seconds the Hun would have him.

The German continued his reversing move as Jimmy expected. Jimmy could only wait as his aeroplane rotated into a near vertical dive. With so little airspeed, it would take crucial seconds for the machine to start moving fast again. Hanging facedown in midair, Jimmy could only hope that the German would overshoot. As the German came around, Jimmy's aeroplane began its descent. Jimmy again pulled hard on the stick to turn away. He could hear a burst of gunfire over the whine of his own engine, and he felt the vibration as bullets and tracers struck his machine.

Jimmy had no idea where on his aeroplane the German had scored. He knew he was alive and his machine was still functional.

The Hun had to have passed him on his right. The reversing move the German had made would have put him on that side of Jimmy's aeroplane, he thought.

The hard turn at such low airspeed had reduced the forward motion of Jimmy's Nieuport 17. He needed this thing to get moving —and *fast*. If the German was on his right and flying away from him, Jimmy either needed to gain separation from his predator or turn and face him. But he didn't have enough airspeed to separate. He started a long-radius turn to his left and looked everywhere for his attacker.

The German had done the same thing. He was turning to *his* left, Jimmy's right. As the two turned back toward each other, they formed a horizontal figure eight in the sky. Jimmy realized they would execute a frontal pass at the center of the eight. Like knights in a joust, the two fired long bursts at each other. Both jinked left and right to avoid being hit. The jinking of the two aeroplanes also threw lead all over the sky between them.

Then Jimmy's Vickers stopped firing. He was out of ammunition.

The aeroplanes passed each other without incident. Jimmy couldn't believe that with all that lead in the air neither ship was going down. As he looked back at his enemy, he noticed that his own tail section was riddled with holes.

His adversary was flying due north toward the spreading melee of the other aerial ships. Jimmy, thankfully, was on a heading that would take him home. Out of ammunition and low on petrol, he could do nothing for the rest of the day. He was thankful that he could breathe fresh air into his lungs. He was fine. His new Nieuport 17 was a little sluggish in rudder control due to the holes in its vertical tail section, but that was nothing that a little canvas and glue couldn't fix. "The mechanics aren't going to believe this one," he said out loud.

Jimmy kept alert for lingering killers in the air, even as he thought back over the total chaos he had just participated in. From the volley of concentrated fire from the first six enemy aeroplanes, to the last burst from Jimmy's dying Vickers machine guns, the action had been fast and furious. Jimmy had never been on a dove hunt *that* wild in his life. He had downed one German, he thought, but he had also seen Sergeant Campbell's aeroplane fall out of the sky.

He flew on. His heart was beating rapidly. His hands were sweaty. Visions of Campbell spinning downward and his ever-menacing adversary trying to turn on him kept coming back to Jimmy. *I'm alive but another good friend and comrade is not,* he thought. *Poor Campbell. What must he have felt spinning into the ground?*

He came into final approach to the aerodrome. As he turned, he noticed that people were standing around a vehicle at the end of the field. He wondered why an autocar would be parked at the end of the field with people milling around it. He had never seen that before. Everyone usually waited at the farmhouse for the fliers to return. He continued his lazy turn around the aerodrome and glanced repeatedly down at the scene. The men around the autocar were patting each other on their backs and almost dancing around the car. One man in the center of the group looked up as Jimmy approached from the air. Jimmy thought he was dreaming. It looked like he saw a ghost. Andrew Courtney Campbell was staring up and smiling back at Jimmy. Jimmy looked again. "Yes," he yelled! It *was* Campbell. "Cort, you son of a gun. You *did* it."

How could that be? Jimmy wondered. He distinctly remembered seeing Cort's lower left wing oscillating in the wind and fall off as his machine spun out of control toward the ground. How could Campbell still be alive?

Campbell was happy to see Jimmy land with only bullet holes in the tail section of his machine. But he was a lot happier to have survived the nearly complete destruction of his own machine.

Jimmy jumped from the machine as the autocar approached. Men were trotting behind the vehicle. As Campbell approached, Jimmy called out, "How in the world did you survive?" They hugged each other. "I thought for sure you were a goner."

"Get this, Jimmy," said Campbell. "The bottom of my left wing fell off. I guess the Germans concentrated enough fire on the wing that it just fell off in my first turn. I started corkscrewing and thought I was a goner. My stricken aeroplane seemed like a rotating rock, it was falling so fast. The left lower wing was completely missing. I was able to bring the machine under control and land it about two miles from here. The only reason I didn't get back to the aerodrome was I ran out of gas."

"I can't believe that. The Nieuport sure can take some punishment."

"No doubt. I'll never forget that one."

Campbell had done the impossible. He had limped back to a field he could land in without the lower left wing of his machine. The wing spar had been cut in two by the fire of the Germans in their first head-on and concentrated pass.

* * * * *

Madison, Wisconsin, U.S.A. - June 6, 1917

"Oh, Eugene, I believe it is a very nice letter," Loraine said.

"My dear, the shear *audacity* of an *Army* lieutenant colonel writing directly to a United States Senator. I will have none of that," Eugene replied as he pointed his right index finger to the sky.

"Dear, let *me* read the letter to *you*," Loraine calmly said as she took it from him. She sat and started to read.

Dear Honorable Senator Eugene F. Stevenson,

I wish to congratulate you on your successful election to the Senate of the United States of America. As a resident of Wisconsin, I ask your support of the United States Army Flying Corps. As America mobilizes for war, I come to understand that she is mocked by her Allies and even more by her pending enemies. Our great country lags the world in aviation. The aeroplane is the future of war. I believe it is crucial to the successful defense of our nation, now and in the future. Your support will deliver this advancement in science and technology to the soldier in combat. As your expectant servant, I look forward to higher production of aerial assets and your support of my desire to organize an effective flying corps for the United States Army.

Sincerely, William B. Mitchell, Lieutenant Colonel, United States Army

"You see? You see there? The audacity of the man to say, 'I look forward to higher production' and '*your* support of *my* desire,'" Senator Stevenson said. He continued, "Loraine, *really!*"

"Oh, Eugene. Don't you think you are taking this a little too far? After all, Mr. Mitchell is from Wisconsin. You voted for war only a few short months ago. Mr. Mitchell is just doing his best to help the war effort. I sense that the effort he proposes could be used to your great political advantage. Why, we *do* have aerodromes in Wisconsin, do we not?"

"'Advantage' you say, my dear? Why, yes, supporting Colonel Mitchell could take on a new dimension in our quest for the White House. As usual, my love, you demonstrate an uncanny ability to see the truth and strength in any endeavor. Let us meet with this colonel and find out what he has on his mind."

"Oh, Eugene, I just *knew* you would see the benefits of Mr. Mitchell's viewpoints."

"Well, the only problem I face is Lenroot. He has already taken up the banner of aviation."

Loraine knew Representative Irvine L. Lenroot to be one of the standing members of the U.S. House of Representatives from the state of Wisconsin and Eugene's nemesis. She knew Mr. Lenroot was upset that Eugene was born and raised in Illinois and had won the election to the Senate from Wisconsin. Loraine was sure it was Mr. Lenroot spreading rumors that Eugene had basically stolen the only open Senate seat available to him, a seat from Wisconsin. Mr. Lenroot also spoke openly of what Eugene's father, Adlai Stevenson, had done to support Stephen Douglas in his run against Mr. Lenroot's idol, Abraham Lincoln. Representative Lenroot was determined to fight against Eugene in everything that the new Senator wanted to accomplish. Eugene knew Lenroot had formed an ominous and most threatening agenda against him. Loraine did not share Eugene's concern. She was confident Mr. Lenroot was no threat to them.

"Oh, Eugene, this is just like a walk in the park. I don't believe the Honorable Mr. Lenroot has taken hold of this Mr. Mitchell. You can use that to your greatest advantage, you know."

"Well said, Loraine, well said. You are not only beautiful, you know your politics."

CHAPTER 10: THE WALK IN THE PARK

Reims, France - August 16, 1917

At 8,000 feet and climbing, Jimmy had an expansive view of the sky around him. The air was crisp and clear. As usual the spinning propeller and floating sensation of flight calmed Jimmy's nerves. They had passed through broken clouds at about 5,000 feet and were on their way to defy death itself. He saw scattered brown areas of the battlefield through the clouds below. *How sad*, Jimmy thought. The ground of No-Man's Land was so churned up. The trees were gone and the ground was barren. The earth was so pockmarked with craters that it looked like the surface of the moon. To Jimmy, it looked like mankind was trying to destroy Mother Nature.

Their flight of four was to separate at 9,000 feet. From there they would form individual but mutually supporting hunter-killers. Each hunter would pounce on enemy aeromachines as soon as they were identified. Adjacent fliers were to join an attack. Each group member was to keep an eye on his adjacent partners throughout the patrol.

Jimmy liked to fly just below 10,000 feet. It was cooler at that altitude, particularly at this time of year. But the air got a little thin above 10,000 feet, and Jimmy didn't like the light-headedness that came with high-altitude combat. But such altitude afforded the advantage that you could accelerate as you descended. His Nieuport did well high in the air, but most of the aeromachines of the times could not climb *and* turn. Some actually lost altitude when they turned. The engines just didn't have enough power to turn and climb. "Go up, Jimmy, go up," his father always used to tell him. Still, Jimmy preferred to fight at about 6,000 feet. Orders were orders, though. And 10,000 feet did give them some vertical separation from the lower clouds. Jimmy didn't want to lose his adversaries in the clouds. He thought that hiding in the clouds was a coward's way out of the combat.

Captain Thenault wagged his wings. This was the signal for the fliers to separate. They all acknowledged the order. Jimmy would support Thenault on his left and Clive on his right. They were heading into the spread formation in which they could cover more ground. But in this formation, one flier might have to fight alone for a while. If anything showed up in his sector, the lone fighter would have to wait for support from his adjacent fliers. Covering a lot of area was important, but the spread formation reduced their firepower and support capabilities.

Jimmy flew in long, horizontal figure eights. He wanted to watch the blind spot below and to the rear of his machine. He also wanted to keep his adjacent fliers in sight. The figure eight covered a lot of horizontal territory, and it made it easy for the flier to protect his rear.

Jimmy always oriented the direction of his figure eights with the sun. He kept his tail section away from the sun. When he flew away from the sun, he did it at an angle so that he could see around the sun without getting vision blackout from looking directly into the glare.

Jimmy saw distant aeroplanes twice while he was patrolling. He could tell the machines were German. Their telltale cigar shape gave them away as Albatroses. But both times the machines were too distant for Jimmy to pursue. Perhaps they were older models used for aerial observation, and the fliers were avoiding the area in which the Lafayette Escadrille was patrolling. Why else would German fliers avoid an engagement?

Jimmy was yearning for a fight. But he controlled his enthusiasm with deliberate and attentive prowling. He never wanted to return to the aerodrome with a full drum of ammunition. But it was beginning to look as if this mission was going to be another walk in the park made up of flying uneventful figure eights and watching elusive observation planes in the distance.

Then he saw them. Two boxy-looking dark figures were slightly below them. *Fokkers,* Jimmy thought. They were at about 8,000 feet and headed toward Captain Thenault's patrol sector. Jimmy looked for Clive to signal to him but couldn't find him. Perhaps he went low to look for some opportunity. Or he might be in a cloud below me. *My guess,* Jimmy thought, *is Clive is hiding in the clouds or shirking his duties.* It didn't matter, he said to himself. Clive would have to figure it out. I need to go *now.*

He didn't like the cold, but with altitude came advantage. He moved in a climbing left turn toward his commander. He could tell that Thenault hadn't seen the Huns. He saw before he heard that the Germans had successfully surprised Thenault. The impact of bullets in Thenault's left upper wing and the tracers arcing past his machine put Thenault in immediate action. The bullets were "walking" along the upper wing directly toward his cockpit. His only safe move was to cut hard right.

Jimmy saw Thenault turn his head as soon as he pulled to his right. Clearly Thenault could tell what was up. The lead enemy flier was trying to turn with Thenault to keep up with him. But the second German was already to the inside of Thenault's turn. The bastards had coordinated their attack. The lead German deliberately walked his bullets toward Thenault's cockpit making him turn to his right. The second German, in trail to the leader, started an early right turn to cut Thenault off. The move put the second German in position to take Thenault to his inside.

Jimmy watched as Thenault reacted immediately. He reversed and turned hard to his left in an unexpected early evasive maneuver. This put the second German on the outside of Thenault's left turn. Jimmy hoped that Thenault's move would surprise the lead flier and make the German pass harmlessly behind him. Hopefully the flying angles between predator and prey would be too great for either German to engage him.

The lead German had anticipated Thenault's early move. Jimmy realized the German had him. Thenault jinked rapidly to his left and right to avoid being killed.

Jimmy had watched helplessly as the Germans shadowed Thenault. They had kept the sun to their rear in the hope that they could sneak up on Thenault from slightly below him. Jimmy saw the entire action continue to unfold as he dove toward the three machines. Thenault cut to his right as the bullets started flying. The second

German adjusted and started coming to the inside of Thenault's turn. Jimmy saw the trap Thenault had entered. Suddenly Thenault executed what Jimmy realized was his only chance of escape. His hard left turn had saved him.

Jimmy checked the relationships between his aeroplane and the enemy machines as he flew. At the right time, he knew that a diving barrel would put him in a perfect position behind one of the German machines. He executed his roll. Up, over to the left, and down he went. Jimmy had plenty of ground to cover before he could come to the aid of his commander.

He aimed his machine at a point in front of the Germans as they flew forty-five degrees to Jimmy's direction of flight. He needed to lead the enemy planes, but he had to be careful. If Jimmy flew too far ahead of the Huns, he would be out of the fight before it began. He could also mistakenly put both German fliers behind him.

Jimmy turned down and to the inside of the lead German. He had to pull back on the throttle or he would overshoot. He had to adjust rudder and turn the right wings up to slide into position. Jimmy knew he had to slide in behind the lead German to get him off of Thenault's tail. He had one chance to cut in and turn away so that the second German wouldn't take him. *So far, so good. The Germans haven't seen me yet.*

The timing was perfect. Thenault would have been a dead man had it not been for Jimmy's bullets and tracers tearing the lead Hun's tail section to shreds. Wood and canvas were everywhere in the air around Jimmy's aeroplane as he continued his turning attack. He knew he had only seconds left to stay in the flying attitude he was in. The second German would soon be on *his* tail.

Jimmy wanted to kill the lead German in his first pass. But he had to fire early in order to keep the Hun from taking Thenault first.

The German did exactly what Jimmy knew he would do. He turned to his left to get away from Jimmy's attack. Thenault saw the move and turned to his right. Jimmy cut in front of the second German. He set up his right turn to avoid being shot down from behind by the second German.

Jimmy and Thenault merged and were now working together. Their parallel turns came too quickly for the second German flier. He fired as he followed his leader but had no chance of hitting anything solid. The hardest shot for a flier to score on is against a crossing aeroplane. A shooter has only a split second to adjust rudder and ailerons to bring his bullets onto a crossing target. The German didn't have a chance at hitting Jimmy or Thenault. The entire action could not have come off more perfectly. But now the two of them had work to do. They had to use their flying skills to gain the advantage. They had to fly in unison and dance with the German killers.

Jimmy knew that the next move would be a head-on pass, two Nieuports flying directly at two very capable German Fokkers. The opposing circles created by the Allied and German flight paths would intersect at a head-on orientation. If either pair turned away, the other pair would win the fight. There were no second chances in a fight like this.

How many head-on passes is this going to take? Jimmy wondered. The converging four fired and jinked to avoid being hit as they advanced. Bullets and tracers were arcing and spraying through the sky in their own Dance of Death. The fliers passed within feet of each other at high speed. Jimmy could smell the cordite and phosphorous odor of his enemy's Spandau machine-gun venom as they passed. He flew through dark pieces of canvas suspended in the air. The odor and particles in the air were proof that Jimmy had struck his adversary again.

A second head-on pass was coming as Jimmy and Thenault flew in perfect formation. On the outside of their parallel left-hand turn and toward the end of the turn, Jimmy straightened his aeroplane and flew to the right, *away* from the action. He knew that Thenault would be shocked as he flew away from him.

Had Thenault turned right with Jimmy, both of them would be dead. The Huns would fall in behind them in perfect firing position. Thenault did exactly what Jimmy had hoped he would do. He pressed on. Thenault made his left turn tighter, hoping to have an angle on the Germans. Knowing Thenault like he did, Jimmy could hear him saying, "To hell with you, Jams. I'll take them myself." Jimmy smiled as he watched Thenault turn toward the oncoming Germans.

As the three started converging, Jimmy turned hard to his left and back into the fight. He wasn't running like a coward, after all. He was using his commander as bait while planning to take the Huns in a surprise assault with a crossing pass.

"That's it, Jams!" Thenault yelled. "Maneefeek, mon-A-mee!"

The Germans trained their guns on Thenault's Nieuport. The two high-speed killers were about to make a kill. But suddenly everything changed for the Germans. The outside German saw it first. Tracers were arcing ahead of them. The Germans would soon intersect with Jimmy's string of lead. Their only move was up. The outside lead flier straightened and pulled hard on his stick. His assistant saw the tracers coming at him a split second later. He too pulled hard, but it was too late. Jimmy pulled up as the Germans pulled. In a rising pass, Jimmy's bullets and tracers cut through the second German's machine from its engine to its tail.

The four converging aeroplanes came dangerously close to collision. Jimmy passed slightly under the first rising Fokker and slightly over the second. *That was close,* Jimmy thought. Only the quick upward move saved one of the Germans. The second German flier had to be covered with engine oil and debris.

As Jimmy crisscrossed with the Germans, he knew he needed to fly over toward Thenault, who was in a quartering pass to Jimmy's flight path. He *had* to merge with Thenault. They were dangerously low on fuel. They had to exit the battle or fall out of the sky without being shot down.

Jimmy executed a rising barrel with a right-hand turn. The move brought him closer to Thenault without sacrificing air speed. They both needed separation distance from the enemy. They also needed petrol. Thenault turned in a lazy right-hand turn as Jimmy came over the top of his roll. He watched Jimmy's move in admiration. *What a flier,* Thenault thought. "Maneefeek!" he yelled again. "Maneefeek, mon-A-mee!" *You have done it.*

The two comrades came easily together. They both turned in their seats to watch the Huns fly away from them. One German machine had been torn to shreds by Jimmy's excellent marksmanship. The machine was smoking, but the German flier was somehow able to keep it in the air. It looked as if one German was coaxing the other on. He sure wasn't going to turn and continue fighting. Either he knew he couldn't catch them or he just wanted to help his friend.

No, thought Thenault. *He knew both of them would die this day if they turned toward these brothers in arms.*

Thenault disappeared from Jimmy's view at the farmhouse of the Lafayette Escadrille aerodrome after they landed. He went inside and told some of the fliers what had happened on their patrol. Many of the fliers crowded around Jimmy and congratulated him on a very successful mission. The excited Americans separated as Thenault slowly approached Jimmy. He grabbed Jimmy's shoulders and gave him a kiss on each cheek. Holding him at arm's length in admiration, Thenault reached to his side and removed his officer's saber that he had retrieved from his office. Thenault took a step back in rigid attention and held his saber at a forty-five degree angle.

"Mon-A-mee," Thenault said, "you are a hero. You are a master flier. I salute you and present you with my saber. Your mastery of the skies saved me so I can continue to kill Les Boche. I am yours."

As Thenault sharply bowed to Jimmy, the group fell silent in respect. Jimmy had saved an excellent aviator and the commander of the Lafayette Escadrille. The American and French members of the squadron were gaining a new spirit of cooperation and trust. They were becoming true comrades and brothers in the struggle to end the domination of the Germans in Europe.

* * * * *

Chicago, Illinois, U.S.A. – October 19, 1917

Eugene and Loraine Stevenson entered the lobby of the well-appointed Hotel du Normandie. They were attending a formal fund-raising dinner with the theme Troops on the Front. Of course, not many U.S. troops had yet deployed to Europe. America had declared war on Germany in April, and the constituents didn't know that the country was unprepared to join combat operations. All the public knew was that troops were headed to the front. So Eugene decided to hold a fund-raiser. Loraine thought it was a truly marvelous idea. This was a special time for the couple to shine. Eugene was just finishing his first year in office. Loraine was one of the most revered of senators' wives. Everything was picture-perfect.

The hotel ballroom was packed with wealthy members of the business community. Shadier characters were also in attendance. When it came to helping the troops, the good and the bad knew how to work a room to their competing interests. Chicago was experiencing a rebirth of illicit business activity. Bookmaking, racketeering, and money-laundering were taking their toll on reputable businesses. Gangs had formed to threaten and control businesses. Gangsters were becoming involved in prostitution and gambling. Lewis Stevenson, Eugene's brother and the Illinois Secretary of State, was right in the thick of trying to stop the ever-growing trend. Eugene did all he could to stay away from the wrong side of business. Or at least he aimed to keep any such connections away from the public eye.

"Well, Senator, it seems like a great turnout for a truly noble cause, wouldn't you say?" Eugene was faced with one of the "undesirable" businessmen.

Loraine deflected the advance. "Oh, Mr. Colosimo, how are you really? It is *so* nice to see you again."

Colosimo's white suite, diamond rings, diamond tie clip, and large diamond lapel pin shined in the light of the chandeliers. The sparkling bravado was more menacing than impressive. It spoke to the sickening success of Colosimo's illicitness.

"Yes, Mrs. Stevenson, it is always nice to make the acquaintance of such a beautiful woman as you."

"Mr. Colosimo, why, thank you. You make me blush *so*. I'm sorry we cannot stay any longer with you and your wife to socialize. Eugene and I must be getting on."

"Of course, Mrs. Stevenson. We hope we can have the honor or your company at *our* fund-raiser next month."

Eugene leaned toward his wife as they walked away and thanked her for getting them out of that unfortunate meeting.

"Oh, Eugene, I know what *that* man does and what he can do to your reputation. We must keep *our* distance from him. His party will be *no* fund-raiser, I assure you. We already know what he has done to our hotels. Your reputation is much more important than what he has done to pay off inspectors and cite the hotels with building violations. He just wants to expand his brothels and gambling activities into our hotels."

Eugene knew what she meant. The inflection in her voice meant "Don't even try it."

Senator Stevenson was asked to say a few words when dinner was concluded. He really wanted to retire to the smoking room so he could discuss his upcoming proposal for helping the troops. What he really wanted to do was help his hotel business and make his constituents more enamored by the prosperity he brought to Wisconsin. After all, he had told them, the war needed Wisconsin.

Giacomo "Diamond Jim" Colosimo left the dinner steaming. He could not believe that a woman such as Loraine Stevenson could brush him aside like that. "Who do those people think they are?" he wondered. "I'm gonna show them. They may like their hotels, but they won't like them when I get through with them. I wonder how much they like the building violations they're getting. That's just the start of things to come."

* * * * *

Southeast of Saint Mihiel, France – September 5, 1918

The men in the trenches needed rest. They had worked hard to improve their defensive positions and had just finished lunch. The hard-baked bread, pickled beets, and smoked meat *must* have some kind of nutritional value, Witherspoon thought. Otherwise, why send it so far forward and at such sacrifice for men to devour? No one ever knew what kind of "meat" they were actually issued. To Witherspoon the food was *issued* not *given* to the soldiers. Today it tasted just like the meat they had been issued yesterday and all previous days. It had no taste but that of smoke.

After the hard work and the meal, with the sun beating down on them, the men started to dose off. Some sat on equipment containers, ammunition boxes, or bails of hay and leaned against the trench walls. Others lay along the trench walls. Each soldier found his own place of solitude, tried to avoid blocking the pathway through the trenches, and hoped not to be disturbed.

After Witherspoon knew his men had eaten, he sat back, relaxed, and reflected on his new assignment. He had been transferred from the 1st Division to the 82nd Division because the newly formed Division needed some experienced leaders to train and lead the young soldiers. As a newly promoted First Sergeant, Witherspoon, his company commander, and many others of the 1st Division were supplying the soldiers of the 82nd with valuable experience. Since the soldiers of the 82nd were assembled from all of the forty-eight states in America, the new Division was called the All-American Division. The first combat experience for the All-Americans was just a month old, and First Sergeant Witherspoon knew it was nowhere near over.

Witherspoon slowly stood, his head cocked toward enemy lines. A faint droning could be heard. He listened for a moment more and then cupped his hand over his ear to listen more intently. Then he saw them and shouted, "Aeromachines! The company will come to arms!" he commanded.

Throughout the trenches of the company sector, men grabbed their helmets. Some took up their weapons and scurried to the front of the trenches. Others crouched low. No one knew what the machines would do. Perhaps they would drop some bombs or leaflets. The machines could and would go in any direction along the trenches. None of the soldiers feared the aeromachines, which were more a nuisance than a threat. Nothing was like the artillery barrages in getting the soldiers worked up.

One of the company lookouts shouted, "Three red machines, 500 yards, right front, approaching."

Captain Sandhurst and Sergeant Witherspoon moved to the front of the company headquarters trench. The commander brought his field glasses up and searched the sky. He saw the distinctive red cigar forms glisten in the sunlight. Each had mixtures of different accent colors—white, tan, green, and blue.

"Albatroses," he said. "They're coming this way."

Sergeant Witherspoon grabbed the company phone and spun the handle. "Three enemy Albatroses, 500 yards, right front, heading this way," he said. "The company shall engage the aeromachines at will in Column Front!"

The soldiers started forming a line facing the attacking aeromachines in the direction of the trench. The normal formation of the company was Line Abreast, where the soldiers aimed and fired at the advancing enemy perpendicular to the trench line. Now the company had to fire along the direction of the trench line in order to defend itself.

The commander and his company sergeant could hear the platoon sergeants give the orders down the line in clear, commanding voices. The soldiers prepared their weapons in rapid action. The bolts of every rifle and machine gun in the company charged forward as the men loaded bullets into the chambers.

They watched the flying machines approach. It appeared that the machines were either on an observation mission or going to attack the southern portion of the trenches away from the company. Sergeant Witherspoon thought the machines were not a huge threat to his men. To the south, another company started to engage the machines with constant rifle fire. Witherspoon could tell that the machines were far out of range and his sister company was wasting ammunition.

The sergeant immediately hit the company phone again. "Chester Company will check its firing," he shouted. He did not want his soldiers wasting ammunition on a target flying out of the range of the rifles.

The command reverberated in the company sector as all of the company sergeants told their soldiers to hold their fire.

"The Company will engage only at the command of the company commander," Witherspoon said into the phone.

The entire company watched intently as the flying machines

approached the American defensive lines. Although they knew they had little chance of hitting the flying machines, the soldiers enjoyed firing at them. It was a way of relieving stress. It felt as if they were getting back at the Huns. Sergeant Witherspoon understood. It was difficult to bring down a flying machine, he knew, but it sure was fun trying to hit the moving targets.

The three machines pealed off into single file over No-Man's Land. Captain Sandhurst called out calmly, "Sergeant, they are lining for an attack. I believe they are on a strafing run. My guess is they are going to turn north and strafe the company. Prepare for action."

Sergeant Witherspoon relayed the command to his sergeants. His voice was calm and deliberate. The men looked on in admiration as Sandhurst and Witherspoon brought the company weapons in line upon the approaching aeromachines. In short order, the company was ready.

Then the enemy flying machine closest to the trenches turned just as Captain Sandhurst had predicted. Sergeant Witherspoon waited for a few seconds and then gave the command over the wire: "First Platoon shall engage the enemy machine at will."

First Platoon opened fire on the Albatros. Sergeant Witherspoon gave commands to each platoon in sequence to engage the enemy. The soldiers fired on the first aeromachine as it flew over the trenches. Green tracers arced down from the aeromachine and struck the dirt around the company. Sergeant Witherspoon could see the rifles move with the machine as his men fired up at it. The action was quick and deliberate. The men worked their trade like experts. Yet the aeromachine flew on. Little did Sergeant Witherspoon know that of all the men in his company, only 15 percent actually fired directly on the enemy. Many men simply fired their weapons into the air in the general direction of the machine. They went through the motions but couldn't fire their weapons directly. They sensed it but didn't know they couldn't actually bring themselves to kill another man. Shooting at fixed targets of red circles in peacetime training made them marksmen, but it didn't make them killers.

Captain Sandhurst raised his voice over the noise of the firing weapons. "Second Albatros in the attack!"

Sergeant Witherspoon relayed the command to fire on the second flying machine. The captain watched as the first machine completed its attack. He saw immediately that his company sector was the object of the attack from all three of the machines. Bullets whizzed around the trenches. Some bullets and tracers from the second machine started finding their marks. Men were hit in some places in the company sector as the red flying machine passed overhead. The infantry firing was deafening. Commands were given in quick order among the screams of those who had been struck. Noise and confusion were constant companions to the action.

Sergeant Witherspoon wondered how many times each flying machine would come around and attack his men. If this kept up, he thought, they were going to get chewed up and spit out.

Witherspoon yelled into the company phone, "Fourth Platoon will bring machine guns into antiaircraft action in Column Front!"

The noise of the machine guns being disconnected from their tripod mounts could be heard around the company headquarters as the command rang out from the platoon sergeants. Witherspoon was bringing the machine guns of the heavy weapons platoon into action. A soldier had to volunteer to stand in front of each machine gunner. The machine guns were placed on a towel on the volunteers' shoulders. The assistant gunners fed the cloth belts of bullets and tracers into the machine guns as the volunteers held the gun barrels on their shoulders. The gunners and assistant gunners were then prepared for action. They and their volunteers would move as one to bring the sights to bear ahead of the flying machines.

The entire action opened again with spraying bullets from the air, the rattle of the machine guns from the company trench, and the massed fire of the individual soldiers. The enemy flier had a much better chance of hitting his targets than did the soldiers on the ground.

Some of the men of Chester Company were cut up by the steel rain from the second German flying machine. As the red devils, each with its different accent colors, circled for another run, Sergeant

Witherspoon ordered medical aid for his wounded soldiers. He could see at least four injured men in the bottom of the trench. Some were screaming and writhing in the pain. One man was hit in the hand. Another had a through-and-through abdominal wound that was smoking from the burning tracer that had sliced through him. Two others were down and unconscious. To Witherspoon's experienced eye it looked as if at least one of the men would not make it. He was losing too much blood from a chest wound.

Witherspoon was searching for a means of downing the Germans or at least forcing them to attack another sector of the lines before they decimated the men in his company. He then spotted movement above the circling Albatros fighters. A squatty tan flying machine dove into the three circling enemy machines, scattering them like bats from a belfry. He noticed that it had a green, tan, and brown camouflage pattern on its topsides.

Sergeant Witherspoon issued the command to cease firing. He didn't want Chester Company to inadvertently down an Allied flier. The noise of gunfire quickly decreased and died. The only sound came from the air, where the flying machines circled in an aerial dance.

The eyes of every man in the company were fixed on the combat above them and to their front. The red bats scurried. The tan and camouflage machine then came to settle behind one of the red machines. The Dance progressed 800 feet in front and only 200 feet above. The men thought from this distance that the Allied fighter was a Frenchman. The machine was a French-built Spad with bright tricolors of red, blue, and white concentric circles on its wings.

Chester Company watched in admiration of the skill with which the Frenchman handled his machine and attacked his adversaries. The four machines, three red devils against a lone Frenchman, played about in death-defying circles above the desolate No-Man's Land. The men cheered as the Dance moved slowly toward the east, toward the German lines. The men were now safe. They watched in great concentration and with great expectation. One against three, they thought, are not very good odds. It didn't look as if the Frenchman could possibly survive the aerial combat.

Sergeant Witherspoon heard the captain say in a low, calm voice, "Magnificent. That Frenchman is a magnificent flier and absolutely fearless."

Captain Sandhurst brought his glasses up to watch as the aerial melee moved farther away from the American defensive lines. As he watched, he spoke to Sergeant Witherspoon.

"Sergeant," he said, "you may report to the company that the flier is actually an American pilot. His machine has the red, blue, and white circles of an *American* flying machine. It also has a screaming Indian painted on its fuselage. That was the symbol of the Lafayette Escadrille, the French squadron of American volunteer fliers. It is painted on some of our machines for those who served as volunteers in the Escadrille."

Sergeant Witherspoon spoke into the company phone. "Announce to the company that the flier before us is an American aviator. Captain Sandhurst has observed the American insignia and a symbol of the Lafayette Escadrille on the flying machine."

The company soldiers started to stir as they received word of what was before them. The men started to cheer as the tan machine continued its dance with the red devils. The French machine disengaged from its three adversaries as it rose above the German lines. Suddenly the American pilot inverted his machine, flew downward toward the enemy lines, and then turned west toward the company.

As the aerial engagement broke off, Witherspoon could hear a rumble in the distance signifying the approach of a new German artillery barrage. He yelled out in a loud command, "Incoming!"

Soldiers crouched low in the trenches as they received the command. Sergeant Witherspoon saw the American aeromachine continue to approach as he too ducked. The *woompf, woompf, woompf* was heard, followed by the shock waves of the explosions. A black cloud of smoke from the artillery barrage rose from the explosions before them.

Suddenly the black smoke parted in a circle, and the tan flying machine materialized like magic. The smoke swirled in counter-rotating circles over the wings of the machine. The men looked up and watched as the smoke parted, the aeroplane appeared, and the flier performed a perfect roll with his machine. The red, blue, and white of the American symbol on the main wings glistened in the sunlight. Sergeant Witherspoon saw the American flier look down at them and pump his fist when his machine was upside down. In a flash, the machine righted itself and flew off toward the southwest.

The company went wild. Men jumped out of the trenches waving their weapons and helmets as the flier swooped overhead. Witherspoon had never witnessed such elation in the front lines before. The men of Chester Company were patting each other on their backs, dancing like fools, and screaming at the top of their lungs. The scene was unbelievable. It was extremely dangerous, yet exhilarating as the dirt and mud from the artillery explosions rained down on the complement of soldiers.

Witherspoon wasn't sure how he could restore order. But he wasn't sure he *wanted* to. This morale boost was exactly what Chester Company needed. These men had endured cold, hunger, fatigue, and fear. They had suffered from lice, trench foot, dysentery, and scurvy. They had seen pain, and some had met death. And they would soon participate in the largest infantry attack in the history of the U.S. Army, a frontal assault on a determined enemy at the Saint Mihiel Salient. The advance would be part of a general attack along the entire French and American sectors of the Verdun battlefield. The men needed their spirits lifted, and the heroics of the American flier might provide more excitement and enthusiasm than the company leaders could muster. Perhaps this one display of bravery would spur them on to absolute victory and the end of the war, Witherspoon thought.

Sergeant Witherspoon looked back at the fading sight of the American flier. A calm feeling overcame him as his eyes met Captain Sandhurst's gaze. Witherspoon had never seen his commander show such a reaction to a combat scene. Sandhurst's face showed amazement at what he had just witnessed.

"Sergeant Witherspoon," the captain said. "That flier is a hero."

CHAPTER 11: "TO ARMS, TO ARMS!" TO ARMS OF THE LADIES!

Luxeuil-les-Bains, France - August 22, 1917

"Gentlemen, the trucks will soon leave," Willie Dugan announced. "They leave in ten minutes, by hook or by crook. All those who are unprepared shall suffer the inevitable fate of complete and utter boredom. To the ladies, gentlemen, to the *ladies*," he shouted.

The few left in the barracks broke out in raucous laughter, shouting back, "to the *ladies*, gentlemen, to the *ladies!*"

Half of the squadron was going on its monthly two-day R&R. The official purpose was rest and recuperation, but the fliers called it "rough and ready," as in rough and ready sex. R&R rarely resulted in any deep relations between the sexes. It did sometimes lead to rough and ready fighting between the alcohol-rich fliers and anyone who rubbed them the wrong way.

The men only yearned for conversation in the presence of the soft and light-skinned French ladies. Some of the ladies even looked very nice. A few of the older ladies were willing and able, as some would say. The young women, who were usually beautiful rather than just very nice looking generally stayed at home. French parents were very protective of their children, particularly during the war years. One never knew what might become of a young woman at the hands of lonely men from the front, the parents worried.

To the fliers who had extra spending money, an R&R could turn into a four-day excursion. Men hoped to have at least one enchanting evening of comfort in the arms of a willing participant.

More often than not, fliers on extended R&R ended up sleeping alone. Some just needed to enjoy something like the comforts of home. Others needed the extra time to recover from their drunken stupors. Hunting for wine more than women, some fliers would drown their fears in drink. After all, the chances of seeing home again after working above the killing fields were very slim. Too many names of Lafayette Escadrille fliers were on the Plaque of Honor. "To Those That Have Honorably Gone Before Us," it said. Those who had *gone before* were the dead.

Most of the R&Rs were in Paris. The participants would board the lories to the closest town and take the train to Paris for an overnight stay. They would take the same route back to the aerodrome after having great meals, great drink, great sleep, and great fun. The trips really settled the flier's nerves.

Jimmy completed preparing his tunic. Dressed in his best uniform, this would be his first R&R. He missed the last one he could have gone on. He was determined not miss the next opportunity when it came up. After missing his first R&R, Jimmy felt he would probably kill to mount the lories bound for their bouncing transport to the short respite from the war. How wonderful it would be, he thought, to get out of the environment of death and destruction over Verdun. He wanted to just free his mind up and relax in a civilized setting. Then again, to meet with and talk to a nice young lady would really top it off.

But this time the small group he joined wanted something more settled and soothing. They wanted to avoid the bustle of Paris and the routines of the men on the prowl. The group decided to go to the countryside. Jimmy enthusiastically headed to one of the waiting motorcars. They were headed to the Vosges Mountains and the quaint little French towns along the Moselle River. The men looked forward to smelling the flowers in the Vosges and enjoying the serenity of the green mountain foliage. Besides, they would have plenty of time in Paris on the next R&R.

The trucks started their bouncing drone toward short-term happiness for the main group.

Jimmy approached the two staff motorcars waiting to take their small group on its journey in the opposite direction. He looked up as he finished buttoning his tunic.

"Willie!" Jimmy shouted. "I thought you were going to Paris with the others."

"*Awwww*, shucks, Jimmy. I almost got myself locked in irons last time I went with them. The Gendarmes weren't putting up with our shenanigans. Besides, I'd rather be with you fellas. I need to take it easy."

"Well, then, what are you waiting for? Hop in and let's skedaddle."

Jimmy and Willie Dugan joined Lieutenant Ray Bridgman, Sergeant Didier Masson, and the newest member to the squadron, Corporal Sam Morris. Jimmy and Ray had grown particularly close. Jimmy had a lot of respect for Ray as a flier and admired him for his honesty and fun-loving attitude. Then there was Masson, Jimmy thought. He was much older than Jimmy but was fun to be around and had a reputation for getting the women.

Morris, the fifth member of the small R&R group, had joined the Lafayette Escadrille just three weeks before. He was a nice man, respectful and quiet and just four years older than Jimmy. But he was not a very good flier. His turns were slow and sloppy, Jimmy had noticed, and he rarely performed barrel rolls. How could anyone *not* want to kick into a tight barrel? Jimmy wondered. No wonder Morris was only a corporal. He's lucky to be a flier and not an aerial observer.

The trip was uneventful except that the motorcars had to negotiate dirt roads and horse trails. Jimmy was flush with excitement. He usually didn't drink much, but he had learned that the French sure could make good-tasting wine. His mouth watered with the thought of the full-bodied Burgundy wine he had sampled before in the hotel. And the bread! Jimmy warmed to the thought of the French bread served with butter and oil containing green leaves. Jimmy had never before had good wine and oil on bread.

The men plowed out of the motorcars from time to time on their trip like lambs running from the wolves. Unlike the large groups of smiling hunter-killers that scattered in Paris, Jimmy's group of five stayed together. They were looking for peace in the hills. They wanted to hunt fun and kill bottles of wine.

Perhaps Sam could fly to a perfect place to attract women better than he could fly an aeroplane, Jimmy chuckled to himself as they continued their travels. If he couldn't, Sergeant Masson certainly could. *Jeepers,* Jimmy thought. *Sergeant Masson was like a magnet for ladies.*

After hours of touring the mountainous area, the five comrades found an elegant and quaint restaurant situated along a small branch of the Moselle River. Charmes, France, looked like a friendly and welcoming place for relaxation. It was a perfect place to stop after touring the mountains. The men hoped it would be a target-rich environment for women like the skies over eastern France were for enemy aeromachines.

Corporal Sam Morris couldn't fly like a bird, Jimmy knew, but he sure could speak French. He stepped up and spoke with the maitre d' when the group of fliers couldn't get her to understand them in their broken French. Hand signals didn't seem to help much. The maitre d' smiled at Sam and nodded when he spoke to her in very elegant French. The maitre d' escorted the group to its tables. An older man was pushing two tables together for the fliers. It became clear to them that the restaurant was a family affair. The husband worked the kitchen and his wife worked the floor taking orders.

The restaurant felt very comfortable. It was a masonry structure with plaster walls painted with grape vines framing scenes of French houses along the Moselle. An elderly French couple seated in the dining room looked up at the fliers as they walked by. The men walked quietly to their tables in respect of the private and very personal atmosphere.

The boys were amazed at Sam. "Where did you learn French?" they asked in a whisper. Masson cut in. "How did you do that? What did you say to her? She was so uptight about us being here until you talked her into letting us in."

"I told her we were American fliers defending France," Sam told them. "I said that we were volunteers who'd joined the French flying resistance to defeat the Hun. I told her we were tired and hungry and that we had heard that this was a magnificent *restaurante*. We wanted to experience the pleasure of the friendly, family atmosphere of this esteemed establishment."

While the other men were joking with Sam about his talent for soothing the maitre d', Jimmy saw a vision. Coming from the kitchen with two bottles of wine was the loveliest creature he had ever seen in his life. Her dark brown hair spilled in flowing waves around her soft and graceful face. *The face of heaven,* Jimmy thought. As she approached the table in short, simple steps, Jimmy saw the warmth of her beautiful brown eyes. For the first time in his life, Jimmy had trouble breathing when looking at a woman.

The young lady poured wine for the fliers, and it seemed to Jimmy that never before had anyone performed such a mundane task so elegantly. He looked at her hands and then at her eyes. *She's a vision,* Jimmy thought. *She must be.* Her graceful fingers and smooth-flowing body worked the bottles of wine like a ballet dancer. *And how she smelled!* Jimmy thought. *She smelled like a rosebud in early spring.*

At that moment the voice of another man called from the kitchen, and it occurred to Jimmy that it might belong to the young lady's boyfriend or husband. The restaurant's proprietors were already wary of these soldiers who wore French uniforms but were actually Americans. The older woman had a concerned look that she scarcely tried to conceal, and the older man who'd arranged their tables had peered at them with suspicion. To flirt with this vision of beauty with the dark brown eyes might cause trouble.

Sergeant Masson might be trouble too. Jimmy noticed he was all over it, staring at the young lady as she moved around the table. But the young woman kept diverting her eyes toward Jimmy and smiled a devious smile as she poured his wine. Jimmy looked at Masson to see that he'd noticed. Jimmy's heart was pounding. To see this woman smile at him while slowly pouring his wine was more exciting than diving toward a hundred German fighting machines.

The light cotton dress she wore ebbed and flowed over her body like wheat in a breeze in the fields of Wisconsin. How her torso moved in slow, rhythmic motion as she walked back toward the kitchen! Jimmy watched her from the corners of his eyes. She walked carefully without making a noise and moved her hips back and forth as she dodged the wrought-iron chairs and tables in the main dining room. *Thank the Lord I have excellent peripheral vision,* Jimmy thought. *Lord, can she move.*

The meal passed like a speeding dove in the hunting fields. It was there. Then it was over. Jimmy even forgot what he had eaten. He couldn't stop thinking about the vision of loveliness that came and went now and again. His heart stopped beating each time the girl appeared.

Jimmy could tell that the older woman spoke to the young lady at times in the kitchen. He was sure she was cautioning the young woman against flirting with the Americans. He hoped she was telling the girl how nice she thought one of the Americans was.

At the end of the meal, Sergeant Masson spoke up. "Lieutenant Smitts," he said, "we all took a vote. We decided that you should stay here after dinner with Corporal Morris and enjoy your evening. Corporal Morris can translate for you. We want to go out on the town and have some fun. We're sure you're tired and need to rest here."

Jimmy hesitantly replied, "No, no gentlemen. I can't take advantage of you."

Bridgman held up his hand. "You and Corporal Morris have your orders. Orders are orders," Bridgman demanded as the others smiled.

Jimmy nodded as the men began to leave. Sergeant Masson came up to Jimmy, patted him on his back, and said in his ear, "My good fellow, I may be a ladies' man, but I know when I'm bested. Good luck hooking this fish. I don't think you're going to get much of a fight out of her."

With that, the men left. Sam went up and whispered something to the maitre d'. As she looked over to Jimmy, Jimmy could tell Sam had told her about him and his desire to meet the young lady. The maitre d' nodded and pointed to a table in the back corner of the dining room.

Sam returned to the table where Jimmy was anxiously waiting. "We're in," he said.

"What did you tell her?" Jimmy asked quietly as they walked to the appointed table.

"I told her the meal was better than we ever expected and we are honored to be in the presence of such a fine family. I told her you were the senior flier and the most honorable man in our unit. I asked her for the privilege of a few moments with her family to thank them all for their hospitality and that your heart would be broken if you could not have the pleasure of at least being introduced to her lovely daughter."

Soon the maitre d', the man from the kitchen, a younger man, and the young woman walked together to their table. Jimmy's heart raced as he deceptively watched the young woman move toward them through the dining room. She was radiant.

The young man spoke first. "Gentlemen, I present my mother Sophia, father Jacques, and my sister Giselle. I am Sharrals, at your service. I mean to say, *Charles* in your native tongue," he corrected.

The fliers stood and shook the hands of the parents and Charles. They bowed their heads at the beautiful young lady. Jimmy was especially honored and thrilled to be with this very nice family. He was overwhelmed to be standing in front of the most beautiful woman he had ever seen.

"We give you our deepest thanks for assistance to France in terrible war," Charles continued. "France has fought the Boche for many, many years. Our people endured constant invasion by the barbarians, and we appreciate greatly your help. Thank you."

Charles translated Jimmy's explanation about America and why the fliers joined the Lafayette Escadrille. Jimmy wanted the family to be comfortable with his presence—and with Sam. He noticed Sophia relax as he explained their dedication to ending the war. Giselle wore a constant smile as Jimmy spoke. Sam broke in by explaining how he and Jimmy flew together to fight Les Boche. Jacques spoke quickly in French, and Sam told Jimmy that the patriarch was honored to make their acquaintance.

An hour passed before Jimmy knew it. Finally Giselle spoke to her parents in French, and a short but pointed discussion ensued between the family members. To Jimmy the discussion sounded more like an argument. Sam leaned slightly over toward Jimmy and whispered. "Giselle is asking her mother to let her entertain us while the family returns to start closing down the restaurant."

Charles then closed with words that Jimmy longed to hear. "We wish you to be comfortable in our "restau-raan." We must attend to our work. But mother agrees to allow Giselle to stay with you for some time. We wish you great honor and comfort for your devotion to France. Giselle can speak some English. Please let us know if you need anything. We will not be far," Charles said, almost as a warning to the Americans. "This bottle of wine is a gift of our family for you to enjoy."

With that, the family left. Sophia and Jacques each kissed Giselle on her cheeks. Then Jimmy was finally together with Giselle. He dreamed she would become *his* Giselle.

Sam spoke first. He told Giselle in French that he was there only to translate if necessary. He wanted Giselle to know that Jimmy was honored and pleased to make her acquaintance. He also told her Jimmy was the best flier in their squadron and the nicest man he had ever met.

Giselle blushed, smiled, and looked up at Jimmy. She said in broken English, "Meet you is my pleasure."

Jimmy was elated. They might actually be able to talk to one another, he thought.

The three of them spent hours in small talk as the others in the family worked to clear and clean the restaurant. During the time, Sam explained to Giselle where he was from. He described where Jimmy lived in Wisconsin and how he had learned to fly at an early age in the United States. Giselle told the two fliers that she learned English in school. Her brother, Charles, studied English in England and returned to France to help his parents with the restaurant.

She shyly told Jimmy, "I was sorry I may not speak English good."

"I understand everything you say, in English or in French. It feels like we have been together for many years." He was so comfortable with her next to him. He really did understand what she was saying just by watching her movements. And what movements they were, so smooth and soft in their appearance. Her eyes and smile melted

Jimmy's heart.

Giselle asked as she bowed her head slightly but kept her eyes on Jimmy, "What is it to fly? Do you have fear in the sky when you are there? How do you fight Les Boche?"

Her mannerisms excited Jimmy. He was sure she was playing with him.

Jimmy told her how exciting it was to fly. She stared at him as he explained the yellow, magenta, and blue sunsets he saw from his machine. Sam translated as she didn't seem to understand Jimmy's words. Her warm eyes and constant smile quivered some as she reacted to Jimmy's description of the beautiful sunsets. Giselle seemed to be in a dream world. *Dream world?* he wondered. *She couldn't possibly be in a deeper dream world than me.*

"You see wonderful things," Giselle said. "I wish one day to be there."

Jimmy couldn't believe it. The night was gone. The family was closing the restaurant and it was time to leave. Jimmy asked Sam to translate something to Giselle's parents.

"I cannot tell you what an honor and privilege it has been for me to make your acquaintance. The food was excellent, and the company was even better. I wish to tell you how wonderful your daughter is. I ask for your permission to visit with your family and particularly your lovely daughter, Giselle, as soon as I can return. I only hope that one day you will come to know the depth of my devotion to the defense of France and to the honor of your Giselle."

"Mon Lieutenant," Giselle's father said, with Sam translating. "I wish to thank you for your service to France. Our family is also very happy to come to know you. We wish the very best for our Giselle. I invite you to join us as soon as you can. We wish you the very best in your defense of France. Vive la France!" he said as he shook Jimmy's hand.

Jimmy couldn't stop his mind from racing on the trip back to the aerodrome. He couldn't keep the young lady out of his mind. It was as if she were standing in front of him as he bounced around inside the staff car. How wonderful she looked. How amazing she smelled. How unbelievable the night had been. Jimmy wondered when the next moment would come when he could be with that vision of utmost beauty. He wondered how he could possibly come back and be with her when they moved the squadron to Ham at the end of September. *Ham is so far away,* Jimmy thought. *This is going to be a very difficult challenge. But I will persevere in my next R&R.*

* * * * *

Washington, D.C., U.S.A. – April 14, 1918

Senator Stevenson was in the battle of his brief senatorial life. He had no idea that the Republicans and most of the Democrats in the Senate would fight so hard against him and his proposed bill. The senator was working to bring government support for federal aid to aeroplane manufacturing in Wisconsin. His argument was that the German and Irish craftsmen of Wisconsin were the best woodworkers in the United States.

He also hadn't considered Senator Paul Husting passing away and giving Representative Lenroot an opportunity to take the open Senate seat from Wisconsin in a special election. But that is exactly what the representative had accomplished.

"America needs aeroplane production. We are relying on the resources of our allies for war materiel. Wisconsin is prepared to bring high-quality flying machines to the troops," Stevenson had declared on the Senate floor and in his campaign speeches. Unfortunately for the senator and Wisconsin, his words were falling on deaf ears. In spite of its vote for a declaration of war one year earlier, the Senate was trying to thwart any effort to federalize war production. Many senators believed that private companies were best suited to produce war materiel and the government had no business getting involved in production.

Representative Lenroot in the House and now Senator Lenroot of the U.S. Senate had been working behind the scenes to keep the war production in private hands. He was entrenched and very well connected in the political circles of Washington. Senator Lenroot worked his influence to try to keep Wisconsin isolated from federal funding. Lenroot disliked his nemesis from Wisconsin more than any other politician he knew. His dislike went beyond reason for Lenroot was basically sacrificing Wisconsin secretly to defeat Senator Stevenson's programs.

Adlai Stevenson fought one of the greatest American leaders of all time, Abraham Lincoln. Lincoln was Representative Lenroot's political idol. He was not about to let this Stevenson family member do well in politics.

"Why Wisconsin?" Senator Lenroot asked often but not before his own constituents. "Why not support Boeing in Washington State, Curtiss in New York, or any other company in say, the great state of North Carolina? After all, isn't North Carolina the birthplace of aviation?"

Senator Stevenson knew Lenroot was behind the failure of the bill he had introduced to put Wisconsin on the aviation map. Even his speech about the needs of the American soldiers and fliers didn't help his cause. He used the fact that General Billy Mitchell, the commander of the American Aero Squadrons in Europe, was from Wisconsin to try to move the bill along. He even considered discussions with the dark side of businesses in Illinois to try to gain some advantage.

Eugene's efforts were fruitless, Loraine could tell. She had to stand by and watch as her husband tried everything to promote the businesses of his constituents. Even her brother, Royal S. Copeland, could not use his influence in the state of New York to help her husband's cause. The government just did not want to federalize war production.

America would not long be in this Great War, people said. Why would the government want to get involved in a short-term venture in wartime aviation?

This was the War to End All Wars, and the idea of federal involvement in private enterprise was not well thought of in the spring of 1918.

CHAPTER 12: ON THE WINGS OF AN AVIATOR

Over Verdun, France - September 2, 1917

The flight of four from the Lafayette Escadrille flew toward its patrol area. This was to be a mutually supporting patrol of individual hunter-killers that they had flown before. They tried not to fly similar missions like this too often each month. The squadron leadership didn't want the Germans to recognize a pattern in its tactics. This was only the fourth time the squadron had ever organized this flying arrangement and the second time Jimmy had participated.

Captain Thenault was to Jimmy's left and Clive to his right. Sergeant Dugan was the only newcomer to their party. He was flying with Thenault and had replaced Lieutenant Bridgman, who was recuperating from a terrible flu.

In typical fashion, Captain Thenault gave his signal for them to separate. Like before, each flier was to watch out for his adjacent comrade. This had worked well in the past, as when Jimmy had flown to the aid of Captain Thenault the previous month.

The sky in their flying area was sprinkled with small clouds. The soft clouds and clear blue sky made Jimmy wish Giselle could see the beauty of it all. It was like he was floating on the clouds. *Oh, if she could only be with me. She would love this,* he thought. *Her lovely smile and soft skin were all that was missing from this wonderful world in the air.*

Thick clouds covered the fliers from high above their patrol area. Jimmy guessed the clouds were about 5,000 feet above their 8,000-foot altitude. Jimmy knew to keep an eye on the high clouds. He wasn't concerned about the small smattering of clouds in the area but worried about the thick clouds above them. He had seen before how a change in the weather pattern could cause more clouds to form quickly at lower altitudes. It took only a small change in air temperature for new clouds to form and give safe harbor to an attacking enemy formation.

Jimmy would accept the safety of clouds if he had to. He didn't like the thought of hiding among them. But he would go to them if he needed to. After all, Jimmy thought, he had to save himself for his beloved Giselle. He kept thinking of how the Hun used the clouds to pounce on unsuspecting Allied fliers. Jimmy would have to watch for building cloud formations as he flew.

The group of four separated. Jimmy kept an eye on Captain Thenault and Clive as he set up to fly his standard figure eights. He didn't need to worry about being blinded by the sun on this mission. It was hidden behind the high clouds.

Then he saw them. There were four dark shapes heading toward his patrol sector. All four had the boxy fuselage shape of German Fokkers. Two of them were larger than the others. They were larger in an odd way. Jimmy couldn't quite make them out. He knew the two smaller aeroplanes were Fokker D models. He had danced with them before. They were maneuverable but not as maneuverable as the Nieuport 17 he was flying. But the German machines were much faster than his. Jimmy knew he would have to use the maneuvering strength of his aeroplane to minimize the speed advantage of the Fokkers.

It occurred to Jimmy that the other two advancing machines were the new Fokker triplanes. He had heard many stories about them from the older fliers at the bar and in the briefing room. The British fliers ranted about these triplanes. According to the British, the new machines were fast, maneuverable, and menacing in their appearance. Jimmy could care less about the appearance of the machines. But speed and maneuverability counted for a lot in aerial battle.

One final thought struck Jimmy as he prepared for the combat. The Hun, like the Lafayette Escadrille, did not issue the most modern, capable, newest aeroplanes to its novice fliers. Jimmy knew he was facing at least two fliers with exceptional flying skills.

Looking right and left, Jimmy realized Captain Thenault had flown behind a cloud bank. Jimmy couldn't find Clive, who seemed to have disappeared from the clear sky to Jimmy's right.

Jimmy adjusted his fighting goggles and pulled back slightly on the stick. He needed to climb without losing too much airspeed to reduce the enemy's advantage. He wasn't scared as he climbed to the challenge. He never really felt scared when he flew. Flying was his dream. Hunting was his nature. Now it was time for his dream and his nature to come together in harmony. He knew he would have to fly and fight as he never had before.

The four enemy fliers closed quickly on their lone target. Jimmy could tell they were setting up to converge their fire upon him. Pushing slight left rudder, he turned to his left and slew his machine slightly sideways. Jimmy wanted his adversaries to think he was inexperienced. He also wanted them to turn to their right, his left. In this way Jimmy would throw off the firing aim of his enemies. He could then maneuver to avoid their concentrated fire and be able to attack them from their sides. He also thought he could maneuver to bring the fight closer toward Clive. He had a better chance of being observed in the clear skies to his right than in the cloudy skies to his left. Clive's patrol sector was in clear air. Thenault might not fly out of the clouds until it was too late.

The head-on pass was going to be hairy. Jimmy was slewing slightly sideways. The arrangement of his aeroplane to the wind cut his airspeed somewhat. But it made the Germans adjust their direction of flight to fire at a point well in front and to the left of him. A few seconds after the Germans turned to their right, Jimmy straightened his aeroplane to gain airspeed. He pushed the throttle all the way forward to turn his engine at maximum rpm.

At the perfect time, Jimmy pushed right stick and spun his wings vertically up to the left. Centering his stick, Jimmy pulled hard, turning his machine sharply to his right. The crisp move surprised the Germans. They had him dead to rights. But he turned quickly out of the line of converging fire that the Germans were setting up. To the Germans it looked as if the enemy flier was trying to run. In fact, the move had reduced the number of aeroplanes that could engage him with fire. It also set him up for his next turn into a proper firing angle with his adversaries.

As the Germans turned to their left to attack, Jimmy quickly spun his wings 90 degrees to his left and pulled up and to the left on his stick. He kicked slight right rudder, which pointed his nose upward in his turn. He opened fire high above and 500 feet away from his approaching enemies. He hoped the plunging bullets and tracers would spray across the front of the Huns and take them all out. Even if he missed, this kind of early attack had scared other enemy fliers facing him in the past. Perhaps it would give him an edge. As the distance between them quickly closed to 200 feet, Jimmy adjusted his rudder to change plunging fire to direct fire. He hoped that his plunging fire had scored. He wanted his direct fire to finish what the plunging fire had started.

The Germans fired too, but Jimmy knew they were completely out of alignment. The German tracers and bullets fell harmlessly to Jimmy's front and below him. But the vibrations from the machine and his excitement in the closing engagement kept him from knowing for sure if he had scored.

As the joust continued, Jimmy confirmed that two of his adversaries were in deed the new Fokker triplanes. As his bullets and tracers flew, Jimmy continued to correct his fire with slight adjustments of his rudder and ailerons. He had to readjust as the oncoming Germans came at him fast. The enemy continued to fire. He pulled up slightly to avoid the oncoming slaughter of lead.

They passed below Jimmy in their diving attack. He passed over them at a slight angle from their left to their right. Hoping the Germans believed he was going to their right, Jimmy executed a quick 270-degree left-hand barrel roll and pulled hard to turn to their *left*. He had totally reversed his direction of flight without their knowing it. He was hoping he could come in behind one of the Huns before the others realized what he had done.

As he came halfway through his turn, Jimmy looked up and over his right shoulder. He wanted to put his eyes on the four. He had expected all four Germans to turn to their right. He wanted them to think he was turning into that side of their formation. But they were splitting up into two flights of two, one going to their left and one to their right. The move was masterful, Jimmy thought. The Germans were forming two leafs in a clover. Jimmy's turn formed the third leaf. As a chess player, Jimmy immediately saw the mastery of the German move. With double cloverleafs, one German cloverleaf could easily turn onto the rear of Jimmy's aeroplane no matter which of the two cloverleafs Jimmy attacked. "So, you have me in check," Jimmy said as he watched the two German groups separate. He knew the only way he would avoid checkmate was to continue to turn inside each cloverleaf as he merged with it.

Jimmy could also tell each enemy flight included one triplane hunter as lead and one biplane wingman in support of the leader. This was not going to be easy, Jimmy thought. These fliers are good and they have an excellent plan of offense supported by excellent defense. He then said under his breath, "Come on, Clive. I need you *now*, more than I ever have before. Where *are* you?"

Jimmy continued to turn hard. He strained his aeroplane to the limit of its capability. He needed to get inside of his next two adversaries as quickly as possible. The first two Germans were turning in Jimmy's direction. He adjusted his turn to climb slightly as they came around. "Go up, son, go up," he kept telling himself as his father had years before. He planned to attack both fighters from slightly above them. The maneuver worked, but the two Germans separated. This made Jimmy's firing solution more difficult.

Jimmy pushed right rudder and aligned on the inside Fokker. It was the biplane wingman. Jimmy let out a long burst of fire. His rounds struck the tail of the flying machine as it rushed passed. *Not good enough,* Jimmy thought.

As a chess player, Jimmy was thinking two to three moves ahead. In the next couple of moves, he knew he would be faced with two groups of two fighters attacking him in converging circles. Cloverleafs always intersect at the stem in the center, thought Jimmy. In this case, each killing circle would intersect his flying path in alternating sequences, one group after the other. He knew the combat would ultimately diverge into individual hunters trying to gain the rear of his machine. He needed help. Jimmy sensed a strong but fleeting moment of true fear. He had never felt it before. It passed quickly up his spine, but there was no mistake about it. He now knew for the first time what it meant to be afraid in the air.

The reality of his situation brought him into action. He knew he had to replenish his ammunition. This could be his last chance to recharge his weapons. Like clockwork, Jimmy disengaged the bolts of both Vickers, allowing the cloth ammunition belts to fall away from the guns. Juggling the stick with his knees, he loaded a new belt of ammunition into each weapon and charged the handles of the guns one right after the other. That quickly he was back in action.

Wow, I would never think to reload a Bébé in combat like that. Wait 'til the boys hear about this. *Reloading while fighting four coordinated German fliers, I'm either really good or downright crazy.*

As the first wingman and his breaking leader continued on beyond Jimmy, he knew he had to turn hard right to face the other group of two. At 1,500 feet away, the triplane flier in the second group moved to the inside of his wingman and was training the nose of his machine on Jimmy. The German in the triplane was clearly taking charge of the action. Jimmy also saw that the German's maneuvers were sharp, quick, and deliberate. He wasn't just a good flier. He was a *great* flier.

Jimmy fired first. His arching fire did not change the oncoming flier's determination. The twin Spandau machine guns of the German triplane opened up. Jimmy could see the muzzle flashes of the barking guns ahead of him. His only hope was to rise up and perform the same passing barrel roll he had executed in the previous pass with the first two. It worked.

But the first group of two was circling toward him. He saw the wingman of the second group turning to the left as Jimmy started his right-turning barrel. The wingman would follow his triplane leader, thought Jimmy. So both of them would be flying away to Jimmy's left. He turned his concentration on the next upcoming pass of two. This was the second time Jimmy would engage the two coming at him. The German machines were in tight formation. They intended to concentrate their fire at a point where they believed Jimmy would fly through. Jimmy fired and knew he had to cut to the inside. They would tear him to pieces if their converging fire found its mark.

He turned harder right, and the enemy passed harmlessly to his left. Knowing the next group of two would be coming around to his left, Jimmy unloaded his machine, turned left, and entered the second turn of the double-turning maneuver he had started. He came around to his left, but he saw only *one* enemy aeroplane where he expected to see two. It was the wingman, the biplane. Turning his head quickly to his rear, Jimmy found that the triplane flier had done what Jimmy never expected. As the leader's wingman turned to his right in the previous pass, the leader turned left, separating from his supporting flier. "Lord Almighty," Jimmy said to himself, "that was a feat of perfection, and it was timed perfectly." The two Germans had planned to fool him into thinking they had turned in the same direction. The wingman had been used as a ruse.

The triplane leader was coming in behind Jimmy. That had never happened to him before. He knew from the maneuvering he had witnessed throughout the fight that the aeroship behind him was being flown by the best flier of the four. On second thought, the aeroship was being flown by the best flier Jimmy had *ever* flown against.

Jimmy saw the bright green tracers coming at him from behind just before they hit his tail section. The fact that Jimmy's machine was at an angle to the Hun kept him alive. He turned harder to his left to keep his tail in one piece. He knew the German would cut harder to try to get inside of him. With that move, the triplane would be set up with excellent lead on Jimmy.

The wingman that had fooled Jimmy was now approaching too. He would soon be in firing position. But he was not a major threat. Jimmy had to concentrate on the triplane *behind* him. He continued to cut left, waiting until the following enemy flier was pulling harder to get inside of his turn. *Lord, can that triplane turn,* Jimmy thought.

At the prefect time, while the German was still turning hard left, Jimmy executed a reversal and turned hard to his right in another double-turning maneuver. The German flew outside of Jimmy's turn and reversed quickly to his right. The Hun was outside of Jimmy's turn but coming around on his tail again. Jimmy knew it was a matter of seconds before his enemy would open up on him. Jimmy also knew that his enemy would expect another turn. At the right time, *Jimmy* did the unexpected this time. He unloaded his machine, flew straight and level, and waited.

The triplane flier was stunned, thinking that his opponent had just made his last maneuver. Flying straight and level was the worst thing he could have done. His enemy had put himself square in the middle of his gun sights. The German would take him in one burst of fire.

"One-one thousand," counted Jimmy. "Now, *execute.*"

Jimmy pulled straight up as the expert German flier watched in amazement. The action was so quick and so perfectly timed that the German leader was totally unprepared.

Vunder-bar, thought the German. *Very good.*

The triplane leader timed his pull and went up with Jimmy, but only after passing harmlessly under him. The German wanted Jimmy's aeroplane to start losing speed before he climbed up after him. The German aviator knew from his vast experience that the first aeroplane to break out of a climb had the least airspeed, the least maneuverability, and could be easily taken as it started to regain its flying ability. The German leader had done this in victory many times against British SE-5 flying machines over the Somme. The Nieuport 17 had similar flying characteristics, the German knew. It was now just a matter of seconds before Lieutenant Werner Voss would score another victory.

This would be Voss' twenty-seventh kill. He was 20 years old and, next to the famed Baron von Richthofen, the best that the German Flying Corps had to offer. And *this* twenty-seventh kill would come with ease when his opponent's machine started to fall backward from its climb.

Jimmy saw the other Fokkers circling and keeping their distance when Voss started his climb. They were obviously giving their leader maneuvering space and expecting their leader to soon take his adversary. They must have done this many times in past engagements.

Before his aeroplane slowed in its vertical flight, Jimmy executed a perfect vertical cartwheel with his machine. He had done this by accident in the past. This was the aerial "mistake" he had made months before. The timing of the maneuver was critical. He had only timed it well once before. This time Jimmy executed the maneuver flawlessly. "Right rudder in the climb, start to slip sideways in vertical flight, push left front stick, wait, close your eyes, spin, push quick right front stick, complete the spin, and recover by centering the stick," Jimmy said to himself in timed sequence. *There*, he saw it as his spinning vision cleared. The other enemy triplane was flying below Jimmy and to his front.

Voss was shocked as he watched his target fall from the sky, turn end-over-end by the cartwheel, and dive toward the other lead triplane. Voss was still in his climbing turn. He was in no position to execute the quick snap roll that would have put him in perfect position if the enemy hadn't cartwheeled like that. Voss could not turn quickly as he would lose airspeed and slip uncontrollably on his right side. He could only watch as the enemy flier with the French tricolors on his vertical tail dove toward his comrade, Feld-vay-ble Meyer. He then had to sit and watch as Jimmy fired controlled bursts into the tail of the triplane.

Pieces of canvas and wood flew everywhere. Jimmy kept firing. He was hoping to continue to pull up and out of his dive and walk his bullets and tracers right up the German's fuselage. The Hun pulled up to get out of Jimmy's diving attack. It was the German's only chance to avoid being destroyed.

Voss' wingman was finishing his turn and started to come back into the fight. Voss was still working to get his triplane to come over the top of its roll. It was just picking up airspeed after its climb. Flying control was coming back to his machine, but he was way out of alignment and too distant from the elusive killer he was trying to kill. Voss' wingman applied full throttle as he turned toward Jimmy. Jimmy had recovered from his cartwheel. He was firing at the triplane and taking huge chunks out of the tail assembly of the German's aeroplane.

Coming in fast, Voss' wingman struck. Bullets hit Jimmy's upper left wing. Jimmy had to cut hard right. He had little airspeed, but that helped him cut harder than the German wingman could. The Hun had too much airspeed and overshot Jimmy's aeroplane. He was out of the fight ... for now.

Jimmy had to find that higher triplane, that leader. He expected the hunter to be on him next. The flying angles and relationships would soon be to the Hun's advantage. Jimmy would have been clear for the moment had the wingman not launched his attack on him.

I don't have much more left in me, Jimmy thought. "Clive, where *are* you?" he shouted.

Then Jimmy saw him. The diving triplane was big and ominous before him. Jimmy was turning to his left. He cut as hard as he could to try to stay inside of the diving triplane's turn. As they passed one another in opposite directions, bullets started flying in front of Jimmy's machine. The triplane flier was almost on target but couldn't match Jimmy's cut to the inside.

As they passed, Jimmy searched for the other group of two. He had the better flier of the four and his wingman behind him and flying away. Jimmy knew he had to concentrate and look for the next threat. Where were they? Where *would* they be?

He found them. They were loitering on the side of the aerial dance that had been unfolding before them. Now it was their turn at a firing pass.

The constant swirling, spinning, and maneuvering of the five machines moved the Dance lower in the sky. The fight had started at 8,000 feet. Jimmy was certain that they had lost at least 500 feet with each turn and passing engagement. At 5,000 feet and still turning, Jimmy knew he would eventually run out of altitude. He also knew that he had to be low on ammunition. Soon he would have to worry about his petrol level too.

The two waiting predators had a good angle on him, Jimmy could tell. They were flying in unison and tracking toward an intersection point between their direction of flight and his. He *had* to do something.

Jimmy started a slow climb. The Germans mirrored his action. They were targeting Jimmy's flying path 200 feet ahead of him. Just before they opened up on him with their machine guns, Jimmy executed an extremely tight half barrel roll. The roll was so tight, it looked like a spin. Upside-down and pulling back on his stick, Jimmy pulled the trigger of his twin Vickers. Lead and tracers barked out of the guns. The bullets sprayed in the direction of the two oncoming Huns as Jimmy spun and dove downward. Then it happened. Jimmy's guns stopped firing. He was out of ammunition.

Clive, where are you? Jimmy thought again. He no longer had any sensation of fear. He felt calm and determined. He wanted support from someone, even Clive, to divert the attention of some of the Germans so that he could best the best.

The oncoming pair hadn't expected Jimmy's sudden upside-down flip. They definitely hadn't expected lead and tracers arching toward them in an open spray of death. Bullets and tracers impacted each German aeroplane sporadically. The unconcentrated fire failed to find a critical spot in the enemy machines. But both fliers got the picture.

Jimmy knew the Huns heard the distinctive sharp end to his firing. They must know that Jimmy's fire would have downed them had it continued. The Germans had to know something was wrong. They probably thought his guns had jammed. Jimmy knew the enemy would attack him like wolves on wounded prey if they knew he was out of ammunition. Now he had only his flying skills left to work with.

Watching the turning and spinning crossing fire, Voss's wingman saw that he had advantage on Jimmy. He was coming out of his 270-degree turn and onto Jimmy. In a quartering attack, the wingman fired. Jimmy was coming out of the second half of his spinning barrel roll. He finished the roll and turned right just as the wingman came onto him.

The wingman watched as his tracers impacted Jimmy's fuselage. The wingman wasn't sure, but he thought his bullets had found Jimmy's cockpit. The two fighters passed within thirty feet, Jimmy going to the right and the Hun to the left.

Looking over his shoulder as he came out of his roll, Jimmy saw the enemy biplane's tracers start their arching flight toward his cockpit. He couldn't believe it. The shots were coming right at him. The bullets struck the padding of the cockpit right behind his back and walked to the rear along the fuselage. Somehow, neither bullets nor tracers found their way to Jimmy's body.

Jimmy knew he had to act as if he'd been hit. He was out of ammunition and in no position to try to reload his machine guns. In the Nieuport 17, reloading was a cinch. The tandem guns of the 17, unlike the Bébé, were right in front of the flier. But Jimmy was outnumbered and outgunned. The Huns would pounce on him harder as soon as they saw he was alive and working his guns.

Jimmy slumped in his seat as though he were dead or dying. He pushed on his right rudder and slowly nosed his 17 over into a lazy dive. He pushed right stick to start a slow downward spin. He wanted to perform a perfect corkscrew toward the Verdun battlefield below. The only problem was that he was flying in the opposite direction of the aerodrome. But he had to maintain the facade of his downward doom. He hoped that the Germans wouldn't finish him off while he was in his dive.

As he corkscrewed, Jimmy could see one of the Fokker triplanes follow him down. The other German fliers remained watchful, aware that other Allied machines were in the air. *Keep your head down,* Jimmy said to himself. He had at least 3,000 more feet to fall. He needed to keep his orientation and avoid getting dizzy. He also needed to make sure the enemy triplane pilot didn't see him controlling his aeroplane. That would certainly finish it.

Jimmy saw from the corner of his eye a tan biplane coming downward. Captain Thenault must have seen Jimmy in his dive. He must have also seen the Fokker triplane. Perhaps Thenault was going to try to avenge Jimmy's "death." *Careful, Captain,* Jimmy thought. *This Hun is one of the best, and his companions are almost as good. They're ready to take you on.*

Jimmy continued to dive, spin, dive, and spin. At 300 feet, he pulled out of his dive and leveled off just before kissing the ground. He made a slight upward left turn to gain separation from the enemy above—and below—him. No need to take chances, he thought. As he started his turn, his engine began to sputter. He knew he could drain more petrol to his engine with a slight downward flying attitude. Unfortunately he was too low to the ground to point his machine downward.

Jimmy looked for a suitable place to land his petrol-starved machine. He saw that he was on the German side of No-Man's Land. *This isn't good,* Jimmy thought. *I can't make it to friendly fields, and I can't land in No-Man's Land. The bombed-out ground of the battlefield will tear my aeroplane to pieces—with me in it.*

Jimmy turned toward the German trenches just as tracers started arching up at him. He jinked as his engine quit completely. He glided downward and continued to jink to avoid the ground fire as he approached his landing spot. *Line up, feather, touchdown, noise, flip, noise, crash, jerk, stop,* he thought. His aeroplane had landed in a meadow. But the fixed landing gear of the Nieuport had struck a downed tree at almost full landing speed. The tree sheared his landing assembly completely off the bottom of the plane. His machine flipped and landed upside-down. The last noise Jimmy heard was his upper wing tearing from its mounting struts. Canvas, wood, and metal collapsed all around him. Something struck him in the head. His left shoulder dislocated, and his clavicle broke when the straps holding him in his seat snapped tight upon impact.

He must have blacked out. He came to hearing words being yelled out in the distance. "Fleeger, Ein Fleeger," a voice said. "Halt!" Bullets struck the ground around the plane. Canvas and wood pieces flew about as bullets tore into the fuselage of his machine. Where was he? What was going on? Everything was so distant and moved in slow motion.

"Nish-t Sheezen," a man called. He could tell someone was yelling, "Flier! Halt! Don't shoot!"

Jimmy heard the sound of boots crunching the dirt as men approached his crashed machine. His head was swimming and his vision was fogged, but he could make out gray forms wearing strange, broad headgear standing over him. Rifles with long bayonets pointed at him. A hand grabbed at the shoulder of his uniform. Jimmy screamed in agony at the rough treatment.

He was in the hands of German infantrymen, Jimmy realized.

"Air ist Mine Fleeger," he heard. It was a commanding voice. "Nish-t Sheezen, Yoong-a. Nish-t Sheezen."

A vision of Giselle, warm and lovely, came to him and then went away again. Lieutenant Jimmy Smitts, prisoner of war, had just passed out.

CHAPTER 13: AT THE HANDS OF THE ENEMY

East of Verdun, France - September 2, 1917

The rough treatment continued as four German soldiers, escorted by two armed infantrymen carried Jimmy over the rough terrain in a gray canvas litter. He passed into unconsciousness but then awoke from time to time from the pain in his shoulder. He was being jerked around in the litter, sending sharp pains radiating through his body.

The soldiers took Jimmy to a wood-framed bunker that was connected to deep fighting trenches. This must be the second or third line of defense in the German front, Jimmy thought. He had flown over No-Man's Land and toward the German rear. He had hoped he would clear the defensive areas and have a chance to escape to friendly lines. Now, seeing the depth of the German lines, Jimmy realized that there was no way he could have gotten to the French side.

The soldiers placed Jimmy on a table in a dark corner of the bunker, which housed communications equipment and maps. Clearly the bunker was headquarters of some kind for the infantry unit in the area where Jimmy had crashed his 17.

After what felt like hours, a man entered the bunker and approached him. "I am medical technician of Imperial German Army," the newcomer said. "I attend to your injuries." The doctor or medical technician examined Jimmy. The technician bent and pulled Jimmy's arm and shoulder into various positions and probed the muscles around his injury. Everything hurt from that point on. The pain was like no other pain Jimmy had experienced in his life.

Jimmy's shoulder was "ge-broken," the technician said. Jimmy's facial bruises and cuts were "Nish-t Schv-air." "Not Bad," Jimmy understood the German to say. He put Jimmy's arm in a tight wrap with a roll of cloth under his armpit. The cloth put his shoulder in an orientation that would minimize the pain. The technician said it would help the break heal properly. At least that's what Jimmy thought he said.

All Jimmy wanted to do was sleep, but the activity in the bunker made that difficult. Just as he had finally nodded off and started to dream of Giselle, a German woke him so that he could eat.

I am a prisoner of war, Jimmy thought. *I will never see Giselle again.*

He struggled to sit up. The pain was hard to endure. He forced down some soup, German sausages, and bread. Refreshed, he lay back on the litter to avoid being noticed and to try to minimize the pain. *A little rest will jump-start my recovery,* he thought.

During the week the Germans blindfolded Jimmy and moved him from one location to another. He felt totally isolated. He didn't know if he would be kept in isolation, moved to a prisoner camp, or just shot. Then a lieutenant escorted him to an ornate French mansion well within the Argonne Forest. Infantrymen, dressed in the best-looking uniforms, guarded the double oak doors of the residence. The Mauser rifles were fine specimens with typical German long bayonets affixed to their barrels. The soldiers had their combat gear on including the renowned German helmets. The helmets had broad brims, double Frankenstein-looking bolts at their sides, and lowered rear portions for maximum neck protection. They looked like the firemen's helmets Jimmy used to see as a boy in Wausau. The helmets appeared to be much too large, and he struggled to restrain a smile as he glanced past the soldiers wearing what looked like oversized cooking pots on their heads.

Jimmy was swiftly escorted through the hallways and past the orderly at the interior double oak doors of the mansion. The German soldiers, he noticed, marched through the building at rigid attention. Jimmy remembered Oma Brigitte telling him how militaristic the German people were. Opa James left his heritage in Land Hessen, she had told Jimmy, because Opa's father lived by military codes and standards as a Hessian mercenary. "Yimmy," his grandmother would tell him, "Otto's life vas v-one of constant orders—'befails,' we called them." Like Opa, Jimmy's grandfather's brothers and sisters were expected to serve "der Fatterland," Oma told Jimmy.

Now, as a prisoner of war, Jimmy was witnessing firsthand what his grandparents had told him about the Germans. The aristocrats issued orders with directness and the expectation of unwavering obedience. German servants and those of the lower classes were expected to take and fulfill the orders. There was to be no conversation or discussion about it.

"Our lives were the lives of order and obedience," his Opa would tell him. "We were German—Hessian Germans, at that. Hessians were renowned as the best fighters in the world. All countries wanted Hessian mercenaries in their wars. That was until Germany defeated France in 1870."

Jimmy was taken into a large study. To his front he saw a large oak writing desk. As with all things in the study, everything on the desk had been placed in perfect order. Papers were in short, neat stacks. The writing utensils were perfectly placed in neat ink holders. The furniture and accouterments in the room were in perfect alignment. *Wow, this is a headquarters on the front lines?* Jimmy wondered.

Jimmy's escort showed him to his left. Jimmy saw a large stone fireplace with a blazing fire in it. He saw an officer sitting upright in a comfortable chair. Next to him was an officer who was only slightly younger than the first. The two officers in their gray tunic uniforms stood up at attention. The younger of the two spoke. "Loynt-nant Schmitts, may I present Oberst Engling. Oberst—excuse me—*colonel* in your army, is the kommandeur of this sector of the front. I am Loynt-nant Burkhardt, the adjutant of the bat-ta-leon." Each officer clicked his boot heels and nodded once as he was introduced to Jimmy. They did not shake Jimmy's hand.

Jimmy tried to hide his astonishment. How did the Huns know the heritage of his name? How did they know he was a Schmidt? Then he realized that Germans could not pronounce the English *SM* as in Smitts. Germans traditionally pronounced the *SM* as *SCH*. Perhaps they didn't know his German heritage after all. *That could put me in a very bad position if they knew*, he thought.

In the corner of the room to his left, Jimmy noticed a young man sitting in an overstuffed leather chair. The man, who couldn't have been much older than Jimmy, wore a light blue-gray tunic covered by a blue-gray cape with a magenta silk lining. Jimmy could tell from his grandfather's stories that this man was of the aristocracy. The young German did not stand with the others.

"Loyt-nant Schmitts, may I introduce Herr Loyt-nant Verner Voss," Lieutenant Burkhardt said. "Herr Loyt-nant Voss is with the Flying Corps of the Imperial German Army." Jimmy nodded slightly but waited to hear someone else speak. He tried to subdue his surprise at meeting the second highest ace of the German Flying Corps. The other two officers motioned for Jimmy to sit as they sat down in their chairs in perfect unison.

Jimmy winced with pain in his shoulder as he sat rigidly in the chair assigned to him by his German hosts. The Germans did not say anything or react to the pain Jimmy had in his shoulder. Burkhardt continued, "I vill be your interpreter. Herr Loyt-nant Voss vishes to speak vis you."

Voss took a slow draw on his cigarette. He held his silver cigarette holder in an odd way, with his hand reversed, his fingertips pointed skyward and the outside of his hand facing toward Jimmy. Jimmy fought back his inclination to laugh out loud. *Do you hold your women like you hold your cigarette holder, hard and with distain?* he wondered.

"Herr Loyt-nant Schmitts, I am extremely pleased and honored to meet you," Voss said as Burkardt translated. "I have pleasure of seeing your aerobatic skills in air. You are excellent flier and respected adversary. My congratulations to you on your many successes."

Jimmy told Voss that he was likewise honored to make Herr Loyt-nant Voss' acquaintance.

Voss continued, unfazed by Jimmy's praise. "*Schmitts.* The name sounds very much like German name, Herr Loyt-nant. You even look German. I could have you shot as traitor to the Fatherland."

Jimmy looked into Voss' deep-blue eyes, remembering that his grandfather said you should always meet the stare of a German adversary. It was hard to stare at Voss' eyes. They seemed to glow with the deep blue color of the sky at dusk. But to look away is a sign of weakness, Opa had told him. *I have to hold my stare. The German people respect strong will and devotion to a cause in their enemies.* *Besides,* Jimmy thought, *this man may wear expensive and very dashing clothes and have my fate in his hands, but he is no better in the air or on the ground than me.*

"I could also have you shot as spy. You are American volunteer wearing French uniform," Voss said.

Voss took another slow draw of his cigarette while returning Jimmy's stare. "You vill not be shot," he continued. "You are honored and respected flier. Your command of skies and daring attacks on my comrades demand that you be given full military honor and respect. As fact, I was surprised to see a Frenchman fly so well and fight with such honor and determination. Your nationality as American only reinforced my knowledge of how cowardly French fliers are. They are no match for my Flying Corps." Voss slowly looked at the Oberst and said, "The Flying Corps of the Army of Imperial Germany vill return you to your comrades when you sign parole. The parole vill state that you agree never to take up arms of your Lafayette Escadrille against the law-abiding and innocent peoples and soldiers of Imperial German Empire. With this parole you return to your country with honor. Herr Oberst Engling vill have your parole written up, and he vill provide for you safe escort back to your aerodrome."

Jimmy only nodded in acknowledgment of Herr Loyt-nant Voss' words.

Burkhardt translated one more order of the young German ace. In this discussion, nothing was a request. Voss was directing everything to be done. "I have one more request," he said. "I vill find out from you how you make this maneuver in the air with your machine. You vill tell me how you spin your aeroplane at the top of your climb."

Jimmy knew little of the German language. He did know from Opa that in German "Ish vill," meaning "I will," was an order, not a request. Only those in authority gave orders, and orders were to be obeyed without question.

Do not show weakness, Jimmy told himself. He raised his chin slightly and continued to stare into Voss' blue eyes. Was it the color of his uniform that made the blue of his eyes so predominant? Jimmy wondered. Jimmy tried to formulate a response to Voss' "request." He had noticed how many times his adversary used the word *honor* in his speech.

"Lieutenant Voss," Jimmy replied, "your reputation as one of the most honorable aces of the German Flying Corps is well known. I *do* believe you can and will easily determine how to perform the maneuver without my help. If I tell you, I will dishonor and discredit myself before my comrades. I will be turning my back on my flying associates. I'm sure you understand and agree that I cannot dishonor my friends and comrades. I will not tell you how I performed the maneuver."

Voss stared at Jimmy as Burkhardt translated Jimmy's words. After moments of tense silence, Voss nodded sharply and stood. The other officers stood as Jimmy rose to his feet. Voss said, "Danka, Herr Loyt-nant. Herr Oberst vill write the order of your parole. I am only sorry to say I will not have pleasure and honor to meet you again in skies over French landscape. I am sure you and I would write more aerial history together. Auf-Veeder-Zane."

With that said, Voss turned and walked briskly toward the door. Oberst Engling marched alongside the German flying ace. The two men faced one another and shook hands as they clicked their heels and nodded. Then Voss was gone.

Jimmy was instructed to sit as Burkhardt wrote the parole. He asked how a lieutenant could possibly make a decision such as Voss had just made. Burkhardt looked at the Oberst, then at Jimmy, and said, "Herr Loyt-nant Voss is of Flying Corps of Imperial German Army. Flying Corps has total authority and control over all fliers, German and Allied alike. Infantry Corps of Imperial German Army has no authority whatsoever in this case." Burkhardt met Jimmy's eyes. "Had you been an American infantry officer, Herr Loyt-nant, I am sure you would not have lived to see this day."

The pain Jimmy suffered during the ride from the mansion to the battlefield's southern front was as bad as when he first broke his shoulder in the crash. The German automachine bounced over dirt roads made rough by holes and ruts. Jimmy was determined not to show the pain. The German soldiers scowled at him, clearly not approving of his presence. He wondered whether the infantry soldiers would honor the Flying Corps order for his safe return.

At the barbed-wire entanglements on the edge of the battlefield, the group left the auto. Jimmy was pushed into a firing trench. The cold of the early fall evening didn't help his shoulder pain. He watched intently as two German soldiers approached the French forward positions under a flag of truce. Jimmy hoped the French would honor the flag and allow the Germans to approach. The hatred between the two peoples could easily explode. *After centuries of killing at the hands of the Germans, the French must hate the Huns beyond belief,* Jimmy thought.

The Germans returned to the firing trenches after a long delay. Jimmy understood only some of what they said in their Bavarian German dialect. He was pretty sure, though, that they would be allowed to pass into the French lines.

The autocar moved forward just as Jimmy sat down. It bounced across No-Man's Land as though the Huns were trying to shake him to death. He moaned with each stabbing pain that shot through his body. The group finally arrived at the French front lines. Jimmy noticed that there was a lone figure in a gray tunic standing by French guards. In the fading darkness, it looked like a dark gray form framed by blue.

Apparently Jimmy was being traded for a German officer. In the darkness he couldn't tell with which corps the officer was aligned. He didn't know whether the German was another flier or an infantry officer. He really didn't care. He was going to safety and medical aid. He needed his shoulder to be put back into place so that the injury could heal.

He had survived. And he would be able to return to Giselle. But what would happen to him beyond that, he didn't know. Would he stay in Europe? If so, would he spend time at a French villa or infirmary? Would he return to Wausau? Perhaps the Allies would not honor his parole and would order him to violate his promise.

As he was escorted to a French medical motorcar, Jimmy realized that all he needed at this point was sleep. His shoulder could wait.

* * * * *

Madison, Wisconsin – June 25, 1918

Senator Lenroot came to realize that he was facing a determined and very capable woman. Her elegance and beauty masked her strength, determination, and powerful influence. She seemed to melt the men around her as she spoke in support of her husband and his agenda. "Eugene Stevenson is a force to be reckoned with," he said to himself. "But I need to watch out for Loraine. She'll cause me to lose my fight to keep Wisconsin's other Senate seat if I'm not careful. *They* adopted *my* support of aviation as their own. I guess I'd better join them. I sure as hell can't beat them."

Looking at Eugene Stevenson, Lenroot said, "Well, Senator, I understand you had a wonderful visit with Colonel Billy Mitchell last month. I take it you found his ideas to be nothing less than outstanding."

"Yes, yes, Senator Lenroot," Stevenson said as he smiled at the others seated in the room. "Thank you. Colonel Mitchell is extremely committed to expanding American military aviation. I believe he's a capable and most worthy flying leader. And, as you may know, he's originally from our great state of Wisconsin." More smiles as Eugene looked at the others.

Lenroot could tell that Senator Stevenson was doing his own form of barnstorming in front of the men and women at the University Club in Washington. It was Mrs. Stevenson's eyes that held Lenroot's attention. They were all over him as if to say, "Don't mess with us!"

"I see, Senator. I'm very pleased to know you had a successful discussion with Colonel Mitchell. I'm also pleased to know that many know he is from Wisconsin. We are all very proud of his accomplishments." Lenroot swallowed hard. He knew Eugene and Loraine were both from states other than Wisconsin. "How dare they act this way?" he said to himself.

"Yes, yes, sir. Colonel Mitchell believes aviation is the future of this country. He believes strongly that the aeroplane can end the Great War and even war itself."

The men retired to the men's lounge. The women turned to the ladies' parlor for tea and dessert. Loraine told Lenroot as she left, "Mr. Lenroot, it will be our extreme honor and privilege to have you with us fighting for Wisconsin in the U.S. Senate. I'm sure there will be many times when we will need to support one another."

Lenroot was at his wit's end as he walked toward the lounge. He merely survived the whiskey and cigars in the lounge. He couldn't wait to break up the banter about the war and how Senator Stevenson was leading the charge for better aviation in American. He also couldn't wait until he had another opportunity to face his adversary.

* * * * *

Saint Mihiel, France – September 12, 1918

The Saint Mihiel offensive had taken its toll on the company. The pouring rain before this attack had taken its toll on the ground. The Allied aerial and artillery bombardments had done great damage to the center of the German salient. The men were mesmerized by the unending lines of Allied bombers as they passed overhead and assaulted the German trenches. But Chester Company had been tasked to attack the right side of the German line. The purpose of the company's advance in the operation was to take and hold the right flank of the entire American Expeditionary Force during its advance.

German resistance was strongest in the Chester Company sector. The enemy trenches and defensive wire had not been disturbed by the massive aerial bombardment. Sergeant Witherspoon ran through the mud of the battlefield with his soldiers behind the limited Allied artillery preparation that preceded them. They dodged German machine-gun fire, cut German wire, and fought and clawed their way up the muddy slopes to the German trenches.

Men fell around Sergeant Witherspoon. Machine-gun fire cut one man next to him almost in half. He saw enemy bullets kick the dirt up around Captain Sandhurst as he ran toward the objective and spurred the men on. The Germans were also laying down a withering fire onto their third platoon to the south. Witherspoon saw three soldiers in the distance go down at one time.

The smoke from the American artillery bombardment obscured their approach and saved many of Witherspoon's men from death. The company was in the German trenches just after the artillery fire stopped. German soldiers pleaded for their lives as the Doughboys jumped them.

Captain Sandhurst told everyone to consolidate. "German prisoners to the rear. Form up on the German trenches and prepare for a counterattack!" he yelled.

Sergeant Witherspoon told his platoon sergeants to bring the Vickers machine guns up and put them into action. He wanted firepower available for the defense of the newly held positions.

The Germans had organized a strong and in-depth defensive area that was now in the hands of the All-Americans. The soldiers were impressed by the depth of the trenches and how they had been constructed.

"Sergeant Witherspoon," Sergeant Henderson said as he looked back along the ground they had just traversed, "look at how organized this position is. The Germans sure had it nice up here."

"The position does dominate the terrain to its front, does it not," Witherspoon replied. "No wonder they were able to put well-aimed fire down on us. I can clearly see all the way across No-Man's Land to where our trenches were."

"I'll tell you what, Captain," Witherspoon said as he slung his Springfield rifle over his shoulder. "We would have been completely cut down if we hadn't walked behind our own artillery barrage."

The First Sergeant turned to his right and yelled, "Platoon sergeants, tend to your men and get this position in shape. We need to collect our wounded and take them to the rear aid station."

Sergeant Witherspoon then quickly walked the line. He wanted to know how many men had been lost in the attack.

When he returned to the company command post, Sergeant Witherspoon told Captain Sandhurst, "Sir, we lost twenty-five soldiers. I'll know how many were killed and wounded in about fifteen minutes."

"Thank you, Sergeant. We need to get some runners to string wire to the regimental headquarters. I think they'll want to know how much the aerial bombardment helped us. We also need to bring up the trains. We need more ammunition, water, and food."

"Helped us, sir? The aerial bombardment helped *us*? I didn't think anyone could have withstood the bombardment we saw hit this hill. But the Germans used these deep bunkers to protect themselves and get prepared to fight us. I'll get started on getting the support trains up after we get this position secured."

The First Sergeant knew what had to be done. He had done it many times in the last sixteen months of combat. The wounded had to be carried by hand in stretchers back to the ambulances in the rear. Then ammunition, water, and food had to be brought up to the line— also by hand. A good bit of hard labor was still ahead of them. Everything seemed to be laborious. Witherspoon could hear the men griping already. He remembered the standard line the men joked about. "I'd rather charge the Germans in their trenches through heavy artillery than carry supplies." At least the supply trains had fresh soldiers with them to help carry the loads.

If anything could be left behind to lighten a load, it was the food. Men needed water to survive. But they needed ammunition more than water. A hungry and thirsty man in combat can wait for food and water. He cannot wait for ammunition.

In anticipation of the long walk back to the supplies, Sergeant Witherspoon took a seat in the German trenches. He, like all of the soldiers in the company, was still spent from the long run during their exposed attack up the hill to the German position. He sat in amazement that he and Captain Sandhurst were still alive. But he knew that twenty-five casualties was a huge loss. It amounted to more than twenty percent of their combat effectives. Units were usually withdrawn from the front when they experienced half that number of casualties. Sergeant Witherspoon knew the standard would not apply to them. They would soon be asked to give more blood, to continue the push to the northeast.

Witherspoon looked around. He saw in more detail how well the Germans had formed their trenches. There were observation and firing positions everywhere along the line that gave the German gunners excellent fields of fire. The trenches were clean and had strong duckboards, the wood floors that let the rainwater drain. He could see multiple wood-formed bunkers along the trenches from his vantage point. He was obviously sitting in a prominent position in the German line, perhaps a battalion headquarters.

He continued to reflect. They had made it through the first real test of an organized American Division assault on well-organized and deep enemy defenses, the German defenses of the Saint Mihiel Salient.

Sergeant Witherspoon grabbed his orderly and four soldiers. They were all exhausted, but the company desperately needed its supplies. So they headed back to the rear to bring the support trains up. Witherspoon was satisfied that wounded were being properly prepared for their long trips across the rugged battlefield to the rear. He needed to make sure the supplies got up quickly. His small group made its way down the hill and started back across No-Man's Land.

The brilliant flash of light startled him. It happened so fast and was so bright that it was almost shocking. But it brought a warm, calm feeling to him. He was relaxed and comfortable in quiet solitude. The white curtain that seemed to surround him slowly faded. It was replaced by a deep azure blue. Soft white clouds moved slowly by, interrupted by wisps of gray smoke. Sergeant Witherspoon started to see dark forms moving back and forth. As his senses returned, he felt sharp needles pricking at his left arm and side. The pricking transformed to a burning sensation. Everything happened in slow motion with the exception of the pain, which came on quite rapidly.

He barely heard someone say, "First Sergeant, First Sergeant Witherspoon..." in a muffled whisper.

He still felt very calm and relaxed but couldn't understand why his right side was so cold and his left side burned like it was on fire. He looked down and saw that the gray smoke was rising from the left side of his tunic, which was torn in some places.

"...Okay? Okay? Are you okay, Sergeant Witherspoon?" he heard someone else ask.

Another yelled, "Get a stretcher. We need to get him out of here *now.*" He couldn't understand why everyone talked in such dull tones. He could not make out what everyone was saying. He moved his right arm to brush the people out of his way. *Why doesn't my left arm move?* he wondered. He looked down at his arm and thought, *I command you to move.* Then a euphoric darkness came quickly to him as he lost his sight and consciousness of his surroundings.

CHAPTER 14: THE DOCTOR AND THE NURSE

South of Toul, France - September 12, 1917

The pain was unbearable. Jimmy was biting down hard on the cloth between his teeth. The French doctor was resetting the shoulder and the break in his clavicle. The procedure was very delicate, the doctor had said.

"Yeah, *right*," Jimmy said. "You and your goons are standing on my side pulling with all your might on my arm. Delicate?" Jimmy said. "If this is delicate, I'd hate to see rough."

The doctor and his assistants finished their assault on Jimmy's body. They wrapped him from neck to waist with cotton and gauze. His left arm was hanging precariously out to his side to allow the clavicle to heal. The doctor said he would be in that position for about two weeks before reexamination.

Jimmy was taken to his second home, the Lafayette Escadrille. He arrived with little fanfare. The aerodrome had heard he was alive but didn't know he was coming back. A majority of the fliers were out on patrol. The squadron orderly looked up in surprise when he saw Jimmy step out of the motorwagon.

"Oh, my Lord of Lords," the orderly said. "You *did* make it out alive, Jimmy!"

"I smell like a pig in a sty," Jimmy told the orderly. "I want to wash up."

Just then Jimmy heard a commotion coming from the maintenance shed. Henri and three of the mechanics were running toward him. They stopped short, noticing his bruised and battered face. Obviously Jimmy had been through an ordeal. They were happy to know that he had made it back from the dead.

After washing and putting a new tunic over his shoulders, Jimmy walked over to the bar. Bill Thaw and Willie Dugan were waiting for him. They had just returned from their mission and had heard he was back. They looked at their watches and said the squadron would start returning in flights of four pretty soon. Jimmy took a drink of whiskey and told Bill Thaw he would like to be seated in front of the farmhouse as the fliers returned. He wanted to watch the majesty of the returning Nieuports as they landed in sequence. The mechanics placed lounge chairs in front of the headquarters building and waited for the show.

Jimmy sat down in anticipation of the returning fliers. He couldn't wait to see their expressions when they saw him. He then thought, *this is going to be quite a surprise to Clive. I can't wait to show him I'll be around for a long time to come.*

The fliers started coming in from the northeast. They rounded the Mark and feathered onto the field. Each flier looked at the group seated in the chairs as he turned into the flying line. None of them could tell why the mechanics were sitting down. Once the fliers were all on the ground and out of their aeroplanes, they realized that Jimmy was alive and back home. How amazed they were to know Jimmy had made it. The last word anyone had of him was from Clive. Clive had told everyone that he saw Jimmy go down in a fireball.

"Fireball?" Jimmy said. "Clive couldn't possibly have seen me go down. But what of Captain Thenault? Did he make it back from the fight?"

The fliers told him that Thenault, who was now home on a family emergency, hadn't seen Jimmy go down. But Clive was sure that Jimmy had been killed.

They retired to the bar. Debriefings would start soon. Then they would eat, sit at the card tables with drinks, and talk about the details of Jimmy's crash, capture, and parole. They had all heard rumors that Jimmy had fought Werner Voss in the skies over Verdun. They were eager to hear about Voss' flying ability and tactics.

Jimmy asked about Clive. He wanted to confront the liar and find out why he hadn't come to his aid during that near-deadly confrontation with Voss and the other German pilots.

Willie Dugan told Jimmy the sad news. "Clive didn't return from patrol yesterday. French infantry reported seeing a tan aeroplane crash in No-Man's Land. We hope the Germans will recover Clive's body and return it to us with full military honors one day."

Clive is dead, Jimmy thought. He had mixed emotions about his death. He would never know why Clive had been so aloof with Jimmy after Jimmy had saved him on their first flying patrol together. He would never know why Clive had stolen his kill. More important, he would never know why Clive disappeared from the skies over Verdun when Jimmy needed him most as he fought alone against four Germans.

As Jimmy ate dinner, his mind wandered. He thought of his battle with Werner Voss, his crash, and his journey to the mansion in the Argonne. He remembered his release and the news that Clive's name would appear on the Plaque of Honor. And he pictured Giselle.

Bill Thaw interrupted Jimmy's thoughts. Sam had told him about the girl and her family. A little special R&R was due him, Thaw said. Jimmy could ask one of the mechanics to take him to Charmes in the morning.

"While you recover," Thaw said, "the French authorities can decide what to do with you."

He was going to see Giselle again. Jimmy was elated. He lay awake much of that night. He was in pain, but it was the anticipation of a reunion with Giselle that occupied his mind.

The next morning he watched as a bystander as the fliers prepared for their daily patrols. Half the squadron was to take off and patrol during the morning hours. The other half would follow three hours afterward. In that way the squadron would keep as many fliers as possible in the air during daylight hours.

Jimmy watched as the first half of the squadron took off. The departure took one hour. Some of the second-shift fliers stood with Jimmy watching the takeoffs. They gave him their best wishes for the short time he would have with his young lady.

"Geez," he said to himself. "The boys are rooting for me and I don't even know if Giselle will be there or if her family will accept me."

Jimmy cleaned his face as best as he could. He knew Giselle

would be shocked to see his face and the bandages around his body and left arm. That didn't stop him from jumping into the autocar for the two-hour trip to paradise. He'd had his fill of the doctor. He was now going to the care of his nurse.

Henri did the honors for Jimmy. He drove as quickly as the roads and trails would allow. Jimmy winced as the motorcar hit hole after hole. But he didn't mind. He was on his way.

Giselle fainted. Her mother and father were also shocked at the sight of him. What must they think of him for scaring their poor little flower? Jimmy wondered. When she came out of her fainting spell, Giselle looked at Jimmy in horror and cried. "Oh, bon Dieu! Mais qu'est ce que t'est arrive! What happen?" she screamed in half-English and half-French. "How they do this? Les Boche are *murderers.*"

Giselle reached out and put the palm of her hand on Jimmy's bruised face. She stroked his forehead and cheek. Her hand was shaking, and tears still welled up in her eyes. She moved closer until Jimmy could smell the fragrance of springtime roses around her. He stood rigid. He had no idea what he should do with her parents watching. Giselle touched each bruise on his face and then kissed each one in turn. Her tears fell on him as she kissed him. Her touch ran through his body like an electrical charge. He started quivering.

"It's okay, Giselle, it's okay," Jimmy said. "I'm okay. I'm hurt, but I'm here with you and I will be just fine. Everything will be fine. We are now together."

She understood some of what Jimmy said, but she couldn't stop shaking. She looked at his arm, and the tears started flowing again. She could hardly stand.

Giselle's mother stood silently watching her daughter. She had not taken her hand away from her mouth. The shocked look on her face told the entire story. But she calmed down as she realized how much Giselle was in love. She had never seen Giselle react to a boy or man as she was reacting to Jimmy now.

The father hurried back from the kitchen. Jimmy hadn't noticed that the father had gone away to retrieve some wine. He motioned for everyone to sit together at a table. Jimmy didn't understand what he was saying as he spoke rapidly in his native tongue, but he sure was animated about it.

Henri had joined them. He sat at the table. A rapid discussion in French ensued. Jimmy had no idea what everyone was talking about. Even Henri was animated as he joined in the banter. Giselle seemed to be in charge. Her parents seemed to be very accommodating to Giselle. Her father smiled and nodded his head at times. Her mother looked like she was somewhat skeptical. Giselle's father twice returned to the kitchen for more wine.

Henri rose to excuse himself. He said he was very happy to have met the family. He shook Jimmy's hand and left.

Giselle finally opened up in her sweet but broken English. "My parents and me, honored to ask you, please to stay in house," she said. "You rest, get good." Jimmy asked about Henri. Giselle said Henri would tell the fliers. He would come back tomorrow. To Jimmy, this was a dream come true. He would be able to spend more time with Giselle.

She and her mother escorted Jimmy through the back of the restaurant. They crossed an alley and entered a masonry structure. Within, Jimmy saw a very comfortable and well-appointed residence. The living room had an overstuffed sofa, side chairs, and billowy window treatments. The pillows of various colors were abundant. "House," Giselle told Jimmy as she spun around, smiling and with her arms out. She apologized that she couldn't speak better English. Charles would be back home the next day, she said, and he would translate their words.

Giselle and her mother prepared a place for Jimmy to lie down in the living room. Throw rugs and pillows formed a very comfortable bed. The extra pillows propped his arm up so that he could sleep in a half-sitting position. The women left him with some wine and cheeses. He felt like a king. Giselle told him she had to return to the "restauraan" with her mother. But she would return every now and then to check on him.

Each time she returned, Jimmy was awestruck by her beauty and gracefulness. She was comforting and caring. Jimmy swam in the feelings she generated.

After the restaurant closed, the family returned to the house. Preparations were made for going to sleep. The oil lamps were doused and the family retired to the bedrooms. Jimmy was comfortable and ready to sleep. Oh, how he needed valuable sleep, he thought.

As he was dosing off, Jimmy heard a noise in the house—a quiet shuffling. A shadow was cast in the moonlit room. Jimmy could tell by the thick-flowing hair that Giselle was coming to him. She eased down beside him. He didn't have to move. Giselle lay down and put her arm softly on his chest. She rested her head comfortably in the crook of his neck. Her hair fell around him. It felt and smelled so good, Jimmy realized.

In the darkness, he could see only the form of Giselle, but he felt the warmth and softness of her breasts through the light cloth nightgown she wore. She stroked his face softly with her fingertips. "Mon cheree," she whispered, "mon amour."

A satisfying feeling of comfort and warmth overcame Jimmy. Giselle was his life's dream, his true love. He now knew for the first time in his life what it felt like to love another. He felt no pain, only peace, as his consciousness faded into darkness.

The early-morning sun brought Jimmy to the realization that his shoulder hurt like hell. He stirred only to feel the softness of Giselle's hands, arms, body, and legs surrounding him. Her warm, soft breath blew across his face. His shoulder might hurt, but this was pure heaven.

Giselle stirred too. She opened her eyes and looked at Jimmy. The smile on her face gave away her feeling that the two had gotten away with something. She sat up, her hair flowing around Jimmy's face. How soft it was, he thought, as it tickled his nose. She arched her back and ran her fingers through her hair while slightly shaking her head. *What a beautiful woman,* Jimmy thought. He couldn't help but see her breasts move as she combed her hair with her fingers. The excited nipples of her supple breasts rubbed back and forth in her light cotton nightgown. She noticed Jimmy's gaze and playfully slapped him on his good shoulder.

"You *bad*," she said.

She frowned as she once again touched his bruises.

"Comment allez vous, mon amour?" she asked in soft tones.

Jimmy told her that the bruises on his face would go away soon. His shoulder would heal in about three months. *If we could only stay together like this,* Jimmy, thought, *I'd be well in minutes.*

Giselle turned her head quickly toward the back of the house from where they had heard movements. She turned quickly to Jimmy and said, "Mamon." She bent and kissed Jimmy on the forehead, then stood and quickly turned toward her bedroom. The movement of her slim natural form as she trotted back to her room excited Jimmy with feelings he had never felt before. In a flash, she was gone.

Lord Almighty, he thought, *this is better than doing barrel rolls!*

Jimmy had breakfast with Giselle and her parents, and then he rested. He dreaded the arrival of Henri and the return to the aerodrome and life among the fliers. He preferred the company of Giselle. The family had many tasks to perform in order to get the restaurant ready for the day, though, and Giselle had to be right in the middle of the preparations. There was no time to waste. Customers would be coming at 10. She was able to bring lunch to him, though, and they ate together, saying almost nothing but looking at each other with sadness and longing.

Henri came too soon. Jimmy's heart sank as he made ready to leave. He entered the restaurant to say goodbye to Giselle's family and then he and Giselle hugged each. They held onto one another more closely and for longer than her parents were comfortable with. The electrifying feeling in him was more painful than it was enjoyable when they parted.

He was into the staff motorcar and gone before he knew it. It would be a hard two-hour trip back to the aerodrome. As Henri negotiated the rough roads, Jimmy sat looking at the passing countryside without really seeing it. Henri informed him that Captain Thenault had arranged for a French doctor to examine his shoulder, but Jimmy didn't reply, and Henri said nothing more. Jimmy was dreaming about his night with Giselle among the rugs and pillows of her parents' living room, about how her body felt next to him, about how she had nursed his wounds.

Giselle was gone. The vision of her standing there crying with her hands to her mouth came back to him. *No,* he thought. *I will be coming back* soon *to you, Giselle.*

* * * * *

Madison, Wisconsin, U.S.A. - July 12, 1918

"Senator Stevenson, how can you stand there and suggest that our men continue to fight 'Over There'? Join me in my plea to stop the killing of our innocent youth. Let's pull our troops out. The Europeans have fought one another for centuries. They just hate each other. What can America do to stop them other than throw its youth into the caldron of death?"

Senator Lenroot was arguing against Eugene's position that Wisconsin should continue to support the troops. He was hoping to gain notoriety and solidify his position as the most junior Senator of the U.S. Senate. It looked like the rural folks of Wisconsin were tired of seeing American boys go off to war.

"My dear colleague from Wisconsin," Eugene began as he looked up at the dark wood ceiling as though gathering his words, his fellow businessmen expectantly looking on. "I must agree with you that it is not and has not been America's mantra to save the Europeans from themselves. But I am for saving our youth from the caldron you speak of by supporting them, not by making them cowards in the face of adversity. These brave, young warriors are the future of Wisconsin and our nation. We climbed out of the quagmire that was the American Civil War and President Lincoln, the great statesman from Illinois, my birth state, saved us from ourselves. I am for saving our troops from those that wish them harm—or those that wish not to give them the fullest support possible in their hour of need. And you, sir. I hear you are for pulling out. Surely you are not for leaving our youth behind now, are you?"

His audience chuckled at the ribbing Senator Stevenson was dishing out to his colleague from Wisconsin. They had witnessed this kind of thrashing from Eugene before. He was an aggressive campaigner and won the day in Wisconsin with his quick tongue just before America entered the Great War. They also knew how cunning Eugene could be. He always seemed to set his opponents up in their attacks against him just before he threw them to the ground.

Lenroot started in a vane attempt to recover, "Senator, I applaud your desire to help our soldiers. But they are in a struggle for their very existence. The Huns are advancing all along the front, and our boys are taking the brunt of it. I believe we should leave the Europeans to their plight and focus our industrial might on the future of machinery like the aeroplane, for instance. Many in our great state are using it to promote business and farming."

Eugene seized the moment. "I too believe strongly in this new technology. I have come to excellent terms with American aviation through Colonel Billy Mitchell, of Wisconsin. But we cannot forget that prosperity comes to those that work hard for it. Machinery alone is not the salvation of production." Raising his voice in excited proclamation, he said, "Prosperity is totally in the hands of the men and women of Wisconsin."

The men stood in the middle of the club and applauded Senator Eugene F. Stevenson. They knew that he was barnstorming in his own right. He was playing the group against Representative Lenroot, and it was working. "Prosperity is *totally* in the hands of the people of Wisconsin." What a capital idea, they all thought. Only Eugene could come up with an idea like that.

Eugene refused to leave it at that. He pointed his finger in the air and said, "Besides, my dear friend, what are we to do? Even your own President Wilson believes America can help the Europeans from future *self*-annihilation. He is talking about a league of some kind to unite the European powers, with the United States as the head of this league. What more could one want? America will be the breadbasket of Europe, and I intend to have Wisconsin be the oven baking that bread."

The men broke up in a roar of laughter. Senator Lenroot sat in solitude knowing he had just been bested.

"Speaking of bread, gentlemen," Eugene said more gently this time, "I believe my lovely Loraine is preparing an excellent Sunday dinner for the household. Please allow me to excuse myself. And a very good day to you all."

With that, the men dispersed from their Sunday afternoon group at the University Club in Madison, Wisconsin. Everyone started for home. Few would stop talking about Eugene and how well he could carve up his adversaries.

Senator Lenroot left the club hoping he still had a chance to make a name for himself in the Senate. *Lord,* he thought. *How am I to act civil with Stevenson? And I have to compete with Loraine by his side.*

CHAPTER 15: PURGATORY

Luxeuil-les-Bains, France - September 11, 1917

The days of the next month went by at varying speeds. Most were like standing in line at a movie house that never opened. The one day he could spend with Giselle each week passed like minutes. The day in the week he spent with a French doctor was a mixture of boredom and agonizing pain. At least his shoulder was healing. But it was healing much too slowly for Jimmy.

Then it happened. The group of American fliers was told that the Lafayette Escadrille would become an American unit. The involvement of the U.S. military in the Great War was swelling. It would not reach Goliath proportions until early 1918. General John J. Pershing commanded the American forces. He constantly fought the French in their desire to mold individual American units into the French "Armees" scattered about the trenches of the battlefields of this horrible war.

Through 1917 the various divisions of American soldiers were fragmented in the defense of France west of the Argonne Forest. General Pershing and the American government had succeeded in merging the units into an organized fighting force, the American Expeditionary Force. American flying units, including pursuit or fighting squadrons, were being organized in the United States. They would soon come with more American infantry and artillery "Doughboys." Up until the later part of 1917, General Pershing commanded individual American units that were scattered along the French front. And there were no American pursuit units in the war. The American war effort needed to mobilize flying units, and the Lafayette Escadrille was the most capable group of American fliers in the world

The fliers were all abuzz about becoming an American flying unit. Jimmy could not wait to be able to join the unit and fly against the Huns again. But he had signed a parole with the Germans. He wondered how the new flying unit might change that. He certainly didn't want to be a bystander in an aerial war.

Lufbery was most ecstatic about the prospects of flying for an American unit. He was hoping that the buildup in the American war effort would bring better resources and investment in France's development of the latest and most powerful flying machines. With new machines like the Nieuport 28 and Spad S model, he told the group, the Lafayette Escadrille could end the war.

All of that was just talk. And fliers liked to talk. The scuttlebutt going around concerned events to the northwest along the British front. The Brits were having a difficult time of it. German fliers were taking their toll on British observation and bombing aeromachines. It seemed as if the British desperately needed to field more of their Sopwith Camel fighters that everyone was talking about. They also needed something to divert the German war machine. American fliers in American flying units could reduce the pressure on the British units.

The talk helped Jimmy get through the days. It hurt to watch the fliers take off from the aerodrome. It hurt more to see them come back with bullet holes in their machines or even victories under their belts. Jimmy was happy that the other fliers were doing well in the air war. But he had to be part of it. He had to do something worthwhile. Sitting and waiting to heal was difficult. "Things are progressing," Jimmy was told during his doctor visits. But that didn't make it any easier for him to sit back and watch.

Then, on September 20, 1917, five American officers and some enlisted personnel arrived at the aerodrome. Jimmy was given a few minutes' notice to get ready to meet them. He had just come back from a doctor's visit. He washed and walked over to the briefing room in the farmhouse.

Standing at the front of the room were some of the best dressed and most dashing military figures Jimmy had ever seen. Compared to the rough and tumble of the various uniforms the fliers wore, the well-pressed olive-drab tunics and trousers of the American officers were striking. Their headgear, the garrison caps with extended backs, and the billowing material of their wool riding breeches were impressive. Jimmy couldn't stop staring at the officers' spit-shined brown leather belts and riding boots. He couldn't wait to recover from his injuries, put on a uniform like that, and return to the air.

"Gentlemen," the senior visitor addressed the fliers. "My name is Colonel Billy Mitchell. I am here representing the American Air Service. The United States has formed a number of American aero squadrons that will soon deploy to Europe."

With that announcement, the fliers stood up, applauded, and slapped each other on their backs.

Colonel Mitchell quieted the group with a gesture and continued. "Legally, your status is still pending. In order for you to have joined the Lafayette Escadrille, you had to join the French Foreign Legion. As such, you are currently not qualified to become fliers in the American units."

The group fell silent.

"However," Colonel Mitchell continued, "the United States government has determined that your acceptance in the American Air Service is a national emergency. My officers are here to enlist you in the Army of the United States."

With this announcement, the fliers broke out into raucous applause.

The meeting that presented the overall concept was adjourned. Each flier was told he would be called aside for an interview. The document with which the flier had joined the Lafayette Escadrille would need to be studied. Fliers in the French Foreign Legion would have to be released by the French government. Then, each flier would sign up for positions in the American Flying Corps.

It seemed like hours to Jimmy before his name was called. He stood before a captain named Johnson, who was casually sitting with one leg up on the corner of Bill Thaw's desk. Like Bill Thaw, Johnson had a half-finished cigarette in his hand. He asked Jimmy a number of questions about his medical status. He also told Jimmy that everyone in Colonel Mitchell's team had already heard how good Jimmy was as a pursuit flier. They also knew Jimmy had three kills. Johnson said they would need to do something about the shoulder injury.

Jimmy asked, "What will become of the parole I signed?"

"We'll work on it," Johnson replied. "As it stands, you will probably have to return to the United States to clear that parole. That won't be a problem because you also need proper rehabilitation. If your shoulder heals, you may be able to sign a waiver saying that the parole applied to your status as a member of the French Lafayette Escadrille. As the Escadrille is to be disbanded, the parole will no longer apply. In that way you could enlist, while you are in the U.S. as a flier in the American Flying Corps."

Jimmy was elated as he left Bill Thaw's office. But he had a fear of the unknown. What happens if "they" determine he wasn't capable of returning to duty? What if his shoulder didn't heal? What would happen to him if he couldn't fly?

His next dominating thought was about Giselle. How would she take the thought of his returning to the U.S.? How and when would they be together after he returned to France? Would she wait for him? He had no answers to the questions. But he knew some of the answers would come soon. He was planning to see Giselle in three days.

Jimmy got another pass from Captain Thenault. Jimmy knew Bill Thaw put a plug in for him and was going out on a limb to help him visit his girlfriend between doctor's visits. But the captain had been given his orders to assist the Americans in the U.S. Army Signal Service as a liaison officer and was now more accommodating. Bill too was more accommodating. After having formed and fought with the Lafayette Escadrille, Thaw would be promoted to major and shipped out to command an American pursuit squadron.

How would he tell Giselle? He was eager to announce that he was going to be a true American flier, but she would be upset about their separation. This was going to be tough. He rehearsed breaking the news to her. No matter how he thought it through, the scene always came out the same. She was not going to like it.

Jimmy spoke in the most direct manner he could manage, looking Giselle straight in the eyes. His return to the United States would hasten his recovery, he said more than once. He had to get out from under the dark cloud of the parole, he explained. He would be back soon.

Giselle cried and her hands shook. Her reaction to his news made Jimmy's heart melt. He hugged her and told her that his going away would help him recover, but nothing he said would comfort her.

"Mon amour, I cannot live without you," Giselle said while stroking his cheek. It was like the time she came to him in the moonlight that first night. It felt so soothing. He closed his eyes and absorbed the moment.

"Giselle, you are the love of my life. I *will* come back to you. I promise," he said softly. He fought back the tears and swallowed the terrible lonely feeling that was welling up inside him. She looked up into his eyes with her own tears flowing. There seemed to be a fear in her eyes that made him shiver.

Oh, what he wouldn't do to stay just one more night with her. But Henri was there before Jimmy knew it to take him back to the aerodrome.

* * * * *

The train trip through Paris to Brest was uneventful. Jimmy just sat in a funk. He couldn't keep his mind from circling from one thought to another. At Brest, he couldn't believe the condition of some of the soldiers returning to America. The wounded were stacked like cordwood and their wounds were ghastly. Many soldiers had the telltale signs of the devastating effects of mustard gas used in war. The hands, faces, and necks of the afflicted were covered with bandages over festering wounds. Some of the men were blind. Many shook uncontrollably. The impact wounds were just as ghastly. Limbs were missing from many. Head, chest, and limb wounds from bullets and artillery shrapnel were everywhere. The white-hot metal fragments of bursting artillery projectiles cut through flesh like a saw, slashing and burning as they passed. The men returning to America were in terrible shape. It made Jimmy remember his thoughts of how he could help end the killing as he flew over the battlefields of Verdun.

He shuddered as he surveyed the misery. He tried to think of Giselle, but the ugliness of it all kept him even from those soothing thoughts. No, the scene did not make him *think* of how he could help. It made him vow to end it. He would return. And he would return with a vengeance.

Jimmy was returning to America with the wounded. It was the beginning of his journey back to flying and Giselle. He was told their destination was the rehabilitation center at Fort McHenry. Jimmy had heard of the fort where the national anthem had been written. He did not know the fort was in Baltimore, Maryland. To Jimmy it really didn't matter where he was going. He cared only that he would be healed, waived from his parole, and returned to flying. Then it would be a reckoning.

* * * * *

Triaucourt, France - September 17, 1918

Sergeant Witherspoon woke from an unrestful sleep. His ears were still ringing, and his entire left side ached. As his vision cleared, he noticed the doctor and nurse returning to his bedside.

"Well, well, our patient returns to reality," the doctor said. "How are we today?"

"I feel like I've been beaten with a hammer."

"Well, honestly, that's basically what happened to you. Actually, that would have been easier on you. You had a lot of steel slivers imbedded all over your left side. We had just enough chloroform to keep you under while we stitched you back to one piece."

"Was I pretty cut up?" Witherspoon asked.

"It could have been worse. It looks like the German artillery projectile exploded far enough away from you or in a crater. You were hit more by its non-lethal force than a direct hit. I think most of the steel shards that hit you were ricochets. You had quite a bit of mud in your wounds."

"Non-lethal? Doc, does that mean I can return to my soldiers?"

"Not so fast, Sergeant. We patched you up. But you need rest and time to heal. Besides, I can terminate your commission as a sergeant and send you home with what you went through. I don't think the hearing loss in your left ear will be permanent. I was told you were right in the thick of things and should consider yourself very lucky to still be with us. Five soldiers that came in with you were not so lucky."

"We lost five?" Sergeant Witherspoon asked. "How many were wounded?"

"Somewhere around twenty. They aren't all from your unit. The machine guns did most of the damage. I understand your unit held its own. Your regiment is supposed to be brought off the line soon to rest and recuperate."

"Right, Doc, that just means we'll be going back in another month. This isn't going to end any time soon. You're going to let me go back, aren't you?"

"Sergeant, I don't know why you soldiers always want to go back to the line. You have a free pass to go home and you just refuse to use it."

"Doctor, my men are out there. I will not leave them. Send us all home and I'll go."

"I cannot do *that*, of course. But I can make sure you heal properly. That is my charge. You need time to rest."

"I'm fine. I ache but I'm fine. You *will* send me back." Witherspoon started to get out of bed. "I'll go myself. I don't need you."

The doctor and nurse both moved toward him to keep him down. "My, my, you *are* persistent. All right then, you win. I'll write the order. I don't have time to argue with a crazy man. Get some rest. We need to finish our rounds with the other patients."

The doctor and nurse turned and proceeded down the line of beds in the open bay. They both seemed to have an ominous look on their faces as they stood by the beds of unconscious, wounded soldiers. Witherspoon lay back and looked up at the cracked ceiling of the French villa that had been converted into a military hospital. Visions of men torn by bullets and exploding shells during the run-up to and attack on the Saint Mihiel Salient came back to him. He was determined to be there with his men and his captain in the next push against the Germans. *Boy, can the Germans fight from those trenches, he reflected. I will be there and I will attack. Attack, attack, attack* were the last words, like the light that faded from his mind.

CHAPTER 16: RECOVERY AND RETURN

Baltimore, Maryland, U.S.A. - October 1, 1917

The troopship moved slowly and rolled like a stone down a hill. The moaning of the wounded soldiers coupled with the seasickness below deck made the two-week trip a miserable experience for Jimmy and everyone else. He felt sorry for the other wounded men and comforted those he met as best he could. *How can mankind do this to itself?* Jimmy wondered. The mangling of human flesh was an overwhelming sight. Jimmy swore he would not return to fly one of the bomber aeromachines. He *had* to return to a pursuit unit so that he could help end the killing.

Baltimore was flooded with ships of all kinds—multimasted schooners, steamers, cargo ships, and local wooden vessels called skipjacks. A maritime harbor was a busy place, Jimmy learned. The troopship sat moored for two days waiting for an open wharf. The harbor looked like a gaggle of wood and metal. There didn't seem to be any organization to it all.

Finally the men were on their way down the gangway. Jimmy couldn't wait to be in fresh air and on solid ground again. His legs felt like they were made of rubber when he first stepped back onto the ground. The swaying and bobbing of the ship had never stopped, even in the harbor. It now felt like the earth was swaying and bobbing.

Baltimore itself was just as bustling and confusing as its harbor. It was crowded and noisy and in disorder. The streetcars were everywhere and went everywhere. It was nothing like living in rural Wausau, Wisconsin.

Jimmy entered the tent city around Fort McHenry. The fort was earthen with brick- and stone-faced walls. It had been built in the form of a star with angular defensive fighting positions at the tip of each point. The positions were arranged to support one another with crossing fires. The fort sat on a dominating piece of land jutting into the Patapsco River. The headwaters of the river formed the Baltimore harbor, the center of commerce for the city and the entire East Coast.

A soldier with heavy bandages covering his shoulder turned to Jimmy as they stared at the fort. "No wonda this fort saved Baltimore," he said with a thick Southern draw. "What naval force could possibly pass by this piece of terrain safely when it was controlled by this type of fort?"

"What was that you said? Oh, yes, yes. This fort does look formidable. But my mind is on recovery. I just want to get through my medical treatment and get back to France," Jimmy said.

"Are you crazy, *sah*? You wan-ta go *back* to that misery?"

"What misery are you referring to," Jimmy asked?

"My friend, you obviously didn't serve on the front. We were the first Americans to fight. I proudly served with the 1st Expeditionary Division, but I have no des-aya to see *that* again."

"The 1st Expeditionary Division? What is *that*?"

"Everyone knows the *1st* Division. We wah the first of all the Divisions of the Army. We wah sent ova there to end the war and that is exactly what we're gonna do."

"I see. So you were in the trenches?" Jimmy asked.

"Oh, yes. I got mine at Verdun. What did you do over thar?"

"I am a flier. I watched infantry attacks from above. At times I strafed German soldiers attacking our trenches, and some of our aeromachines bombed the Germans."

"You did? Strafin help us some, but the bombin didn't much. We wah attakin the Germans and that's how I got mine."

"Bombing didn't help, you say? How's that?" Jimmy asked with surprise in his voice.

"My good friend, only the infantra can take the ground. Aerial bombin is good for poppin eardrums when men go to ground. Why sure, the bombs, like artillery shells, fall directly down onto the trenches. But one only needs to dig deepa to find safety. The infantra has to suffah in its attack over open terrain to dislodge the fiend. Bombin only takes lives and makes men suffah in the open. It takes real leadership to spuuur men on to fight. I got mine fightin with my

First Sergeant. Now *that's* a leader."

"First Sergeant, what's that?" Jimmy asked.

"First Sergeant, sah, is the highest rankin' sold-ya in the company —fightin' sold-ya, that is. Of course the captain fights too. But the First Sergeant is a man's man. Mine was First Sergeant Ralph Witherspoon, the best fightin' soldier on this earth, I can tell yah. What a leader, that man. I wish him and my friends Godspeed."

"I see. And your name, sir?"

"Roberts, Jack Roberts, and I'm proud to say, I fought with Witherspoon."

They walked together for a short while, looking around as they went. The land around the fort was covered with tents and hastily built wooden buildings. The large brick building to the north of the fort was the main hospital. Jimmy was led to an area around the wooden buildings. His friend went on to another area of the tent city. Jimmy had heard that they would finally end up in the tents. So this is my new home during my "vacation in pain," he said.

Processing through Fort McHenry was a slow, boring, and depressing process. Constant pain and agony permeated the atmosphere. Men with life-changing combat wounds were everywhere. Jimmy could tell he needed to get out of there as soon as he could. He needed freedom and fresh air. He needed to fly.

Jimmy was at his next medical review station. He was about to be interviewed at the hygiene station. *Hygiene?* Jimmy wondered. *What do they mean by* hygiene?

Then he saw her. He watched the nurse work with confidence and reassurance. She appeared to speak to the wounded soldiers in ways that made them relax and nod in attentive agreement. Jimmy was still five soldiers away from her desk thinking how she looked very much like Giselle. She was slim and had fine facial lines. He could feel the nurse's presence as much as see it from that distance. Her command of the station was very impressive.

Winifred Alvather's hair, uniform, and white shoes were immaculate. She spoke in soft but deliberate tones. Jimmy felt the air of confidence she had about her.

"So, Lieutenant Smitts, is it? Where were you stationed overseas?"

"I was a flier with the Lafayette Escadrille. We were stationed at the Lux, I mean—I'm sorry—I mean Luxeuil-les-Bains. It's in—"

"I know," she interrupted. "It is located just southwest of the Vosges Mountains and the French lands of Alsace and Lorraine."

"Wow, how did you know that, Ma'am?" Jimmy asked.

Winifred raised her chin slightly and said with a devious smile on her face, "I know that because I am … an *educated* woman. Also, I am a Miss, not a Ma'am or a Madam, and my name is Winifred, Winifred Alvather. May I have the pleasure of knowing to whom I am speaking?"

"Jimmy, Miss Winifred, Jimmy Smitts."

"So, Mr. Jimmy, you were a flier," she said flirtatiously. "How wonderful! I always wanted to learn how to fly."

"You mean you always wanted to have someone take you up in a flying machine."

"Mr. Jimmy, you will soon come to know that I say what I mean and I mean what I say. I said I always wanted to *learn* how to fly. There was no inference to the contrary. Now, if you don't mind, I believe we should get down to business."

How she acted so much like mother, he thought. She had that same confident and inspiring way about her.

As a dietician, she asked him about the kinds of foods he had eaten while in Europe. She seemed intrigued by his duty as a flier. She seemed to be even more thrilled just to hear Jimmy's voice.

Jimmy shook his head as he walked away from her interview. His mind was racing. Thoughts of flying, Giselle, and Winifred whirled around in his head. Lord, this was confusing. When would it clear up so that he could get back into the air against the Huns?

Jimmy saw Winifred a number of times during the week. He passed by her dietician station as he went to the doctor and physical therapist. He paused many times to chat with her. Her demeanor and confidence soothed him. Her soft voice and reassuring knowledge of health and hygiene were comforting to all the soldiers, Jimmy noticed. He was intrigued by Winifred. She knew so much and carried herself so well.

With each visit to Winifred's station, Jimmy worked himself closer to asking if he could spend more time with her. His heart raced each time he saw her. He just couldn't bring himself to say something. He was confused. He didn't know if he wanted to avoid rejection or he felt guilty about trying to be with Winifred while he had Giselle in his heart. But he remembered Roberts telling him, "Hell, Lieutenant, just ask the woman. She won't bite."

Toward the end of one of the workdays, Jimmy finally asked, "Miss Winifred, would you mind if I walked you to the trolley?"

"Well, Mr. Jimmy, I would be honored to have the privilege of your escort. Thank you so much for asking."

She seemed pleased to be in his company. That first walk turned into more frequent visits. They started taking lunch together and meeting after Winifred finished work. The only interruptions, when they were together, came in the realization that misery was all around them. The wounded men just didn't stop coming. Injury to the flesh and damage to the mind permeated the neighborhood around Fort McHenry. Jimmy wanted to be away from it all. And he wanted to take Winifred away from it. He could tell the stress of seeing and dealing with the wounded every day was having its affects on her. Her demeanor was completely different at the end of each day than it was in the morning. She was quiet after work and stopped speaking of the needs of the soldiers. He had to do something to cheer her up. She was brave but he could tell the strength of the misery was overpowering the strengths of her cheerfulness and determination.

They frequented Federal Hill on the south side of the Baltimore harbor. The view from the hill was breathtaking. From their perch, they could see far to the north into Baltimore. The air was fresh and free from the pungent odor of burning coal that permeated the harbor.

"Winifred, this is an amazing view," Jimmy said. "Can you tell me a little about those buildings in the distance?"

"The building to the west that looks like a stone lighthouse is called the Bromo-Seltzer Tower. Its narrow square appearance, peaked with a narrower round tower, is similar to the Islamic minarets of the

Middle East and North Africa."

"It looks out of place in the middle of the flat buildings that dominate the hill in the middle of the city."

"The buildings of Baltimore rise up from the harbor to Mount Vernon, the hill that is peaked by the Washington monument. The view to Mount Vernon is framed by the Bromo-Seltzer Tower to the west and the Shot Tower far to the east of the city, over there. The city continues up to Mount Royal, the second hill within the city and beyond Mount Vernon. The hills of the city are very enjoyable to walk."

"The Shot Tower? What is *that*?"

"It was built during the Revolutionary War," Winifred said. "It has a moat at its base. Men would melt lead at the top of the Shot Tower. The molten lead was dropped down into the moat. The lead formed balls that cooled as they fell and hardened just before hitting the water. In that way, Americans made round 'shot' for muskets and cannon. That's how the tower became known as the Shot Tower."

Jimmy could only stare at her as she gave him a detailed history lesson about the city.

They often walked arm in arm from the trolley up to their favorite place on Federal Hill. The early dinners on the hill were a great relief from the suffering they witnessed in and around the fort and the effects it was having on her. Winifred was determined to help the soldiers in their recovery, she told him. Their devotion to the cause of freedom and for the oppressed in Europe gave her great strength, she said. All of the soldiers took their suffering as well as could be expected. Many of them took their pain quietly to their deaths.

Jimmy had no idea a woman could be so smart. Winifred was extremely well read and knew a great deal about health and hygiene. She also knew about American history and world events. She had a Southern heritage and knew a lot about the Civil War. She was also a student of the Great War and American politics.

On their fourth trip to Federal Hill, Winifred gave Jimmy a lesson he would never forget.

"My ancestors fought for the South during the Civil War. Federal forces occupied Federal Hill during the war because Maryland and particularly Baltimore were pro-South. The Federals placed cannon in the exact spot where we're now sitting."

"You mean the government was so concerned about the loyalty in the city that it occupied portions of Baltimore?"

"Oh, yes. The Federal government worked throughout the early 1860s to keep Maryland from seceding from the Union. The first shots of the Civil War after Fort Sumter were fired at Camden Station, the rail station here in Baltimore. Baltimoreans were the first civilians killed by Federal soldiers at the start of the war. Fort McHenry itself has a storied history. The war of 1812 was basically stopped by the brave men who fought and died at the Battle of North Point and the bombardment of Fort McHenry. North Point is just southeast of Baltimore. The militiamen and regulars of the newly formed American Army stopped the British from advancing to Baltimore by land after the British burned Washington. Fort McHenry was the last stand for America in its fight to end British barbaric domination of the seas."

Jimmy found that Winifred's knowledge wasn't limited to history.

"I'm glad it happened, but I don't understand why I was given this parole," he said. "The Germans paroled me, but I just sat there while they talked about it. I had never heard of a parole before. Now that I think about it, I have never heard of a parole before or since."

"Oh my dear, Jimmy," Winifred said. "Military paroles have been in existence for centuries. They're unheard of in this war. But they were commonplace in other wars, particularly in Europe. The American forces gave paroles from time to time."

"Really?" Jimmy asked.

"Let me quote a letter to you. 'In accordance with the substance of my letter to you of the 8th instant, I propose to receive the surrender of the Army of Northern Virginia on the following terms, to wit: ...The officers to give their individual paroles not to take up arms against the government of the United States until properly exchanged and each company officer or regimental commander sign a like parole for the men of their commands. The arms, artillery, and public property to be parked and stacked and turned over to the officer appointed by me to receive them. This will not embrace the side arms of the officers nor their private horses or baggage. This done, each officer and man will be allowed to return to his home not to be disturbed by United States Authority so long as they observe their parole and the laws in force where they may reside. Signed, U.S. Grant, Lieutenant-General.'"

"How do you know *that*?"

"My dear, that letter was the salvation of our family. It was the beginning of the end of the War for Southern Independence."

"You mean the Civil War," he interrupted.

"No, Mr. Smitts. I mean the War for Southern Independence. *Northerners* call it the Civil War. General Grant gave a parole to the entire Army of Northern Virginia at Appomattox Courthouse in Virginia on the 9th of April of 1865. The letter was most controversial at the time, but ended the terrible destruction of our heritage. It also started Reconstruction."

"And you know it by heart?"

"My granddaddy was standing in the fields near the Appomattox River on that day. He faced three Union cavalry divisions with his friends. Had General Grant not been so gracious and given paroles to the men, General Lee would not have surrendered his army, and I would probably not be sitting here at your side. My granddaddy would not have survived more than two or three days after Generals Grant and Lee met. Because the letter was our salvation, the children of my family have all been expected to recite the words in that letter."

"But why did Voss parole *me*? What was his purpose in doing *that*? As I said, I have never heard of a parole before or since."

"My dearest, Mr. Voss obviously held you in very high esteem. You must have been the best flier he had ever flown against. I'm not sure I have ever heard of a parole in this war before or since either. But he gave one to you. You are here now, sitting beside me as proof of his respect for you."

She and Jimmy talked for hours more about the details of recent events overseas. Winifred knew more about the military command structure of the French, British, and German armies than he did. She told him of the vastness of the Great War. Jimmy knew of the Eastern Front, as Winifred called it. She told him she did not believe the Russians would stay in the war. A man named Lenin was leading a group called Bolsheviks in revolution against the czar of Russia. Winifred was sure the war to the east of Germany would end as soon as Russia's czarist government fell.

In Jimmy's small aerial world above Verdun, he was not aware of the ramifications of the fall of Russia. Until Winifred told him, he had no idea that the Germans could reinforce the Western Front and launch new attacks against the Allied Powers with reinforcements from the east.

He knew from his discussions with the fliers that the Germans were advancing in Palestine and North Africa. Jimmy was amazed that Winifred's knowledge of those military operations was so advanced. She told him of the total carnage during the Battle of Gallipoli in the Dardanelles, a land in the Middle East that Jimmy had never heard of. She told him of the devastation the Turks brought onto the British and Canadian forces as wave after wave of men charged into the direct fire of the Turkish machine guns. The damage wrought by the guns did not stop the Allied commanders from ordering their men to certain death throughout the day.

Winifred continued, "Stories have been told of men impaling letters to loved ones in the wood forms of the trenches with their bayonets before going over the top. Men sent their last words of love and hope on to their loved ones right before they ran into the maelstrom."

"Why did the soldiers simply run into machine-gun fire like that?"

"They probably did it because they were ordered to do so and their friends were going and depended on them. You've told me many times how you fought for your comrades. Sometimes we do strange things when our friends are in danger. So the men probably continued to run into the caldron of fire because they had a great sense of loyalty to those they fought with. Once ordered, they all went in hopes of helping their brethren survive.

"I can believe that, but why order it? Why did the soldiers not go around the Turks?"

"Jimmy, the murder of soldiers like that should never be forgotten in the annals of military history. Commanders have a duty to God and mankind to know their craft and command effectively in war. The egotistical attitudes of the Allied commanders in the current war are like the egos of the men at the university I attended. The unfortunate difference is in the destruction of human life in war rather than advancement of male ego in society. For you see Jimmy, ego is the torch that lights the fire of hatred and discrimination in mankind throughout the world."

In Winifred, Jimmy finally came to know what a college education and devotion to learning really meant. He felt somewhat naive and uneducated but understood that Winifred had followed a different path than he. Winifred was one of the first women to attend the newly formed School of Hygiene and Public Health at the Johns Hopkins University located in the center of Baltimore. Coming from an aristocratic family of Virginia, Winifred's parents sent her to Baltimore to private school so she could attend one of the most prestigious universities in America. She wanted to advance herself and make an impact on society and others, she told him. Coming from a rural family, *he* wanted to advance his *flying* skills.

A feeling came over Jimmy that he was facing a very strong and capable woman. In some respects, he felt inferior, almost as though he could never meet the standards of excellence that she set for men. "What do you mean by saying the men at the university had egotistical attitudes?" he asked her.

"The university leadership and American society as a whole do not accept women as a moving factor in human existence. Male dominance in society, education, and business is the norm rather than the exception. Johns Hopkins University was no exception to the norm when I enrolled and attended the school."

"What do you mean by *male dominance?*" Jimmy asked. His feeling of inferiority turned to slight aggravation at hearing the words *male dominance. Dominance,* you say? He wondered. Perhaps no man could live up to her standards.

"The other ladies and I had to attend classes by sitting in the coat closets of the classrooms. The very few women that attended the university were not permitted to sit with the men in class. We had to wear our hair up in buns and dress in high-collared long dresses. We were also required to take more classes than the men in English literature and the sciences. That was because women were restricted from public speaking. We were not allowed to present our theses before the men in the classes."

"Why would they do all that to you?"

"The men at the university were probably threatened by our presence," Winifred said with a giggle. "They were probably afraid that the women would prove to be better students. And we *were* better students," she said with smiling conviction.

So that's what she meant by "male dominance." Surely the men at the university felt threatened. Why else would they cage the women up like that? How absurd. Then again, I feel a little threatened by her and how she knows so much more than me about almost everything.

During their visits to Federal Hill, Jimmy's amazement of Winifred's ability to speak in great depth about any subject only grew but in a reassuring way. She spoke inspirationally like his mother and was refined and well mannered beyond anyone Jimmy had ever met in his life. And she was beautiful. Winifred, he could tell, was falling in love with him. Her eyes showed Jimmy a deep and warm connection with his. Perhaps he too was falling in love.

Jimmy lay back in his cot under the olive-drab cotton tent. He thought of Giselle and Winifred as he watched the tent canvas rise and fall in the late October breeze. How different the two were in many ways, yet they were similar in many other ways. He loved both of them, but his feelings differed. *Love sure is confusing,* he thought.

The tranquility of his rest was interrupted when he heard the tent flap get pulled back as someone shouted, "Anyone in here from Wisconsin?" As the intruder quickly started to leave, Jimmy rose on his good arm and shouted, "Yes. I'm from Wisconsin."

"You are? What's your name?"

"James, James Smitts," he replied.

"Smitts? What's your rank?"

"I'm a flier."

"Not your occupation, mister, your rank."

The man entered the tent. He wore an olive-drab dress uniform and had captain's bars on his collar.

"Lieutenant. I am Lieutenant Smitts."

"'I am Lieutenant Smitts, *sir'!* I am a *captain*. I hope you're not forgetting that I outrank you," the captain said smugly. "All right. Lieutenant, you'll do. Come with me. Someone important wants to meet with you and the others."

The captain led Jimmy and a group of fifteen other wounded soldiers to a meeting room in the main administrative office located in the stone and brick halls of the lower level of the main fort.

"Gentlemen, please keep your seats," a major said as he entered the room. The gold oak leafs on the epaulettes of his tunic shined brightly in the dimly lit room. Jimmy looked around at the others and noticed they too seemed confused by this assembly.

"It is my pleasure to introduce you to Senator Eugene F. Stevenson. Senator Stevenson is your representative to the U.S. Senate. He is here on a fact-finding mission from Washington and wishes to have a few words with you. Gentlemen, please stand as Senator Stevenson joins us."

The men in the room all stood up.

"Thank you, thank you, Major," the senator said as he rushed into the room. "Gentlemen, please take your seats. Relax. We are all friends here."

Jimmy saw three men walk in behind the senator and sit down in the front of the room. All three were dressed in handsome suits. A white card was tucked into their hat bands and said, PRESS. The senator continued as though he had not been interrupted by the other men. The men concentrated on their notepads and appeared to take copious notes.

"As the major said, I am on a fact-finding mission looking at

219

what the government can do to help our *very* honored wounded soldiers. I thought I would take this opportunity to meet with soldiers from our great state of Wisconsin. As you may know, I have promoted a new initiative called Food for the Troops. I wish to help promote support for our troops while advancing the prosperity of our home state, the great state of Wisconsin."

Jimmy sat dumbfounded. He had no idea Wisconsin had a senator in Washington and could not believe he had been pulled away from his rest just to hear this tall, egotistical man talk about *his* initiative. He certainly had no idea there was some initiative to feed troops. Now Jimmy was watching firsthand what Winifred said of male ego and dominance play out in real life.

"I also came here to give you thanks from all of Wisconsin for your devotion to our country. You have given your all for America and most importantly for our great state of Wisconsin. I'll tell you, we are going to win this war. We are going to win because we will do it for you. We will defeat the German hoards and keep those people from doing what they have been doing to Europe ever again. Thank you for your service and your sacrifice. If any of you need anything or want us to pass a message onto your mothers and fathers in Wisconsin, just let my staffers know about it. They will be around presently. May God bless you for your dedication to this Great War, this great country, and the great state of Wisconsin."

Jimmy watched silently as the senator rushed from the room. It seemed to Jimmy like the senator had no stomach to be with men with bloody and festering wounds.

"Thank you, gentlemen. You may return to your duties," is all the major said as he too left the room. Jimmy casually walked back to his hospital tent to get ready for his next visit with Winifred. He realized he had not seen any staffers come around to anyone. *The audacity*, he thought, *of this man saying, "We will win this war."* The senator sure wasn't wounded from shrapnel or mustard gas. Then he pondered, how many times did that senator say the words *the great state of Wisconsin?*

The beauty of the fall colors of the trees in October turned to the cold breezes over Federal Hill in November. Jimmy and Winifred planned to have Thanksgiving dinner together. Perhaps that would be the right time for him to tell her that he had a beloved in France. Jimmy was thrilled to be in Winifred's company, and he knew he loved her—but in a special way. She was the closest thing to a true friend he had ever had. Jimmy had never before been so honest with anyone about his innermost thoughts and feelings. But he knew he had to stay true to his love in France *and* be honest with this lovely new friend of his in Baltimore.

Winifred prepared a wonderful Thanksgiving dinner at her apartment on Fort Street. Jimmy had never eaten turkey and glazed ham that tasted so good.

"Lord, Winifred, you sure can cook."

"Well, Jimmy, an important part of any meal is the balance of the diet. A good, balanced meal is the basis of a long and healthy life."

Jimmy had never heard of "food groups" before. Winifred was the first person to tell him a balanced diet helped people get well from sickness and injury. The balanced diets she prescribed to the wounded soldiers were critical to their recovery, she said. Her intelligence, confidence, elegance, and grace never ceased to amaze him.

She received his message about Giselle with the same confidence and grace that she showed in everything she did. She paused for a moment as if forming her words ... or perhaps trying to control her emotions. She understood Jimmy's predicament, she said.

"I respect your openness and honesty, Jimmy. I'm sorry we can't be closer. But I would be very disappointed if you didn't keep your promise of love to Giselle. I expected nothing less than this kind of honesty and devotion from you."

"Thank you, Winifred. You are the most special friend of my life."

"I will hold you very dear in my heart for the rest of my life," Winifred said, holding back the tears that were welling up inside of her. "No matter what happens in your life, I want you to consider me as your closest and most devoted friend and confidant."

With their new personal pact, Winifred and Jimmy hoped they would enjoy the coming weeks together. As Christmas approached, his recovery was going well. Many others weren't so lucky. Winifred, who knew so much about the devastating effects of shrapnel and bullets on the human body, described to him the agony many of the soldiers suffered.

The worst cases, she said, were those who'd been gassed on the battlefield. The poison gas destroyed flesh and affected the nervous system, she said. Her descriptions of the injuries chilled even him. Winifred, with her understanding of chemistry and biology, was an angel of mercy to these men. Jimmy stood in wonder at her amazing grace toward the afflicted. Had he not fallen so deeply in love with Giselle, he thought that he and Winifred could have had a wonderful life together.

His enlistment in the U.S. Army Air Corps was completed in early December, and he was ordered to deploy to France. They waived his parole because he would no longer be a member of the Lafayette Escadrille. He was now in the 103rd Pursuit Squadron. And he was ready for action against the Germans.

Winifred was supportive but also scared for him.

"Please use all your skills to stay alive, Jimmy," she said. "You're a wonderful man. I see in you a level of integrity and moral courage that I see in few men. You *must* stay alive, Jimmy. You *must* follow your heart back to Giselle and to your destiny. I will always be with you. I will be there protecting you and guiding you in your hours of hope, love, and need."

Christmas of 1917 was the most wonderful holiday Jimmy had ever experienced. The bustle of the harbor and streets of Baltimore were great contrasts to the calm and comfort of Winifred's small apartment. Winifred had knitted him a sweater and given him a silk flying scarf, a flaming red scarf. Her thoughts of comforting him in combat touched his heart. He choked on his words as he told her he would always remember her care and love for him. Then Jimmy turned and brought out from behind a chair a long paper-wrapped box.

"Oh, Jimmy, you shouldn't have. My, my, what could it be? Did you get a box of long-stem roses for me? You know how I love long-stem red roses. That is why I gave you a red flying scarf to protect you and have you fight harder to live in remembrance of me. No one has ever given me roses before." *Roses for the heart,* she thought. *How wonderful.*

When she opened the present, Winifred broke down. "Jimmy, how could you do this?" she said through her tears. "How could you give me such a wonderful Christmas present? This isn't a Christmas present. It is a present for all times."

Winifred lifted the French officer's saber out of the box as though it were a fragile bag of eggs at the market. "Captain Thenault's saber," she said. "This is the most cherished object of your life. I am so honored and yet humbled. It symbolizes everything about you."

"I want you, of all people in my life, to have this saber, Winifred," he said. "You may never know how deeply I love and care for you. This is only a small token of my feelings for you. Please accept it and display it proudly."

Winifred couldn't control herself. *How could he give me such a symbol of courage in combat and compassion for his fellow fliers?* she thought. She knew he loved her. She was madly in love with him. But he *had* to return to the war and his flying comrades. He *had* to return to Giselle and find his life's pathway. She knew he could not commit himself to her until he came to know that pathway, his *destiny.*

"Love by bondage from one's path is not love," Winifred had told him a week earlier. One had to follow one's dreams no matter where they led. If his dreams led him from her, then he had to go.

They spent their last moments together on the 25th of December. She said they both knew it had to be. His destiny was with the endeavors on the other side of the Atlantic Ocean. Jimmy had to serve and help end the misery and killing and finally bring peace to the world.

* * * * *

He could not have been more cold and miserable. A troopship in the North Atlantic Ocean in the wintertime was a miserable place for human occupancy. Ice formed on the decks and railings. An icy spray bit at the hands and face of anyone who went topsides. But sometimes it was necessary to go there for relief from the stench and ugliness of the gloomy troop holds below.

Words that Winifred had spoken to him came into Jimmy's mind as he stood in the wind and ice-cold salt spray.

"You have to find and follow your destiny."

CHAPTER 17: THE SHOCK

North Atlantic Ocean – January 15, 1918

The last thing Jimmy ever wanted to do was travel across the ocean again in one of the metal boxes. They were cold and dark like coffins. They rolled constantly. The ship he was on shuddered with each swell. The crew told everyone to stay calm. The periodic shudder was from the rotating propeller as it broke the surface of the waves when the ship passed over a swell.

The body odor and stench from seasickness made the trip a trip to hell. Jimmy was on his way to the hell of the killing fields through the hell of the clanging and shuddering metal coffin. And the *food*, he thought. Lord, the food was terrible. He played games in his mind in order to make it more comfortable for him through the unbearable mess. He would dream each time he ate in the ship's mess that he was having Thanksgiving Day dinner with Winifred. He would dream of flying sensations he used to feel in the air each time the ship rolled.

The troopship stopped in Great Britain. Jimmy had no idea where they were. It really didn't matter to him. The ship was taking on supplies. Additional coal for the boilers and nondescript boxes of all sizes were added to the ship's cargo holds. They would be there for two days. Jimmy could not have been more bored by the excursion. Thoughts of Giselle and Winifred comforted him and helped him pass the time. He could feel Winifred's comfort, warmth, and love. She was right. She was always with him.

Disembarking at Brest, France, was a welcome relief. Jimmy knew the harbor and the city well. He had passed through them twice before. He prayed his efforts as a flier would help stop the war. Only in that way could he be with Giselle and return to America and his destiny. He hoped to take Giselle home with him.

He went by troop train through Brest to Paris. He was on his way to the French School of Flying Preparation for the second time. He wondered whether the school now had more modern flying machines. *Please don't have me fly those slow and sloppy Cauldrons again,* Jimmy prayed.

Paris was amazing. It was full of soldiers coming and going. Many were on their own form of rest and recuperation. Others were on their way to or from the front. Jimmy could easily tell which way soldiers were headed when he met them. Those who were headed east toward the front had an ominous and frightened air about them. They knew they might be headed to doom. Many said that if they were to be hit, they preferred to die on the spot. Nothing was worse than suffering for the rest of your life with miserable war wounds, they said. Jimmy kept his knowledge of the suffering at Fort McHenry to himself. He didn't want to confirm the thoughts of the worried soldiers. Those who were happy and smiling were either on a pass for R&R, or they were going home.

Jimmy was different. He was excited about returning to the war. He longed to return to the air. He knew his ability to fly would keep him safe. The sweater that Winifred had knitted for him and the red silk scarf she had given him would comfort him in flight. They would give him the charge he would need to sustain himself.

The flying school had not changed much. There were different instructors and administrators than the first time he attended the school, but the school itself was the same. American instructors had been added to the staff. Some of them had flown in combat and would give the student fliers excellent advice. The instructors found out that Jimmy was a returning flier. Everyone at the school including the administrators was surprised to hear that Jimmy had three kills to his name.

The instructors hid their surprise and respect for Jimmy's previous aerial successes. The instructors would quickly change their attitudes when they saw Jimmy fly the French Breguet two-seaters in training. They found out that Jimmy didn't need someone behind him watching him and telling him what to do. His first turn was as tight as any of the instructors had seen the large Breguet turned by anyone in the past. The Breguet was big and somewhat slow but was quickly becoming the French standard machine for aerial observation and bombing. Jimmy could snap it around like a whip, a feat done in a bombing machine only by the best.

He was quickly sent to the School of Final Preparation. The aerobatics and practice strafing runs were easy things for Jimmy to master. He was surprised, though, by the improvements in the flying machines. They had more gauges indicating altimeter, oil pressure, engine temperature, and flying direction in the cockpit. They were more powerful than anything he had flown in the past. And their flying controls were much tighter than the Nieuports. Aerial tactics had changed considerably in only the four months that Jimmy was out of action. Mutual supporting fliers, stacked formations, and attack angles were discussed in great detail in the classrooms. The instructors were egotistical and standoffish to the students. That didn't bother Jimmy. All he wanted to do was pass each stage of his retraining and move on.

He knew he would be going to the American 103rd Pursuit Squadron. So he was comfortable with what he had to learn and practice. Some of the new students didn't know if they were going to be observers, gunners, bomber and observation fliers, or pursuit fliers. The final destination of each flier would be determined by the instructors based on how well the flier performed. Some fliers washed out. Those who couldn't cut the mustard were sent to communications, ambulance, and staff duties. Jimmy watched some turn ghostly when they got sent directly to the front. He felt ill at ease remembering those at Fort McHenry. The front meant death or, worse, permanent disability.

His training was almost over. The staff and administrators were planning Jimmy's passage on to the 103rd. He desperately needed— no, *demanded*—to have a few days off before going to the squadron. He had to go to Charmes. He had to see Giselle. Jimmy constantly planned what he would do as soon as he saw her. He couldn't wait to get his training over so he could go to her. What would Giselle think once she was in his arms? How would she react to seeing him? He constantly told himself, "Lord, I hope she hasn't found new love."

The training squadron administration did not want to hear that Jimmy wanted a few days off from training. He tried to get permission to take a training flight to the southeast. But it was not to be, he was told. The school absolutely could not spare a machine for personal use. The Allied buildup in men and materiel had taken off. Every man and every machine was needed for the war effort. A flier in training could not be spared to take a two or three day R&R just to go on a wild goose chase.

Jimmy was constantly planning how he could get to Giselle. He would soon be shipped to Issoudun with the 103rd. He needed to get to Giselle. Otherwise it would take forever for him to make it to her side. There is no way to know what the squadron would do once he got there, he thought. He could be sent directly into combat, kept at the aerodrome until everything was in order, or ordered to stay at his post. He had no idea how he would get to see Giselle. He wanted desperately to see her. He planned to ask her to marry him.

Toward the end of his training, Jimmy was called to the school headquarters. He walked into the main briefing room only to see a U.S. Army officer. Bill Thaw turned and smiled. It shocked him to see Thaw. "Bill Thaw," Jimmy said, "how in the *world* are you?" Then he saw the gold oak leaf of the rank of major on the shoulder tabs of Thaw's olive-green tunic. Major Thaw told Jimmy a lot had changed since he was shipped out of the Lafayette Escadrille. Thaw was now the commander of the new U.S. Army Air Corps Pursuit Squadron 103. Jimmy was elated. He would fly with his old friend, one of the best fliers of the group.

"Jimmy, we're now flying the new Spad. It stands for The Societe pour L'Aviation et ses Derives, or the Society for Aviation and its Derivatives. It is France's answer to the powerful and well-built German fighters. We're facing newer and more powerful Fokker's, and they are taking their toll on the British," Thaw said.

Major Thaw then told Jimmy that Raoul Lufbery had been given command of the U.S. 94th Aero Squadron but had been killed in action just after the first of the year. Jimmy could barely keep the tears away. He swallowed and tried to get himself under control. It made him get that much closer to the reality of his own mortality. Thaw told Jimmy he would be transferred to his unit in about two weeks. The unit was currently building its barracks, hangars, and other buildings at Issoudun. They would be fully operational in early February. Then his new commander asked Jimmy if he needed anything. Jimmy told his friend he would be obliged if he could find a way to help him get to Charmes.

"I see," Thaw replied. "I do remember something very important, something *very* French in that town."

Major Thaw called one of the French lieutenants over to the briefing room. He started to speak to Jimmy with the lieutenant listening. "Lieutenant Smitts, I'm going to send one of our new Spad S pursuit aeroplanes to this station. I want you to take a couple of checkout flights in the machine. The Spads are very touchy on takeoff and landing. But they're fast and agile. They're the best the world has ever seen. I need you to learn quickly. I need you to be the best you've ever been."

Thaw paused, and Jimmy said, "Yes, sir!"

"After you take a couple of checkout flights and you're comfortable with the machine, I want you to take a solo orientation flight to our old aerodrome at Luxeuil-les-Bains," Major Thaw ordered. "You are to reconnoiter the area of operations and report back to this aerodrome no later than the 25th of February instant. Is that understood, sir?"

"Yes, sir!"

Major Thaw then looked at the French lieutenant and said, "Sir, do you have any questions about my orders to Lieutenant Smitts?" The lieutenant said no and the orders were written.

Thaw shook Jimmy's hand and stepped briskly out of the briefing room. Jimmy couldn't have been more happy and impressed with his old friend. On the twentieth of February, the student fliers stood in awe as a camouflaged squatty pursuit aeroplane with a large engine cowling turned into final approach toward the landing field at the school. The fliers had never seen such a sleek and impressive flying machine before. The Spad S VII skidded and stopped near the administration building.

A flier left the machine and entered the building. Jimmy walked in behind the flier. He was none other than First Lieutenant Ray Bridgman, Jimmy's friend from the Lafayette Escadrille. In the building Lieutenants Bridgman and Smitts jumped at each other and hugged one another.

"*Bridgman!*" Jimmy yelled. "How are you? I thought I'd never see you again."

Bridgman told Jimmy a little about the developments in the Lafayette Escadrille. The unit had not yet been disbanded. But that was on paper. Many of the fliers were still together, but they were formed into a new American flying unit. Bridgman told Jimmy how much work they were doing just to get organized and operational. No one was doing much flying, he said.

The members of the French school were astonished and studied the new Spad S model. As he gave Jimmy an orientation of the cockpit and controls, Bridgman told him he had to be very careful. The new aeromachine was very temperamental. A couple of the guys had flipped the machine on landing. It also had a tendency to slip when turning hard to the right at slow speed, Bridgman told Jimmy. Jimmy and his friend then talked about how sad they were that Lufbery had been killed. Ray told Jimmy how horrible it was. Many in his squadron watched it all unfold. Lufbery had been hit by a German observation gunner. His petrol tank had burst into flames. Lufbery had tried to jump out of the machine and into a pond to save himself but had fallen to his death.

Bridgman told Jimmy he had five days to check out on the aeromachine. Someone would be back to retrieve it. Then, remembering Jimmy's previous exploits in the French town of Charmes, Bridgman said, "Give Giselle my best, Jimmy. Don't get too deeply in love. We need you." With that, Lieutenant Bridgman left. He took a staff car back to their aerodrome at Issoudun.

Jimmy took his time with the machine. He understood exactly what Ray had told him about the Spad. Jimmy noticed how heavy the engine was up front as he threw the throttle forward for takeoff. Wow, the machine could accelerate, Jimmy thought. But it sure did bounce forward with a weird, unbalanced feeling. It seemed as if the Spad would flip forward with each bounce.

Pulling back on the stick, Jimmy felt the surge of power and lift in the machine. It seemed to take off with a mind of its own. *Wow,* Jimmy thought, *this is amazing.* He pulled the throttle back to slow the machine and banked a number of times to find out how the Spad would slip under him. He wanted the machine to be a part of his body and soul before he did any sharp cuts and turns with the ship. He adjusted the throttle in various turns to fully understand the range of the machine's speed at different flying attitudes. At full throttle, the machine could turn *fast*, he found.

Two days later, Jimmy was ready to take the machine on the long-distance checkout that Major Thaw had ordered him to execute. It had been so hard for him to restrain himself. In the first two days that he had the machine under his command, he wanted so much to fly south to Charmes. But he had to follow orders. He also needed to understand the capabilities of the machine.

Now it was time for him to go to his beloved Giselle. The machine responded to Jimmy's every move. It was a very capable and powerful aeroplane. Jimmy hadn't yet tried tight barrels and double-turning maneuvers. He wanted to be sure that he and his machine were one. Before he knew it Jimmy was passing over the checkpoint he used to use as a member of the Lafayette Escadrille. He turned just west of Epinal and toward the church steeple he knew so well. Then he looked for the Mark, the numerous ponds just north of his old aerodrome.

Buzzing the aerodrome and turning into final approach, Jimmy realized that the facilities of his old home had changed. In only five months the aerodrome had nearly been deserted. There were a few observation machines on the ground. But the constant buzz of the Lafayette Escadrille had become an isolated, rundown support field. Jimmy landed and turned his machine into his old spot on the landing field. He walked to the farmhouse and approached the operations desk. The mechanics and few fliers at the field had already reported that a new camouflaged pursuit machine was landing on the field.

The French captain sitting behind the operations desk looked lazily up at Jimmy. Jimmy told him he was on orders to reconnoiter the area north of Epinal. He needed a staff car and a driver for two days to complete his mission. Jimmy presented his written orders to the French captain. After much debate among the French staff, the captain told Jimmy he would have his staff car in an hour. Jimmy couldn't have been happier. He would be with Giselle in only three hours.

The ride to Charmes was as long and bumpy as it ever had been. The French driver did not speak any English. So the trip was taken in silence. The French driver performed his duties with no emotion. Jimmy knew the driver was wondering what was going on. It would soon be dark and he had no way of knowing whether he would have a comfortable and warm place to sleep.

The staff car entered Charmes. The small town seemed eerily quiet and serene, Jimmy thought. It was usually abuzz at dinnertime, and the restaurant was at its busiest. Jimmy told the driver to stop. He wanted to walk the last two blocks. Jimmy had yearned for this moment since he'd left Giselle in September, almost five months before.

As he turned the last corner, Jimmy couldn't believe his eyes. The restaurant was quiet and dark. There was no activity either in or around the building. As he approached, he noticed that there was some light on the inside of the building. He walked through the front door and found the restaurant in complete disarray. He looked up and discovered that the light on the inside of the building was coming through its roof. The building had been damaged by some kind of explosion. Jimmy believed it had been bombed.

The French driver approached in total confusion. He had no idea what the American officer was doing. Jimmy turned to him and started to speak to him loudly. Where is she, he asked? What has happened? *Go.* Go talk to someone and find out what has happened to this building, he ordered. Find out what has happened to the family that lived and worked here.

The French soldier seemed to understand. He left and searched up and down some of the streets. Jimmy went inside the restaurant and looked through the mess that was once a place of comfort and love to him. He ran to the back of the building and looked across the alleyway. The house that Giselle had lived in was also damaged. Jimmy couldn't believe it. Everything in his life had just changed. His *destiny* that Winifred so enthusiastically spoke of had just ended. Giselle and her entire family were gone.

He searched the house. There was some damage to it, but it looked as if it could be repaired. *Where are they?* Jimmy wondered. *How am I to find them? Where is my Giselle?* The driver returned and spoke to Jimmy in French. Jimmy couldn't understand everything the driver said. "Boche ... bombardier ... Epinal," Jimmy heard him say. It seemed that the Germans had bombed the town from the air. They were apparently trying to attack the markets of Epinal and dropped their bombs on Charmes. Jimmy sat for a second. He had to think. What was he to do? It was getting dark. They needed a place to eat and sleep. And he had to find out where Giselle had gone.

As they drove around the town, Jimmy realized that many of the merchants had left. None of the happiness that existed in the town was evident. Charmes was a ghost town with nothing to offer the two soldiers. Jimmy told the driver they would go to Epinal. They would eat and spend the night there.

Jimmy had the driver pass through the town once more to ask everyone they passed whether they knew what had become of Giselle and her family. Only one person recognized the name Giselle. The merchant spoke in loud and animated tones in French. The driver seemed to understand but couldn't convey to Jimmy what had happened and where Giselle was. Apparently the family had left Charmes for the safety of another town, and the merchant did not know where they had gone. At least that's what Jimmy thought had been said.

It was late when they arrived at Epinal. On the way Jimmy believed that no one in her family, especially Giselle, could have been killed in the bombing. He was sure the merchant would know if a beautiful young woman had been killed in the aerial attack.

At breakfast in Epinal, Jimmy came to understand a little more of what had happened. The proprietor of the hotel could speak a little German. So the French driver explained things to the proprietor. The proprietor tried to translate and tell Jimmy about events in Charmes. The proprietor's ability to speak German was almost as bad as Jimmy's. But Jimmy was able to confirm that the town had been bombed by large German flying machines. The merchant that the driver had spoken to the night before really did not know where the family had gone. He thought perhaps they had traveled to southern France. The family elected to leave without cleaning up. When they were bombed, everyone in the town thought the Boche would come to invade their town. Why else, the proprietor said, would the Germans bomb the quaint little town?

Jimmy was heartbroken. But somehow, he hoped, he would find Giselle.

* * * * *

Issoudun, France – May 15, 1918

His train trip from the flying school to the squadron ended in constant briefings about the developments in the war. Bill Thaw was obviously trying to get the men ready for the worst. The briefings were constant and so intense that Jimmy had no time to socialize with and befriend the other fliers. The briefings certainly kept him from looking for Giselle.

The massive killing in the trenches across central and northern France had taken on new heights as 1918 unfolded. Bill Thaw continued his dissertation. "The British have reported that this month the Germans have fielded the most menacing and capable fighting machine in history. The Fokker D VII has arrived in great numbers all along the front. The machine has the most powerful engine of any fighter in the world. It can climb rapidly while turning, and German fliers are beginning to rack up kills with the machine. Be careful, gentlemen. German aces are now everywhere in the air, and the Germans are throwing up groups of twenty to thirty machines at a time."

Bill continued with his briefing on the overall situation that faced them. "Hydrogen-filled airships have been made by Zeppelin. Built to deliver bombs to Allied rear-echelon lines of communication, the machine is now being used to attack London. So, if you see a large airship, attack it immediately. Zeppelin has also built large flying bombers. So keep your eyes open for those massive war machines. The Germans have built some of the largest cannons ever devised. Bombing distant places such as Paris, the guns have scared civilians more than hurt the Allied war effort. Just leave the big guns alone. Go after the flying weapons. Various gases are still being employed along the battlefields to maim and destroy men in all aspects of attack and defense. If you do not have any other targets during your mission, attack the source of the gases. That could stop the German use of the weapon for the moment."

To Jimmy it is as though the Germans have found new ways to maim more than kill. Gas is less effective than artillery bombardments in killing but can permanently injure soldiers over wide expanses of the battlefield.

The news of German successes in the war made Jimmy wonder if the Allied endeavor had a chance of a positive end. They made him wonder if the initiative of that senator from Wisconsin was actually doing something to contribute to the endeavor. *We need more than just Food for the Troops,* Jimmy thought. *We need more aerial assets if we are going to persevere.*

CHAPTER 18: THE COMBAT

Issoudun, France – May 15, 1918

Jimmy loved the Spad. This machine could *move*. He worked with it, training with greater determination than any of the other fliers in the newly activated 103rd Pursuit Squadron. He came to know the Spad and could take it to its greatest capabilities with sharp, deceptive turns and barrel rolls that looked like corkscrews to the other fliers.

But there was more to success in the air than having a fast machine and knowing how to operate it, Jimmy had learned. The most important attribute of a good flier was his ability to shoot. He had to take his adversary with the first few shots in an engagement. Only by accurate shooting could a flier down his opponent and survive to fly again. The flying machine had become a means of delivering weaponry to the aerial battlefield. And in Jimmy's hands the Spad became a weapon beyond the designer's greatest expectations.

Lieutenant Smitts was a highly regarded flier. The other members of the new American squadron were glad to fly with him. He was capable, and he was willing to do what needed to be done to protect his fellow fliers and kill the enemy.

Jimmy knew, though, that the pilot had to be careful in a Spad. The machine could easily lose flying control in tight turns. When he'd flown the Nieuport for the Lafayette Escadrille, he had sensed the torque of the engine as it rotated. In the Spad the torque dominated the control of the aeroplane. Its 220-horsepower Hispano Suiza engine was almost too much power for the machine. The engine torque pulled the aeroplane through a left barrel. To the right, the engine fought the roll and even a turn. One had to maintain speed through the turn in order to keep the machine from slipping. These characteristics of the Spad caused many aviators to lose their lives while trying to turn to their right on landing. Others fell from the sky in slow turns during combat.

The 103rd was still training with the new machines. Major Thaw knew from firsthand experience that the fliers needed to be at the peak of their performance. The Germans were well trained and capable of downing any Allied flier, he would tell the men. "Watch the clouds, watch out behind you, and watch out for the other fellows," Thaw would say.

* * * * *

The four Americans flew in a spread formation at 6,000 feet before separating. It was a tactic that Jimmy knew well. Captain Thenault had developed it with the Lafayette Escadrille. The pilots were on the hunt for observation machines and the Gotha and Zeppelin bombers that the Germans were throwing at the French trenches.

It was cold in the early morning. Jimmy was flying with two of his Escadrille buddies, Sergeant Dolan and Bobby Rockwell, Kiffin Rockwell's brother. A new flier, Sergeant Livingston Irving, was Jimmy's wingman. Jimmy had sensed that he would be asked to take the squadron's newcomers as his wingmen. Jimmy was just too good. He knew Major Thaw wouldn't waste the efforts of the experienced fliers by pairing them with him.

Jimmy had a comfortable, almost commanding, sense of his surroundings as he flew. He could see everyone in the formation around him while watching the broad expanses of the clear sky. The scene below him was amazing. The small hills poked up through the dense fog in the shallow valleys of the battlefield below him. The battlefields were eerily quiet as though the fog blanketed the dead ground below. His last view of the battlefield in 1917 was of a brown river of destruction in a sea of green foliage. Now, in the cold spring morning, the brown river of death was a dark shadow meandering through the French landscape below the fog. Infinite tracks in the ground to the east and west of the dark shadow told Jimmy of the massive efforts underway to supply the killing fields. But he had to concentrate on his command of the sky rather than the surroundings below.

Jimmy saw them first. He waved and moved his hand down and to the right signaling to Irving and Rockwell that the large observation machines were 2,000 feet below them. Jimmy led Irving to the right to increase their separation from Dolan and Rockwell. He headed straight toward the rear of the three German machines as they made their way to the trenches.

Irving was struggling to stay with Jimmy as he flipped over and toward the German machines. Jimmy opened with a stream of machine-gun bullets and tracers. As Jimmy pounded the German bomber, three arching tracers rose from the rear seat of the bombers. One machine was well out of range. Jimmy continued to fire as he kept his eyes on the other two machines.

Then Irving's engine started to smoke. Jimmy's inexperienced wingman had been hit. Both fliers exited the fight and started back toward the aerodrome. Jimmy knew that Irving forgot to jink his machine left and right as he attacked the Germans. He realized he would have to bring the younger fliers up from below the two-seat German observation and bombing machines in the future. The Germans had too much firepower and could easily take out an inexperienced flier.

Jimmy could tell that Irving's engine had been only partially hit. His machine was flying much slower than normal, but he would be able to make it back to the aerodrome. Jimmy yearned to return to the fight. He had plenty of ammunition and petrol. But he had to stay with Irving to make sure he returned safely to the aerodrome at La Noblette, where the squadron had moved.

Briefings, flying missions, debriefings, dinner, drinks, discussions, tactics, and sleep were the constant cycle of life of the pursuit fliers. Jimmy missed some of the opportunities that others had enjoyed in the air. He was still struggling to lead inexperienced fliers through the menacing skies over the trenches. Others in the new squadron had scored a couple of kills. Rockwell had taken down one of the Gothas they had attacked the week before, and Frank Hunter had made a kill on a German Pfalz. Jimmy seemed to linger on the three kills he had to his name. After all these missions, he had been successful in only a few.

Jimmy was never jealous of the other fliers. His youthful desire to simply rack up kills changed through Winifred's soothing guidance. He now desired to do all he could to help end the war. He wanted the best for each flier in the squadron, and his comrades could sense Jimmy's desire to help them. They knew they could rely on him to support them through each mission. Only through his support did Jimmy feel closer to his desire. Only through his support could he help end the war and move on to find his love *and* his destiny.

On his fifth mission with the 103rd, four German Albatroses attacked Jimmy. The action was swift and Jimmy had to use his best maneuvers to avoid being trapped. The enemy had come out of the clouds just above him. Jimmy saw them and turned into them sharply. The Germans realized that they were attacking an experienced pilot. The screaming Indian in full headdress on the sides of Jimmy's machine told them that they were up against an American that had considerable experience. The German leadership had told their fliers that the Americans were easy pickings. But the symbol told them otherwise.

This flier was no pushover. The four Germans were totally outmatched by Jimmy's maneuvers. He was able to hit two of the German flying machines as he rolled and turned around them. He could tell the Germans were trying hard to disengage from the fight. Jimmy was just too good. Each German, in turn, vacated the combat zone. Jimmy was low on petrol toward the end of the engagement and needed to return to the aerodrome. Otherwise he would have pursued the enemy.

As Jimmy returned, he couldn't help but think that the German machines must be extremely durable. He had scored many hits on his adversaries, but none of the machines had smoked or fallen under his fire. He would talk with the other fliers and see if they felt the same way. He remembered how Lufbery used to complain that the Germans must have a guardian angel. Lufbery would say he would pound the German flying machines with continuous fire, but they seemed to take the bullets like a prize fighter took jabs. To Lufbery it looked as if the bullets just bounced off of the German machines.

Late spring brought constant clouds and thunderstorms to the battlefields. The fliers had difficulty finding enemy machines to attack. The skies were rarely clear enough for anyone to fly. Throughout the spring the Germans tried a number of drives that were decimating French and British ground forces. The Battle of the Somme had started in early April. The Battles of Lys and the Aisne followed.

The German ground forces took full advantage of the bad weather, making advances when few Allied aeromachines could strafe and bomb. French and British trenches were pushed back in numerous areas of the front. The situation became desperate, and Marshal Pétain wanted more American units brought up to halt the German advances. He also demanded more support out of the fliers, French and American.

The weather cleared during the first week of June, and Jimmy was finally able to take off in search of the enemy. The squadron had left La Noblette in February and moved three times since then. The spring thaw and constant rains in central France caused havoc at the aerodromes. The fliers could barely find a dry field on which to land. Bray-Dunes had been a disaster. After only four days there, the fliers had moved to the slightly higher ground around Leffrinckoucke.

As a lone flier on patrol and after weeks of weather delays, Jimmy found what he was looking for. He approached from below and behind two German Zeppelin Staaken bombers. *Lord Almighty,* Jimmy thought. These dark forms are massive and cast huge shadows.

Aligned perfectly on the first bomber in his attack, Jimmy fired in front of the propeller of the engine that was mounted between the left upper and lower wings. His attack position kept him farthest from the rear gunner in the second German machine. That gunner had to avoid hitting his German partner while aiming at Jimmy. The position also kept the gunner of the first machine from being able to effectively open up on Jimmy.

The tactic worked. The engine of the rear Zeppelin flamed. As the bomber lost its left engine, the machine started rolling to its left. Jimmy cut hard right to avoid being shot at by the gunner in the doomed machine. He had just downed his fourth kill – with only twenty rounds. He hoped that the soldiers on the ground would confirm it. He would *like* to take one more kill, but he cared most that the Germans lost another one of their killing machines.

Jimmy heard the rattle of four German Spandau machine guns as he snapped to his right. He could see the tracers spanning across the sky from the twin machine guns of each of the two gunners. One gunner was in straight and level flight but was too far away to be a threat. The other was out of position as his machine turned and fell. He kept up a steady stream of fire as he plummeted toward death. The determination of this gunner differed considerably from the salute he received by another in 1917. The war sure has changed from an honorable endeavor to constant and determined killing.

Jimmy turned toward the second bomber. He slowed some and used the Spad's tendency to slip down and to the right as he continued his turn. The turning slide would bring him onto and below his target. He used the spin maneuver taught at the French flying school to get into an attack position. The German had already turned to his right toward the safety of friendly lines. As he started merging with the bomber, Jimmy saw four dark specks approaching the scene from above. Faced with four German fighters and the machine-gun fire of the gunner in the bomber, Jimmy withdrew.

He found a number of opportunities during June. The first was a lone flier in a Fokker F I. Jimmy's Spad easily outclassed the slower German machine. It went down in flames with only a few bursts from Jimmy's dual Vickers machine guns firing in tandem. Then Jimmy put bullets and tracers into the wings and fuselage of a German Halberstadt D. II fighter as his wingman watched in amazement. Sergeant Edgar Tobin was proud to fly as Jimmy's wingman on that mission and was impressed by what he saw Jimmy do to the German machine.

The Halberstadt looked much like the Albatroses that Jimmy had engaged many times before with the Escadrille. But the Halberstadt had a triangular vertical tail section, whereas the Albatros had a large rounded tail. More important, the Halberstadt was much slower. Knowing this, Jimmy conducted his attack simply and without alarm. The triangle flipped up suddenly. Another German spiraled to his death under Jimmy's expert marksmanship.

The German attacks on the French and Americans from March through May would later be called the Battles of the Three German Drives. The Three Drives would turn into a total of five throughout the summer of 1918. The Germans were determined to gain as much ground as they could. Only by gaining territory could the Germans possibly demand Allied capitulation. The Germans were working hard to end the war before the Americans started influencing the action.

It was plain to Jimmy that the Huns were pushing hard. Formations of six to eight German flying machines would head toward the front to strafe Allied defenses or support the bombers that were attacking the trenches. Everything the Germans flew seemed to be committed to hitting the trenches. German fliers would attack any Allied aeroplane, but their priority was to kill soldiers on the ground.

Marshal Pétain kept up his demands that the Allied fliers stop the German aerial bombardments. The German observation machines were being used to direct overwhelming concentrations of artillery fire. The aeromachines made in 1917 and 1918 had been adapted by the Germans to ground attack and were having devastating effects. Aerial and artillery attacks during the German Drives were pulverizing Allied men and materiel.

Jimmy flew constant missions with the others. The task was exhausting but invaluable. He had little time to try to find Giselle or even write to Winifred. He had to concentrate on flying. Only in this way could he finish his reckoning and get on to his destiny.

One day Jimmy caught one German flier completely by surprise. The Hun was evidently returning to his aerodrome from a strafing run. Jimmy had the setting sun to his advantage and ended the life of another German airman with one short burst. A Pfalz D. V and its pilot found the ground in a vertical spin under Jimmy's machine-gun fire.

Jimmy paid little attention to how many kills he had. The recent unconfirmed kills, plus the confirmed and unconfirmed kills he had with the Lafayette Escadrille, would put his total at around twelve or thirteen. He must have shot down seven or eight enemy fliers over the last three months alone, but only a total of four had been confirmed. The numbers didn't matter to him. He was on a mission of mercy, though. He wanted to stop the killing on the ground. The silk red scarf that Winifred had given him the Christmas before was with him whenever he flew. It was a warm reminder of the mercy she had shown the maimed soldiers at Fort McHenry.

The spring and early summer German offensives were quagmires of killing and devastation. From the air Jimmy witnessed wide, linear explosions as concentrated artillery fire impacted on both sides of No-Man's Land. He could see exploding shells of air burst technology kick up dirt and dust in huge circles on the battlefields. One shell could tear up a lot of ground. At times the dense, black smoke of the largest explosions came close to reaching him at flying altitude.

Jimmy wished that he could find the artillery pieces and end the misery in the trenches. *How the soldiers must be suffering!* he thought. Even if they weren't split by shrapnel spinning through the air around them, they would suffer concussions and hearing loss. But Jimmy couldn't think too much about the carnage below. He had to keep his eyes in the skies. He had to manage his machine and end the killing from the air. Many fliers said they refused to look at the ground at all. To watch the artillery concentrations from the air made them sick to their stomachs. Sicker still, the German artillery was launching air bursts at the Allied fliers at times. One flier reported he was at 10,000 feet when a black burst erupted near his machine.

Just after takeoff in early September, Jimmy saw three German flying machines circling above the Allied trenches. He didn't know whether the trenches were manned by French or American soldiers. All he could see was that the German machines were taking turns strafing the trenches.

Jimmy dove on the Germans. He opened fire on the closest

machine. The flier cut left as pieces of his machine littered No-Man's Land below him. Jimmy saw the middle flier turn right toward his own lines. He had an inside track on the Hun machine when it turned to the right. He slightly overshot the enemy as the German turned harder into Jimmy. But he knew he would ultimately make the turn onto the German's tail.

As Jimmy's enemy flew over the German trenches, he banked again to his right toward the south. Flying low behind enemy lines, Jimmy realized he had been lured into a trap. Inside their lines, the Germans had set up heavy antiaircraft machine guns. They were arrayed in line abreast from north to south and parallel to the trenches. Soldiers wearing dark gray uniforms and broad helmets were manning the guns. Jimmy saw them at close range.

The killing zone Jimmy was flying into had been well coordinated between the Flying Corps and Infantry Divisions of the Imperial German Army. He was caught low and in the middle of a line of gunners on his right *and* left. The right gunners were German infantrymen with rifles and machine guns in the trenches. The left gunners were heavy machine-gun squads trained to bring Allied fliers to the ground.

Jimmy jinked left and right as he tried to avoid the intersecting bullets and tracers that were arching up ahead of him. The gunners were firing at the tail of the German aeroplane as it passed, expecting their aim to miss the German to his rear and take Jimmy in a crossfire. Jimmy did what the Germans least expected. Instead of turning right toward friendly lines, he turned left. This forty-five degree move would put him farther away from the trench gunners. The angle of his departure from the killing zone caused him to fly over the heavy machine guns before the gun crews could readjust the direction of their fire.

Jimmy also knew he needed altitude. He brought the nose of his machine up to about eighteen degrees and slowed his machine to about ninety miles per hour, the angle and speed at which the Spad climbed most efficiently. He looked back to see the German antiaircraft gunners struggling to bring their burden onto Jimmy's flying direction. As he climbed, Jimmy had an eerie sensation that bullets were passing through his body from below. The sensation tingled all the way up his spine. He squirmed in his seat to rid himself of the feeling. He spurred his machine on and concentrated on his actions to rid himself of the feelings. *Come on, baby, get me higher— and fast!* he thought.

Looking about quickly, Jimmy saw eight enemy biplanes high and to the southeast. The three fliers Jimmy had attacked over the Allied trenches were merging low and to his right.

"Okay," Jimmy said out loud, "you have me in check!"

The Germans had him in a three-sided box. He could be killed by the gunners on both sides of the killing zone if he turned toward his own lines. He could be shot down by eight enemy machines above him to his front left if he continued to climb. He could also be engaged by the three fliers merging to his right.

His only safe exit was to the east, farther over enemy lines. Jimmy had no idea what was lurking for him in that direction. Whatever it was, it couldn't be friendly. If he turned toward that escape route, all eleven enemy aeroplanes would have a chance to close on his rear. No matter which way he turned, high, low, left, or right, he would be in trouble.

Jimmy kept climbing. He watched as the eight Germans above him and to his left front adjusted their direction of flight. They were aligning to intersect Jimmy at a point farther to the south. The three lower Germans were flying in parallel to Jimmy's direction. They would take him if he turned westward away from the eight and toward the safety of his lines.

As the game of aerial chess kept unfolding, Jimmy spurred his machine on. He adjusted his throttle to keep the engine screaming at its most efficient rpm and hauling him skyward. All eleven German fliers adjusted their points of intersection with Jimmy's machine. Then he figured out exactly what he had to do. He smiled, realizing that this was actually going be fun.

Jimmy suddenly spun his machine and turned upside-down in his climb. When he was suspended in his shoulder straps at 1,000 feet, he pulled on his stick and performed a tight inverted Immelman. The half-loop put the Spad in a screaming dive—in the opposite direction of all eleven of the enemy fliers. Pulling his throttle to conserve critical fuel, Jimmy performed a quick and very small double-turning maneuver in his dive. The left then right turns aligned Jimmy's machine right down the center of a line formed by the heavy German antiaircraft guns. His machine entered its final alignment with the Huns on the ground only 75 feet above them.

"Checkmate!" Jimmy yelled.

Jimmy watched as the German gunners scrambled from their defensive positions. They were feverishly trying to put their guns back into action. As the gunners scrambled around their guns, Jimmy opened up on them. The hail of bullets rained down on both men and materiel.

Jimmy didn't particularly like shooting at soldiers on the ground. But if this helped end the killing or saved many of his comrades in arms, he was all for it. He interrupted his attack only to rise up to avoid hitting the ground. Each time he rose, he stopped firing. Then he would quickly lower the nose of his machine and fire again. As he adjusted his machine and fired his Vickers in the quick seesawing flight path, he saw German soldiers spin, fall, and explode at the end of his line of tracers. The ground around the Germans kicked up in all directions. His bullets and tracers passed through or bounced into their marks. Dirt, bodies, and metal parts of machine guns flew everywhere. The scattering masses of men before him reminded him of the strafing run he made on the Germans with Didier Masson in 1917.

At the end of his run, Jimmy made a slow left turn toward his own lines. He wanted to turn slowly to maximize his air speed. He also wanted to increase the distance between himself and the enemy fliers who were determined to bring him down. Jimmy flew on with great satisfaction. He knew the German airmen were forced by his unexpected maneuver to watch as he destroyed their comrades on the ground. The reverse Immelman he had executed put all of the enemy fliers out of the fight.

Jimmy's machine screamed across No-Man's Land at 50 feet above the ground. He suddenly heard a pulsating rumble above him. He looked back and could tell he was safe from the German fliers. He just couldn't make out what was causing the noise above his head. It must be thunder from an early fall rain, he thought. As he looked forward, dark black explosions detonated on the ground directly in front of him. A German artillery barrage started pounding the area about the friendly lines he was fast approaching. Jimmy nosed up slightly to climb up and over the black mass of smoke as it rose above the exploding shells. The rumble he had heard was the noise from spinning artillery shells as they flew in ballistic trajectory toward their deadly end. He realized that he had flown *under* the artillery projectiles.

Big sky, little bullets, Jimmy thought. Only this time there were a lot of the little devils.

Just as he approached the Allied trenches, Jimmy flew directly through a wall of black smoke. He continued to rise as his aeroplane parted the smoke. He rolled over the top of his climb as he passed the first line of trenches. Upside-down, he looked up at the ground to see troops shouting and waving their arms in elation at what they had just witnessed. They were celebrating his success.

Jimmy could tell from the olive-drab uniforms and pith helmets that the soldiers in the trenches below him were Americans. He smiled and joined their celebration by pumping his fist as he continued to roll his machine over them.

CHAPTER 19: ARMISTICE

Vaulcouleurs, France - September 10, 1918

The room of fliers came to attention. Brigadier General Billy Mitchell had just entered the room. Major Thaw told the fliers that morning that the American Commander of the Air Service of General Pershing's American Expeditionary Force was going to tour the aerodrome. General Mitchell was on a tour of the various American Pursuit Squadrons of the Force. He wanted to speak with the American fliers. Apparently, Major Thaw said, the American forces were going to make a major push in the Allied center.

General Mitchell told the fliers they could take their seats. He was immaculately dressed in olive drab. His general's star on his shoulders shined as did the brass of his leather cross belt. He was confident and direct.

"Gentlemen, I applaud your escapades in the air. The missions you have flown since the weather cleared have helped the cause immensely. I am also very satisfied to tell you that General Pershing was successful in keeping the American Expeditionary Force as an independent American Army."

The men in the room rose to their feet and yelled and clapped in celebration. General Mitchell continued when the men had calmed down.

"The combined forces of the AEF will soon advance on a general front. We are preparing our artillery and supporting arms to engage the enemy as it has never been engaged before. General Pershing sent me here to give you his congratulations for a job well done so far. He asks that you give it your all as we confront this dastardly but very capable enemy."

The men broke up into groups to discuss the upcoming effort of the AEF. Every flier in the squadron was thrilled to be a part of this noble endeavor.

Jimmy was called to Major Thaw's office. He entered the room to see General Mitchell and another staff officer sitting on the sofa. General Mitchell stood and shook Jimmy's hand.

"Lieutenant Smitts, I bring General Pershing's sincere thanks and congratulations to you for your excellent and successful pursuit of the Hun in the air. Word has it from the front that you disrupted the enemy's attack upon our soldiers and took the aerial battle to the German lines. The All-American Division gives you its warmest regards for your courage and deep devotion to duty. Sir, you are heralded as one, among few, that deserve all the respect and honor of the AEF."

Jimmy didn't know what to say. He looked as professional as he could in front of one of the most well-known American military figures in the AEF. General Mitchell was one of the greatest advocates of American military aviation.

"Sir," Jimmy started. "It is my honor to be acquainted with you and to receive such esteemed words of respect from my comrades. I mean only to do my duty and the small part I can play in ending this terrible conflict against man and nature."

General Mitchell told Major Thaw and Jimmy that he was going to put Jimmy in for an award. General Mitchell said he looked forward to hearing about Jimmy's future successes in the air and in this endeavors for international peace and prosperity. He said he hoped to have the honor of Jimmy's presence again sometime.

With that, General Mitchell and his entourage of staff officers and enlisted men left. Jimmy knew there was a cloud of doom in the air. The massive formations of soldiers were already gathering, and they would soon move toward the killing fields. The real action was just about to begin. Jimmy only hoped that the Great War would end and it would *really* be "The War to End All Wars," as people had declared.

Word made its way to the squadron that the American forces had started an advance and were pushed back by the Germans. The fliers heard rumors that American soldiers had come under devastating artillery fire and massed machine guns but held their own in around

Belleau Wood. Was this a foretelling of events to come? Would the newly formed American Army merely hold its own and not defeat the Hun? Jimmy and the other fliers wondered how the upcoming push would turn out.

August 1918 had not gone well. The Fokker D VIIs were taking their toll on Allied fliers. August became the most devastating month in aerial-combat history and made Jimmy continue to wonder. He also wondered what it meant for him and his flying comrades in the air. The Fokker D VII alone accounted for 565 victories against Allied fliers in just three months of operation. The facts were ominous.

American soldiers were taking punishment in the trenches in the French center. The British were being pushed back along the Aisne-Marne area and along the Amiens River. The only telling message that Jimmy noticed was it was harder to find enemy aeroplanes to attack over the south-central portions of the front. Apparently most of the Fokker D VIIs were flying in the British and French sectors to the north.

The U.S. Marines and soldiers of the 1st Division gave the Germans a thrashing at Château-Thierry. That was the deepest penetration of the German spearhead in the final assault by the Huns in the Great War. In the middle of August, it sounded as if the French and British were starting to keep a foothold against the Germans. The Germans were struggling to mass enough forces to continue an effective frontal assault.

Then orders came down to the aerodrome. Major Thaw called all fliers to the main briefing room to make an announcement.

"Gentlemen, the American attack on the German defenses that General Mitchell talked about is soon to happen. And, gentlemen, the aerial assets of the American Flying Corps are going to take on an effort of massive proportions."

General Mitchell had organized an aerial assault of almost 1,500 Allied machines. Wave after wave of bombers and fighters were going to attack the Saint Mihiel Salient. The strong German defensive position would be decimated by the aerial assault, Major Thaw declared.

Jimmy couldn't believe what he was hearing. Flying machines were going to be a major influence in a land battle for the first time in history. And he was going to be part of it.

"In preparation of the upcoming aerial attack, the 103rd, 94th, and other American pursuit squadrons have been tasked to clear the skies over Saint Mihiel."

Major Thaw told everyone that the squadron would take to the skies in groups of four and fly continuous missions over the battlefield. The fliers were not to strafe the enemy on the ground. Enemy ground forces were to be left to the artillery and aerial bombing. The mission of the squadron was to clear the skies of enemy aeroplanes by any means.

The flying activities of the last week in August through the first week of September had been exhausting. The machines and the pilots were pushed to fly almost continuously. As one landed, the flier's Spad was turned over to another with only an hour between flights. The mechanics couldn't stop working. Lights in the hangars at night kept the service and maintenance on the machines an around-the-clock effort. Everyone throughout the squadron was exhausted.

Jimmy took off on his second mission of the day. There really wasn't much activity over the Salient. Enemy fliers seemed to avoid the area altogether for some reason. At least the Allied fliers were keeping the enemy away "by all means," he thought.

As he approached the battlefield, Jimmy could see that the Germans had a number of older Albatros machines in the air. They were in the distance and keeping it that way. He had seen the cigar-shaped fuselage and swept-back wingtips of the German Albatros so many times, Jimmy thought he could make them out even if they were flying in China. Apparently the Germans were flying high behind their lines to try to see what was going on within the Allied lines. The Germans wanted to know if the Americans were up to something.

Jimmy started planning his attack. There were at least four Albatros machines in the air. They had probably been modified for observation use with two seats. Even so, the machines could be very dangerous. The aerial observers also served as rear gunners. Jimmy knew the German rear gunners had gotten very good at their trade in the last six months, and they were firing dual Spandau machine guns.

As he planned his attack, Jimmy remembered that Hoskier and Lufbery of his beloved Lafayette Escadrille had both been shot down by back-seat observers. Hoskier was the first to die at the hands of a rear gunner just after Jimmy had joined the squadron. Then there was the loss of the legionary Lufbery.

Jimmy decided to attack the Germans from high above them. The German gunners had a hard time aiming vertically. Also, he had the advantage of the mid-afternoon sun. By coming in from above and in front, Jimmy might have a chance of taking two Hun aeroplanes in the same pass. Jimmy continued to climb. He wanted to come in from as high as he could. That way he could set up the alignment of his guns and sweep his bullets and tracers across the German machines.

It was not to be. One of the observers must have seen Jimmy approaching. The lead Albatros turned and dove toward the east. The other three followed the first. Jimmy could tell they had no stomachs for a fight. *Lord, gentlemen,* Jimmy thought. *There are four of you and only one of me.* He then turned toward the aerodrome. He had to get some rest.

Two days later Jimmy could not believe the massive formations that were entering the airspace above and before the Saint Mihiel Salient. He was flying a screening mission with eight others from the squadron. *American aviation sure has come to new heights of technology and mission control,* he thought. *Here we are, screening massive formations of Allied bombers stacked one on top of the other.* Jimmy could clearly see the entire array of aeroplanes. They seemed to be following each other, stacked well to the rear of the Allied lines in successive advancing waves of coordinated death and destruction.

The sight was breathtaking. There were lines upon lines of large Caudrons, Handleys, and Breguets. The sun's rays played through the clouds and made the magnificent colors of the different aeroplanes glow across the sky. Dark green, light green, tan, and brown camouflage colors danced in the light – high above the ground.

Different concentric circles of red, blue, and white, the insignias of the various Allied nations in the aerial assault shined brilliantly in the camouflage.

The colors just kept coming.

In the distance Jimmy could see formations of the new Vickers Vimy bombers as well. The various squadrons of bombers were stacked in successive lines, one behind the other and far behind friendly lines waiting for their turn in the Salient. It was as though the sky was packed tightly with floating figures, their arms extended claiming their aerial space.

There is no way any army or nation can withstand a massive bombing attack like this, Jimmy thought. *The Germans are about to experience devastation beyond human endurance.* The upcoming bombing, Jimmy thought, was going to end this war. The threat of aerial bombardment might even end the practice of war itself.

Jimmy had to keep a diligent watch. He had to make sure the bombers were not attacked by German fliers. He had to protect himself and his comrades. The German aces were still out there, and they might prefer to take on single Allied fliers rather than the massed machine-gun fire from the tight formations of bombers. The Caudrons and Vickers Vimys had two gunners, and there were so many of them that they appeared to be flying wingtip to wingtip. Each gunner controlled the fire of two Vickers machine guns in tandem. Jimmy could see how a mass of Allied bombers could send out a formidable spray of lead and tracers at an oncoming enemy.

Nothing happened. Not one German aviator attempted to stop the oncoming masses of Allied bombers. The Germans seemed to be willing to just sit back and take the onslaught. Had the Hun devised a new way to absorb such punishment? Jimmy wondered. Did they just want to take it and keep their fliers safe behind their lines? Jimmy thought it was suicide not to do *something* to stop the bombardment that was about to be delivered. There is no way the Germans soldiers should be left unprotected in their trenches.

Jimmy watched as wave after wave of aeroplanes dropped their bombs. The trenches were covered with black, brown and grey smoke.

Lines of bombers turned ever so slowly into then out of their attack. The entire mass of aerial machines seemed to turn in unison over the battlefield like a horizontal wheel of death. *Lord, have mercy on the German soldiers, the men in those trenches,* Jimmy prayed. His determination to end the killing suppressed his compassion for the Germans as men but with limitations.

Jimmy and his group had to return to the aerodrome. The bombing took so long the fliers were running out of petrol. They returned without any chance of engaging enemy aerial machines. The bombing campaign of September 12th was the start of the American advance through Saint Mihiel. The doughboys would soon go over the top, Jimmy knew.

* * * * *

Argonne Forest, France – October 7, 1918

The whistle blew. Captain Sandhurst yelled a yell that Sergeant Witherspoon didn't want to hear. He knew the command would send shivers down the spines of his men. They had been pounded by enemy artillery shells, shot at by snipers, bombed by German aerial machines, and pushed to their utmost limits. But this advance could be worth it all. *One more push,* Sergeant Witherspoon thought, *just one more push.*

"Over the top, men!" yelled the captain. "Follow me!"

First Sergeant Witherspoon had just returned to the company after his meeting with the artillery projectile at Saint Mihiel. He was still in bad shape but able to run and carry a sidearm. His left side hurt so much he could not lift a rifle. So he carried the newly issued M1911, 45 caliber semiautomatic pistol. Captain Sandhurst "procured" one from regimental headquarters so his company First Sergeant could contribute to the cause.

Witherspoon had left the hospital long before the doctor wanted to release him. He heard his regiment was going back into the line. The Allied "Grand Offensive" had been going on for ten days, and things were not progressing well. The 82nd Division was called up from its assembly area at Varennes-en-Argonne to fill a large gap between the 1st and 28th American divisions in their assault on Montfaucon.

Sergeant Witherspoon knew the attack across open terrain up the Meuse River and to the front of the Lorraine Forest was going to be another bloodbath. He vividly remembered how the Germans had put down withering machine-gun fire against his regiment during its attack on Saint Mihiel.

"Sergeant Witherspoon," Captain Sandhurst said as they advanced toward their objective, "I believe the artillery bombardment put the German defenses in very poor condition. I cannot imagine any soldier withstanding the bombing and still being able to fight."

"Sir, we've withstood one hell of a pounding many times before. The Germans were able to sustain their fire on us after that massive aerial bombardment at Saint Mihiel last month. It seems to me that the Germans will be ready for us again. I hope you're right. But I know the kind of punishment men can take. I think we need to be ready for the worst. After all, we still have to cross that open ground and deal with those obstacles."

The company followed as closely to the rolling artillery barrage as it could. The line of explosions was about 200 yards in front of the men. It was the second and last pounding the German gunners would have to endure before the company attacked the trenches.

Suddenly the German artillery opened on the division. The men of Chester Company watched as explosions rained down on their sister company to the south. Each soldier in the company knew that it was just a matter of minutes, possibly seconds, before the rain of steel would descend on them.

"Incoming!" yelled one of the platoon sergeants. The men hit the dirt and fell into the bomb craters that were everywhere. The tingling in Sergeant Witherspoon's left side reminded him of how close to death he had been in a German artillery attack like this before.

The company continued up the hills after the artillery explosions ended. Everyone knew the only way home was through the Argonne Forest. After years of trench stalemate, the war now became a land battle of fire and maneuver.

They passed Fleville to La Forge and Cornay along the Aire River and left wounded and dying friends on the fields behind them. Sergeant Witherspoon continuously worked his craft as he led men under fire and kept supplies advancing with their attacks. The unit found German units everywhere. Some put up heavy resistance. Others capitulated after only a few short bursts of fire from the All-Americans. This was a fluid, moving combat that Witherspoon and his men had not experienced in the trench warfare to this point. To some it brought its own dangers as one did not know the enemy's intentions. The pressure from all angles and in all ways constantly affected the men and brought many to uncontrollable shaking and tears.

They struggled up and down the rolling hills at the western foot of the Vosges Mountains. As they reached the area around Saint Juvin, Sergeant Witherspoon knew his men could not take much more of the advance. He and Captain Sandhurst struggled with another challenge. The company was given fillers of inexperienced soldiers from other divisions so that it could replace the wounded and dead and continue to press the attack toward Ravin aux Henris. Witherspoon constantly worked on his junior leaders to try to keep the fresh young soldiers alive.

Finally, on November 10th of 1918, Sergeant Witherspoon and the few soldiers who remained with him since he joined the regiment sat down to a hot meal at Bourmont. The war ended the next day as Sergeant Witherspoon and Captain Sandhurst took stock of what they had been through. It was a welcome relief. But in reflection, it was anticlimactic. They had endured things no man should have to endure. They had worked hard as an effective team under life-threatening circumstances to kill the enemy. But now there was only silence. Sergeant Witherspoon talked with many of his soldiers to keep their focus on the future as they sat back and shivered from their combat experiences. He too became lost in a depressing mood at times as though he were in a fog. He understood how the combat had changed him and everyone he touched.

"Captain, it's been a pleasure for me to have served under you. The men—what is left of them—know that you kept them alive. You were an inspiration to us all."

"First Sergeant, I believe you and I and some of our sergeants should be extremely proud. We have the distinction of being the few to serve the longest in combat in the U.S. Army in this war. We started this in the 1st Division in May of 1917 and have made it through terrible atrocities. I first learned about war in my classes at West Point. But nothing prepared me for what we've been through together. I hope this war will end it all. I can't fathom another go at something like this."

* * * * *

Foucaucourt, France – November 11, 1918

Jimmy had few chances at aerial combat in October and early November. Word spread that the Germans were suing for peace. His aerial-combat experience ended officially when the Armistice was signed at 11 a.m. on the 11th of November, 1918. "The Eleventh Hour of the Eleventh Day of the Eleventh Month," the newspapers had written. *What poetry*, Jimmy thought. To turn the misery of this war into poetry seemed downright cruel.

He was satisfied that he had helped end the carnage and he had survived. The unknown future was to him somewhat scary. He worked one day at a time to get through the boredom of the beginnings of occupation duty. Jimmy was exhausted. He had lost ten pounds over the last six months. He had been overtaxed but was in very good shape. They were now going on a mission that he knew he would thoroughly enjoy.

The entire squadron was flying at 5,000 feet and following the Moselle River to the northeast for extended demobilization and occupation duty on the German soil for the first time. The clear skies of winter over the river valleys and the remnants of snow on the hills along the rivers made for spectacular views. Jimmy saw from above the beauty of the Moselle and Rhine River valleys and their rows and rows of vineyards along hillsides. He passed over the numerous German castles along the Rhine and approached Ehrenbreitstein, the stone fortress high above the Rhine River in Coblenz. Jimmy would shortly land on the plateau next to the fortress in the land of his grandparents' heritage, Rhineland-Phalz. As he relaxed in flight, he reflected on what he had accomplished and thought about Winifred and Giselle. *Please Lord,* he prayed, *be gracious and give me strength to look for Giselle. Help me find her.*

He knew the demilitarization was going to be a massive undertaking. The squadron had a lot of work to do. It also had to wait for millions of American soldiers and millions of dollars in materiel to be returned to the homeland. It had been almost four years since Jimmy had seen home. Perhaps during the lull and before his return to the U.S., he could search for and be with Giselle. Hopefully they would let him take her back to Wausau with him. Wausau was a quiet town surrounded by plains and rolling hills that were similar to those around Charmes. Perhaps Giselle would feel at home in his hometown.

He interrupted his thoughts to concentrate as he came into final approach on the plateau of Ehrenbreitstein.

* * * * *

He braced himself against the cold winter wind that constantly swept up the Rhine and over the fortress. Jimmy enjoyed looking down at the Moselle and Rhine Rivers as they merged and continued their course to the North Sea. *I never thought I would actually see the Deutches Ecke that Oma talked so often about,* Jimmy thought. *The view of the two river valleys and their wineries is breathtaking. I wish Giselle could be here to warm me and see this amazing sight. I hope the Army will give me a machine to go search for my love. After all, we have demobilized a good bit of—what did Voss call it?—the Flying Service of the Imperial German Army.*

An orderly approached him. "Lieutenant Smitts?"

"Yes," Jimmy said as he turned.

"I have a telegram that has come for you."

The orderly saluted and turned back to the warmth of the squadron headquarters building after Jimmy accepted the telegram. The short but direct words brought home to reality. The Western Union telegram said, MOTHER ILL. STOP. COME HOME. STOP. Thelma Smitts, Jimmy's beloved and supportive mother, was in very poor health.

Jimmy tried but failed to get a flying machine of some kind to travel to the south in search of Giselle. The Army was kind enough to give him orders for an early return to America to be with his mother. After all, Major Thaw had said, it's the least the Army could do for such a dedicated and devoted soldier.

Right, Jimmy thought. *It was the least the Army could do, but it didn't seem fitting to issue me a machine to look for Giselle.* The U.S. needed to organize the return of its war-fighting materiel, he had been told. The logisticians had no time to rearrange their planning so one soldier could fly around the south of France in the name of romance.

Jimmy was torn between searching for Giselle and going to his mother's side. As painful as it was, there was no question about what he had to do. He had to go to Mother. She gave him his life. She was his inspiration. She raised and supported him in everything he wished to do. Jimmy had to go help his mother in her time of need. *Please keep her safe until I get home,* Jimmy prayed. *And please keep my Giselle safe and secure until I return.*

* * * * *

Through Brest, Jimmy started another ugly jaunt across the North Atlantic Ocean. He was headed to New York City. The ship would not moor at Ellis Island like his grandfather's ship had done in 1873. But he would see the city Opa Smitts had passed through. Via New York, Jimmy would also be closest to the most direct trip to Wisconsin that the Army could offer him.

There were masses of people everywhere. People massed in the streets. Soldiers massed in the ships and shipyards. Hotels were swollen with returning servicemen. Hospitals were swollen with wounded and dying heroes. The only thing that was hard to get was a good meal. There were so many people in New York City, including newly arrived soldiers, that good food was scarce. But everyone was happy. Everyone was celebrating no matter where Jimmy turned.

Celebrating was the last thing Jimmy had on his mind. With this trip he was losing the love of his life in France. And he was headed toward losing one of the three women in his life he had ever really cherished.

CHAPTER 20: THE FLIER

Wausau, Wisconsin, U.S.A. - December 1, 1918

Jimmy already felt lost without the love of Giselle. But now he lost his understanding of life itself. The vision of the family friends carrying his mother's coffin over the crackling ice and snow in the cold Wisconsin breeze to the gravesite and finally lowering it kept coming back to him. Yes, he had to accept the fact that his mother had died. *But why?* Jimmy constantly asked himself. *Why would a gracious God end the life of such an amazing woman?* She was so caring, supportive, and inspirational. Maybe God didn't end the life of his mother any more than He had called for death and destruction on the killing fields of Europe. Death was the normal course of human existence. Life and death were God's gifts, he had been told. God giveth and God taketh away.

"Son, I know you're distraught," his father told him. "You're away from the French girl. You're away from the woman in Baltimore. And Thelma has passed. But you need to get your life in order. You keep talking about some kind of destiny. Go find it, son. Don't sit here and brood. I don't know what this destiny thing is you speak of. But whatever it is, I can tell it is not here in Wausau."

Jimmy struggled with the answer. He tried often to write to Winifred but couldn't start even the first sentence. Their conversations were so fluid and open when they were together. But now he seemed lost in his words as he was lost in his life. After months of sitting and wondering, with mad reflection, about the war and the death of his mother, Jimmy realized that he hadn't lost the answer. He had lost his life's direction, what Winifred called his pathway. Winifred had once told him to go to his destiny. Winifred, like his mother, possessed strength, courage and the spirit of life. Without Giselle, perhaps he should go to Winifred and see if they could build a life together.

"Father, you're right. I really don't have much going for me here in Wausau. I'm not a farmer. I'm not a businessman. I'm not a merchant. I'm a flier. I need to fly."

James Earl Smitts looked at his namesake with the hint of sadness and said, "Jimmy, I purchased this one-way train ticket from Wausau to Baltimore last month for your Christmas present. Go fly. Fly to this Winifred you speak so highly of. I can easily tell, your destiny is in Baltimore. I want you to be free to pursue you life's dreams. I don't want to keep you here and away from your future."

Jimmy looked down at the ticket in his father's weathered hand. He felt many emotions swirling around him as he reached for it. The death and destruction of the war, the death of some of his comrades, the death of his mother, the death of his dream of being with Giselle, and the possible death of even his destiny all came suddenly to him like the snowstorms over the plains of Wisconsin. The feeling was cold and lonely. He knew the only way he would feel warmth and salvation from that cold was to travel to Baltimore.

"I've got some money saved from my service with the 103rd. I should have enough to live on for a month or two without a job. If I get a job, I'll settle on an apartment and look for Winifred."

"Send me a telegram, son, and let me know you're safe," his father said. "Let me know if you find her and where you end up settling down."

The train trip was grueling. It was slow and stopped every twenty to thirty minutes at various small towns between Wausau and Cincinnati, Ohio. It was like they had nothing else to do but allow individuals to mount and dismount the bucking cars. The train was loud and uncomfortable. When it left Cincinnati, the train was packed. *Where was everyone going?* he wondered. *The war was over. Wasn't everyone settling down to normal life?*

* * * * *

Baltimore was crazier than Jimmy remembered. There were people everywhere. Many of the soldiers had returned through Baltimore. Thousands decided to stay in the city. Everyone was fighting for a job. Many of the soldiers tried their hands at the dockyards near Dundalk, just southeast of the city. They had to compete, sometimes to the point of fighting, to get steady work. Some men turned to the hot molten world of the Bethlehem steel mill.

Baltimore was becoming a rough town, a place for the hardy. Soldiers and sailors fought for work as longshoremen. Some found jobs on the oyster skipjacks, the wooden boats with the single swept-back mast that sailed the Chesapeake Bay, and others shucked the oysters as they were hauled onto the docks. Many men joined public-works projects. But few men in Baltimore could *fly*.

Jimmy *had* to fly. But he had no idea how to get a job as a flier. The Army certainly wasn't hiring. He'd read in the newspapers about how Congress was dramatically reducing military services, including the aviation units.

Jimmy then heard that some companies were looking for fliers. An aerial circus had been formed. He could fly in aerobatic shows, Jimmy thought. The Postal Service seemed to be interested in fliers to move important and time-sensitive mail. Some aeromachine companies needed fliers to test new technologies. The only problem was that there weren't many flying companies in Baltimore.

Bracing against the cold winter wind off of the Patapsco River, Jimmy came upon a seafood distribution center called Aaron Straus Fish and the acquaintance of Mr. Aaron Straus III. Mr. Straus was the third generation of owners of his family's distribution center and needed materials to get to New York, Philadelphia, Washington, and Richmond quickly. The bulk of Straus' business was delivering fresh fish to seafood restaurants and markets throughout Baltimore. His biggest market was on Thames Street in Fells Point.

"Jimmy," Mr. Straus said, "I can vastly expand my business if I can get fresh oysters to the seafood markets in other cities along the East Coast. Fish can last on ice traveling by train. But oysters will spoil on the slow train trips to distant cities. They're a delicacy to the rich. I can sell a bundle of them if I can get them to the other markets on time."

"Well, I'm your man, Mr. Straus."

"Unfortunately I already have another flier in mind for the work. Right now I only need one flier. But keep in touch, son. If things go as planned, I'll need more fliers."

Jimmy searched for work for two weeks. He also searched for Winifred with more determination than he had looking for work. Jimmy was down on his luck. He was also down on his cash. He knew he needed to find work soon. He needed Winifred.

Jimmy took the trolley to Mr. Straus' booth at the seafood market. *I don't want Mr. Straus to think I'm desperate, but I'm desperate. I hope his business picked up and he needed another flier.*

"Well, well, what have we here? Haven't seen you for a while, Mr. Smitts. Come to buy some rockfish?" Mr. Straus asked as Jimmy walked up to him at the market.

"Good afternoon, Mr. Straus. I was just wondering if your business picked up and you needed another flier."

Mr. Straus continued to arrange fish in the ice bed of an open-air display. He put his hands on the wood frame of the display and looked up at Jimmy. Jimmy thought he had a sad look on his face.

Mr. Straus spoke solemnly. "Well, my boy, my seafood flier was killed in a crash on landing just two days ago. The flier had to land in bad weather and hit some treetops as he came in too low. As long as that doesn't scare you, you have yourself some employment. I do need a flier."

"Mr. Straus, I am very sorry to hear that. But I saw a lot of fliers lose their lives in the war. It doesn't scare me. I *am* your man." Jimmy finally had a flying job.

Moving oysters was a miserable experience. The oysters smelled. The boxes they were packed in leaked constantly, and they barely fit behind the seat of the de Havilland biplane Mr. Straus had purchased.

"This isn't working out so well," Jimmy thought. "The oyster season is going to end at the beginning of March. I have to find other work for myself."

Jimmy spoke with four major banks seeking work as a courier. None of them wanted anything to do with fliers. Aeromachines were just too risky to use in trying to get orders and paperwork to the banks in New York. Why would anyone risk losing business to a machine that fell out of the sky? he was asked.

Continuing his quest for funds in the cold winter in Baltimore, Jimmy approached the National Bank of Baltimore. Jimmy was sure this was going to be another rejection.

The bank manager sat behind his oak desk looking solemnly at Jimmy. He reluctantly said he would call the president of the bank, "given this is a business matter," he said. Jimmy scanned the twenty-foot-high colored-plaster molded ceiling as the manager spoke on the intercom to a Mr. Welsh. The manager finally escorted Jimmy into a large conference room where he found a man sitting at the head of the table. The man stood, shook Jimmy's hand, and got right down to business.

"Well, well, Mr. Smitts," Welsh said, "I'm very pleased to meet you. I've heard about you already. It seems like you've approached just about every banker at my club. I will tell you, I've given this a lot of thought since I heard of your attempts to get my friends to support you."

"Mr. Welsh, I assure you, I can get your bank documents to New York faster than any other means. It's one thing to send information by telegram. But nothing is as solid as a signed contract in the hands of the New York bankers."

"Well, sir, I have been thinking of using aeromachines to move my important business notes. If this works out as you say it will, I can hire you out as a flier to the other banks in Baltimore. I've heard the U.S. Postal Service is working on flying mail between cities. They plan to call it Airmail. The postmaster said it has great potential. Perhaps I can hire you out to the Postal Service in Baltimore as well."

"Mr. Welsh, the only problem I have is I need an aeroplane."

"You mean you have been propositioning my friends without a means of getting your promises fulfilled? Bully there, sir."

"I thought if I had a loan, I could pay off the loan as I flew."

"A loan, you say? I'm in the banking business, Mr. Smitts, and that is music to my ears. I'll give you a loan. But you need to tell me your plan and how you are going to get your hands on a worthy machine. You also need to find a suitable place to take off and land this worthy 'contraption,' as they call it."

"Mr. Welsh, I know aeromachines are flooding the market. But high-quality machines are not so easy to find. The European powers and the United States Flying Service destroyed many good flying machines at the end of the war. I would like to get my hands on the Fokker D. VII due to its sturdy construction and powerful engine. But the Allies destroyed that very capable war machine to keep the Germans from recovering and using it to their advantage."

"You must know that I do have concerns, sir. Few people understand the machines. They refer to them as little more than flimsy, canvas-covered toothpicks."

"Word has it, Mr. Welsh that the Army is going to sell surplus aeroplanes at auction in Long Island. I assure you, I will find a very capable machine and be in business in no time."

Mr. Welsh made his decision, stood, and shook Jimmy's hand. "I give you my blessing, son. The manager will disperse the funds in a new account for you. You can use some of the bank's cash to buy yourself a *one-way* train ticket, mind you, to Long Island, New York. Congratulations, you are on your way to a flying business."

He was off to take his chances at buying a surplus flying machine.

After convincing Mr. Welsh to back him, Jimmy searched for a landing field where he could conduct his business. He approached many of the local farmers. Mr. Straus suggested that he contact Mr. Rutherford, a farmer who provided considerable produce to the Thames Street Market. His farm was located in Windsor Mill just a short trolley ride outside of Baltimore. A middle-aged man with a lot of farmland, Mr. Rutherford was keen to Jimmy's idea. He had some fields in fallow and was more than interested in allowing a flier to use them. "I'll tell you what there, young man," Mr. Rutherford said, "I may be a farmer, but I'm a *contemporary* man. I think it'll be fun to have a flying service in my unused fields." Jimmy was soon on his way to his new flying business.

* * * * *

The surplus flying machines in front of Jimmy were the worst lot of canvas and wood he had seen in a long time. He wasn't sure whether any of them even had functional engines. There were ten Curtiss Jennies. Jimmy knew the Jenny inside and out. The examples before him were far from being reliable aeroplanes, he knew. *I might be daring,* Jimmy said to himself, *but even I wouldn't fly these crates.* Two other machines caught his eye. One was a Sopwith Pub. The Pub was small and slow. He wasn't sure if this bag of bones would get off the ground with even a small bag of papers behind the flier's seat, he thought.

Then he saw it. It was a Royal Aircraft Factory S.E. 5. The S.E. 5 served the Brits extremely well during the war, he remembered. The machine he was looking at had to have been a training machine at one time. It had been modified from the single-seat pursuit plane to a two-seat trainer or observation machine. Now it was stripped to its bones.

Jimmy put a bid on the aeroplane and became the proud owner of an S.E. 5. It looked as if it would never get off the ground. Thank goodness the buyers at the auction had never heard of the Wolseley Motor Company engine and were afraid of the machine. He bought it for a song.

"So, mate, you're the owner of this bag of bones, eh? I'll tell you, this machine you've purchased is a wonderful phenomenon of flying excellence. Have you ever flown before?"

"I'm sorry, sir, what was your name?"

"Phin, sir. Scot Phin. You can call me Scotty."

"That's quite an accent you have, Mr. Scotty. Where are you from?"

"I'm a Canuck from Toronto. Canadian, that is."

"Oh, and you have experience with S.E 5 flying machines, Mr. Canuck?"

"Sir, I am the best engine mechanic on the face of this planet. I can whip that Wolseley into shape in no time. And, I beg your pardon, sir, this machine is actually an S.E. 5 - *A*. That engine is a 200-horsepower Wolsely Viper. It's a high-compression, direct-drive motor and the best aeroplane engine in the world."

Two weeks later, after many hours of rebuilding the engine, Jimmy and his newfound engine mechanic were on their way to Baltimore. "Bring on the commissions," Jimmy said to himself. "This Canuck and I will take you on. The Smitts flying company is on its way. I was a pursuit flier, Jimmy reminisced as he flew south. How about if I call it the Pursuit Aero Company? 'We'll Pursue Your Packages as You Pursue Your Future.'"

The jingle sounded pretty good to Jimmy.

The S.E. 5A was a very capable and strong flying machine. Jimmy learned that the machine and the engine he bought lived up to their reputations as dominant factors in the air over Belgium and northern France. He was very happy with his purchase and looked forward to many years of reliable and safe flying.

Jimmy's flights for Mr. Welsh blossomed into other commissions. He started building up a reputation as a reliable asset that businesses could count on. Scotty saw to the reliability of the engine. Jimmy saw to the reliability of the company. Jimmy's honesty and integrity put him in high esteem among some businessmen. The U.S. Postmaster in Baltimore was interested in using his services. The Postal Service was putting together its own flying service. But the Postmaster said he would use Jimmy for a while until organized Airmail service was operational.

Between flying and promoting his business, Jimmy searched for Winifred. She had been transferred out of the U.S. Army Nurse Corps before Jimmy returned to Baltimore. He couldn't find her anywhere. The constant attention he had to pay to putting his business together kept at bay his disappointment in not finding Winifred. But he was committed to continuing his search whenever he could make time to do it.

Jimmy had found the perfect location for his business in a field Mr. Rutherford had in fallow. Nearby was a rundown shed that Jimmy could use as an office and hangar. With his newfound enterprise, he rented an apartment on Hanover Street in Baltimore. The location was central to Jimmy's business clients, who were near the Baltimore Harbor. He could pick up packages and take them to the field by trolley very easily.

Jimmy and Scotty were working in the shed at the field, Jimmy on paperwork for Mr. Welsh and Scotty on the Wolsely, as they called the machine's engine. They both looked up as the wind whipped into the shed when the door creaked open.

"Mr. Smitts? My name is Vernon Stevens. I've organized a flying circus. You may have heard of it. It's called The Amazing Pursuit. It's about American fliers in the war that dominate the skies over Germany."

Jimmy and Scotty looked at each other skeptically. Scotty wiped his hands as Jimmy looked over at the intruder. "I'm sorry, Mr. Stevens, I have not heard of your circus."

"*I* have heard a lot about your flying business. I also heard rumors that you may have flown in the war. If you aren't afraid of performing aerial stunts on the side, I'd like to talk to you about flying for me."

"I'd be willing to fly in some shows. But my flying business is most important. I can't lose business because of the circus."

"No, no, of course not. I would never think to harm your business. Our circus shows are only on the weekends. We fly from a field on the east side of Baltimore, near Essex. The show is starting to attract quite a following."

"I'll come by and see what you have. What do you have in mind for me to do?"

"Well, I need an experienced pilot to fly a Jenny painted red to look like a German Albatros. The flier I need will be the German, the villain. The villain is called 'Hanz the Hun' and is always shot down by 'Al the All-American,' the greatest American fighter in the skies over Germany. Do you know the Jenny, Mr. Smitts?"

"Sir, I grew up flying a Jenny and I know them like the back of my hand. I think it will be very interesting and I'd love to give it a try."

They shook hands and Mr. Stevens started to leave. "Oh, Mr.

Stevens," Jimmy interrupted. "The aerial war in Europe wasn't fought over the skies of Germany. It was fought over the skies of France."

"Right, right. Well, the circus is just that, sir. It's a circus. I don't want to have to change the story line right now. People seem to like it as it is." Jimmy didn't bother to tell his visitor that he was used to shooting Albatroses down rather than flying something made to look like them only to be shot down. And Jimmy knew *he* was the greatest fighter in the skies over France.

Scotty looked at Jimmy with a raised right brow. "Mate, how are you to look for this lovely lady you speak of *and* be Hanz the Hun on the weekends?"

"Scotty, I've found neither hide nor hair of Winifred. If she's here, I'll find her. But the business could use a little more cash, and I can't afford to lose my skills in the air. If I lose those, you lose a boss."

"Balls on the boss there, mate. If you kill yourself, I'll lose my source of income," Scotty said, causing both men to break out in laughter.

Through the summer of 1919, Jimmy flew alternating missions for his business and the flying show. Scotty continued to keep the Wolsely in prime shape. He also kept an eye out for someone he had never met, some perfect woman his boss constantly yearned for.

True to what Winifred hoped he would do, Jimmy read the newspaper daily. He wanted to learn and be knowledgeable in current events. He read often of how the old soldiers and sailors were having great difficulty landing and holding jobs. The shell-shocked soldiers couldn't relate to civilian life, and many of them suffered from nightmares and the sweats. They couldn't handle the pressure of work, and many failed to show up on time. Others argued with their bosses. Baltimore was tough and getting tougher as fired workers and unemployed ex-soldiers roamed the streets looking for some way to make a living.

Jimmy was immersed in his business and the stunt flying. He really didn't make much money with the flying circus, but it was *some* money and he could make it on his time off from the business. The stunt flying wasn't challenging, but it kept an edge on. You could never be *too* sharp. Sometimes the weather wasn't suitable for humans on the ground. It could be devastating to an unprepared person in the air.

Jimmy was doing well in his business and was making a name for himself. The circus promoted Hanz the Hun well enough. People took note. Even though his name wasn't in lights, people would surround him at the end of the shows and find out that he was actually a real person. He also had a real person's name.

The flying business was more dangerous than flying in the circus. Jimmy had many near-accidents. Telegraph wires were showing up everywhere. None of the landing fields had lights on them. Some of them didn't even have a wind flag to show the strength and direction of the wind on landing.

Jimmy flew along certain flying routes. He would follow the Chesapeake Bay and many of the tributaries that fanned out from the Bay. Then he would follow the railroad tracks through Philadelphia, Newark, and New York. Navigating during the day was a cinch. But the Chesapeake Bay was susceptible to squalls, particularly in the spring and fall. Nighttime flying, particularly in bad weather, could be deadly.

At times Jimmy had to land when it was dark out. Landing without lights and lining up on unfamiliar fields made him wonder whether it was worth it. He was flying, but he didn't need the business to end his life and any hope of finding his destiny. He also didn't want it to stop him from looking for Winifred.

Jimmy was a stickler for good service and maintenance on his machine. The Wolseley 200-horsepower engine of the S.E. 5 was very reliable. Jimmy's mechanic was as reliable as anything Jimmy had ever been exposed to. Thank goodness Scotty was available. Scotty could also wield a hammer. The shed looked like a very efficient and up-to-date maintenance hangar due to his carpentry skills.

Scotty even helped Jimmy stay alive one night. A delivery to Curtiss Field in Long Island one day took too long to unload and refuel. Jimmy flew back in the hopes of making it before the thunderstorms started and it got too dark. His plan didn't work out that way. Fighting heavy winds, driving rains, and overcast skies, he struggled to find his landing field in Windsor Mill. As he approached the field in pitch blackness, he noticed a light hue over the field. When he turned into final approach, Jimmy saw the distinct outline of burning items about fifteen feet apart along the tree line next to the field. Scotty had placed paper bags with lighted candles in them along the wood line so that Jimmy could see the trees and line up to his final approach. Jimmy wasn't too sure he would have landed safely under those conditions without Scotty's help.

Time seemed to stand still sometimes. Jimmy was active with his business and his "hobby" of flying with the circus. But there were many things missing from his life. He missed Giselle dearly. He knew he would probably never see her again. He also missed Winifred. His love for her might not be the same as his love for Giselle, but Winifred was very special to him. As he knew almost two years before, he and Winifred could have had a wonderful life together. If he could only find her, he thought.

In Baltimore, people were still struggling to make ends meet. Soldiers and sailors were being left behind by their government, which wasn't interested in maintaining a fighting force. It certainly didn't believe that the nation needed airpower. The war was over. It was The War to End All Wars. At least that's what everyone was saying. Why spend money on defense when there wasn't anything to defend against?

In his sparsely appointed apartment, Jimmy read the news each morning over a cup of coffee. He read of the negotiations in Europe about German reparations for causing the war. Each of the Allied powers wanted Germany to pay dearly for what it had done. "To the victor go the spoils" was the historical mandate. He remembered Winifred's description of how reconstruction was in large part a drain on Southern resources after the Civil War—no, *the War for Southern Independence,* as she had called it. The demands coming from every nation on the winning side of the Great War were no different. Jimmy also remembered Winifred telling him of the German advances in North Africa. Some of the nations of North Africa were involved in the negotiations to bring about heavy German reparations.

The amount of money the nations were demanding of Germany astounded Jimmy. Where would any nation come up with that kind of money? He had seen how the German forces were whittled down toward the end of the war. Surely the country had exhausted its resources. How could even a rich nation afford to pay such reparations? The French were demanding that Germany pay millions into a fund for the European wartime widows. They *did* need support, but how could Germany do what was being demanded of her?

He folded his paper, took another sip of coffee, and looked out the window to the blossoming spring flowers in the field across Hanover Street. He reflected on the loneliness of Germany among her victors. He reflected on how lonely Winifred could be without him. He reflected on his own loneliness without her. Jimmy was in a funk. He wasn't depressed. He didn't suffer from shell shock or any of the other afflictions common among soldiers. As a matter of fact, he enjoyed thinking about what he had accomplished overseas. But there was something missing in his life. He really didn't know what direction he would go in. Was it all worth it? He wondered. The challenges he and Scotty faced on the ground and in the air helped make it seem worth it. He was inspired knowing that nothing came along that he and Scotty couldn't handle. But that didn't help sort out what direction he was headed in his life.

The square, gold envelope with black trim that fell to the floor as he opened his mail changed all that. Jimmy had no idea how anyone of significance in this world knew his address. He understood as soon as he opened the envelope and read its contents.

The Honorable Senator and Mrs. Eugene F. Stevenson
From the Great State of Wisconsin
request the honor of your presence at
A Ball
in recognition of:

William B. Mitchell
Brigadier General, United States Army Air Corps

on the twelfth day of the month of September
in the year of our Lord of 1919

1422 Pennsylvania Avenue
Washington, D.C.
Black Tie

I wonder, he thought. *Is this the same senator with that food initiative? Yes, yes, that's him. How many times had he said the words "the great state of Wisconsin" at Fort McHenry? I have no desire to meet this Honorable Senator from the great state of Wisconsin. But I've got to go for General Mitchell. After all, the twelfth day of September is the anniversary of that massive aerial bombardment I participated in. I've got to go. Perhaps I can stay away from the Honorable Senator and enjoy myself.*

CHAPTER 21: THE PLEASURE

Washington, D.C., U.S.A. - September 12, 1919

Just another train, Jimmy thought. Riding on trains was nothing like flying. One floated in an aeroplane and had the freedom to go in any direction including up and down. The flier could even travel upside-down if he wanted to. In a train, one sat in a dark car with no orientation as to its intended direction of travel. The train was extremely loud and disturbing to Jimmy.

He had found a black tie to wear to the ball. He rented a top hat too. But the tailor said, "No tails." The tailor told him tails were for *very* important black-tie affairs. Recognition of an Army officer, no matter who he was, the tailor said, is not up to the standard of tails. Jimmy didn't bother to correct the tailor. He knew the tailor had no idea of who General Mitchell was.

The twelfth of September. What a great day to pick for a ball in honor of General Mitchell. Jimmy was excited about seeing his old comrade in arms, even though he was a general. Jimmy was more excited about recognizing the massive aerial bombardment of the German lines in 1918, the bombardment that started the American attack on the Saint Mihiel Salient. That bombardment was the largest in the history of mankind. It made the attack on the Salient as easy as it could have been. From that moment on, it was just a matter of time before the American Army pushed the Hun back in the Battle of the Meuse-Argonne.

It was fitting and proper to recognize a leader of men such as General Mitchell and to do it on the twelfth of September. But Jimmy had received two telegrams requesting his attendance at the ball. He wondered why anyone would take the time to ensure that he was there. How had anyone even tracked him down in the first place?

Jimmy arrived a little early and spent some time sitting for coffee near the large stone meeting hall on Pennsylvania Avenue. The building, with its great Roman columns and ornate capitals, was almost as dominating in appearance as the nearby White House. Jimmy entered the massive oak doors of the great building. It was as though he was entering a Greek temple. Then the vision of the mansion he had entered as a German prisoner of war in the Argonne Forest suddenly came to him. On either side of the doors stood sharp-looking U.S. Army soldiers in olive-drab full-dress uniforms with bright white gloves and white ankle leggings called "puttees." Their weapons were immaculately clean, the bayonets highly polished. With the exception of the lack of those broad gray cooking pots on the heads of the soldiers, the sight looked shockingly like that in the Argonne.

Jimmy handed his invitation to a sergeant at the front door. The sergeant handed Jimmy's invitation to a sergeant major at the front of the receiving line. The sergeant major announced Lieutenant James Smitts, aviator, to Senator Stevenson's staffer. The staffer whispered Jimmy's name to Senator Stevenson.

Senator Stevenson smiled at Jimmy. He held and shook Jimmy's hand for a good while longer than Jimmy expected. Senator Stevenson thanked him for his service to his country. He said General Mitchell had told him that Jimmy was a war hero and one of the best aviators that the U.S. Army Air Corps had ever had in its ranks. Jimmy realized that Senator Stevenson was spending more time with him than he had with anyone before him. *Oh, yes,* he thought as he recognized the senator, *this is the man with* the initiative. Jimmy sized up the senator in the long minute he stood before him. *The man isn't quite as egotistical as he seemed at Fort McHenry. But he does think highly of himself,* Jimmy thought. He could see Mrs. Stevenson in his peripheral vision patiently waiting for the next "victim."

Senator Stevenson passed Jimmy onto Mrs. Stevenson by quietly announcing his name again. Mrs. Stevenson was stunning. Her welcoming grin exploded into a huge, friendly smile.

"Why, Lieutenant Smitts," she said, "I am so happy and honored to make your acquaintance."

"The honor is all mine, Mrs. Stevenson."

Next, Jimmy was standing before the man he held in highest esteem. General Billy Mitchell shook Jimmy's hand.

"Lieutenant, I mean *Mr.* Smitts, I'm honored to have you join us and the activities of the evening. It has been quite some time since we have seen each other."

"General Mitchell, the honor is all mine. I am humbled to have been thought of."

General Mitchell closed by saying, "Stay close, son. I believe you are going to be thought of again in a short period of time.

The receiving party stood there for an hour. People came through almost without end. They must have been standing out on the street waiting to enter the building. Jimmy was amazed as he looked at the guest list. He found out that Eddie Rickenbacker, the highest scoring American flying ace of the war, was in attendance. Many of the most heralded leaders in aviation were there, as well as many current and past soldiers of the American Expeditionary Force. Senators and congressmen were present. Jimmy felt as though he was a very small cog in a large wheel, and the wheel was turning quickly. He wasn't too sure whether he really belonged at this ball. He sure wasn't very comfortable being in the ballroom with *the senator with the initiative*. But it was in honor of General Mitchell and the great aerial campaign he had organized and that Jimmy had witnessed from the air exactly one year before.

The sergeant major from the receiving line touched Jimmy's arm. "Excuse me, sir. The honor of your presence with General Mitchell is requested. Please follow me." The sergeant escorted Jimmy to a room adjacent to the ballroom.

The first thing Jimmy saw as he entered the oak-paneled room was a beautiful young woman in a pearl-white formal dress. The collar of her studded gown smoothly transitioned from its high back to a front vee that revealed nothing but suggested everything about her firm youth and comforting beauty. The young woman turned slightly as if to say she did not notice him, but he did see her look away quickly and smile as he entered the room. Her high cheekbones were only slightly noticeable within the smooth features of her soft face.

But it was her eyes that captured Jimmy's attention. They had a fascinating slant to them. He had seen the kind of deep royal-blue color only once before, in the eyes of Werner Voss two years before this event. Jimmy was speechless. She was so beautiful and moved with such elegance, he could hardly breathe.

The young woman stood next to Mrs. Stevenson and smiled as though she really enjoyed the conversation around her. Jimmy couldn't stop looking at the pearl color of her form-fitting gown as it glowed against the wood paneling. He also couldn't stop noticing the smooth waves in her form.

An Army captain interrupted Jimmy's gaze at the young woman. He escorted Jimmy to Senator Stevenson and General Mitchell. The captain refreshed Jimmy's introduction to the senator, Mrs. Stevenson, and General Mitchell. Mrs. Stevenson touched Jimmy on the arm and said, "Lieutenant Smitts, may I have the pleasure of presenting our daughter? Lieutenant Smitts, Miss Victoria Stevenson."

Jimmy took her hand and bowed slightly. "Miss Stevenson, I am extremely honored to make your acquaintance. The pleasure is mine."

Victoria slowly looked up into Jimmy's eyes, bowed her head slightly, and said with a smile, "The honor and pleasure are *all* mine, sir."

General Mitchell broke the trance that was forming between the two.

"Ladies and gentlemen, I would like to start the proceedings. Lieutenant Smitts, would you kindly approach the front?" General Mitchell faced Jimmy and continued. "When I first met you in September of 1918, I knew you were a hero and an excellent leader of aviators. You taught, defended, and saved untold numbers of Allied fliers. But your attack on the German fliers that were strafing American soldiers in the trenches has to take its place in American military aviation as a stroke of exceptional courage and flying genius."

After a slight pause, General Mitchell continued. "First, it is my honor to present to you military awards bestowed upon you by the French government."

General Mitchell presented Jimmy with the French Ribbon of

the Croix de Guerre. He then placed the French Medaile Militare, the highest military medal that could be bestowed on an American soldier, on his "black tie" tuxedo. General Mitchell told everyone that Jimmy had to return to the U.S. so suddenly at the end of the war that the French did not have time to present him with the medals.

The small group clapped after General Mitchell said, "It is my pleasure to be a representative of the French government this evening."

General Mitchell nodded to the American captain who announced, "Attention to orders!"

Everyone stood upright as the captain continued. "For conspicuous gallantry and extraordinary heroism during combat operations in the Theater of Operations of the American Expeditionary Force of the United States of America and in the face of overwhelming numbers of German flying machines in their attack upon American forces and with great disregard for his personal safety in defense of the American soldiers of the 82nd Division of the American Expeditionary Force on September 5th, 1918, having dived into the attacking machines then executing an aerial maneuver in the face of the enemy to spur the American soldiers on to combat, Lieutenant James Smitts is hereby awarded the Distinguished Service Cross of the United States of America. Signed this tenth day of August 1919, Newton Diehl Baker, Jr., Secretary of War; John J. Pershing, General of the Army, Commanding."

Jimmy was stunned. He had no idea he was going to be honored at the ball. This was, after all, a gathering in honor of General Mitchell. General Mitchell turned, pinned the medal of the U.S. Distinguished Service Cross on Jimmy's chest, saluted him, and shook his hand.

"Sir," General Mitchell said, "on behalf of the President of the United States and General Pershing, I wish to thank you for your gallant action in defending our soldiers. I know the soldiers of the All-American Division could not have continued their brave attack on the German line without the inspiration of your heroic action. Congratulations."

Jimmy couldn't clear the fog that surrounded him as the others in the room shook his hand. He noticed that the command sergeant major had a look of shock on his face. He also had tears welling up in his eyes.

Command Sergeant Major Ralph Witherspoon approached Jimmy and saluted. The sergeant wore the combat patch of the All-American Division on his right shoulder. It was a place of honor on the uniform signifying the unit in which a soldier served in combat. The bright white double back-to-back A's stood out in a red circle of a square royal blue patch. *Double A's. I get it. The All-Americans,* Jimmy realized. The colors were so vibrant that they dominated the sergeant's uniform. The red, white, and blue ribbon of the Distinguished Service Cross pinned in another honorable place on the sergeant's uniform shined as brightly as the patch of the All-Americans. The sergeant was almost in tears as he thanked Jimmy for what he had done in the skies over the 82nd Division trenches.

"Sir, I was in those trenches when you flew over our position. I saw firsthand how your attack upon the German fliers saved many of my men. Our regiment was downtrodden and being torn to bits by those aeroplanes until you dove into the enemy. Your action completely changed the attitude of the entire line. After your attack, we were all charged and ready to take the fight to the Germans. And we won. Thank you, sir."

The sergeant wheeled about quickly and stepped to the side of the room. Jimmy could tell the sergeant had lost many friends and comrades in those trenches.

The people in the room started moving into the ballroom. The captain spoke next. "Sergeant Major Witherspoon, I will escort the members of the head table. Would you kindly escort Miss Stevenson to her table?"

Sergeant Witherspoon, Jimmy thought as he walked behind the sergeant and the beautiful young woman. *Where have I heard that name before? Yes, I heard it at Fort McHenry. That soldier with the Southern accent said, "I'm proud to say, I fought with Witherspoon," That's what that soldier said at Fort McHenry.*

Everyone in the ballroom had been busy socializing. The music, drinks, and appetizers kept the attendees entertained as the small group of people watched General Mitchell recognize Jimmy with his medals.

The Army Band started up a march as the receiving party approached the head table. As he walked toward his table, he watched Sergeant Major Witherspoon escort Miss Stevenson to her table. Jimmy couldn't help stare at her as she gracefully moved across the ballroom. To his pleasant surprise, he was assigned to the same table as Miss Stevenson.

As Jimmy moved toward the table, Eddie Rickenbacker approached him and shook his hand. "Congratulations, Lieutenant. I understand you were recognized tonight for your exceptional performance in the air. I welcome you to the few that have the honor of wearing the Distinguished Service Cross. It is the second highest medal for valor to the Medal of Honor. I proudly wear the seven crosses that have been bestowed upon me. My compliments, sir."

"Thank you, Mr. Rickenbacker," Jimmy replied. He didn't fail to notice Rickenbacker's self-serving recognition of his own achievements.

"I now work for General Motors on their new automobile, the Sheridan. Word has it GM is going to set up an arrangement, some kind of affiliate relationship with Fokker. They may develop larger aeroplanes together. Talk has it that they may develop aeromachines for civilian transport. Then again, I am considering venturing out on my own. You should consider joining us. We can always use some help."

"Thank you, Mr. Rickenbacker. I appreciate the offer, but I have already started my own flying business."

"Your own flying business, you say? Well, then," Rickenbacker said, "I wish you well. Just don't do too well competing with us," he jokingly said as he slowly walked—almost swaggered—away with a half-smile. Or was he joking?

Jimmy was stopped and congratulated so many times that he was slow getting to his table. Many attendees were puzzled when they noticed the young man who wore military decorations on his civilian tuxedo and followed the senator's daughter around the room.

Attendees stood at attention behind their chairs. Jimmy, unsure of what he was supposed to do, just followed along. Color bearers marched the flags of the United States of America and the United States Army into the room. The color guard stood at attention and saluted with their rifles as the color bearers placed the flags in holders behind the head table. After the color guard marched out, the captain at the head table announced, "Ladies and gentlemen, I wish to propose a toast to the United States of America."

"To the United States of America!" everyone in the room said and raised a glass of grape juice, the staple of toasts after prohibition was ratified in January 1919.

Eugene F. Stevenson, the host of the ball and influential senator from Wisconsin, smiled with a sick feeling in his stomach as he raised his glass. He felt as though he had made a pact with the devil. "Diamond Jim" Colosimo's men had gotten to him. He had changed his vote *for* Prohibition in December 1917, only one year after arriving in Congress. His vote stopped the flood of building violations his hotels in Chicago had been receiving. His vote also brought upon him the wrath of his German and Irish constituents. But he had to do what he had to do.

The toasts continued. "To the United States Army!" "To our comrades in Arms, the forces of the great nation of Great Britain!" "To our comrades in arms, the forces of the great nation of France!" The toasts concluded with "Gentlemen, to the ladies!"

Jimmy raised his glass of grape juice to Miss Stevenson in reply to that last declaration.

Jimmy noticed little during the remainder of the dinner. Plates came and went as waiters delivered a variety of dishes. Glasses were raised. Guests gestured and conversed. But Jimmy's attention was drawn to the beautiful face of Miss Stevenson, that wonderful crown of Gibson-styled light-brown hair, and the form of her body in her pearl-white gown. *How can I get to talk with her?* Jimmy asked himself. *What would I say?* He could barely dance, but if he had to step all over her toes to get to speak with her, he would.

Toward the end of dinner, young men and lieutenants in uniform came up to Miss Stevenson. Each one seemed to ask her something. When she nodded, they wrote something down on a card pinned to her left hip. Jimmy had no idea what was going on.

The lady next to Jimmy leaned over and asked him, "Young man, aren't you going to sign Miss Stevenson's dance card?"

Dance card? Jimmy wondered. *What's a dance card? I guess I should go up and sign the card.*

Jimmy approached Miss Stevenson and asked her.

"Why, Lieutenant Smitts," she said, "I thought you'd never ask. As a matter of fact, I saved the top reservation just for you."

Jimmy realized he had just committed himself to dancing with the most beautiful woman in the room. He was going to be the first to dance with her, and everyone on the list after him was going to notice. *They probably want to make sure I know how to dance,* he thought. *Or maybe they want to make sure I don't steal her heart.*

Miss Stevenson glided along the floor and eased Jimmy through his steps. They weren't very close to each other as they danced, but Jimmy moved through light clouds of wonderful French perfume. *I hope this never ends,* he thought.

As they returned to the table, Miss Stevenson said, "Thank you, Lieutenant Smitts. That was the *best* dance I've ever had the pleasure to accept. May I call you *James?*" she asked, looking up at him as she sat down. Her smile was radiant and her beautiful eyes never left Jimmy's gaze.

"Miss Stevenson, my friends call me Jimmy," Jimmy replied. "My father goes by James."

"Well, *Jimmy,* I hope *I* may be one of your friends. I would be extremely pleased if you would call me Victoria. I am very impressed and honored to make your acquaintance."

The night was like living in a dream. Jimmy had been given military honors for his service during the war. He got to meet some of the greatest fliers in America. He was in the presence of the most respected commander in Army aviation. But the most exciting thing of the evening was watching Victoria float over the dance floor. She moved as though her feet never touched the floor. He really didn't care that she was dancing with other young men. He just enjoyed watching her move.

Toward the end of the evening, the captain rang a bell and announced, "Gentlemen, the smoking lamp is lit."

With that announcement, everyone relaxed and started mingling around the room. Men lit cigarettes and cigars. People came up to Jimmy to ask him what he had done in the war. People mumbled to one another that he was obviously "someone" with all those military medals. Jimmy couldn't find a way to evade the questioning. He *had* to find his way over to Victoria.

"Mother. Mother," Victoria whispered to Loraine, touching her arm.

"Victoria, please, I am engaged at the moment. Father needs me to socialize with some of his colleagues. What *do* you want?" she whispered back.

"Mother, you must invite the Lieutenant to breakfast with us tomorrow."

"What Lieutenant, Victoria? What on earth are you talking about?"

Loraine looked across the room with satisfaction at Jimmy when Victoria said, "*the* Lieutenant, Mother. The one that got the medals tonight. We *must* have breakfast with him. I insist. I will not take no for an answer."

"And why *must* we, my dear?"

"Mother, he is the only man I've met that cared about *me*. He asked me constantly how I was doing, what my goals were in life, and if I planned to have a family. He actually thought about *me*. All the other suitors only thought of themselves. They all looked upon women only as a means of rearing their babies."

"Victoria, *really*. Not here, please. This is a social event, not a parlor for gossip. All right, then," she said as she noticed Victoria's disappointment. "I like the young man and will ask him to breakfast."

Victoria's eyes lit up and her smile radiated as she curtsied slightly and said, "Thank you, Mother, thank you. Oh, and you must have Father join us. Father *must* meet this young man."

"I take it you insist on *that* as well. All right, then. I will also speak to Father."

Jimmy realized he didn't have to struggle to find her. Victoria moved ever so slowly toward him as she spoke to different guests. He could smell the perfume as she made her way toward him. He started to sweat. He could feel his neck turn warm from his excited expectations. She turned and smiled at him.

Victoria could barely keep her eyes off of Jimmy as she worked her way through the ballroom and back toward Jimmy. She was interrupted at times, although the interruptions failed to keep her from the object of her periodic gazes. She was finally next to him again.

"So, Mr. Jimmy," she said, "have you had an enjoyable evening?"

"Miss Victoria, the evening has been many things to me."

"Oh, yes? Would you please tell me what the evening has been to you?"

"It was humbling and thrilling to be honored by such famed leaders of the American effort in the war," he said. "But most important, Miss Victoria, the evening has been a wonderful pleasure in making the acquaintance of such a beautiful woman as yourself."

She blushed and smiled that devious smile she showed when he first set eyes on her. They continued to talk about nonsense as people interrupted each of them at different times. Some of the younger men approached her every now and again. Most of the suitors realized that they had been beaten. They didn't mind because they had actually been bested. After all, Victoria seemed to enjoy the company of the civilian awardee standing next to her.

The evening ended all too soon for Jimmy and even more so for Victoria. He knew he still had a long train trip back to Baltimore. It was going to be a very long night, but it was definitely worth it. Victoria knew she would have the pleasure of his company again as Mrs. Stevenson came to them. Victoria could tell that her mother was enthralled by this honored hero of the Great War and knew she was going to fulfill her mission, the mission to extend Victoria's acquaintance with *the Lieutenant* before they left.

"Lieutenant Smitts, where are you staying for the night?"

"I am going to take the train back to Baltimore, Mrs. Stevenson."

"Oh, my," Mrs. Stevenson said. "Absolutely not, Lieutenant Smitts. We won't have any of *that*. I insist that you stay at Eugene's hotel. We will put you up in the presidential suite for the night. *And* I insist that you take breakfast with us in the morning at the hotel. I won't take no for an answer, Lieutenant."

Jimmy was elated as he said, "That is so kind of you. Thank you very much. I look forward to breakfast with you in the morning." The words made Victoria feel like she just melted inside. *Thank you, Mother, thank you,* she thought.

Her radiant eyes told Jimmy she was happy to know she would see him again. To Jimmy it was one thing to get a good night's sleep without having to take the train that night. It was another thing altogether to get to see Victoria again in the morning.

General Mitchell approached the small group. Victoria stayed close to Jimmy. The general told Jimmy he hoped he would consider joining the Army's Flying Corps again. The Army needed his service, especially his excellent flying abilities, General Mitchell told him.

"The hardest duty for a soldier is at war," General Mitchell said. "The second hardest duty for a soldier is preparing for the next war."

"Oh, General Mitchell, you must be mistaken," Mrs. Stevenson said. "This last war surely was the last. They say it was the War to End All Wars."

General Mitchell said out loud to everyone in earshot that there would always be wars. That was the way of the human race.

"Please seriously consider it, Mister Smitts," the general

continued. "Your country needs you. I also have to admit, *I* need you."

With that, General Mitchell left as quickly as he always did. His departure meant to Jimmy that he was just one more moment closer to being with Victoria in the morning.

The hotel was well appointed. It was an older Victorian hotel with excellent décor. Jimmy felt overwhelmed as he walked into the presidential suite.

What a night! he thought as he drifted off to sleep. *What a woman!*

CHAPTER 22: HIS DESTINY

Washington, D.C., U.S.A. - September 13, 1919

"My, Lieutenant Smitts, it is such a pleasure to see you again. I wish to congratulate you on the awards you received last night," Mrs. Stevenson said to him as she shook his hand. "I trust Eugene's hotel staff has done its duty and taken very good care of you."

He was a little humbled by what Eugene's staff had done for him. They knew exactly what to do. *Not only did they bring toiletries to me, they measured me last night as soon as I arrived. A new gray tweed suit with a starched shirt was waiting for me when I woke up. I guess money and influence can do many things,* he thought.

"Mrs. Stevenson, the staff was excellent. They took very good care of me. I cannot thank you enough for your hospitality and for everything you've done for me."

"Oh, Lieutenant Smitts, you *are* too kind."

At least he didn't have to wear the tuxedo he had worn at the ball, he thought. It was a little disheveled and would have been completely out of touch with the moment. Compared to how these ladies looked, he would have appeared foolish in a wrinkled tuxedo.

Mrs. Stevenson and Victoria were immaculately dressed. Mrs. Stevenson had a coral dress on and wore a matching wide-brimmed hat. Every hair on her head was in perfect alignment. Her makeup and nails were impeccable. He was thrilled to be with them again.

Victoria was even more beautiful than he remembered from the night before. Her light-green chiffon dress formed perfectly to her body and hung in amazing flutters of light-flowing material below her waist. The lace behind her neck made the soft, smooth skin of her beautiful face radiate.

Thank goodness, the hotel provided the suit and had toiletries for him to use. Otherwise he would not have been able to get ready and look presentable for breakfast with these two lovely ladies. He would have canceled breakfast with the women if he hadn't been able to shave. Then again, he realized, nothing would have kept him from being here. *This vision of loveliness before me was well worth every minute of embarrassment,* he thought. *I definitely would have come no matter what I looked like.*

The parlor where they sat was framed in wrought-iron entwined with grape vines. It was light and airy with plaster walls and terra-cotta flooring. The scene reminded Jimmy of the French restaurant of Giselle's family. He suddenly had mixed emotions of yearning to be with Giselle and a burning desire to get more involved with Victoria.

Mrs. Stevenson decided she would break Jimmy's pause. She sensed he was thinking about something. But she just couldn't make out what was on his mind.

"Lieutenant, may I call you Jimmy?"

"Oh, certainly, Mrs. Stevenson. I'm sorry I didn't think to ask you. I must admit, I've been remiss. I am also a Mister now. I was a lieutenant in the war. Now I'm a civilian. I forgot to mention all that. Your beauty and hospitality have me somewhat stunned."

Victoria giggled again as her mother blushed.

"Well, thank you, Jimmy. That's very kind of you. I must say, I was impressed by the honors that the French and American governments bestowed upon you last night. To me, at least for now, you seem to still be a lieutenant of the Army."

"Thank you, Mrs. Stevenson. I was extremely humbled by the medals that were awarded to me. But I am even more humbled by the honor and pleasure of your company this morning. Thank you so much for your invitation to breakfast with such lovely women."

He could tell Mrs. Stevenson was very happy to hear him compliment her. Victoria wore the same devious smile she had worn the night before. She was obviously having a wonderful time.

"Mr. Smitts," Victoria said, "you certainly can dance. Thank you for a wonderful dance and a wonderful evening last night."

Victoria was trying to placate her mother. He did tell her last night that she could call him by his first name. She smiled an inner smile knowing she was lying like a rug. He stepped on her feet three or four times during the dance. *She* almost had to carry *him* around the dance floor. If it hadn't been for her, he would have tripped a couple of times. But, she remembered, he had been such a very nice gentleman last night.

"Thank you, Miss Stevenson."

"Oh, come-come now, children. Please allow yourselves to call each other by your first names. Victoria, I will make sure Father is fine with it as well."

"Thank you, Mother. And thank you, *Jimmy*, for your compliments."

The breakfast was excellent. He tried hard to avoid spilling coffee and food all over himself as he hid his attempts to admire Victoria. He knew he would totally mess this up if Mrs. Stevenson saw him staring at her daughter. But it was hard for him to stop. Victoria didn't mind if her mother saw her looking intently at Jimmy. This was, after all, *her* breakfast. Mother would just have to put up with it.

It was evident that Mrs. Stevenson deeply loved Victoria. She respected her daughter and her opinions. It was also evident that Mrs. Stevenson was very protective. Both women were intently listening to Jimmy's every word, especially Mrs. Stevenson. She was surprised to hear that Jimmy took his first solo flight in a *real* aeroplane at the age of thirteen. She seemed pleased to know his father was an entrepreneur. Jimmy deliberately didn't tell her that his heritage was German. He'd leave that for another time.

Victoria tried to control her inner excitement as Mrs. Stevenson asked Jimmy about his time in Europe during the war.

"Please, *Jimmy*, tell us about the camaraderie between the fliers and the difficulties that you had to endure," Loraine said.

Victoria constantly smiled as Jimmy explained some of the action he had seen. She was about to cry when Jimmy told the women of his broken shoulder and capture by the Germans. His parole and safe return to Allied hands was a huge relief to Victoria. Both of the ladies were amazed at how Jimmy had recovered and voluntarily returned to the war effort.

"My, my, Jimmy. You were extremely brave to have gone back to the war after having been wounded and captured by the Germans. I know I speak for Victoria too when I say we are so happy that you made it through those terrible times."

The interrogation didn't stop at Jimmy's involvement in the war. He answered question after question about the new company he had formed. Mrs. Stevenson was particularly concerned about "the safety of it all." Victoria just kept smiling and told him how wonderful it must be to be in the air. Her smile got bigger when Jimmy told her at times he felt as if he was one with God when he flew.

Mrs. Stevenson melted when he said that. "How romantic," she said.

"Jimmy, the Senator couldn't join us for breakfast because he had an early committee meeting he had to attend at the Senate building. But he should be here presently. Eugene wouldn't dare miss the opportunity to join us and spend some time with you on our first visit," Mrs. Stevenson said as Victoria looked on with that devious smile of hers.

He felt a slight tingling run down his spine when she told him Senator Stevenson would join them. *I completely forgot about the senator,* he thought. *I don't want his ego to ruin the beauty of this moment. Then again, nothing can ruin the beauty. It definitely can't ruin the beauty of these women.*

Jimmy couldn't help but think that something was up. He'd been given a room, with all the trimmings, at "Eugene's hotel." And he had the impression that someone had demanded that "Eugene" be present at breakfast.

Victoria felt satisfied that her mother was able to convince her father to join them. To her it was another small victory. *Father might weasel out of coming to breakfast if Mother or I ask him to join us,* Victoria thought with a smile. But he can never say no when Mother and I both insist on his presence.

Victoria could tell Jimmy was strong and self-assured, but he had a warm side too. Even this morning at the breakfast table, she could still feel his comforting but firm support and guidance. It felt as though his arms were still around her as they were when they danced the night before. She glanced at Jimmy and smiled between sips of tea as she thought about how he tried so hard to please her in everything he said and did.

"Father agreed to join us last night. He is really looking forward to seeing you again, Jimmy." Victoria said.

"Oh *really*, Victoria. Jimmy, Victoria *ordered* the senator to join us," Mrs. Stevenson said with a smirk as Victoria blushed. "Then again, I must say, I too asked Eugene to get out of his committee meeting and spend some time with us."

Jimmy heard a disturbance in the lobby. Senator Stevenson strutted through the hotel. He had finally made it. "What a committee meeting," Jimmy faintly heard him say to the hotel manager. The manager and the staff doted on him as he walked toward the parlor where the three were entertaining each other. The manager escorted him to his seat.

Jimmy stood up. He shook Senator Stevenson's hand after the senator kissed his wife and then Victoria on their cheeks. The senator's voice was direct and clear. "Lieutenant, I am honored to meet such a hero of the Great War."

"I couldn't be more pleased and honored to be able to make the acquaintance of you and Mrs. Stevenson," Jimmy replied. "I have to admit, Senator, I am extremely pleased and honored to meet Victoria."

Victoria raised her chin slightly and smiled as her father looked at her as he sat.

"Father, Lieutenant Smitts was telling us how wonderful it is to fly. His descriptions of the sunsets were just marvelous. How nice it must be to be in the air," Victoria playfully said.

"Yes, yes, my dearest. It must be very nice," he replied.

Man after man in the hotel interrupted them to say hello to the senator as he tried to be attentive to his daughter's desire. Some talked to him briefly about a bill or some event in politics. Jimmy could tell Senator Stevenson got more disappointed and aggravated as the time went on. Victoria could tell her father just wasn't going to stay. He loathed being interrupted like this.

"This just won't do, my dear," the senator said to Loraine. "I need to get out of the hotel and go back to the Senate where I can get something done. Perhaps you and Victoria can have a more enjoyable time with the lieutenant without me and these constant interruptions."

Victoria felt satisfied as he stood to leave. Father was able to change his plans at *her* request. She knew she would be able to tell him all about it before bedtime. She also felt confident that he would get it from both sides. Her mother too would tell him how wonderful the man was. Victoria would tell him how she felt. She was determined to make sure this wouldn't be the last time her father would see Lieutenant Smitts.

Senator Stevenson rose to leave. "I'm so sorry, everyone. I must get back to my duties in the Senate. Lieutenant Smitts, it has been a pleasure and I look forward to the next time we can meet again. Don't worry, young man. I know I will hear everything about your breakfast. I have two lovely ladies in my life, and they don't hesitate to inform me of everything they want me to know. All my best to you, sir. I'm sure we will see each other again—and *very* soon, I'm sure."

Things were looking pretty good. Even though he did not have enough time to get to know the senator, Jimmy was pretty comfortable with what he had seen and heard. He hoped the senator felt the same about him.

"It will be my pleasure, Senator Stevenson," Jimmy replied, disguising his fib.

The senator kissed his wife and daughter goodbye. He nodded as he kissed Loraine. After he kissed Victoria, he held her arms in his hands and gave her a special look. Jimmy saw the reactions but had no idea what was going on.

Mrs. Stevenson broke the silence as the senator left. "Lieutenant, we must schedule another time together. Perhaps you have time to join us next weekend."

Jimmy couldn't be happier. He wouldn't have to beg to see Victoria again. And Victoria was grinning and seemed to be nodding in agreement.

"Mrs. Stevenson, it would be my absolute pleasure to be able to call on you, Senator Stevenson, and Victoria next weekend," Jimmy said. He hoped his words had come out right. He didn't want Mrs. Stevenson to know how eager he was to join them again. He did hope that *Victoria* sensed how eager he was.

"Well, then, Lieutenant Smitts, I suppose we will see you next Saturday for dinner," Mrs. Stevenson said as she stood up.

Victoria stood slowly hoping she could extend the visit. She had so many things to find out about this intriguing man. But her mother had ended the visit and it was not to be. *Oh my*, she said to herself, *the time came and went so quickly.*

Jimmy couldn't stop thinking about how wonderful the weekend had been. He met an amazing woman with her amazing family. *And* he actually liked Mrs. Loraine Stevenson. He didn't have enough time with the senator to know how a relationship with him would work out. But it really didn't matter. He was set up to see Victoria again. *Life is good and getting better,* he thought.

Victoria couldn't be happier either. She was finally going to be in the company of a man who cared about her needs and desires.

Jimmy took two special trips in his machine to Washington during the week. He wanted to see whether there were any suitable landing fields. He planned to fly to Washington Sunday morning to visit the Stevenson family. He noticed a field near the Potomac in central Washington. There were ten aeromachines lined up at the field. That was good. He could land there and take a carriage to the Stevenson's residence. Perhaps he could take one of those new motor-taxis.

* * * * *

The door to the hangar at the Aero Pursuit Company opened to reveal the darkening sky of dusk. Scotty looked up at Jimmy as a strong figure walked across the hangar and over to Jimmy.

"Hello, Sergeant. I believe we met at the ball in honor of General Mitchell, is that not right?" Jimmy asked.

"Yes, sir. I hope you don't mind the intrusion," Ralph

Witherspoon said. "I wanted to know if you needed any help. I have left the army and would like to join you in your aero business."

Jimmy saw Scotty frown at the sergeant's request. "Scotty, this is Sergeant Witherspoon of the United States Army." Turning to Witherspoon, he said, "Well, right now it is just Scotty and me. But business is booming and we could use some help. We just purchased our second aeromachine and need help making rounds to the customers and doing paperwork. How are you at paperwork, Sergeant?"

"Please call me Ralph. I am now a civilian like yourselves. I did paperwork throughout my military life. I can run errands and help with anything you need done. I'm also a very good mechanic."

"How's that you say, *mate*? You say you want to join *us*?" Scotty asked as he moved closer to Jimmy.

"I'd like to help you build your business. I can also help *you*, sir," Witherspoon nodded to Scotty, "I would be honored to assist you in your work."

Jimmy and Scotty went to the office and discussed the expansion of their business. They both knew that they could not keep up with the workload by themselves. Jimmy and Scotty returned to the hangar bay. "Ralph," Jimmy said, "you are now a proud member of the Aero Pursuit Company. Welcome to the club."

It seemed like it took forever for the week to finally end. Jimmy flew into the Washington landing field. He was shocked to learn that there was a five-cent landing fee and a ten-cent takeoff fee. If he wanted to keep the machine at the field overnight, Jimmy would have to pay another five cents. *Wow*, Jimmy thought, *20 cents is four hours' wages for Scotty, so this is going to be expensive and I now have Ralph's pay to worry about.* He knew the only reason the takeoff fee was so high was because the field *could* charge that much. It made perfect sense to a businessman that the takeoff fee was so high. Once you landed, you *had* to pay the ten cents to take off. There really wasn't much chance that the field would not make the full fifteen cents.

But the high fees were worth it. Jimmy would have paid a lot more if he'd had to. The flight got him to Victoria much sooner than the train could.

Dinner was everything he thought it would be. Being across from Victoria at the table gave him a fantastic view of her innocence and great beauty. To Victoria, being with Jimmy was absolutely dreamy. After dinner, Senator Stevenson invited Jimmy to join him in the study. The women disappeared. He and Senator Stevenson sat with a cognac. Senator Stevenson offered Jimmy a cigar, but Jimmy said he didn't smoke.

"Good thing, sir," Senator Stevenson told Jimmy. "Bad for the heart. I should stop one day."

They spoke about the war and future business. Jimmy deliberately stayed away from politics. For one thing, he didn't know the first thing about politics. He also thought Senator Stevenson had enough of politics at work. The senator didn't need some young kid like Jimmy asking him what was going on in Senate chambers.

The senator was happy with the young lieutenant. He sure did seem young, Senator Stevenson thought. But he also was very well read and had great business sense. The senator was impressed—very impressed—that Jimmy was able to convince a banking organization in Baltimore to loan him money for his aero-company investment.

"The damn bankers don't loan anyone any money these days," the senator said.

The best part about the conversation, Senator Stevenson thought, was that Lieutenant Smitts had not asked him one thing about politics. Senator Stevenson hated talking politics at social times.

Jimmy started making many weekend trips to Washington and back. Sometimes he and Victoria were even able to get away and take private summertime walks together through the Georgetown neighborhood of Washington. *This is the woman for me,* Jimmy thought. *I just have a lot to do to get things ready. I need to get more business for the Pursuit Aero Company. I just pray Victoria feels the same way about me as I do about her and she will wait for me.*

The weather turned cold. The days were getting shorter. Jimmy kept pushing his departure time from Washington. He sometimes landed at the field at the Rutherford farm a little later than he wanted to. It was dangerous. But it was worth it because he could maximize his time with Victoria. Then again, Victoria had a firm grip on his departures too. She enthusiastically hoped he could stay longer at each visit. To him the landings in darkness were nowhere near as dangerous as the squalls he had flown through over the summer.

He smiled as he walked down the cobblestone walkways of Georgetown with Mrs. Stevenson. He was thoroughly enjoying the shopping trip with her. He actually liked walking about looking at women's merchandise. The shops were quaint and the proprietors very accommodating. They were all pleased to see Mrs. Stevenson walk into their shops.

"Ah, Jimmy, I just *love* to shop. I particularly love to shop for Victoria. She gets so excited each time I bring her something from the ladies' store. It warms my heart to see her so excited."

Jimmy was happy to hear Mrs. Stevenson tell him, "I must say, young man, it is a pleasure to see Victoria excited as she waits for your arrival. I wouldn't say that to a young man if I didn't know I could trust him with the sanctity of *that* information."

"Oh, Mrs. Stevenson, you can trust me. I will also admit that the feelings are mutual."

When they returned to the Stevenson house, Victoria couldn't control herself. She just had to know where they had gone and what they had done.

"Now, now, Vitoria, you know we were shopping for you. You are just going to have to wait until Christmas before finding out what we were up to."

"Mother, I *must* know. Christmas is three weeks away. I cannot wait that long to know."

Victoria turned to Jimmy when her mother failed to respond and said, "Jimmy you *must* tell me. I *must* know what you got for me. I *insist.*"

"Victoria, I would love to tell you, but it will ruin your Christmas. You will love it that much more if you wait." Jimmy said with a smile knowing the coral dress, matching hat, and white laced gloves are perfect for her. Not only did it suit Victoria's skin color, but he remembered that Mrs. Stevenson had worn the same color the first time they'd had breakfast together.

* * * * *

Christmas of 1919 was a wonderful time for Jimmy. Victoria said Christmas had been everything she had ever hoped for in life. Jimmy had given her wonderful Christmas presents. He was ecstatic when he opened his presents and found a long brown fur coat with matching fur gloves sitting before him. Victoria wanted him to be comfortable in wintertime flight. And he knew he had hit the mark with her presents. Both Victoria's mother and father were happy with him. They could see how happy he made their daughter.

Victoria made Jimmy promise he would take her flying when the weather warmed. She couldn't wait to get into the air and see what it was like to *fly*. To her, though, it was an opportunity to spend more time with Jimmy. She wanted to see him work the controls of the aeroplane, but she was a little scared. Her eagerness to be with Jimmy made the risk of an aeroplane flight worth it.

As the months passed into the year of 1920, Jimmy continued to fly delivery missions to New York, Newark, Philadelphia, Washington, and Richmond. It seemed like the bankers were moving a lot of business. As far as Jimmy was concerned, they could move cows, as long as they commissioned him to move them. Business was great and his social life with Victoria was even better. He couldn't wait until each week passed so that he could take the short trip to the landing field near the Potomac River in Washington, D.C. As soon as he landed each Saturday morning, he knew he would soon be in paradise with Victoria.

* * * * *

Northern Maryland - April 12, 1920

At 4,000 feet he noticed that the color of the daylight seemed to change. He saw hues of yellow all about him. It was a color in the sky he had never seen in the nine years he had been flying. Then he saw a dark wall materialize out of the haze before him as he crossed the Susquehanna River into Maryland. Jimmy was carrying a load of bank notes from New York City to Baltimore and could see he was going to be challenged by another Chesapeake Bay squall. The weather had been unusually hot during the last week, and this would be the third time he had hit a wall of water since he started flying out of Baltimore. He started his climb thinking how odd it was to see a squall in mid-April even over the Chesapeake. He wanted to get as high as possible. The wind in a squall was less forceful at about 10,000 feet. At least that's what he hoped it would be with *this* narrow storm front as it had been in the past. His side of the dark front made the squall deceiving. It was so calm where he was. The sky was blue and there was no wind. Jimmy knew from experience that the other side of the storm, only a few hundred yards or so beyond the front, was just as calm as it was where he was now. But the yellow hue about him turned the blue sky to green. How odd, he thought.

The buffeting started at least half a mile short of the front. He got concerned because he was passing through 7,000 feet, hit rough buffeting well before the front, and still could not see the peak of the storm. For a second he considered turning around and landing in a field until the storm passed. Suddenly his S.E. 5A climbed faster than he had ever climbed in an aeromachine before. He was at 9,000 feet before he could even look down at the altimeter. White puffy clouds surrounded him as he was pushed higher. Then it happened.

He entered a black form. Bright flashes of lightning were everywhere and he could hear the loud rumble of the thunder about him. It cracked like a whip at times. His machine was kicked around in just about every direction like a ball in an arcade game. He could feel his aeroplane roll. Even though he was totally disoriented, he sensed that the machine was flipped upside down and put by some unknown force in a nose-down attitude. Then it seemed to spin uncontrollably and flip end over end at times. Jimmy knew the machine could not possibly flip end over end, so he focused on the instrument panel in front of him. He didn't want his blind senses to deceive him or make him dizzy. Looking outside of his machine was useless because he saw only spinning white streaks of mist in a black void. He turned his engine off, let go of every control device in the cockpit, and grabbed the cockpit padding to brace himself in the rattan seat. Closing his eyes made him seasick, so he opened them and watched the dials of every instrument in the cockpit turn in various directions. The altimeter passed through 5,000 feet, and he couldn't tell if he was right-side up or upside down. He just hoped his machine would stay together so he could recover and restart his engine when it cleared the menacing black stew he seemed to be boiling in.

The vision of the beautiful woman he first saw in a brilliant pearl-studded formal gown against the oak paneling flashed before his eyes. "Victoria, I *will* make it through this and be by your side—*always*," he shouted, almost in defiance of the menace that was around him.

He heard the crack of something that sounded like lightning below his aeroplane. The machine shook violently, and he saw out of the corner of his eye the black form of his bottom right wing pass then disappear into the swirling mass behind him. "Campbell," he shouted, "I need you now to tell me how to fly this thing without a wing. You did it with the Nieuport over France. I guess I can do it now."

Concentrating on his instruments, he noticed his altimeter suddenly show a higher altitude. He was now at 7,000 feet again, and it seemed like the sky around him was getting lighter. He popped out of the clouds like the cork of a French champagne bottle. He was in a vertical nose-up position and realized the best maneuver he could make was the cartwheel he had performed in aerial combat against

Werner Voss three years before. The cartwheel to the vertical nosedive would help him get his machine under control and restart the engine. The Wolsely, like most water-cooled engines, didn't restart as fast as the rotary engines of the Nieuports, so altitude was everything. He grabbed the controls and noticed they were very sluggish. He tried the cartwheel maneuver, but it took a long time before he sensed any response in his machine.

The S.E. 5A finally started coming around. Jimmy looked over his shoulder as the machine started its cartwheel. He was shocked to see the glistening waves of the Chesapeake Bay much closer to him than the 7,000 feet the altimeter had recorded only seconds before. Now in the clear air, he could tell he was only about 3,000 feet above the water and falling sideways. The altimeter must have registered the wrong altitude in the belly of the storm, he thought. The machine flipped around. Jimmy's engine restarted after his second attempt, but he had lost valuable distance between him and the churning water waiting below to devour him. He pulled on the stick as he gained airspeed and noticed that the aeroplane responded much more quickly by her left wings than her right. *Ah, yes,* he thought, *I don't have a bottom right wing. I need to make more adjustments if I'm going to make it safely to the ground.*

The aeroplane flattened out at about 200 feet above the water. He could tell he had some flying capability, but the aeroplane slipped to the right constantly. He had to hold the stick to the left and work the rudder to keep the machine in a slight right-hand turn. Only then could he avoid spiraling to death.

Adjusting ailerons, rudder, and engine rpm, Jimmy brought the machine under control. He started looking for the closest landing spot but faced 200-foot-high cliffs at the banks of this northern section of the Chesapeake.

He finally saw his only opening. There was a field to his left just beyond a low area in the cliffs. But he knew the wounded bird could not go to the left. He had to make a right-hand turn out over the bay and hope he could make landfall without crashing. The turn actually helped him gain some altitude as he slowly banked the machine. *Lord, don't make this landing end up like the one I made behind enemy lines in 1917,* he prayed. *Give me a flat and open place to set down.*

The touchdown could not have been better. The aeromachine came in somewhat high, but he wanted to make sure he kept the wings level at touchdown. Surprisingly the bird feathered nicely and landed as though it rested down on a pillow.

Jimmy sat for a while and took stock. He never felt it during the flight but realized as he sat in the cockpit that he was completely soaked. Small balls of sleet lay in his lap and on the floor of the cockpit. Where did they come from? He wondered. He sat back, put his head on the cockpit padding, took a deep breath, and realized he was lucky to be able to see Victoria again. The comfort of visualizing Victoria and the realization that he had survived soothed him senselessly.

* * * * *

"So Jimmy, don't you just love springtime in Washington? Oh, yes, how *is* your business doing? Is it *really* safe? I am so concerned for your welfare," Mrs. Stevenson asked at their usual Sunday-evening dinner at the Stevenson's Georgetown home.

"Everything is fine, Mrs. Stevenson," he answered, trying hard to avoid looking suspicious in his little white lie about things being so *fine*. Well, then again, everything *was* fine. It would be much finer after Scotty rebuilt the lower wing of the S.E. 5A.

"We just purchased our second aeroplane, an Airco D.H. 4, and the business is doing extremely well. My mechanic, Scotty, keeps everything in very safe working condition. He even souped up the Rolls Royce engine of the Airco to give me more horsepower, which makes the aeroplane much stronger and safer to fly. We are doing so well, we hired that sergeant major that was at the ball commemorating General Mitchell last year, Sergeant Major Ralph Witherspoon."

"Oh, I see. I don't know much about souping up aeroplane engines. I also don't remember this Witherspoon. But everything sounds very comforting to know."

* * * * *

He looked to his left. At 1,000 feet the early spring setting sun was a wonder to behold. The flaming red, bright yellow and deep blue hues of the sunset were amazing. Jimmy reflected on the pathway he had taken to this moment. He thought of Opa Smitts, his hunting days in the dove fields, his early days in the Curtiss Jenny, and the thrills and dangers he'd experienced in aerial combat in France. His meeting with Werner Voss and the death of so many of his friends gave him the mixed emotions of extreme highs and deep sorrows. The faces of Genet, Hoskier, Johns, and his beloved Lufbery flashed before his eyes. The horrifying seconds as bullets and tracers struck Sergeant Walters in his first engagement of the war were as clear to him now as if they were happening again right before him. He shuddered as he watched the artillery projectiles explode over the trenches. He felt elated as he sensed rising up and over the top of those explosions only to see the celebration of the American soldiers below him. The elation turned to excitement as his heart raced in retrospect. He relaxed in the comfort of the recognition he'd received from France and the United States for his bravery in combat and as he watched the sun continue its explosive westerly end and he flew on toward his landing field. His last brush with death in the sudden squall over the Chesapeake Bay made his stomach churn as he rode the wind.

The visions of Giselle coming to him in the French summer moonlight of 1917 and Winifred sitting with him on Federal Hill in Baltimore as the wind whipped through her soft, brown hair made Jimmy feel the glory of life and the pain of loss. The revolving memories of horror, love, and death made him wonder if it was all worth it. What did it come down to?

It all comes down to *this*, Jimmy realized.

It didn't matter that her family was wealthy. It didn't matter that her father was a well-known businessman and influential politician. It didn't matter that her father agreed and her mother was elated with him. Well, all those things really *did* matter to Jimmy. But there was one thing that mattered most to him at this point in his life's journey. She had enthusiastically said yes. Miss Victoria Stevenson, aged 22 years, said she would marry him.

As the crimson-red sun started to fade away over the horizon, he reflected on all he had witnessed and experienced in his life. Remembering the same sight over the landing field at the Lux, he cut a sharp barrel roll and turned into his final approach to the Pursuit Aero Company.

Jimmy Smitts, flier, had found his destiny and it was *her*.

Alden Smith Bradstock, III was born in Baltimore, Maryland in 1955. He graduated from the United States Military Academy at West Point, New York and served with the 82nd Airborne Division at Fort Bragg, North Carolina. A Field Artillerist, Master Parachutist, and U.S. Army Ranger, Mr. Bradstock commanded soldiers in Germany during the Cold War. He received many military awards and decorations during his career including the Meritorious Service Medal and Germany's Ehrenkruez der Bundeswehr in Bronse, the Honor Cross of the German Military. With a Master's Degree, he left the military service and became a partner in a successful business in Maryland. He enjoys time with family and friends and the pleasures of the Chesapeake Bay with his wife, Samia. They have two sons.

CPSIA information can be obtained at www.ICGtesting.com
Printed in the USA
BVOW07s0030070813

327620BV00004B/12/P